ACID CONNECTIONS
PART 1

A Novel By:

DEANNE T. SMITH

This is a work of fiction. Names, characters, businesses, places, events and incidents are either the products of the author's imagination or used in a fictitious manner. Any resemblance to actual persons, living or dead, or actual events is purely

coincidental.

Deanne Smith
465 Columbus Ave
Boston, MA 02116
deannethewriter@gmail.com
http://www.deannetsmith.com

Cover Designed By: Devon Guillery

Dedication:

Acid Connections is dedicated to my sons, Dylan and Ehsan. Thank you for changing my life and my world. Thank you for your unconditional love. Thank you for a reason to always smile. You are the reason my heart beats and the reason I dare to dream and reach big. I love you boys with all my heart!

Acknowledgements

This book has developed over time. It's been a process and a journey to get to this page right here. I never thought I would see my dream become a reality, but I am now, and I want to thank some very special people!!

I want to thank my heavenly father. GOD, you have watched over me, guided me, protected me, and most of all, made my dreams come true. I give you all the thanks, praise, and honor for this blessing.

NaNa, you are my rock, my world, and my backbone. You are the guardian angel that GOD gave me to protect me and always love me. Words will never express my gratitude and appreciation for all that you have done for me. I LOVE YOU.

Daddy, we don't always see eye to eye or understand one another but I LOVE YOU!

To my sisters, Sydney, Adrianne, Diamond, Raya, and Ashley, I love you ladies to the end of the world and back. I know when the rest of the world is cold and turns their backs on me, I have my SISTERS....I AM MY SISTER'S KEEPER!

To my sister/cousins, **Latoya, Nikki, Krystal, and Kiefa**, I love you and the unbreakable bond we share.

I want to thank ***ALL*** my family, immediate, extended and those who have adopted me as family.

Aunty Veronica, a special thanks to you. You're my aunty, my supporter, and my voice of reason. Thanks for your love and support at times when I've felt lost and alone.

The following ladies are special and dear to my heart: You all have loved me for the person I am, AS I AM. You ladies hold a dear spot in my heart.

Monica, Monique, Tia, Kizzy, PJ, and Kim... yawl are my day one crew and I thank you for being my friend through the good, the bad, and the ugly!! Words, time, nor distance can change the love I have for yawl. You ladies have set the bar for my expectations in a friend and you've set that bar high. I love you!

Michelle C, Nomi, Michelle H, Chelsea, and Angela, my SSU crew, college wouldn't have been the same without yawl... I love yawl, you ladies have left footprints in my heart forever and taught me that real friends don't have to see each other or speak every day.

Latasha, you are my sister from another mother. Thank you for always being brutally honest and telling what I need to hear even when I don't want to hear it.

Kim Yai, Nadia and Lamara you ladies are special kind of friends: I'm happy GOD blessed me with yawl. Thank you for all the love & support.

Jaly, you are so special. I love you for showing me that I can still be ME and love my GOD!!

Star, I take your words to heart and have learned a lot from you. Everyone needs a friend like you.

Gerty and Ciara, you ladies are my always honest, loyal, fashionista Virgo Sisters. I have a special love and bond with yawl.

Daphne, thank you for pushing me and pushing me from the moment that you heard I was writing a book. Many didn't believe from day one but you did, thank you!

Tonya, you are so loving, caring, giving, and supportive. I love you for always being in my life. You are consistent; tolerate me and a real blessing. Thank you for coming along on this ride to make this dream a reality.

Aisha, I love you. You are my sister, cousin, and friend. I love, respect, and adore you. You never let me down. You support me, keep me sane, and the bond we have is undescribeable. I love you and thank for you helping me on this journey!!

Jermel, I appreciate you. You're not just my son's father but also my friend. I thank you for being a real man, a father, and a friend. But more importantly for showing how great life can be when you walk to your own beat!

Shizz D, Johnny, Majors, Bernard, Jamie, Chucky and Wale I love you! God didn't bless me with a brother but he gave me yawl!! I couldn't have asked for better brothers to teach me how a man should be and treat a woman.

Brent, I owe you a special thanks. Six years ago I said I was going to write a book, that very day you went to Barnes & Noble and got me a book to assist me. You believed in me from day one, so thank you from the bottom of my heart, my dear friend.

~ 3 ~

Kaenzjie, words can't describe the love, admiration and respect I have for you. I'm blessed with a friend like you. Thank you, for always being in my corner and being there for me.

Chanae, GOD does amazing things with the people he places in your life. I will never be able to thank you for the support and motivation. I appreciate you on another level.

Renarda, with your assistance and foundation support I became an AUTHOR. You are an amazing woman. Thanks, beautiful.

Sir, I love you! God gave me a lover and a friend when he gave me you. I will forever love you, and am blessed that we are friends although no longer lovers.

Most importantly, my **READERS**!! Thank you for supporting me. I couldn't do this without you. As long as you read I will continue to write, so thank you!!!

PROFESSIONAL THANKS

<u>Photographers</u>: Sydney Smith & Troy Dixon

<u>Web Designer</u>: Nicole Tongue

<u>Editors</u>: Sara Joy and Charlee Redman

<u>Graphic Designer</u>: Devon Guillery

~ CHAPTER 1 ~

Play to win, and don't make a habit of losing.

Boston, Summer of 2009

It was a Sunday, and Washington Park was rocking.

"Damn…the park is crazy today," Tavares said, looking out the window of her apple red Acura TL, stuck in bumper to bumper traffic, watching her surroundings.

"Tell me about it," said her right hand, Jazz. "Everyone's out in full effect today."

Tavares loved the park because it reminded her of what home was all about. "I love going away to school, but this shit right here is why I love being home for the summer," Tavares said with excitement. Tavares was born and raised in Boston, but had been obtaining her bachelor's degree in Georgia for the last three years.

Kids were everywhere, running up and down the streets, weaving in and out of the already tight-knit crowd.

All the gangbangers, hustlers, and old heads were tryna bag broads. Some chicks were tryna their best to be seen and stand out, while others were simply tryna to get in where they fit in.

Chicks were groomed to perfection and had on their Sunday best, or so they thought. A new outfit was a must if they were going to be the shit on Sunday. They didn't stop there. They made it their business to sit in the overcrowded hair salons for hours on Saturdays or Sunday mornings. They had to if they were going to be flowing and blowing when Sunday afternoon came. The nail salons made you mad that you even played yourself and stepped foot in them on a Saturday afternoon or

Sunday morning. It was nothing but pure chaos, with hood chicks tryna tighten up their nail and toe game and or get their eyebrows waxed. Figuring that with their hair looking good, nails and toes glistening, and a new outfit to lace them, they could seal the deal and bag the nigga of their choice. But really they were just doing way too much for a simple afternoon at the park.

Niggaz had their new cars out showcasing them. There were BMWs, Benzes, Hummers, Escalades, Tahoes, Jaguars, Acuras, and even souped-up Hondas with blaring music going down MLK Blvd and busting U-turns at the end of the island that separated the two sides of the Blvd to show off their cars on each side of the street. Even the ugliest niggaz looked fly as they rode in their hot boy whips. Motorcycles had their own spots. They were parked at the corner of MLK Blvd and Walnut Avenue, usually parked about fifty to a hundred deep. Motorcycle riders were the pick of the litter. Women tended to find them sexy even if they were shabootie ugly.

Looking at all the cars triple-parked, creating traffic, Tavares asked Jazz, "Where the hell are we going to park? I got on these high ass heels, so we ain't diddy bopping from too far."

"Just park in the Joe," Jazz suggested. The Joe was a housing complex right behind the park. "Them Joe niggaz ain't going to let nothing happen to the car," Jazz assured. "We'll just enter the park on the Dale Street Side. That ain't a long walk, Miss. I gotta wear my highest heels to the park," joked Jazz. "We can walk down past the softball field and the pool, and we'll be right in the mix of things at the basketball courts."

Washington Park was huge. There were four basketball courts and four games were going at the same time, with women, men, and children spectating around each court. The courts were connected at an angle. On the inside of the park there were widely separated stairs that connected each small tier. On the top level, where it became a flat surface, was the last basketball court. Next to it was the tennis court, only no one was ever playing tennis. Usually on a Sunday, DJ Roxbury was rocking the mic something hard. People were set up around him with their grills, tables, and chairs—cooking out and socializing. At the edge of the park was the nice, oversized, secluded playground for kids to run wild, which they were doing a good job of.

The food vending trucks were taking up the most room on the two-lane boulevard, backing all the traffic up to a single lane. There was Al B's famous iced tea truck. Al B's line for iced tea was always down the block. His iced tea was straight homemade, perfectly sweetened, with a fresh lemon. Al B's iced tea was worth the wait and the $2.00 he wanted for it. There was the fried dough truck that had fried dough, funnel cakes, candy apples, cotton candy, and freshly made lemonade.

You could smell Chef Dee's soul food truck long before you got to it. Eating their collard greens, mac and cheese, ribs, and caramel cake was just as good as, if not better than, Sunday dinner at your grandmother's house. There was a slush lady on the sidewalk, stationed under her same shaded tree every week. She made over thirty flavors and had prices as cheap as fifty cents, which made you have to treat yourself. The old timers had coolers on the edges of the sidewalks. They were selling Heinekens and Coronas for $2.00 a piece. Hustling between the people in traffic and the people on the sidewalk, they were making a killing.

Tavares and Jazz approached the basketball courts and couldn't help but notice all the chicks who might as well have had on nothing.

"Yo, but are those her daughter's shorts or her underwear?" Tavares asked, looking at a chick with purple shorts on so small and tight that they may as well have been her underwear. "They're so small they look like she borrowed them from her five-year-old," Tavares laughed. Tavares was disgusted, but couldn't help but laugh because the chick thought she was hot shit, in her mind and in her world.

"Bitch, don't get brand new," laughed Jazz. "You know it be the same shit every summer. Bitches come to the park thinking they're getting right and getting tight, and be looking a hot fucking shitty mess."

"They be acting like they took hours to put together a $20 dollar production," Tavares said to her best friend. "You go away to school then come home and act like you done forgot how these two-dollar hoes rock. I can dig it," Tavares said. "I ain't coming out like that, though. It ain't that serious," laughed Tavares as she looked around at a good amount of damn near naked women.

The duo were falling back, watching the games and the live scenery, sitting on the brick wall facing all the basketball courts.

"I need an iced tea, let's walk around to the iced tea truck and get one," suggested Jazz, really just wanting to walk and be seen.

"Damn, we just sat down," Tavares whined, hip to the reason Jazz wanted an iced tea. "Why can't you just sit your ass still for a minute?"

Sucking her teeth, Jazz said, "Just come on."

Tavares liked to play the cut and didn't wanna move. She didn't like to be in the spotlight. "If you was a star, the spotlight light came to you," was her motto. Jazz didn't mind finding the light. Tavares didn't feel like looking at Jazz pout. "Fuck it, let's go, puffy face," Tavares said to her best friend.

Tavares and Jazz strolled pass the crowd sitting on the back wall watching the games and could feel all eyes on them.

"Ooowe, there go them Lenox Street Niggaz," Jazz said as they reached the middle tier on the stairs. She spotted her crush and got a tingle from wanting to give him the business so bad. "Uhh, who cares?" asked Tavares, not impressed by what was heading their way except for the oddball in the group.

"What's up, Jazz? Who's your girl?" the yellowest of the crew asked, nodding his head like he was giving the lady the seal of approval.

"This is my girl, Apple."

"Hi," Tavares said, not wanting to speak but figuring, why be rude. The guys nodded their heads in a "what's up" motion.

"What's your real name?" the oddball of the crew asked.

Taken aback, Tavares snapped her head and asked, "Why? You writing a book?"

"I might be," he responded, right on cue.

"You got too many questions," responded Tavares, snappingly polite.

"Nah, sweetheart, that was just my first. I'm tryna get my info up for that book you asked about." He wasn't intimidated by her small, feisty ass even though she had the right combination of beauty and bark.

"I'm Balile. I want you to come walk and talk with me." Tavares eyed the brown-skinned, at least six-foot-tall, lanky, scruffy-bearded, handsome guy with a sexy lineup. Tavares could see he was bold and real different, just how he had went in on her from the door. The waves in his head were so serious that Tavares thought she was gonna be seasick.

"No thanks," Tavares said to the truly fine dude, who came across as an edgy black skateboarder. He had on True Religion jeans, LV belt, white tee, and custom-made creative recreation sneakers. His dimples were so deep they made you melt every time he smiled.

"We about to go in the trees if yawl wanna come," he offered, still trying to lure Tavares into his presence. Behind the short brick wall there were three acres of beautiful, towering trees. Through the trees were walkways, paths, and benches everywhere.

"Nah, we don't wanna go," Jazz said, not liking that she got shot down by her crush before she even got a chance to holla at him, seeing as he had tried to holler at her friend. They said goodbye and went their separate ways.

"Oh, shit! There goes Damien," Jazz said.

Tavares's eyes got big when she spotted her boyfriend on the tennis court. "He got his back to us, so he don't even see us. You can calm down. I'm far from worked up over Dame being up at the park. Stop playing," laughed Jazz's partner in crime.

"I'm surprised he's even up here though," Tavares said, wondering what had her boyfriend at the park. "He don't really play the park like that," she said, shocked to see her boyfriend who swore he was the shit no matter where he was.

"Your boo thinks he's fresh to def in his charcoal grey cargo shorts, the white tee, and white and grey and red Air Max '95s," Jazz commented. "And I can't front, he definitely is," she admitted.

Damien was speaking to and giving dap to all the most well respected hood niggaz like he was a celebrity or something. Tavares lost him in transition through the crowd, but didn't care because they did their own thing outside the house. Public displays of affection were cool, but not when they were out separately, doing their own thing. They rationalized it that they knew who they were coming home to, so they didn't sweat each other out in public if they weren't out together.

All the hoods came out, and for the most part niggaz kept it drama-free. Enemies lurked and watched one another but it was rare that it got popping at the park. It was only every blue moon that an asshole would shoot and mess up the Sunday fun for everyone. The hood was on fire with dudes shooting every day, but the park was like an unspoken truce.

Major hoods and projects all had a professional sports team behind their street or project's name. The Academy Braves, Humboldt Raiders, Magnolia Steelers, Franklin Hill Giants, Orchard Park Trailblazers, St. Joseph Saints, Egelston Timberwolves, Heath Street Heat, and not to mention all the other hoods without team names. Affiliates Franklin Hill, Academy, and The Timberwolves were sitting up on the rocks that overlooked the whole park.

They had to be the center of attention. They were overlooking everyone and everything. Together they had created an alliance and were getting the most money in the city of Boston. They had the hustle game on lock, and not by selling drugs. They had been there and done that. Flipping all their illegal money into legal money, they owned a little bit of everything. They owned any and everything they could get their hands on. Property, clothing stores, hair salons, laundromats, cell phone stores, book stores, and they even had three franchises of McDonald's and two Dunkin' Donuts.

They were the money getters and it showed in their iced out jewelry and pricey cars that niggaz in the hood could never afford. They were dem dudes and they knew it. Cocky was their middle name. Money was the only reason chicks messed with their extra cocky, rude asses. Money was a motherfucker in the hood. Chicks in the hood were usually chasing a nigga's pockets, confusing it with love.

"Shorty, why you looking so mad?" a fella yelled down from the rocks. "Give a nigga a smile or something."

Tavares couldn't help but smile and make her face shine. Gemini was handsome. His tall, muscular frame, smooth toffee-colored skin, and strong, handsome facial features made him the finest cooley, handsome pretty-boy Trinidadian man. His perfect, pretty white teeth and hazel eyes were sick with it. The drop-dead crispy line up, wide bright smile, and thick, pretty full beard made you just want to run your hand across all the gorgeousness before you. He was always dapper to death in some plain but high-end stuff. Gucci this, Prada that. He was way too into the money he paid for his stuff, but Tavares had to admit he always looked good.

"What's your name?" he asked Tavares, who had to stop. In Tavares's book there was never any harm in a little flirting.

"Damn, and you got a fat ass," his friend said.

"Watch your disrespectful fucking mouth, PLEASE," Tavares said with her icy eyes and a tone that he had no choice but to respect.

"Don't act like that, Blue Eyes." Tavares could feel her face turning red from his rude friend's comment.

"Nah, he don't be like that with his fresh ass mouth." Gemini liked Apple. He loved that she was a smart, beautiful girl in school, but that she was in the hood and down to earth. It turned him on that she moved so under the radar that the average person would never imagine her to be a hustler. He had seen her very far in between, but had done a background check on her. He loved the exotic, soft-on-the-eyes beauty and that she was from the streets but flipped it and used it to her advantage for something more. "So you gonna let me take you on a cruise?" Gemini asked, serious as could be.

"Damn, that's how you do for first dates?" Tavares said with a genuine school-girl laugh. She couldn't hold back blushing. "I don't know if I could be stuck with you that long," Tavares said, only half telling the truth.

"You won't know unless you take me up on the offer," he said, smooth and cool with his slight Trini accent, not really giving a fuck about her man that he wasn't too fond of. Had Apple been single, she would have been right there on a cruise with him. A vacation to nowhere was a vacation with him. Tavares knew what she was missing, because the streets talked, and Gemini was the man, not the man next to the man.

"I can't, baby doll. I just stopped because I wanted to tell you how handsome you are. You see me here and there, and you always look from afar with a hard stare, so I just wanted to tell you my name's Tavares. So now you ain't gotta look at me all icy when you see me," Tavares said with a sexy chuckle.

Jazz's eyes were all over Sweezy. Sweezy was the poster child for dickhead. Money and power had conquered him a long time ago, so cocky was all he knew how to be. He was a fine motherfucker but a supa dupa disrespectful, arrogant jerk.

"What's up with you Jazz?" asked Sweezy, since Tavares was talking to Gemini.

"You know how Sweezy do, baby, I'm just out here trying to take over the world. Why you trying to get down wit your dude?"

"Did I say all that?" Jazz snapped, knowing in her mind he was right. "Can't a chick just ask what's up with you and be friends?"

"Yeah, we can be friends, Ma. But how about you turn around and let me see what you working with first," Sweezy said, disrespectfully as always.

"Nigga, please," Jazz said, ready to go off but knowing that Sweezy would slap the shit out of her, since she witnessed him slap more than a few chicks who got fly with him. She saved herself the embarrassment.

"Oh, boy," Tavares said, "here they go. Let me go," Tavares told her flirt buddy.

"I'mma see you again, Pretty Lady," Gemini said, meaning it and not making a general statement.

Making their way across the first court where little kids were shooting hoops, Tavares saw Copeland Street on the benches along the court. Thumbs down, out of all the hoods they were the rudest and most disrespectful bunch of drug-dealing ass niggaz you ever wanted to meet. They weren't flashy niggaz with their jewelry, money, or cars, even though they had all three.

They chose to use their foul mouths as their way to be flashy. Only it was never nothing good coming out. Chicks didn't even like walking near them or down their block. Copeland Street was infamous for throwing bottles at bitches, as they always called them, when they walked down the street and thought they would pass without being social to the dude talking to them.

Tavares thought she was cute one summer day. She had run to Washington Park Mall to the cleaners when she had to go visit a person who lived off Copeland Street. It was nice out, so Tavares thought she would stay parked at the hood mall that had a discount grocery store, bank, cable spot, furniture store, hair store, bootleg clothing stores for men, low budget clothing stores for women, a Reebok Outlet, and a convenience store to play your numbers and do money grams. Tavares strolled across the street and, upon spinning the corner, regretted even walking down the treacherous block filled with no-respect-having, barbaric, money-getting animals.

"Hello, beautiful," said a cute, stocky, well-groomed and well-dressed dude with perfect white teeth and a huge smile.

"Hi," Tavares responded, being friendly, not even wanting to go through the bullshit.

"How are you doing today?" he asked, eyeing Tavares up and down in her fitted knee-length jean capris and a simple white tank top that had her melons sitting up real pretty, with flat gold sandals and matching gold accessories, her hair curly and wild. Tavares was looking real exotic.

"Good, and you?"

"I'm good now that I've seen you. Can you stop and talk for a moment?" he tried to ask very politely.

"I can't," Tavares said as she passed him and his friends who were snickering about her.

"Shorty, I ain't worth two minutes?" he said very humbly.

"If I had the two minutes to spare, they would be yours," Tavares said, looking over her shoulder.

From there, Tavares became every stuck up, blue-eyed bitch to him and his friends. They went postal for nothing. Tavares just kept on going about her business, not paying them any attention.

Coming back up the block, Tavares walked up and checked them in a real calm voice. "You can call me every fucking bitch in the book you want, but guess what? Who gives a fuck? That shit don't make or break no real chick. Yawl look fucking crazy screaming and carrying on because some fucking bitch in the streets doesn't wanna holla at you. Who fucking does that, yo? If you're this so-called fucking big balling ass, getting money nigga, then why do you give a fuck? Pussy is like #28 bus. If you miss one, there's another one right behind it. If you gotta call me a bitch because I came on your block and spoke and was polite, by all fucking means please do so. I could give two fucks," Tavares said, spinning around and walking away.

They were shocked, sitting there with their mouths open at the fact that shorty had the heart to even walk back up the block after they had bitched and dogged her out. They were even more shocked that she didn't hesitate to tell them about their selves on *their* block. That was a first, because chicks dreaded them because of their *I don't give a fuck about disrespecting you* attitude.

"Ayo, come here," the big, stocky, cute nigga said.

"Hell fucking no. You walk down here if you got something to say to me."

He did as she said. "I just wanted to apologize. That was some foul shit."

Tavares just listened with a blank facial expression.

He pleaded hard enough that Tavares was convinced. She walked away, gaining a friend that she was cool as shit with to the present day. From that day, they never gave her a hard time and always spoke to her and kicked it with her when and wherever they saw her.

Orchard Park Projects were lined up along the fence of the second court, going back and forth with Mission Hill Projects. Their hoods were always deep in the game with every nigga trying to coach. "That's how you dunk, nigga," Shizz D from Mission was bragging in his naturally loud, cocky voice. Shizz D was funny as all hell when he coached, with his tall basketball frame and mahogany skin.

Everyone who knew Shizz D knew he lived for basketball and talking shit when his team was winning. He loved the kids and basketball. That was how he gave back to the community. He was the head sponsor of the summer league that had over three age ranges and involved kids from every inner city project and housing development.

"Yawl's hood ain't seen a nigga dunk like that, since when? Oh…never," Shizz laughed.

Sole from O.P. was across the court with his innocent high yellow, freckled Jesus face turning red. It was funny to see his freckles when his face was red. "Shizz, are you for real? Nigga, you can't be serious," said Sol, with his bright cheeks flaming red. "That dude is like seven feet, literally. He should be able to dunk, since his big ass can't shoot."

Shit talking was the norm between these two hoods and all in the fun of the game for them. They bred all the best basketball players in Boston. Most b-ball players out of Mission and O.P. always ended up getting a ticket out of the hood on basketball scholarships, and nine times out of ten went pro or overseas. Glad that they were able to slide past them, the ladies finally made it to the street.

Heath Street Projects and the Humboldt Street Raiders, who were archenemies, were both on the front side of the park. They were holding up the Blvd, pulling bitches left and right, giving each other the stare down in between. Chicks loved their hoods the most, so with all the chicks flocking them, they had no reason to fuck with each other. Tension was thick, but thus far they had yet to be the ones to shut the park down, even though off the park grounds they got it in, gunning each other down every other day.

Heath Street was the pretty boy niggaz who loved to live by the *ball till you fall* motto. It was a known fact that fucking with a nigga from the "Heat" meant there was always going to be a come up. If they liked you, then kind generosity, or tricking as some would call it, wasn't nothing to them. Shopping, clubbing, traveling, and having a good time was what they did every day. To them balling was like taking a bath every day, it was a need in their eyes, so if they fucked with you, you were balling too.

The Raiders were doing it big and living large too, but their swagger differentiated from the Heat because they didn't trick just for the hell of it. Their swagger was too fucking mean to have to. All they had to do was step in a room and it was all eyes on them, from women and men. Admiration, genuine love, jealousy, envy, and hate always had people's eyes on them. They were getting money on top of money and had a nice sized team that wasn't too large, so their money flow was long.

Rocking thousands of dollars worth of canary diamonds was their trademark. They stayed with an immaculate presentation in their dress game. It was always flawless and crispy. Hat, shirt, and shoes always matched with the perfect pair of jeans. Their feet only stepped outta the hottest whips. A Beamer, Benz, Porsche, or whatever they thought they wanted for the season. Their arsenal was full of handsome, yet rugged men to choose from. It was hard to not give them credit.

"Yo, babygirl, it ain't too often I step to a lady, but I dig your swag and your movement," said D White. "You know you're beautiful but you not cocky. I like that," he smiled. "I find that to show just how beautiful you are skin deep and that shit enhances your outer beauty, for real, babygirl." His voice was sincere but his eyes were even more so. They cosigned that he was telling the truth. D White was looking right in his chocolate brown Nike Airmax sneakers, tan cargo shorts, and a brown polo shirt with an orange horse and Orange B fitted hat.

He was with his crew, Kevin Day and Landell Jackson. In the streets the ladies called them the Tasty Three. Because tasty they were, with Kev Day looking like a chocolate delight. Landell was silky, looking like a straight caramelized Puerto Rican, when he was straight black. D White was all the flavors mixed in one because he really was mixed, but had dark chocolate skin, green eyes, and long, pretty hair. He was Costa Rican born and American bred and raised. What made them different from a lot of hood dudes was that they didn't just fuck with anything or anyone. They were smart enough to know that fucking with random broads that the wind blew in was dangerous when trying to survive in the game. *Women are conniving and will set you up* was their motto, thanks to their mothers. Their mothers had all instilled in them not to trust bitches in the streets. It wasn't too often you would catch them giving chicks anything other than airtime. Past conversation, they weren't pressed, like dudes from the Heat were.

D White looked at Tavares and was like, "Yo, I just wanna treat you, not cheat you. I wanna get to know you. This park shit is rec to me, Babe Girl. What I love and what I do is get money so that I can enjoy my true passion of traveling. Let me take you to Paris, Greece, or Geneva. I just wanna look into those innocent, soft and sexy eyes."

Being that he was sexy and so fucking swagged up on top of polite, Blue Eyes decided to entertain him. "You know what, if I ever get single, I just might have to do that," she said. "You got a real air about you that I dig," Tavares admitted. Tavares had to go because she would have been in trouble fucking with D White.

Exactly what Tavares didn't want to happen happened—she got stopped by one too many hood niggaz. She hated attention. Jazz was mad on the inside because no one was offering her trips or going hard to get at her. Tavares and Jazz passed everyone and finally made their way to the iced tea truck. Standing in line, they kicked the shit.

"Tavares, I don't know where you got them eyes, but they are bananas," Jazz said. "You be having niggaz from every hood at you. Girl, if I had those eyes, I wouldn't say shit but 'get back, yawl don't know me like that' and be straight coming up," Jazz laughed. "Niggaz really go crazy over them fucking eyes. It's like one look and they're hooked, ready to go hard with you. They be all over your exotic-looking ass. Your family has to be white or something close to it, because black chicks don't have eyes like that. We know for sure that Dolonda wasn't black, so whatever you are it sure as hell ain't black."

"Whatever," Tavares said, not wanting to discuss her eyes nor her other side of her family that she didn't know. It was just Tavares and her mother growing up. No talk about a father except that he bounced on her Dominican mother. Tavares felt like her funny-colored blue eyes had been the curse they gave to her. Never liking that they were different from all the other kids, she grew up with a complex. She felt like her eyes were too much of an attention getter and she hated it. Tavares was ready to get her iced tea and take a seat, because Jazz had just aggravated her with the conversation at hand.

"All I know is that I wish I had eyes like yours," Tavares said, meaning what she said from the bottom of her heart.

"Are you fucking—" and Jazz stopped her words short.

"Finish your fucking sentence, retard."

"I need that nigga right there in my life," Jazz said with her mouth hanging open.

"Damn, hooker, close your damn mouth. Who?" Tavares said looking around. "There are fifty million niggaz out here, which one?"

"That nigga down the block, talking to Majors from Franklin Hill. Damn, that nigga is fine," Jazz said, referring to a six-foot-six-inch package of fineness. He was the color of extracted honey. He was showing off his muscles and twelve-pack to everyone. His sexy, cut up body had tattoos on every nick and cranny of it. His inked back, neck, and arms were glistening under the sun. He had an egg-shaped head, with clean, glistening, bald skin. He looked like a thugged-out, handsome Boris Kodjoe. Tavares wanted a closer look at the fine, tattooed God. He was a hood nigga to his heart. His hood swagger was mean and screaming. It could be seen as soon as you laid eyes on him. Dressed so simple but so fly, Tavares was thinking, *god damn.* Dressed in dark denim blue jean shorts, some Red Versace shades, a red B-fitted hat, and some crispy red, white, and blue Jordans, with his wife beater in his hand and a rag over his shoulder, he was hurting chicks' eyes.

Jazz looked at Tavares, knowing what she was thinking. "Yeah, he's that dude," Jazz said, knowing her best friend all too well.

"Tell me about it," Tavares said. "I wonder where he came from," said Tavares, real curious.

"Not here," Jazz said, like she knew for sure.

"He might be, you never know," Tavares said optimistically.

"Bitch please, if that nigga was from here, I would know him. The hood is not that big. You know I be out and about, so even if I didn't know him, I would have seen him before. So stop it. I have never seen that nigga in the hood a day in my life. His fine ass would have been my baby's father way back when," Jazz said jokingly, but really meaning the words that had come out her mouth.

"You're a fool," Tavares said, sipping on her sweet lemon iced tea as they walked even closer to the eye candy.

Making their way down the block a short distance, Tavares said, "Damn his sexy ass got sleepy, almond-shaped green eyes."

"Girl and do you see his side burns that come down his strong jaw line and chiseled cheek bones and connect to his full beard?" Jazz said like she was overheated.

"Oh hell yeah, he is scrumptious as hell," Tavares cosigned. Tavares tried to find another word, but that was the only one that she could get to come out.

Walking past him, not wanting to be obvious, they made it their business not to look his way. Out the corner of their eyes, they could see that he was even finer up close than he was from afar.

"I guess we aren't the only ones on him," Tavares said, referring to all the chicks standing around the new eye candy. Just as they got past the mystery man, someone yelled, "Damn, Apple, you going to walk past me like that. How about I slap you real quick?" Turning around, Tavares knew that it was Majors who was yelling at her. Stopping to speak, Tavares was glad that at that moment she had played that one like that.

"What's up, Big Head," Tavares said as she gave him a big bear hug. "To be honest, we were so engaged in conversation that I didn't see you. You know I wasn't trying to be rude, so stop it."

"Whatever, Tavares, save the bullshit with your funky attitude ass," joked Tavares's friend. Majors and Jazz exchanged hellos.

Looking at the chick, who was light as the sun with a deep bronze tone, with high, perfectly round, thick cheek bones and nice full lips that had a beauty mark above the corner, Tavares's admirer was impressed. He was loving the mole that was a gift from GOD and not bought at Walgreens, and her natural big, bright blue eyes had him overly impressed. Something few chicks had that ability to do, and especially not without trying.

Standing at five feet even, with a thick, curly sandy brown mane at the moment, gorgeous face, beautiful teeth, and sky blue eyes, Tavares was flawlessly beautiful. She had a natural beauty that didn't even need makeup. Wearing it just heightened her beauty over the top. *Damn, ma looks tanned but she can't be a black girl with blue eyes. She definitely got some something in her,* Dora thought to himself before letting it go. He wasn't going beat himself in the head trying to figure out what it was. At least not right now. Not to mention she was thick as hell, with no waist, wide hips, and a huge tight butt.

"When you got back from school?" Majors asked. Dora made a mental note—she wasn't only pretty, but shorty was in school, getting her education on and not just a pretty hoodrat.

"I got back a few weeks ago."

"Damn Apple, summer is almost fucking over now. Oh, shit, my bad," Majors said, snapping his fingers pointing at his friend. "Apple and Jazz, this is my man, Abdora."

Turning around, Tavares looked him in the eyes and said, "Hi, nice to meet you," in a very proper and articulated voice.

Captivated by each others' eyes, Dora replied likewise, "Mumma."

Jazz walked over and shook his hand, saying, "It's a real pleasure to meet you," with flirtation all in her voice. Jazz was at him. It showed in the sexiness of her words. She played no games when it came to going after what she wanted.

Chuckling, Dora responded, "Thanks, same to you too."

He looked at the female who had long, thick legs with a petite upper body and a cute face, and thought she was definitely doable. But she wasn't holding a candle to her blue-eyed friend.

"Apple, I can't believe you been back home and ain't hit me up, sucker."

"Naw, not even," Tavares defended. "I'm taking a summer class at U-Mass Boston at night and working at Roxbury courthouse during the day on a paid internship. I be too tired to come out and rock in the streets after all that—which is why I'm out today. Usually I'm in the house doing homework, laundry, cleaning, or sleeping, but since it's nice out, I dragged myself outside. Plus I missed the park, so I definitely had to slide through."

"I see you still looking good," Majors said, teasing Tavares about her red button-down baby doll shirtdress and matching platform peep toed, sling-back red Dior leather heels. The simply but prettily dressed lady was iced out. Her four-carat princess-cut diamond studs, ten-carat tennis bracelet, and five-carat single-stone princess-cut diamond ring were clear, with not a cloud in sight.

Her jewelry screamed, "I got money" to Dora. It was nice and expensive but it didn't look like something a man picked out and bought. He had flawless taste in jewelry and didn't think he would have picked out something so classy yet flashy at the same time for a woman. The jewelry screamed "I'm a bad bitch," and yes she was, Dora had to admit.

You could see the effort she put into her jewelry. She had good taste and Dora was digging it. But her face said that she couldn't be doing anything more than being a square, so how was she so iced out, wondered Dora.

"Oh, boy, here you go," Tavares laughed. "Shit, shopping is my only enjoyment in my crazy life. So yeah, I'm always gonna look good," Tavares said, rolling her eyes.

"I ain't mad at you," Majors said, "with your 'pretty little ass.'" That was his coined term for Tavares.

"Don't be, because I sure as hell ain't," she laughed. "Don't hate the game, hate the player," Tavares said, giving her homegirl dap. They all fell out laughing.

Ok...and Ma got a little cockiness in her, Dora thought as he took notice, liking her swag more and more.

Jazz decided to spark a conversation with the new love of her life. "So, where are you from?" questioned Jazz.

"I'm from Jersey," responded Dora as he tried to not obviously stare at her friend—her friend, who wasn't stunting him like all the other chicks staring him down.

"So what brings you to Boston?"

"A little bit of business and a little bit of pleasure."

"Oh, so how long will you be in town?"

"I'm leaving tomorrow."

Majors interrupted. "My bad yawl, but when yawl walked up I was about to tell my man that we are having a pre 4th of July party tonight."

"What?" Tavares asked sarcastically, with her face screwed up as she snapped her neck back. "Did I miss the memo or isn't the 4th in two weeks? Sounds like a pre pre party to me," Tavares laughed.

"Yo, Apple, you got a smart ass mouth and can't even help that shit."

"I wasn't trying to be smart. For real, I wasn't," Tavares laughed. "I was just asking how you have a pre party two weeks in advance," Tavares laughed again. This time not on purpose.

"If you must know," Majors said, looking at Tavares with his head sideways as she was talking to him, "people have different plans, leaving, coming, and going, and we wanted everyone to come. Since you must know," Majors said blankly.

"I didn't need to know, but thanks for sharing," Tavares said sarcastically, accepting the explanation.

Being inquisitive is a good quality to have, Dora thought as he listened to the young chick. Mama had just a little too much swag for her own good.

"With all that explained, I know you're bringing your ass to the Backstage tonight, right?" asked Majors.

"I don't know..." Tavares answered, like she was seriously debating on a hard decision.

"What the fuck you mean you don't know, Apple?" Majors just started laughing. "All that shit talking and you ain't even coming?"

"Nah, it's not like that. I gotta work tomorrow."

"Apple, you better get off that funny shit and come through. I'll even put yawl on the VIP list. Just tell that nigga of yours to let you out the house," Majors joked, knowing that Dame had Tavares on lockdown. Dora knew she was too fine not to have a man.

"Majors, don't start nothing. It won't be nothing," Tavares said, playfully nudging him. "I can get out the house. Don't worry about me. You just worry about putting us on VIP because you know I sure as hell ain't paying to get into nothing you're giving," Tavares cried out in laughter. The funniest part was that he knew she meant it. "So put our names on the list just in case we make it," Tavares said, batting her ocean blue eyes jokingly at Majors.

Jazz was trying to make sure she was there tonight. "Will you be there?" Jazz asked the absolute finest man she had ever laid eyes on.

"I would love to party tonight, but I doubt it, Ma. I got an early morning. Partying wasn't really in the plans. But you never know, shit happens," Dora said nonchalantly.

"Well, we aren't going to hold yawl up," Tavares said, not wanting to feel like she was lingering for too long. She felt like all eyes were on Dora, and she was in the crossfire. Everyone exchanged goodbyes.

"You better come out, Apple," Majors said as the ladies walked off.

I hope so, Dora thought, but didn't say it out loud. Dora was definitely in the building tonight, if it meant bagging shorty. He watched the young, pretty girl walk away, knowing he had major plans for her.

"What's up with Shorty Wop?" Dora asked no sooner than the ladies were out of earshot.

"I don't really know Jazz. I know her through Apple, but she's cool. Apple's my nigga though. As cool as she is, you would think she's a nigga. You see she talk cash shit. She likes sports, falling back, getting money, and will kick it with you about bitches, like she got a dick and some more shit. Only thing that saves you from thinking she's a man is that there ain't nothing manly about that face, hips, or sweet little juicy booty," laughed Majors. He was high yellow with a big frame that he always kept fresh to def. He was like six-two, 280 pounds. But he wasn't fat, he just had a big frame that he would never be able to shake, so he kept it tight. He was crispy in his wife beater, khaki shorts, and fresh out of the box Prada sneakers. A new pair on every Sunday was a no doubt about it. He had on some stunting ass DG shades and wasn't nothing to fuck with, big boy or not. He was always fresh and dressed to def. Not to mention his handsome baby face and long beautiful hair touching the middle of his back that he inherited, being black and Puerto Rican.

"Nigga, and that's who I'm asking about?" Dora said, as if Majors should have known better. "Her girl is cute. Don't get me wrong, but she don't got shit on that blue-eyed bandit. Apple looks like she's sweet pie, and I need a taste of her in my life," Dora laughed.

"Apple's a bad little bitch, ain't she?" asked Majors. "I was at that, but now that's just my homegirl. Apple be on the move, doing things. She got a crib down in the south end, one of the most expensive parts of Boston, with her man. She goes to school down in GA but she got the hood in her heart because she raised herself out here. Apple gets her hustle on and everything. I mean shorty gets paper."

"I knew it," Dora laughed to himself as he listened. "She's dumb down low with it, because of trying to be a lawyer. Only if you know her, you know she gets paper. So a nigga better know—to fuck with her, they better come correct, because she don't need him for shit but hard dick and bubble gum."

"So she's a good girl who ain't afraid to get a few dollars, huh?" asked Dora, who grew more impressed each moment that his boy gave him the rundown. "My type of girl," Dora sang. "Shit, she sound like we got a lot in common." He liked chicks who were doing their thing, had drive and goals. He was attracted to a woman always striving and reaching for more. A lazy bum bitch, just sitting all day at home on some bum bitch shit smoking weed, yelling at her kids because she's mad that she had them, wasn't his style. If a bitch didn't have a job, they couldn't even talk to him. Dora felt like he had too many jobs to be carrying someone who wasn't trying to carry one job.

"Nah, my nigga, not at all. She goes hard or goes home. Apple came from nothing and grinded her way up. And when I say nothing, my nigga, I do mean nothing. She was homeless at one point and some more shit. You wouldn't look at her bad ass and think it, but word she was."

Dora got a flash of her face and couldn't even imagine such a thought. Who would leave a face like that out in the cold? "Where you meet her little bad ass at?" Abdora questioned.

"I met her on the late night, at an after hour spot. Like four years ago. I could tell she was mad young. I think Apple was like seventeen then. You know usually, young bitches go for anything," Majors said like he was stating a fact. "And she was bad, so I was on it, nigga! I was trying to push up on her hard. Apple could have had all my money that night if she wanted it. But shorty wouldn't budge," he laughed as he thought back to that night. "She wasn't moved by what I had, what I was offering, or none of that. All the bitches love me, but that night Apple showed me that some chicks really are loyal and ain't moved by a few dollars. We ended up just kicking it and laughing and shit. We both bought rounds and just took the moment for what it was, laughing and having a good time clowning. I always saw her after that and we got cooler and cooler. I came to love her like a little sister. For like the last three years we been cool as fuck. Yo, she's a good girl. And I can't lie, I love having her as a homegirl. Apple's my nigga, dawg. She's a chick, but I rap with her like I would one of my mans and them, and to be honest I might fuck with her a little harder."

Majors continued, "My chicks used to complain about me not being up on the gifts and shit. And I don't be fucking having time for that shit, and she stay in the mall, so she became my personal shopper for my chicks. She stays holding me down with some hot shit. She be having my bitches go outta their mind with the shit she picks out. She'll come back with a purse, perfume, shoes, clothes, lingerie, chocolate-covered strawberries, or whatever she feels like that day. I love that little bitch. I'd lay a nigga down behind her."

"Damn, that's some real shit," Dora said, respecting that he had a genuine love for her.

"Not that I give two fucks about son, but what's got her so into her man?"

"I guess because he's like her first boyfriend and the one to hold her down. I can't hate on the nigga, though. He's a real nigga, who gets dough. Not like you get it, but he definitely gets his. He's been with Apple for years. That's his bitch and he takes care of her. He just don't appreciate her or know what to do with a real bitch like Apple. He thinks fucking mad bitches that together can't compare to his one bitch at home is fresh or some shit. The nigga get money, but he got it fucked up in the bitch department. He be out here fucking with mad bum bitches and don't even give a fuck that he got a winner in his bed. She's a real ride or die bitch, not to mention she's bad as hell," Majors said, somewhat envious of Dame.

"Yo, I need her in my life," Dora said, definitely feeling her after all that his man had just told him. Shorty reminded him of himself in so many ways. "I don't know her man and don't really give a fuck about him, but his chick done fucked the game up. So now he got a problem on his hands," Dora laughed. "Are those really her eyes, or is she rocking contacts like no other?"

"Nah my nigga, those are hers."

"Say word, Majors," Dora said, totally fucked up in a good way. "I'm a hood nigga who just really experienced love at first sight," laughed Dora, but meaning it. "Word to my mother, nigga, shorty is gonna be mine."

Majors didn't want to hurt his man's feelings, but he had to warn him. "My nigga, don't even waste your time. Apple don't give niggaz airplay for nothing in the world. She might kick it, laugh, joke, and maybe even flirt, but that's it...I ain't heard of a nigga yet to get her to fuck around on or leave her man. And she got a hell of a fan club trying. Her man got that on lock."

"Alright," Abdora replied nonchalantly, "but just remember. I play to win and ain't never made a habit of losing."

Tavares and Jazz made their way down the block, but not without being stopped by ten dudes in the process. They were trying to talk to Tavares for the most part. Jazz was feeling a few of the niggaz who tried to holler at her, but Tavares wasn't ever enthused by men telling her how beautiful she was or how pretty she was. She wanted someone to say something else, besides that, to her.

Tavares was into something that most men, at least hood niggaz, didn't know how to do. Fuck her mind. Tavares liked someone who, in other words, could stimulate her mind and not just think about how good of a fuck she would be because she had a big ass and pretty eyes.

~ CHAPTER 2 ~

Good guys make mistakes too.

Tavares and Jazz were at the park until about 8:00 mixing and mingling and getting in where they fit in. Ending the innocent, good fun, the ladies headed home.

Getting in the car, Tavares drove her candy apple red Acura that she called Apple around the corner. She arrived at the top of Highland and Fort Hill Avenue to drop Jazz off in the housing development that everyone in the hood called Highland Projects for short.

Tavares hadn't even made it home to get dressed, and knew that she was going to be tired in the morning. "Damn, hookerbutt, if we're going out then I need to go home and get my stuff ready for tomorrow and go over some notes for a test."

"I can't believe you go to school all year and then want to take classes in the summer. It's not even like your ass had to," laughed Jazz at the fact that her friend just had a good square nature in her heart. "Just so that it can be one less class that you have to take in your last year."

"I know, but it's nothing, just a few hours in a class and a little work to occupy some of my free time," Tavares said nonchalantly.

"Do the damn thing, girl," Jazz said, sincerely proud and happy for her best friend. "I'm not mad at you, girly. I want to go to school," Jazz said, admiring that her girl was about to graduate from college after all that she had gone through in her life.

"I wonder if Leslie, Randee, and Mona-Lisa will be back in time from Six Flags to go out," Tavares thought out loud.

"You know they ain't gonna want to go out when they get back. They're going to be tired and exhausted after being in that park for over eight hours," Jazz reminded her.

"I know, right?" Tavares thought, after realizing what their nerves must be like at the moment.

"Call me when you get home," Jazz said, getting out of the car, ready to go prepare and conquer the man she had met earlier.

Tavares pulled up to her brownstone and was mad that someone was in her parking space. Damien's car was in his spot, so parking there was out too. Parking on the street rather than behind the house, Tavares walked up the stairs through the French doors mad as hell.

Stepping into the oversized stainless steel and black kitchen, Tavares screamed, "Damien, are you home?!" With no answer, Tavares knew she was home alone, as always.

"They parked all their fucking cars here, and now they're MIA. Ain't that some bullshit," Tavares said out loud to release her anger. Tavares went in the refrigerator and grabbed the honey chicken, candied yams, and collard greens she had cooked for dinner before she went out. Heating the food up, Tavares sat in the tall, black swivel chair at the island.

No sooner than she sat down, her mind drifted off faster then she could catch it. Tavares's mind rolled backwards to the events that unfolded that lead to such a rollercoaster of life over the last ten years. Tavares hadn't seen her mother, who she secretly thought about often. She wondered what it would have been like to have had her mother when she needed her most. What path would her life had gone on, instead of the direction it did.

The first ten years of Tavares's life had been straight. Her mother had always taken care of her to the best of her ability and held it down. Dolanda was a young single mother who managed working, partying, and being a mother better than most her age. Tavares didn't know what happened to her mother and father because her mother never spoke of it. All she knew was that the few times she asked about her father, her mother had a sad, broken look in her eyes before she told Tavares that her father was a good man who made a bad decision. Never nothing more or less. After the age of eight, Tavares never asked about her father again because it was clear it was just her and her mother against the world.

Tavares was very well taken care of. Maybe not everything she always wanted, but definitely everything she always needed and never nothing cheap. Tavares went to private school, the best camps in the summer, and never a birthday or a Christmas that wasn't over the top, so in her eyes her mother was the only person she needed.

When Tavares turned nine, she saw a change in her mother. Dolanda no longer wanted to spend time with Tavares or do the various activities she did with her, like the park, the zoo, the movies, shopping, skating, or anything for that matter. Dolonda suddenly went from outgoing and energetic to always tired or angry. She was giving Tavares freedom to go outside, ride her bike or hang out with the local kids. All stuff that she had never been able to do before.

Dolanda went from cooking and baking cookies to buying take-out or telling Tavares to just make herself a sandwich or get something out of the fridge. Tavares was cooking full meals by the time she was ten. Sandwiches and noodles got old real fast. She had watched her mother enough while she cooked to learn how to do it herself. It was nothing for her to whip up some scrambled eggs and make some bacon and waffles if her mother was asleep.

Ten ago years ago Tavares awoke to her mother slightly shaking her small frame. Groggy, she asked "Yes, mummy?"

"Wake up and slip on your black sweat suit and princess slippers. You're going to go down to Ms. Verlinda's house. I have to run out for a minute."

"No, mummy, I'm tired."

"You can go to sleep down there."

"Noooo," whined Tavares.

"I am not going to tell you again, get up," Dolonda said in her thick Dominican accent.

Getting up half asleep, Tavares did as she was told. Going down the dirty, smelly stairwell, one flight of stairs, Tavares was mad as hell. She didn't like Ms. Verlinda. Everything about her was a mess.

Tavares and her mother approached Ms. Verlinda's apartment. Walking into the drab house that didn't have one piece of matching furniture and was decorated with bags of smelly laundry everywhere, Tavares's eyes got big. It smelled like one big clothes hamper. Tavares had always played outside with Verlinda's daughter, but had never been inside their house and now she was glad.

Oh my God, please help me, Tavares thought, looking around the house. "Mommy, I can't believe you want me to sit in here, never mind sleep in here."

"Watch your mouth, Tavares," her mother tried to whisper, knowing that Verlinda had heard her daughter. Ms. Verlinda was the ugliest person Tavares had ever seen. She was a short, wide munchkin with no hair. It was so short that she should have just had a fade and not a weave ponytail on top of the four strands of hair she pulled in a ponytail. She had lips that were bright pink and bigger than Wanda's from *In Living Color* and had the nerve to decorate them with bright red lipstick.

"Hey Tavares, just make yourself comfortable."

Is that possible? Tavares thought to herself but told Verlinda with her facial expression.

"Me and your mom will be back," Verlinda said, ignoring the uppity child's dirty face. "You can turn on the TV."

Is that a TV? Tavares asked herself, looking at the TV that had to be older than she was.

"My two friends are going to stay here with you and Maysha till we get back. If you get tired, you can just go lay on my bed."

Yeah right, Tavares thought. Tavares looked at her mother with pleading eyes, begging her not to leave her in this dump of an apartment. Her mother didn't catch her hint because she had a monkey on her back. Plopping down on the plaid brown and orange couch, with no bounce and holes everywhere, Tavares was too upset.

Looking around the room, Tavares couldn't believe that people really lived like this because her house upstairs was the complete opposite. Tavares scanned the house once over in total disbelief. In one corner was a kitchen table with three legs. There was a recliner chair that looked like if you stood next to it, the dirt would jump on you. There were sheets hanging where the blinds should have been, and what was supposed to be a TV had no color and had a metal coat hanger coming out of it, with foil around the top. Tavares sat and stared at the two people sitting at the table, who looked like they were homeless and smelled like they had just crawled out of the dumpster out back. Tavares was watching the news on the TV that had more snow than TV coming across the screen.

Though she tried her best to stay awake, she fell asleep. Awoken by a man who was trying to whisper but failing terribly, Tavares just lay there and listened. "I'm not getting high with no kid in the room. I don't know about you two bitches, but I got some morals."

"Come on, Junie. It's cool," said the oversized woman with no teeth and a lonely-tail in her head.

"No, the fuck it ain't cool. I can't believe her mother left her here with you two buckethead fiended out bitches."

"Shit, her stuck up ass is off getting her own shit," the other equally smelly, ugly woman said. Never realizing Tavares was awake, she scared the hell out of them.

"You're right. My mother left me here with two dirty, dumpster-smelling crackheads, so yeah how much does she love me?" Tavares asked sarcastically.

"Go lay your ass down!" the toothless lady screamed.

"How about you get some teeth and then you tell me what to do?"

The gentleman couldn't help but laugh. The little girl had a lot of fire and was going to be a tough cookie when she got older.

"What, you think your mama is better then us?"

"What?" Tavares asked the woman. "You really don't want me to answer that," Tavares snapped at her. "You're a bum. You look dirty, smell dirty, and just look real crazy. And when I woke up, you were begging for drugs. Imma call you Betsy the Begging Bum," laughed Tavares.

The man just sat and watched this little girl with two long thick pony tails and killer eyes have so much attitude and smarts that she shut the lady down in her tracks. At that moment, the front door swung open and in walked Tavares's mother and Verlinda.

"What's going on?" Verlinda asked, looking from the table to Tavares and back to the table, where there was crack out.

"This smart mouth little girl needs to learn to stay out of grown folks' conversation."

"Mummy, she thought I was sleep and was talking about you."

"What the fuck was you saying about me?" Tavares's mother asked the toothless woman.

The woman responded with too much attitude. "I told her that you ain't no better then us," the lady said, with her toothless mouth curled up.

"That's where you got life fucked up, Tootsie. I ain't a motherfucking thing like your broke, sleeping from house to house, jobless, begging for a hit ass. I got a house, a car, and a job."

"Yeah and your ass got a habit, too," the toothless lady tried to mumble.

Just as the pretty lady lunged for her neck, the man grabbed her in an attempt to stop the madness that was going on in front of a little girl.

"Yo, Miss, this ain't the time or the place. Take your daughter and go. Handle your business another day," the man said in a sincere but authoritative voice.

"Verlinda, let me fucking go before I have to beat this bitch up in front of my daughter," the woman said in her thick accent as she raged with anger. "Well, go on then," the toothless lady said, itching to get the shit slapped out of her.

Arriving upstairs, Tavares's mom asked, "What else did she say, Tavares?"

"That you get high, so it was okay to smoke in front of me."

The older version of Tavares's eyes popped out her head, and she was at a loss as to what to tell her way-too-smart daughter. She learned at that moment that raising her daughter to be so mature had just backfired on her. It hit her at that moment that her habit had spun out of control.

"Don't listen to her," was all that the sad mother could muster up. "She's a sick lady and needs help."

Tavares was no fool. She was a whiz who loved school and was street smart from watching the world she lived in, so she knew her mother was lying. It didn't matter, because Tavares loved her mother and knew her mother loved her.

Three weeks later, there was a heavy knock at the door. Walking past Tavares, who was in the living room watching TV, paying no attention to the knocking, her mother made her way to the door, ready to cuss out whoever was on the other side. She snatched it open, ready to go in, until she saw who was on the other side. It was a lady in a stiff plaid suit escorted by a uniformed police officer.

"Hi, my name is Magdalina Theyus, I'm from the Department of Child Services. Someone called the Department of Child Services and informed them that drugs were being used in the home and done in front of the child."

When the police searched through the house, crack was found in the apartment on their initial visit, and Tavares was taken away. She was more like dragged, kicking and screaming.

That didn't stop Tavares's mother from smoking; she went on a binge in the days to follow and lost her job after she didn't show up or call for three days. After losing her job, she binged a little harder. Every week she told herself just another week of trying to smoke the pain away, then she would do what she had to, get clean, and get her daughter back. She couldn't pick herself up—she was brokenhearted and smoked out. Not knowing how to face the fuck up, she wallowed into a long road of crack smoking. She left Tavares to raise herself in a system that didn't care about the kids, while she nursed her soul with crack.

Tavares didn't get her mother for leaving her, because she wasn't the type to just leave her kid. Tavares didn't understand how she was where she was in the world that she was in. She went from being a normal child living with her mother to living with strangers who weren't nice and didn't even like kids. People who always wanted to yell and made the kids eat nasty food and wear cheap clothes. Tavares couldn't keep track of how many times she had sat at the table with her foster home cronies and watched the foster mother's real kids eat good. Foster home kids ate sugarless cereal, oatmeal, noodles, and hot dogs and beans. Never did they wear cute clothes, only clothes bought at the Goodwill that were rotated among the kids.

Tavares couldn't believe the cruelty that she was enduring. Tavares had always kept to herself, quiet and in a book, so the foster parents really never bothered the polite, quiet, pretty girl. But some foster mothers got gutter with it. They restricted kids to taking baths on certain days, having to wear the same four outfits, made them walk, while they drove their kids to school. Tavares did her thing in school no matter where she was or how she was being treated. School was her outlet and it paid off. Tavares went from foster home to foster home being quiet and just dealing with whatever wrath and blows came her way. Tavares was always a fighter, so fighting in the foster homes just upped her skills and made her a beast.

At twelve, Tavares was placed in a foster home with a lady who drank too much coffee and had no patience to have three foster kids on top of her two sons that lived at home. But overall she was the most normal and nicest foster mother Tavares had. Her sons were Dusty and Russy.

Dusty was never around. He was only home long enough to eat, shower, and get dressed. Russy was the younger of the two sons. He was two years Tavares's senior. For the first year, he made sly comments to Tavares and checked her out hard. Tavares wasn't feeling or hearing him or his bullshit. Screwing his hot dick ass was the last thing on her mind.

One day, Ms. Octavia had gone to the store and took the two smaller foster kids with her. Taking advantage of the moment, Russy made his way to Tavares's room, where she was laying on her stomach reading a book.

"Damn, you looking all good in them capri jeans. Won't you stop playing and let me taste it?"

"Russy, please. You ain't tasting or touching shit. Get outta here," Tavares snarled.

"Tavares, I'm about tired of your stuck-up ass playing hard to get."

Before Tavares knew it, Russy's 235-pound ass tackled her small frame full force, taking the only thing that Tavares could say she had, her virginity.

Fighting and trying to claw his big frame drained Tavares, so he won. He took what he thought he had a right to.

After finishing with Tavares, he got up and said, "You can waste your time telling my mother if you want to. I'm her son, she ain't going to put me out for you. You're just another income in the house."

Just like that, she was no longer a virgin. For two years, Russy slid in Tavares's room and took advantage of her whenever he wanted, stealing her insides every time. Tavares liked Ms. Octavia. She was the coolest foster parent she had, with the exception of her son being a rapist. But Tavares couldn't take it. She was losing her insides more and more. Unable to take another night of Russy, she ran away with nothing but what she had on her back.

Tavares was downtown on the Boston Commons trying to figure out her next move as she was curled up on a bench. It was late, it was cold, and Tavares was starving. Before Tavares appeared a strikingly handsome chocolate dude. All his facial features were strong and gave him a distinct look with his big, dark but bright eyes, thick eyebrows, and dimples that stole your heart.

"Are you straight?" he asked the dirty bum, trying to get off his last two rocks so that he could bounce from downtown. Rattered and tattered with no coat on, he assumed the lady was a fiend. After looking into her face and seeing her beauty, he knew there was no way she was an addict. At least he hoped not, because the girl wasn't more then sixteen.

"Yo, what are you doing out here in the freezing cold, with no coat on?"

"I don't have a coat or anywhere to go," Tavares said, with tears starting to come down her face. Her voice was calm as she sat up. "I've been on the streets like this for five days," Tavares said with a deep draining look on her face.

"Where are your moms and pops?"

"I don't know where my mother is. She left me fucking with that shit you just tried to offer me," Tavares said snidely. "Don't have a father. I just ran away from my foster home. My birthday just passed, and I decided that I was going to stop getting raped for my birthday. I'd much rather live out here than with people taking advantage of me."

Dame was amazed at how nonchalantly she was speaking as tears steadily trickled down her pale cheeks and her bright eyes stayed strong. He was floored because she was so beautiful underneath the dirt and dishevel. Instantly feeling a soft spot for the dirty beauty before him, Dame knew he couldn't leave her out in the cold. He wanted her and was going to clean her up and have her.

After a lot of hesitation, he convinced Tavares to let him take her for a hot meal. After taking off his wool pea coat and putting it over her shoulders, he led her to his Navigator Truck and took her around the corner to South Street Diner. After filling her belly, he gave her a deal that she couldn't refuse.

The more Tavares ate, the more Damien stared at her and couldn't believe that she was on the street homeless and with no parents. She was too pretty for that. He wanted her and he was going to breed her into a bad bitch. She was going to be his bitch. "Alright ma, this is what we going to do. I'm going to get you set up in a crib. I'll furnish it and all that."

"So just like that, you're going to put me in an apartment?" Tavares asked blankly, but with a confuse tone.

"Then we'll get my moms to make up some fake papers like you're in her custody to enroll you into school. Just how old are you anyways?"

"I turned fifteen two days ago," Tavares said with a hidden sadness.

"Damn, you gonna have a nigga catching a case," Damien said, shocked that she was younger than he'd thought.

"Why, how old are you?" Tavares asked, since he was implying he was a grown man of some sort.

"I'm eighteen, but been a man since I was twelve."

"I don't think a boy should be a man at twelve, but that's nice," Tavares sarcastically complimented.

"Alright, smart ass, back to the school shit. My aunt got some connects in the school department, so I'll have my mom hit her up and make something happen."

Tavares had been through a lot, seen a lot, and knew that everything came with a price tag. "And what do you want from me?" she asked, knowing there was a catch. "Because I'm sure that this isn't coming without a catch," Tavares said, rolling her eyes and biting her toast. "I'm not being no prostitute, so if that's what you think, thanks for the food but no thanks."

Damien liked this girl because she had spark and it just needed to be lit. "The only catch is that you're going to have to take your young ass to school and get money the way I'm going to eventually teach you."

Tavares had the skeptical look in her eyes again. "Hustling, ma, fucking hustling," Dame snapped in a whisper. Damien knew what she was thinking. "I ain't no fucking pimp. That ain't my thing."

Tavares thought about it and knew that at that point that was the best she could do.

From that day forward, Tavares and Damien had been together. They were inseparable. Where you saw him, you saw her. Damien fell in love with his molded creation. They each held up their ends of the deal. Tavares took his lessons, went to school, and mastered cooking coke and hustling better than any nigga. He combined book smarts, street smarts, and something natural in her, and produced way too good of a hustler.

In the time she had been with Damien, her life had completely changed. They had seen a lot of good times, but also bad and crazy times. From drama with the bitches, him getting arrested, Tavares beating bitches up, to him being kicked out the brownstone that he bought when he turned twenty-one for days at a time. It was always something.

As tears started to stream down Tavares's face, she hopped up, turned off the food, and kept it moving to mask her pain like she had been doing since the last time she saw her mother. Just as Tavares reached the second floor, she could hear her phone ringing on the third floor. Sprinting to the third floor, Tavares picked up the phone, out of breath.

"Damn, what the hell are you doing?" Jazz asked. "You and Damien over there being nasty, ain't yawl?"

"No, bitch, he ain't even home. I was on the first floor and heard the phone just as I got to the second floor."

"Well, I'm about to get in the shower. I just called to see if you had started your studying."

"Nah, I was heating up dinner. You know I had to feed my big baby. I don't want him acting all crazy about me going out," Tavares said, laying out on her king-sized bed that was up on a platform. "Imma 'bout to bang my studying out right now though. I know what I'm wearing, so all I have to do is shower and slip my dress and sandals on and we'll be on our way."

"Alright, call me when you get out of the shower," Jazz said, ready to get the night started with her partner in crime.

Very shy, Tavares didn't have many friends in school. From kindergarten at the age of five, when Tavares and her now best friends entered school, she wasn't a friend of theirs or many others. At recess, instead of playing hand games, tag, or hopscotch with the other girls, Tavares read a book in a corner.

By the time they skipped ahead two classes to first grade, Jazmine, Mona-Lisa, Leslie, and Randee, who had been down from their first day of pre-school, took a liking to the quiet, smart girl. All the way up until the fifth grade they were thick as thieves. Foster care wasn't covering private school tuition, and bouncing from foster home to foster home made it hard for Tavares to stay in contact with the only people who she knew loved her like family.

After going to live with Damien, life became good again. Tavares was a normal teenager, even balling out to be her age. They spent their weekends being typical teenagers on the phone, shopping, skating, clubbing, going to the park, and just doing what they felt like.

Needing to escape the pain that Boston had brought her through, Tavares made a hard decision when she graduated from Lincoln Sudbury High School with Honors. Leaving all the schools that had reputable names in Boston, she went to school down south in Georgia. Tavares just needed a change for a little while. The beautiful, quiet, small, rural town of Savannah was going to be a nice change of pace for Tavares.

Oddly, she was never in GA unless she was in class. She was always home on the weekends or when something was going on. Being home from school at least twice a month made Tavares feel like she really wasn't gone.

Wrapped in a towel ready to take a shower, Tavares's phone rang. "Hello?" she answered, aggravated.

"Damn, what's your problem?"

"Oh, hi, boo. Nothing. I was just about to take a shower and the phone started ringing."

"Where are you going?"

"Me and Jazz are going out. The rest of the crew is tired from taking the kids to Six Flags today."

"So what's popping tonight that you're going out on a Sunday?" drilled Damien.

"The Backstage," answered Tavares, knowing he knew the answer to his own question.

Sucking his teeth, Dame asked, "So you're going to fuck with them buster niggaz from the Hill, huh?"

"Here you go. I saw Majors up at the park and he invited us. It's not like it was planned, and I'm just now telling you about it. Dinner is done. The house is clean, and I'm ready for tomorrow, so leave me the hell alone," Tavares said, feeling like she had to defend herself. "Plus I haven't been out since I got home. I've been grinding hard with school, work, and hustling, so I'm overdue for a night out."

"You don't need to be out," Damien said, far from buying it. "You need to be in school and at work and hustling in between the two."

Knowing that Tavares was a hot commodity, thus far he had done good keeping her out of the streets.

"But you rip and run all day and all night," Tavares said, not even feeling the raining on her parade. Turning the tables, Tavares questioned, "Well, where the hell are you?"

"I'm down the projects, shooting the shit with niggaz. My niggaz said they saw you doing your thing at the park too. I was up there, but didn't see you."

"I know," Tavares responded with a sneaky tone. "But I saw you," Tavares said and busted out laughing.

"You're always somewhere watching, like a stalker," Damien laughed. "I don't know how your boys saw me. They were clearly doing them. I thought I crept by them," Tavares said, disappointed at her failed attempt.

"Never that, I got eyes on you wherever you go," Damien joked.

"And you talk about me being eye spy," Tavares joked.

"Baby, I need you to step on it before you go out."

"Damn, it's always something," Tavares whined. "I'm about to get in the shower. Bring your lazy ass home and do it yourself."

"You don't mind spending the money but you always complain when it comes to making it," Damien chastised her.

"Whatever," Tavares said, not wanting to hear the bullshit. "What am I stepping on?"

"Some mingmee." That was their phone word for weed.

"Damn, you got a stash of mingmee and didn't tell me?" Tavares said, snapping.

"I just got it, so kill the noise. But look at you, always wanting in on getting mingmeed up but just a second ago you didn't even want to step on it."

"Where is it?" Tavares asked, not even mad that she had to bag the smoke up. Now she was getting something out of the favor.

"Downstairs in the corner bedroom that's closer to the bathroom. Open the closet door in the right corner of the room and lift the floor up. When you step on the mingmee, deuce it," Damien said, letting Tavares know to break them down into ounces.

"You got it," Tavares said, ready for him to get off the line so she could get the weed stash up. "I'll call you before I go to the club."

"Yeah, do that," Damien said, not feeling that his girl was going out.

Going downstairs, Tavares grabbed the weed, did as she was told, and wondered how much more of this life she could take.

When she met Dame, he offered her a deal she couldn't refuse because she had nothing to her name. Something was always better then nothing. He had even loved her and taken good care of her over the years, but now she wanted more: to be totally and completely in love against all odds, and Dame wasn't doing that. He came with baggage that she was tired of. The drugs were bad, but she could deal with it for the time being. But the streets, the baby's mother drama, drama with other chicks, and his extra bullshit were just too much.

Tavares bagged up while also weighing the good and the bad of being with Dame. The bad always won, no matter how hard she tried to make the good outweigh it. Tavares put the bagged up ounces in a canvas satchel and left it next to the door. Tavares took her two ounces of weed and headed to the shower.

~ 49 ~

Stepping out of the shower, Tavares called Jazz. "What's up, chick-a-Rita?"

"Nothing, girl."

"Well, I just got out of the shower. I was calling to see what type of progress you done made."

"I was laying here watching videos making my booty clap. I been took a shower and curled my hair," Jazz said, still into what she was doing before the phone rang. "I need to figure out what I'm wearing though. What are you wearing?"

"Fuck what I'm wearing. All that time you been making your flabby ass bounce, you could have had an outfit picked out. I need you to get that together and work that out," Tavares said, sarcastic but serious. "I told you I'm wearing a dress and some sandals."

"Well, I'm about to get up now. How long before you get here?" Looking at the clock on the side of her bed, Tavares said in forty-five minutes. "I'll call you when I get down Dudley, so you can be ready to walk out the door."

Tavares walked into her walk-in closet, grabbed her dress, threw it on her king-sized bed, and went to do her make up. Making her face up with bold, smoky pink eye makeup to accentuate her blue eyes, some lip gloss, and a spray of Dior Addict, Tavares was ready to roll as she slipped on her extra sexy dress that was three shades of pink. Every time Tavares moved, the dressed looked like it was a different color pink. Tavares took her thick hair down out of her scarf, pulled it back in a ponytail, and put it in a bun.

All you saw was her beautiful face, sparkling diamond studs, and funky yet sexy eye make up that screamed, *I'm sexy, come get me.* Grabbing her matching hot pink sandals that tied around the ankle in a perfect bow, Tavares slid them on. Knowing she was drop dead sexy, Tavares walked out the door and was ready to party.

~ CHAPTER 3 ~

The game is to be sold not told.

Pulling up to Jazz's house, Tavares watched Jazz come down the stairs in some black, fitted Capri pants, a black and silver shimmer wife beater, and some silver wedge-heeled slide-on sandals. Her hair was curled extra curly in an upsweep to show off the funky blue shadow she was wearing.

"Okay, Sexy Lady," Tavares said as Jazz climbed in the front seat with a rolled blunt. "I know you ain't talking, because that dress has major breast action going on. I can only imagine what your ass looks like in it."

"Shut up, heffa," Tavares said, playfully slapping Jazz. Making their way to 93 north, they kicked it while they blew it down.

"I bet Damien didn't see the sexy production," teased Jazz, loving how sexy it was.

"And so what if he didn't? I'm grown and can wear what I want," Tavares said, knowing Damien wouldn't have loved it.

"Uh huh," Jazz said with a look that read, "convince yourself, not me."

Exiting the highway at Fanual Hall, they parked in the garage. "I can't believe Fanual Hall wants fifty dollars to park," Jazz said as they exited the garage toward the club.

"Girl, this is the number one tourist place in Boston. They have the hottest stores, restaurants, history, and the aquarium, so of course they want dough to park," reminded Tavares. Trying to not get their heels stuck in the cobblestones, they carefully walked past the long rows of stores on each side of them toward the club.

The Backstage was on the corner of the row and the line was about two stores down. "Thank God Majors put us on the list," Tavares said.

Hearing people sucking their teeth and niggaz trying to get their attention, Tavares and Jazz walked to the front of the line. "Miss, the line is back there," the bouncer said, pointing to the hundred people behind them.

"Oh, no, sir, I'm on the VIP list."

"Oh, well, in that case, what's your name?" asked the overly muscular high yellow bouncer with freckles. Placing two VIP bands on their hands, the girls entered the club for free. Walking up the two flights of steel stairs, the girls could hear the Lil Wayne, as always, going hard body on the track. He was roaring through the club.

"Damn, it's damn near packed in here," Jazz said after seeing the large amount of people already inside.

Backstage wasn't all that big. It was a restaurant that was converted to a club at night. It was the shape of a square. There were leather-seated booths on the front exterior, and a bar on the back exterior. The sides were empty to linger about and had a set of stairs on each side. The center of the room served as the dance floor. Above the bar was an upstairs area that was the VIP lounge, which overlooked the small club. Making their way up the stairs to the VIP section, Tavares spotted Majors, B Rude, and Choppy from the Hill, popping bottles and surrounded by tons of groupies.

"Bitches kill me," laughed Tavares as she watched the chicks surround the hosts of the party.

"They're on them niggaz hard body," said Jazz, looking at all the thirsty bitches around them. Chicks were always trying to score as arm candy with the Hill due to all the dough they had. They didn't care if they looked like hood groupies because the Hill were the hood celebrities.

Tavares just chuckled and said, "Watch this." Tavares made her way over to the corner they were holding down and said, "Excuse me" with a real nasty tone so that all the chicks' attention was got. "I'm looking for the three fathers of my six kids," Tavares said to the women. "I tend to find them where the street urchins are lurking. B Rude, Majors, and Choppy please don't look like yawl don't know who the fuck I am! I got babies with all you trick dick sons of bitches. Ladies, how did I get all three ballers is what you're thinking, right? I know, I sometimes wonder myself. But, ladies, the game is to be sold, not told, so yawl hold that thought. You three hot dick, no good, always tricking on bitches motherfuckers, you got time to flirt, then you each got time to come pick up each of your motherfucking kids and be fucking fathers," Tavares said, rolling her eyes and snapping her neck so hard that you would have sworn she was for real.

"Fuck you," Majors said first, falling out laughing at his homegirl, who had the bitches definitely believing her.

"Don't mind this nut," B Rude said, "she just likes to be an asshole."

They watched the pretty chick steal their shine in a matter of seconds. Choppy loved Apple because she pretty as all hell, but she was so fucking cool. She wasn't no dick-riding chick, like the chicks who were giving her dirty looks right now. Exchanging short conversation with her homeboys, Tavares let the mad onlooker groupie broads have them back.

Making their way to get a bottle, the ladies sipped and watched the jam-packed crowd below them. B Rude, who got his name because all he knew how to do was be rude, came over. Even when he was being nice and polite, he still seemed to be rude, so the name stuck.

"What's good, hookers?"

"Chillin'," said Jazz, loving how fine B was. He was out of Jazz's league, but he was still fine to admire. There was nothing that wasn't fine about him. His color, hair, smell, looks, style, swag, dress game, even his fucked up mouth was a turn on to Jazz. He was the poster child for pretty boy gangster. Tavares never blinked or responded to his greeting.

"What the fuck, you don't hear me or something, Apple?" B Rude asked, real snappy. He knew what she was doing. "If you don't, then clean your fucking ears out."

"Fuck you, I can hear you. But I ain't no fucking hooker, so address me by my name. I know you stay laying up with a stinking ass hooker, but don't get us confused," Tavares said, rolling her eyes and looking B Rude up and down. They both burst out laughing.

"You always talking shit, Apple."

"No, that be you starting shit."

"Okay, I'm sorry," he said, doing something he never did— apologize. "Apple, what's up? You know I don't be giving a fuck about chicks' feelings and shit right?"

Tavares started smiling, because she had beat him, as she always did with his fucked up mouth. "Ain't shit, just enjoying the festivities of the Hill being big ballers, shot callers," Apple sang as she two-stepped.

"Ahhh, here you go, Apple."

"What?" Apple asked innocently.

"You got a lot of nerve talking about someone balling," B Rude said to Apple, in a manner that read between the lines of—if don't no one else know, you know I know your money flow. "Look at that sick-ass ring on your finger and that bracelet. Let me hold something, homegirl." You know you got stacks on deck," B Rude laughed.

"Whatever, B, I don't have shit. I'm out here starving, just like everyone else. I'm a squirrel trying to get a nut. Not everyone can be out here big balling and doing the shit yawl do," Apple said, motioning for him to just look around. "Yawl are dem dudes. Yawl got ladies, chicks, whores, and gold diggers playing to win!"

"Shit, well when you going to leave that buster and come fuck with a real nigga like me?"

"B, please. You got more game than a fat kid has cakes. Why am I going to leave one asshole for another? I watch you dog these weak bitches out with your rude mouth. You like to act craaaazy and that mouth is too out of control for me. You don't care who you talk crazy to, so why would I subject myself to that?" Tavares asked, really curious to hear his answer.

Mr. B Rude didn't answer though. He knew Apple was right.

"Don't you remember when you shut Major's birthday party down because you gonna tell that girl, 'Bitch, shut up!' Your high-pitched squeaky fucking voice is irritating the fuck outta everyone in the room. So close your fucking mouth or go to another room in the house."

B Rude burst out rolling at the fact that Tavares was still talking about that night. "Damn, Apple, you ain't still talking about that, are you?"

Tavares couldn't believe her ears or her eyes that night, as she witnessed her boy be a straight disrespectful asshole for no reason, in a serious but so calm tone. "Yeah, I am, because you was just doing too much. Then when she gets mad, which she should have, you going to tell her: 'Look here bitch, either shut up or go get your brother, your father, your boyfriend, or whoever you think is tough, because I don't slap women or bitches like yourself.' I don't want to hear your bum bitch lips squawk another minute," Tavares said, just shaking her head. "Then your punk ass going to turn around and go back to gambling like nothing ever happened."

"Shit didn't happen, except she did as I said and shut up. Then she let me take her home that night and bust her down," laughed B Rude. "But I told her she couldn't talk because ain't shit changed, I still didn't want to hear her fucking squabble."

Tavares and Jazz just laughed because B Rude was one of a kind.

"The dumb bitches you fuck with actually be pretty but they ain't too smart, I swear they ain't," Tavares said. They act like it's cute and cool how fucked up and mean you act. I ain't got time for that shit." B Rude had to smile because, although he was fine as fine got, Apple never fell for his game. She had just hit the nail on the head. "Apple, I'll give it to you, you be on your shit."

"How can I not be, hanging around niggaz like you?" laughed Tavares.

"Well, when you're ready, you know where to find me," B said, giving Tavares a kiss on the cheek and Jazz dap; then he went back to his groupies.

Jazz and Tavares were in their own world. They were around the corner from drunk as they danced and took shots of Patrón. Majors came to join the private party. The ladies stopped diddy-bopping to give him a hug.

"So what's up with your man?" Jazz questioned, without even saying hello.

Majors just laughed and shook his head. "I can dig it Jazz, you're trying to get yours off top. Ain't nothing wrong with that," he laughed. He admired her drive but felt bad that the man in question was at Apple, not her.

"He's a good nigga. I met that nigga through my Bajan mans and them. Dora gets crazy paper. And I do mean crazy stupid paper. And not even just in these streets. He got mad legit businesses popping. He's a real stand up nigga. Will go to the end of the earth to help or do anything for anyone. But he's a stomp down gangster that be on his shit and takes very little shit in these streets. He's a real ass nigga that I have mad love for. I done came across a lot of niggaz in this game in my day, but he's one of the realest. He got real stand up qualities and ways about himself."

"Damn, so you ain't got nothing bad to say about the nigga?" Tavares said sarcastically, cutting her boy off before he could say anything else.

"Damn, Apple, why, you want me to say some fucked up shit about him?" laughed Majors.

"He's got a flaw, trust me he's not perfect," Tavares said as if she knew it for a fact.

Jazz probed Majors a little while longer, trying to figure her angle to come at Abdora, while Tavares took shots and laughed at how serious her friend was. Tavares thought he was fly, no doubt, but she wasn't in stalkeratzi mode like her girl.

"I'm going downstairs," Tavares said to Jazz. "Are you coming?"

"Fuck that, ain't no way in hell I'm going down into that crowd to get outside," answered Jazz. "That Patrón got me nice, I'm good."

"Suit yourself," Tavares said and spun around to make her way outside. Tavares walked down the stairs of the VIP section. *I need a stupid cigarette,* Tavares thought to herself, exiting the club. *Thank goodness I bummed one,* Tavares thought, fiending for the cigarette as she walked down the outer stairs. Buying cigarettes was a no-no. She didn't smoke unless her intoxication was climbing toward drunk. For some odd reason, it was the only time Tavares wanted or could stand the taste of a cigarette.

Getting outside, Tavares realized she didn't have a lighter. "Damn," she said out loud, mad as hell. Turning around to go back in, she bumped clean into a six-foot-six, bald-headed, light-eyed, long-lashed, bow-legged, clean-cut god.

"Excuse you," Tavares said with her glassy, sky blue eyes, still stunned at his gorgeousness. "I didn't even realize you were right behind me."

"You wasn't supposed to," he shot back with just enough cockiness. "But it's more than a pleasure to see you again."

"Twice in one day," Tavares thought, but said out loud, "Likewise."

Dora admired that Tavares looked even better than she did earlier. *Something about her I like*, Dora thought as he looked Tavares up and down. She was so bad that earlier she conquered him at, "Hi, nice to meet you."

"As beautiful as you are, I wouldn't mind having the pleasure of seeing you every day."

Laughing, Tavares responded that was cute. "Excuse me though," Tavares said, attempting to excuse herself.

"I'm not ready to move," he said, looking down at the shorty he towered over by more than a foot and a half, as he rolled his eyes and sucked his luscious bottom lip. His tone sounded like he was trying to enforce his gangster that Tavares wasn't going for, even though it was definitely to be recognized.

"I didn't know people had the right to stand in other people's way," Tavares shot back, with her blue eyes icy and more sass in her voice than he had just tried to use on her. His sexiness was giving her a run for her money. Tavares was having a hard time with his succulent lips, soft eyes, and gangsta demeanor.

"I wasn't in your way, Lil Mama. I was stepping into your life. I wanna giftwrap the globe and give you the world after I make you my queen."

Tavares laughed, but was kind of flattered at his slick words. "I bet! How often do you use that line?" Tavares asked as she gave a sarcastic chuckle. The joke was on Tavares, though.

"Never, till I met your blue-eyed ass," Dora laughed, but was more than serious.

"Ooooh, excuse me," Tavares, having no other response

"Your eyes are hot to death, what are you?" Her skin was the color of an olive-toned white woman or a light Spanish person. Her thick features were those a white woman wouldn't have, though. She definitely had some black somewhere, with all the hips and ass she was carrying. It was even more confusing when you got to the long, thick, wavy hair and blue eyes.

"I'm Dominican, Italian, and Trinidadian. Although I can only verify the Dominican," laughed Tavares.

"Hmmm…that's a very interesting combination," Abdora said, knowing that he would have never got that right. Tavares realized that this stranger was the first person that she had ever shared the one fact that her mother had shared with her about her father—his race.

"Do you know that you're beautiful?" Abdora asked.

"Where did that come from?" Tavares asked, looking at him like he had lost his mind.

"I want to know if you know that you're beautiful, what's wrong with that?"

"Yeah, I do," Tavares said, looking at him like he was crazy. "Imma need you to not be getting all sentimental on me after only a few minutes. I know that I'm soft on the eyes, but don't melt on me just yet."

"Now who got the jokes," he laughed at the wittiness of the pretty lady.

Tavares was digging the overly sexy, handsome guy, but he was off limits for her. Trying to put in a good word for Jazz, Tavares said, "My girl is going to be happy to see you showed up." Walking around him, not even wanting a cigarette anymore, Tavares needed some space because he was making her hot all over.

"Why's your girl going to be happy to see me?" he asked, trying to play it off that her girl was feeling him.

"Boy, don't play with me," Tavares said giving him the evil eye. "Why do you think we even came out?" Giving him no room to answer, Tavares said, "Because my girl wanted to see you."

"That's the only reason you came out?"

"Absolutely. I don't go out during the week. To be honest, I don't really even go out at all."

"Why's that? Your man got you tied up in the house?"

"If so you say," Tavares responded.

"I don't so say. I'm asking—trying to figure out what has a beautiful, young woman such as yourself all cooped up in the house."

"I never said I was cooped up in the house. What I said was I don't go out. I do a lot of stuff other than go to clubs and mingle in the streets," Tavares said, shutting him down.

"Okay, Miss Apple, don't hurt me."

"I won't," Tavares said, "as long as you don't make me." She flashed him a sexy smile.

"So tell me how you got the name Apple." Tavares batted her eyes.

"Stop it, I'm sure you have figured out why they call me Apple," and they both laughed, knowing he had. Her butt was large, solid, and perfectly round, like an apple.

"I like that," he said with a sly grin. "Who gave it to you?"

"Long story," Tavares laughed, not wanting to expose that one day her friends sat an apple on her butt and when it didn't fall they began calling her Apple.

"So Apple, how can I get to know you?"

"You can't. I have a boyfriend, and I don't do the cheating thing," Tavares said with a serious face. "But I told you my girl wants to holler at you." Dora and rejection usually didn't go hand in hand.

"I'm not trying to holler at your friend. I'm trying to know you." Dora was loving this cute, sexy, sassy, blue-eyed monster in front of him.

"Well, I'm taken, so I don't know what to tell you, playboy."

And she was loyal, not a hoe for a cute face and a few dollars. He was liking her more and more. "Well, tell your man I said 'don't slip up,' because I'm in the wings waiting. But before you go, what's your real name?"

"Tavares."

"That's different, yet pretty."

"Thanks, but please don't ask where my mom got it."

"I won't. But for the record you're wearing the hell out of that dress, Ms. Tavares."

Dora was referring to the pink halter-top dress that was made like Marilyn Monroe's famous white dress. Tavares's was changing shades of pink every time she moved.

"Thank you, you don't look to bad yourself," Tavares said, winking and loving his hood swagger that was present even when he was dressed up.

"I hope I get to see you again, Ms. Tavares," Abdora said, throwing a hint, hoping Tavares caught it.

Blushing, Tavares said, "I doubt it, but have a good night, sir." She excused herself and made her way back to the VIP lounge to throw back a few more shots of Patrón.

Damn, he thought as he watched the thick, tri-racial woman with more ass than the Lord should allow walk back inside. *I want her.*

He wasn't used to getting rejected. Broads went through all kinds of crazy tactics to get at him, so he could respect the tables being turned. Even though he didn't like it, he could appreciate it. Dora liked her. Not too many walked away from him—actually, she was the first, and that was the first point for her in his book

"Damn, where you been?" asked Jazz, realizing that Tavares had been gone for more than a hot minute.

"I was outside running my mouth, talking to ole boy that was at the park today."

"Tavares, you bitch!" Jazz yelled all crazy, with her eyes damn near popping out her head. "I'm at that. You better not have been out there trying to bag him."

"Damn bitch, is it that serious?" Tavares said in disbelief at how her girl had just come off. "Relax, thirsty, you can have him. I got a man at home, remember? You know damn well I don't do the cheating thing, so trust me I was def not out there doing anything other than conversing."

"But I gotta question for you," Tavares said, looking utterly confused, as her eyes squinted real low. "Were you really just acting all crazy over a nigga you seen once?" she asked.

"Shut up, bitch," Jazz said laughing, after she realized she had gotten kinda serious about her crush. "I didn't mean to, but you know one look into them eyes and you have them hypnotized. I didn't want you reeling my boo in with them ocean blue eyes. My bad, Tavares. I'm sorry."

"You should be, Jazz, because you got real aggressive," Tavares said, still a little confused by her girl's actions.

"And FYI, bitch, if I was down there hollering at him, you better know he hollered at me. I don't do *NO* hollering, that ain't even in my swag," Tavares said, clarifying to her homegirl while letting her also read between the lines at the same time. "So calm the fuck down and stop acting all crazy," Tavares said, letting her girl know she had just been dead wrong.

Knowing that Abdora had been out there with Tavares, Jazz felt like she was under pressure. "I'll be back," Jazz said, wanting to make her move on Abdora. Making her way downstairs, she saw him at the bar and went straight for him. "Hey, Handsome."

Turning around, Dora saw Apple's girl.

"I see you made it out," she said with a pretty, beaming smile.

"I came out to support my man, before I head back home."

"Well, I'm glad you did. I was hoping I'd bump into you."

"Is that right, uhhh…" Dora said, totally blank to what her name was. "Forgive me, I'm bad with names," Dora lied.

"It's Jazz and I'm not gonna beat around the bush. I'm trying to get to know you. I want your number so that I can come check you in Jersey, one on one. I'm sure you got mad chicks on your team, that's cool," Jazz said, overly nonchalant. "I just gotta be the captain."

Tempting as she was with her striking boldness, Dora knew who he wanted and it wasn't her. She was a mean time chick and definitely not worth her girl that he was trying to keep for the long haul. Seeing an out across the room, where his man was arguing with a chick, Dora said, "How about you holler at me a little later. I need to go take care of that real quick."

Unsatisfied, Jazz said, "No problem," and made her way upstairs to inform Tavares that she had just kicked it with Dora. Jazz must have been a little clouded or intoxicated, because she told Tavares that they had talked and confirmed she was getting his number to go to Jersey to check him one on one.

Tavares wasn't a hater, so if Jazz did her thing and bagged him, that was what's up. She wanted Jazz to make it happen with Dora. Tavares figured since she couldn't have him, someone should. Tavares was a little impressed with him. He made your eyes wanna melt when you looked at him, had it going on in the business department, and was sexy as hell with his ruggedly gangster swagger. *What wasn't to be impressed by*? Tavares asked herself.

Dora was downstairs rocking with his boys. They had a corner occupied, throwing back shots of Hennessy, with chicks flocking to them like celebrities. Dora wasn't amazed, neither were his boys, but they let the chicks do them and got rec off of them. All the chicks breaking their necks to get at them were clearly materialistic and had shovels on their backs. The fellas chatted with them, bought them a drink, and sent them on their way in a nice, diplomatic way.

Sipping on Moet and taking Patrón shots while two-stepping, the ladies enjoyed the evening that was going by too fast. Both were eyeing Dora as they stood diagonally from him. Tavares was doing her thing and merely observing the interesting scene of all the chicks throwing themselves at him. Jazz was clocking Dora's every move while trying to size up her competition.

Before the ladies knew it, they had drunk and danced their way to 2:00 a.m. The lights came up, and from above, Tavares watched people start to whip out their phones and call their late night thang thangs. Dudes were lingering around, trying to see what was popping with the chick they had bought the most drinks for. Loud, drunk women conversed their way to the ladies' room for one last release before they made it home. Others were making their way to the door and running their mouths in large and small crowds.

Tavares and Jazz were definitely wavy. They realized their level of intoxication while walking down the stairs that they both had to hold on tight to. Neither was falling all over the place or slurring, but the Patrón and Moet had definitely done a job on them. Tavares was trying her best to keep her "Imma bad bitch" walk straight. She wasn't struggling for balance, but her walk definitely felt like it was in slow motion.

They were finally outside, heading to the car when someone yelled, "You need me to carry you?"

Turning around, Tavares knew it was who she hoped it wasn't. "No thank you," she answered. Her uncontainable blush said the opposite. Jazz was crushed that he was on Tavares. She wasn't going to hate on her homegirl, though.

"Well at least let me walk yawl to your car." Dora waved for his friends to meet him at the car.

"Sure, why not," Jazz said, looking at the dressed up gangster in white linen pants with the matching shirt that wasn't buttoned, a new fitted crispy white tee, and some out the box Gucci bowling ball sneakers.

"Did yawl have a good time?" the sexy man asked.

Answering for both of them, Jazz said, "Yeah, we had a ball, how about you?"

"Yeah, it was cool. Coming out served its purpose," Dora said smugly.

"What was that?" inquired Jazz.

Deflecting her question to avoid answering, "to get Apple," Dora asked, "Tavares, why you so quiet?"

Jazz realized that he had called Apple by her real name. *Okay, they were getting real acquainted,* Jazz thought.

"No reason." Tavares was drunk and knew it, so her words were limited. "I'm tired and ready to get home." The Moet and Patrón had her to her limit and she wasn't about to make herself look a fool in front of this fine ass dude. "I'm just tired and letting yawl talk."

"Don't be so tight-lipped," Dora said, pulling Tavares's bun.

Finally approaching the car, the ladies got in and said thanks. "So Apple, are you going to let me call you?"

"I don't think that would be a good idea."

"Nah, it wouldn't. You're right," Dora said. "It would be a great idea," he said, like he was learning her something new.

Blushing, Tavares said, "Maybe it would, but really I can't. I would if I could. But I can't, so I won't," Tavares said, with puppy dog eyes for the both of them.

Tavares never saw the car parked two cars down, watching her every move.

"I'm out of here tomorrow morning, so please don't send me home without your number," he said, trying to extend his phone to Tavares.

"If we see each other again, it will be a pleasure to encounter you, but for real, I can't take your number."

"You drive a hard bargain," Dora said, "but Imma see you again. Believe that."

Tavares doubted it, but said okay anyways.

Jazz sat in the passenger seat, salted. She couldn't believe that the nigga of her dreams, who she had just went at hard, shut her down and then hollered at her girl—her girl who already had a man and a happy home.

Tavares dropped Jazz off and was damn near home when her cell phone rang. Fumbling to watch the road and dig for her phone, Tavares finally found it. "Hello?"

"Bitch, I saw your trick ass all in that nigga's face, giving him your number."

"Excuse me?" Tavares said. "Yeah, hoe, you was in the parking lot all in that nigga's face. I bet you Dame don't know his sweet little schoolgirl is a hoe."

"Well how about you let him know, then. I don't got time for this shit, Shaunda."

Shaunda was Dame's baby's mother. She and Tavares hated each other with a passion. They hadn't got along since day one. She was the last person that needed to have seen her tonight, even though she didn't give her number out. "I think I will do just that. Then my baby's father can be back home, loving me and his kids."

Tavares laughed so hard she was crying.

"What the fuck is so funny, bitch?"

Tavares was still laughing. "Bitch, you're funny! Is that what you think, Shaunda? Dame wouldn't fuck with your bum bitch ass if his life depended on it."

"That's what you think, but we'll see when I get to his stash house and let him know what a trick bitch you are."

Two minutes from home, Tavares busted a U-turn on Mass Ave to head to the projects. Tavares knew she had to beat his petty baby's mother there. Making it there in three minutes flat, Tavares was so tired of the bullshit.

Getting out of her car and rushing up the stairs, Tavares went to ring the bell but was stopped short by a blow to her head. She fought hard to keep her balance. Screaming from the pain, she turned around to see Shaunda and what was about to be a sucker punch. Kicking Shaunda backwards, Tavares laid on the bell one good time and came down the stairs before she could be attacked on the cement stairs. Tavares knew it was about to be on, and Dame would never know it, because fighting was the norm in the projects, so people never paid it any attention. As Shaunda's girls picked her up, Tavares was squaring up, knowing that they were about to jump her. Tavares punched Shaunda one good time, and the blows started to come from every direction. With the bell ringing and no one answering, Dame looked out the window and saw his baby's mother and her girls were trying to tear into somebody who was holding her own.

Oh, this bitch is buggin', Dame thought as he threw on his wheat, construction Timberlands, and t-shirt. Coming down the three flights of orange, dirt-filled steel stairs, Dame came outside and was in shock when he saw the chick they were jumping was his girl. Tavares was holding her own, for four bitches to be on her. She was swinging every which way, catching them where she could. Dame busted his 9 mm Glock in the air and everyone stopped.

"You fucking hoodrat bitches got the nerve to be out here jumping my shorty and making my spot hot. I should shoot all you bitches."

They were all shook to death. He walked to the car they were in and shot all the tires out instead. "Now you bum bitches can walk home."

No energy, and blood all down her face, Tavares caught her breath. No one was going to make another move because they knew Dame would really shoot them.

"That bitch can't shoot the ones with me, so they had to jump," Tavares said in pain.

"Dame, I came here to tell you that she was at the club tricking all in some nigga's face. You don't need a bitch like her. They were in the parking lot and your hoe bitch gave him her number." From nowhere, Tavares had a newfound rush of energy in her weak body and slapped the shit out of Shaunda's lying ass.

Pointing his gun, Dame said, "I dare one of you bitches to move and get shot tonight." He knew that a fair one was only right.

Tavares was beating the shit out of Shaunda one on one. Tavares was giving her body blows with her knees in between punching her in the face. Shaunda fell backwards. Hitting the ground, Shaunda curled up in a ball. Tired from all the drama, Tavares just stopped and spit on Shaunda and said, "Babe, let's go."

Mad that he had to be in the middle, Dame left his baby's mother right there on the pavement and hopped in Tavares's car and headed home. Shaunda had got what she deserved for the sucker move she pulled by jumping Tavares.

Getting home, Damien couldn't believe what had just happened. Pouring alcohol on her open cuts, Tavares screamed.

"So what is this bitch talking about you were at the club tricking and giving your number out?"

"Your baby's mother is dumb and blind! I wasn't fucking tricking. I was upstairs in VIP all night. I didn't even see that bitch at the club. Yes, someone asked for my number in the parking lot, and I clearly told him no. That bitch didn't see me doing shit. I was headed home, and the bitch calls my phone talking all types of shit about how she's on her way to tell you a whole bunch of bullshit. I get there, and just as I was about to ring the bell, the bitch hits me from behind."

"Well, you whooped her ass, one on one, so that's what matters." Hurting, Tavares knew she was not going to be happy at work tomorrow.

Dame crawled in bed and tried to hold her as close as he could without hurting her. With Dame kissing her eyes and her face, Tavares drifted off to sleep before she knew it.

~ CHAPTER 4 ~

You do dirt, you get dirt.

Tavares woke up and Dame was gone. Knowing that he was outside making his morning money with the fiends in the projects, she turned her head to the right of the bed.

Looking in the mirror, horror was Tavares's first feeling. Her face looked just like she had expected. Her once pale face was now purple and blue. *Thank God for MAC makeup*, Tavares thought. She was in twice as much pain as she had been in last night.

Rolling out of bed, Tavares made her way to the shower and just let her thoughts run wild as she stood under the hot water. Tavares was too tired of Damien's baby mama drama. All her and Shaunda did was fight and argue, and it was getting old. She loved her man but hated the drama that came with loving him.

As Tavares sat on the bed, she picked up her cell phone. Noticing that she had seven missed calls, she called Jazz. Tavares told her what happened.

"Bitch, why the fuck didn't you call me last night?"

"For what? It was over. It's not like I knew they were coming there to jump me."

"We could have gone to that bitch's house and gave her the business. That bitch better hope I don't see her, because it's on—on site," Jazz said, only imaging how bad her friend's face looked.

"It's cool, Jazz, because I shot the ones with her after they jumped me. Trust and believe I got my money back."

"Tavares, that bitch is a real sucker. How did she hear that nigga ask you for your number? We must have been so fucked up that we didn't even see them in the parking lot."

"I know, right?" Tavares said sluggishly. "Girly, let me motivate. I'll call you when I get to work."

"I can't believe you're going to work and your face is all messed up."

"I'm going to cover it up with some makeup and it will be fine. My body is what hurts more than anything."

"Well, hit me up later," Jazz said, and the line went silent.

Ready for a long day, Tavares pulled into the parking lot, sipping Starbucks French Vanilla coffee, and parked her apple red Acura.

Monday at Roxbury Court House was always busy. Doing intakes at the counter and in the cellblock of the busiest court house in the state was the worst way to start a Monday morning, especially in the condition she was in.

"Excuse me, how do I fill this form out?" asked a smelly, blond-haired, freckle-faced, oversized woman with three kids.

Tavares was not in the mood and it showed in her attitude. "What are you here for?" asked Tavares.

"My son got arrested and asked me to come."

"Well, you don't need to fill out that form," Tavares said, agitated. "Grab the log, look for his name, and it will tell you what courtroom he's in."

"Thank you," the lady said, and turned away.

"Miss, I can't afford no lawyer, so what's going to happen?" said a tiny Hispanic woman with too many track marks on her arm.

"Ma'am, just fill out the form and a judge will determine if you are indigent and eligible for a free lawyer."

Looking crazy, the woman responded, "What is ingent?"

"I said indigent, and it basically means poor, needy, or destitute. All things that you seem to be, so you should be okay," Tavares snapped.

After clearing the counter of the variety of people checking in on various charges, Tavares headed up to the cellblock to do intakes there.

"Why me?" Tavares asked as she climbed her way to the third floor of the courthouse.

As soon as she stepped past the first smelly, dim cell, Tavares questioned why she came into work today. As she walked, all types of things were hurled from the cells. "Yo...Sexy." "Damn, she got mad ass." "Don't act brand new, like I don't know you and your man." "I would take that ass on my face." "That bitch is mad stuck up." "That's Dame Sharkin's girl, don't waste your time." As usual, Tavares left those cells where they were talking shit for last, which meant they would see the judge last.

"Apple," a voice said down the hall and she stopped in her tracks. Walking toward where she had been called, she spotted her favorite cousin, Carlos, in the doorway. He was really Dame's cousin, but you couldn't tell because they were hella close.

"Nigga, don't you ever call my name out like that. You had me nervous."

"When I heard all the niggaz yelling, I got happy as hell. I knew it had to be you coming."

Tavares just laughed. "What the hell are you doing in here?"

"Man, for some fucking bullshit. My baby's mother straight pulled a stunt. She was playing on my girl's phone and threatening her. My girl goes to her house, checks her and fucks her up, and then she calls the police and tells them I fucking did it and that she fears for her life. Next thing I know, I'm in the crib in my boxers and the police come and arrest me."

"Aww, man, cuz, that's a bad hit. But you should be good as long as your girl says you were home all night and tells them it was her."

"Yeah, she's downstairs ready to hold daddy down!" They both laughed because Carlos swore he was the man.

"I'll put your intake form on top so you can go first and get out of here."

"Good looks," Carlos said. "Cousin, that suit you have on is nice as hell," he said, looking his cousin's girl up and down. "I see you been breaking that nigga Dame's pockets," referring to Tavares's chocolate linen capri pants and double-breasted jacket, with her cream camisole and cream platform peep toe sandals.

"I don't break his ass for shit. He gives me what I deserve. But let me go. Hit me up later on tonight," said Tavares. "I have to finish these intakes."

"Aight, thanks again cousin."

Walking to the largest tank, Tavares was glad that she was just about done. She stopped in her tracks, blinking twice. She thought she had lost her mind.

"We have to stop meeting like this," the man said, looking at Apple and thinking he wasn't happy to be seeing her like this, but he was still happy to have bumped into her again. He couldn't help but think she was still okay with him, even though she was the law.

This is not happening to me on a Monday morning, Tavares thought.

Half jokingly, Tavares asked, "Where did you come from and why don't you go back?"

After she did his intake, Dora said, grinning, "Even though you're down with the law, I still like you, Ma."

Damn scruffy, talking shit and all, this dude was still fine.

"So you hang out with criminals at night and crucify them by day, what type of shit is that?" he joked, but he was serious.

"Excuse you," Tavares said, not even going to entertain his smart mouth. "What did you do?"

"They say I was drinking and driving, but I was hardly doing that. I was more like DWB: driving while black. He only pulled us over because we were in a Bentley. I offered to take a breathalyzer and everything, and he didn't want to give it to me, because he knew better. I start talking shit so he hits me with disorderly conduct and drinking while driving, because there was an open container in the car. The pig just wanted a reason to arrest me."

"Sounds good," Tavares said. "Unfortunately I'm not the judge, gorgeous. But the good news is that they'll probably just slap you with probation."

"Damn, so will you be my probation officer?" he asked like he had just hit the jackpot.

"Not a chance in hell, but good try," Apple said, walking away.

Doing the intakes of over 150 weekend arrests took the whole morning. Tavares placed her cousin's on top and made her way back downstairs to her office to get caught up on paperwork. Deep in her work groove, her phone interrupted her thoughts.

"Good afternoon, Probation, Tavares Del Gada speaking."

"Oh, bitch, please! What the hell are you doing? I know you ain't working. You ain't been at your desk all damn day, so please don't front like you been working," said Jazz.

"Bitch, this is the courthouse, so my working requires more than sitting on my ass. And if you even had a fucking a job that didn't require partying, you would know that. Now, what the hell do you want?"

"I want you to look up someone's record for me."

"No."

"Why not, Apple?"

"Because I said so."

"Please," begged Jazz.

"Hell no, but how about dude from Jersey got arrested?"

"For real? For what? Is he alright? Is he going to get out? Does he need bail money?"

"Oh god, would you fucking calm down, that nigga got you wide open. He said something about drinking and driving."

There was a tap on Tavares's office door. "What's up, Phil?"

"You got two new clients out here."

It's always something, Tavares thought. Work never had any down time.

"Tell them I'll be out in a few moments. I gotta go, Jazz. I'll hit you back in a little while."

"Make sure you do, because I need to know what's up with my baby daddy."

Walking to the counter, Tavares said, "Who's here to see Probation Officer Del Gada?"

Dora's face lit up and his hand went up in the air like he was in first grade again.

"You, come with me. You hold tight," Tavares said to the dingy white man who had also raised his hand. "I'll be back."

Following her, Dora couldn't help but think that he couldn't have lucked out better. The judge knew he wasn't guilty, but Dora volunteered that he needed to take a class and would do administrative probation for two months till he completed the class. He figured that was all it would take to get close to Tavares. The judge was dumbfounded but agreed.

"Have a seat, Mr. Santacosa."

"Mr. Santacosa, huh?"

"Well, we are in the court house and now you're officially one of my clients," Tavares said, not knowing if she should be happy or sad. "How would you like for me to greet you?" she said, signing his paperwork, not even looking up at him. "Sign on the dotted lines."

"Apple, come on, this is some bullshit, I did this bullshit just to get at you. I ain't feeling your brandnewness. Now you want to treat me like some criminal that you just wasn't kickin' it with last night?"

"Are you kidding me?" Apple asked, turning beet red. "I didn't tell you to get arrested and I sure as hell didn't tell you to take no probation on account of me, so you can forget the guilt trip."

"Guilt trip? Ain't no one trying to guilt trip your ass. I'm just saying that you ain't gotta be all funny style with a nigga and shit. Do you know what I had to go through to get *you* as a P.O.? You don't even want to know," Dora said, shaking his head.

He had just paid the public defender two grand to pull some strings and get Apple as his probation officer. She was one of the four people handling administrative probation for the summer, but the court appointed someone else, so the lawyer worked his magic and got Dora on her caseload.

"What do you want from me?"

"Apple, I don't want shit, I'm going to do my corny ass probation and stay clear of the law. Are we good?" he asked, mad as hell at how bougie she got on him.

"We are good, please report every other Monday. I need proof of residency and employment. Lay off the drinks and have a good day."

Tavares had to flip on him because she was feeling him and knew she had no business. After the Monday Tavares was having, she couldn't wait for Friday to come.

This weekend some serious partying was due. Shit was crazy and only going to get crazier with Jazz feeling dude, him feeling her, and her being his new probation officer for two months that seemed like forever.

Dora picked up his property and headed out of Roxbury Courthouse mad and happy at the same time. Whipping out his phone, Dora called Middeon.

"What's good, my dude?"

"Ain't shit, my nigga. Just on standby waiting to hear what's good with you."

"I got off with probation and guess who the fuck my probation officer is?"

"WHO?" Mid asked, confused because he didn't fuck with the law on a personal level.

"Shorty from the club!"

"Get the fuck out of here," Middeon said. "Shorty that you was feeling or shorty who was on you?"

"Nah, the shorty that I'm trying to wife is the law."

"Damn," Middeon laughed. "Go figure, a boss trying to wife the law," he laughed, "That shit don't sound like it's a good mix, but big bro, stay right there. I'll be there in ten minutes. We need to go get up wit Holton."

"Hell yeah. I was thinking that shit when I was in that nasty, funky smelling cell. I was supposed to go see that nigga this morning. I'm right out front of the courthouse waiting for you."

Dora never saw Tavares looking at him through her office window as he waited for his ride to pick him up.

Damn, he's fine, Tavares thought, trying to figure out why she was getting stuck with him for the rest of the summer.

Going through his messages, a dark skinned, chunky woman with too much acne approached him and asked for a light and his number.

"Naw, Ma, I ain't got neither, but you have a nice day," he said and turned around.

Dora wasn't in the mood to be nice, so fuck the fat bitch, he thought to himself.

Middeon arrived and saw Dora sitting under a tree. Getting in the truck, he asked Dora, "Who was that chick looking at you all crazy?"

"Some busted down bird, but I'm not fucking around in the Bean unless it's with my new probation officer," laughed Dora. "I got to come back every other week to check in with her. But it's cool because I'm going to wear her down slowly."

Driving forty miles to Taunton, Dora and Middeon pulled up to a huge grey house with a perfectly mowed lawn, huge windows, and a two-car garage. Ringing the bell, they were greeted by the maid.

"Hi, we're here to see Holton."

"Señor Holton is in the study. Follow me."

Walking through the spacious mansion, they finally arrived at Holton's office. The business man and supplier for a large portion of the US was sitting behind his mahogany desk, speaking fluent Spanish, pointing to the chairs for Dora and Mid to have a seat.

"What's up, gentlemen? I been waiting on your asses all day. What happened?"

"Ain't shit, just had a run in with the law," said Dora. "Just leaving the courthouse."

"Oh no, that's not good for business."

"Nothing major. Just a drinking and driving that I could have beat. I copped out to probation because I was feeling the P.O."

Holton laughed. "Ain't that some shit. She must be bad as hell?"

"More bad than you know. If shorty gives me a chance, I might marry her little fine ass. If I get her, you'll definitely meet her," Dora said, proud about something that wasn't even his yet.

"But let's get down to business, because I need to get back to Jersey. You know shit don't move without the King," Mid said. Mid handed the bag to Holton.

"This is why I fuck with you, Dora, never is your shit short and never are you looking for any handouts."

"Nah, Holton, but I'm going to need an additional hundred bricks when I come back in two weeks. I'm trying a new business venture in the Bricks, so it requires more product."

"I got you," said Holton. "What I will do is give you fifty on consignment, and you can pay for the other fifty upfront."

"That's what's up, Holton, thanks."

"Well nigga, just keep having my money and we'll be good. Your shipment is in motion right now. So by the time you get back to Jersey it will have been dropped at your stash houses."

"Fellas, I'm having a huge Christmas slash birthday party for my wife. Leave your addresses with Consuelo because we're doing it way big. I need to get the list worked out now for the party planner, so be sure to give the addresses to Consuelo." Sealing their business deals, they hopped on 95 South and headed home.

"Damn, my little shorty is bad, but if she becomes a boss's wife she got to kick that job," Dora thought as he laid back and drifted off to sleep.

In the days to come, Tavares's life went back to normal. She was hurting less and less and was back on her grind without misery. Being mad about the fight, Damien wasn't getting any nice treatment. Tavares wasn't arguing with him. Nor was she asking him to come in and just chill out with her or cussing him out about the late nights he was keeping. She was being cordial because they were in the same bed but she wasn't going the extra mile with him or for him.

Hearing the alarm, Tavares got ready for work and knew that Damien would be walking in any moment to take her there. Tavares only drove to work if she had to. Which, if she had it her way, would be never.

Damien came in from servicing his morning clientele with Dunkin Donuts in hand, like he did just about every morning.

Grabbing the french vanilla iced coffee and bagel, Tavares said, "Oh, no, we gots to go. I'm going to be late."

"You kill me how you rush a nigga and got a whip outside, a fly ass whip to be exact."

Sucking her teeth, Tavares said, "Okay, well this conversation might be something that I'll consider tomorrow, but right now, I need you to pick your breakfast up and come on."

"Tavares, I got more than enough time to shower and dress for the day, so I don't have to come back home."

"Damien, I have to stop and pick up a cake in Uphams corner for a party that we're having. That's why I am rushing you."

Damien didn't even hesitate. He just did like she said. He picked up his food and went out the door.

Damien had been up since 5:00 in the morning and knew that he wouldn't be slowing down any time soon. He hoped he even made it back home to get dressed. His phone never slowed down. Even when he was asleep, his trap phone was blowing up. It was a nonstop thing, seeing fiends and serving weight.

Dropping Tavares off at work and putting everyone on hold, Dame headed home to get dressed before he spent the day moving a mile a minute. People didn't know it, but hustling was more than a full time job.

It was 4:00 p.m. and Damien was on Blue Hill Ave headed to pick Tavares up from work. His trap phone went off.

"What's up, Dollar?" Damien answered.

Dollar was a pretty lady who'd let crack ruin her life. But as much as she smoked, she always had money and a place to call home. Dame respected that about her. She just needed to kick the crack habit that had claimed her, because she was pretty and smart underneath all the damage from the crack.

"Damien, I need you to come see me. I was out all morning running and shit so now I need to smoke."

"Dollar, what was your hustle today?" Damien asked, always amused. "You know you stay with a come up."

"I gots to. I was boosting and selling meat. You know I gots to eat, smoke, and keep a few dollars. Other than that there ain't shit for me in life."

Damien respected Dollar because she was always on a paper chase. Smoking was her enjoyment and what got her through the next day, so she maintained it with her street smarts and book intelligence.

"Dollar, I gotta go snatch my shorty from work. Then I'll be through there to see you."

"Alright," Dollar said quickly, in the moving-fast voice that fiends used when they wanted to get high.

Damien pulled up on Warren Street and waited for Tavares to come out of the courthouse. Tavares came out tired and exhausted, ready to go home.

"I got a play out in Brockton, do you wanna ride with me?"

"Nope, not at all," Tavares said. "I want to go home, take a shower, and cook something."

"Alright, well Imma drop you off, take the ride, and come back in the house since you have no summer class tonight."

"That works for me," Tavares said, getting comfortable, with the wind blowing through her thick, curly hair.

Dropping Tavares off, Dame hit the highway. Taking the forty-minute round-trip ride to see Dollar was nothing. Dollar was Damien's favorite fiend. He'd been dealing with her for a hot minute. No matter where she moved, she stayed a loyal customer.

Dollar got her name because she was all about getting a dollar. She had hustle in her blood. Dame got to Dollar's house and saw that she had a house full of people. That made him even happier that he had taken the ride. Collecting $2,000 and some porterhouse steaks and chicken breast, Dame was happy he took the ride.

Damien headed home to his number one girl. He knew that he wasn't always faithful, but he definitely loved his girl. Damien decided that he was going to stay in the house for the weekend and kick it with Tavares, who he'd been neglecting.

Walking in the kitchen, he found Tavares making plates in some tiny grey cotton shorts that had money-green colored handprints on each cheek and a green wife beater. The phone was glued to her ear and she wasn't paying Damien the least bit of attention. When he grabbed her firm, round apple bottom, Tavares screeched loudly into the phone.

"Get the hell out of here, Dame, before I spill the food," Tavares said, slapping his arm.

"Oh shit, bitch, I see Big Papa is home," Mona-Lisa teased on the other end of the phone. "You know it's time for you to go. I'm about to bathe the girls anyways."

Sucking her teeth, Tavares said, "Yeah. He always wanna come in the house and thinks he should be the focus of my attention. He's like a big ass kid, yo." Tavares talked about him like he wasn't standing right there. "Let me fuck with him for a little while. I'll call you back when he goes back outside. Which we both know will be shortly."

After eating dinner, Tavares and Damien did what they did best: they crawled on their couch in the TV room, popped in a movie, and went to blowing down some good sour deez weed.

"Damn, tell your boyfriend to stop calling you, tell him Big PaPa is home," Damien joked, but he was feeling some kind of way about Tav's phone blowing up and she wasn't answering.

"I wish I had a boyfriend on the side, then I wouldn't even have to let you stress me out," Tavares laughed, knowing that he was about to get mad.

"Don't get the shit slapped out of you."

"Whatever," Tavares laughed. "You always talking about what you want to do to people. One day you going to do something to the wrong damn person."

"Fuck is that supposed to mean? I ain't scared of getting touched. You do dirt, you get dirt."

"Okay, but you're going to fuck with the wrong person and it's going to really come back and bite you in the ass. You can't always be so ready to jump the gun."

"And this is coming from the prettiest but craziest chick I know, get the fuck out of here," laughed Damien. "One would never know what I go through in this house, but you're for sure crazy."

"Only as crazy as you make me," Tavares said, wondering who was calling her back to back like that. "Damn, my phone is blowing up," Tavares said, getting up to see who was calling her like a crazy person.

Stepping out of the TV room into the kitchen, Tavares grabbed her bag off the island. She rummaged through her denim Chanel bag till she found her phone. Looking at the number, Tavares definitely wasn't picking up. She didn't pick up numbers she didn't know, on a good day or a bad day—especially not from a weird area code. If your number wasn't programmed, you were shit out of luck if you thought she was going to answer. Tavares and her friends had a system if they were calling from a number that the other didn't know. They would send a text letting it be known it was them calling before they even wasted their time calling. Tavares knew for sure that her friends weren't calling from the odd number coming across the screen, so she wasn't messing with it. Tavares powered her phone off, tossed it on the counter, and headed back to her place of comfort.

Sitting on the couch, Tavares could feel the thickness in the air. "Oh, so you turned your shit off," Damien asked, trying to start. He was trying not to get jealous and mad, but he didn't like that Tavares had just turned her phone off.

"Yeah, I did. Is that a problem?" Tavares asked, confused about what had him up tight. He turned his phone off all the time and Tavares didn't give two fucks about it.

"Nah, but why'd you do that?" he asked hesitantly, like he really wanted to say something else.

"Because the shit was blowing up and I didn't know the number. You know as well as I do. If the number doesn't pop up with a name, then they're assed out."

"But why turn it off? It makes it look like you do know the number and just ain't answering. What if you miss an important call?"

Tavares couldn't believe her ears. "Damien, I hate to burst your bubble, but if someone important is looking for me, we got a house phone. Lastly, they know to call you and I'll be findable for sure. Now that we've finished with your interrogation, can you please roll up a blunt?"

Spending the whole weekend in the house, Damien and Tavares had a vicious cycle going on of eating, sleeping, and sex, with their phones off and no one to bother them.

Abdora was in his car, headed to pick up his brother, and figured that he would try his luck at the phone number that his man had given him. *It pays to be a good nigga, word it does*, Dora thought. When you were so good to niggaz that they would do anything for you, no questions asked, that was a good feeling.

Whether it was a million dollars or something as simple as a phone number, when niggaz came through it was a real rewarding feeling. After calling Tavares six times and getting the voicemail, Abdora felt like a stalker. Sucking his teeth, he gave up for the time being. He was going to have some words for her when he got her on the phone, though. He didn't leave a message, but he was going to catch her sooner or later. Dora didn't chase and she had him chasing, so she was definitely in for some choice words.

Abdora felt like one of the sucker ass niggaz that he'd clowned his mans for being when they were too entangled with a chick. Tavares didn't know that he'd never in his life been open for nothing with a pussy. Money made him bust a nut before a chick did. But she had him all the way open. Tavares was finer then a motherfucker, but Majors giving her that super boost had him going hard. Not only did he cop to probation with her, he had to take an AA class and check in with her every other week. She had a nigga going real hard, to be acting like he wasn't worth her time of day.

Tavares was sitting at her desk when there was a knock at the door.

"Delivery," one of her coworkers said, as Tavares was doing her weekly reports.

"Ooooh, those are so pretty," Tavares said, truly surprised. They were two dozen long-stem roses and a pretty tall, clear red vase that had hearts all over it. Tavares knew that she and Damien had been cooling over the weekend, but she didn't know that they were doing it like this. He hadn't sent her flowers since Valentine's Day, which was the only time he sent them. "Let me find out my boo is stepping his game up," Tavares said to her coworker as she took the delivery and sat it on her desk. Opening the card, it read: *Have a nice day, beautiful... Your Secret Admirer.*

Tavares was shocked, because she had really thought that they were from her boyfriend. Tavares didn't have to guess who they were from. Only one person would go this hard. Tavares had to smile, because not only was the gift thoughtful, but the flowers were beautiful and lit up her office.

Tavares pulled his file and was about to search for a phone number to call and say thank you, but stopped.

"Actually, no, I'm not calling him," Tavares said, and threw the file back in the drawer. He was trying to bait her in a nice way and she wasn't going for it.

All week Tavares received a daily flower delivery. She wanted to call him but didn't. Every time Tavares watered her flowers, she smiled and thought about Abdora being off limits.

~ CHAPTER 5 ~

Sometimes you have to play nice.

Dora was the founder of the Murder Mafia. He was a stomp down gangster raised in the streets of Newark, NJ. Being a gangster was never his plan, but it was in his heart and what he was bred into.

The son of a crack addict, he was forced to turn to the streets at an early age. At ten, he was on the corner hustling for older, well-respected niggaz. Dora had to feed his brother. He had watched and observed O.G. niggaz in the process. He soaked up all their knowledge and, pairing it with the true gangster he was at heart, started soaring in the streets. Being the provider was what he had to do, so he was forced out of his cocoon. The streets had bred a monster.

Dora acquired the name Murder when he was fourteen and started laying niggaz down that older niggaz in the streets couldn't touch. By sixteen, his name was ringing bells all over the state on the streets and throughout the prison system. Dora was notorious for pushing a nigga's shit back—although he never did start shit, because he was humble. But when the occasion called for it, he would be sure to finish it. Not too many crossed him, at least not if they valued their lives.

Dora started the Murder Mafia at eighteen with just five soldiers in Jersey, and now had over two thousand people that he had networked with and brought onboard. His crews were in jails, on the streets hustling, gangbanging, working, and had businesses in mad states like New Jersey, Pennsylvania, Virginia, DC, Florida, and Georgia. His reach was far and long. He had a movement behind him that couldn't be stopped. Most hoods in Jersey were with him, and the few hoods that were against him didn't scream too much noise in the streets. They knew the Murder Mafia was as big as an army and moved like the mafia, so never would there be any beating them if a war broke out. It was nothing for a body to come up missing or dead if someone played with the Murder Mafia's money, tried to disrespect them, or went against them. Anyone who wasn't with the Murder Mafia or supported them was a minority, because they ran all the way from North Jersey to South Jersey and were slowly taking over the East Coast.

The justice system hated them for being so organized and operating in a way that kept them from getting caught up. It also worked in Dora's favor that he had beat cops, detectives, and even a few captains on his payroll. They got paid every first of the month, just like every other bill. They were his security blanket, although there was never any eye witness to finger them. Never would people snitch on the Murder Mafia, because the consequences were too high to cross them. People feared they or their families, even their mothers or children, would end up dead. People disappeared or recanted their stories before telling on the Murder Mafia. If you didn't fuck with them, they didn't take your life. So the New Jersey penal system was at their wit's end because they never had anything to charge them with.

Anyone who encountered Dora loved him. Grandmothers, pastors, kids, community residents, and activists were all among those who loved him. They loved him because he respected and took care of the community and because of the way he carried things out in the streets. As cliché as it was, he was a gangsta with morals, respect, and values, and it showed no matter what he did.

Dora never let shit go down recklessly in his hoods. His niggaz didn't shoot shit up or get out of pocket when old people or kids were outside. When kids didn't go to school, parents located him to talk to their kids, and without a doubt their kids listened, because he was their hero. Never did he allow kids to chill in his hoods during school hours.

When the kids were doing what they were supposed to do, he rewarded them with gifts, new clothes, sneakers, money, or whatever he felt they deserved. His Christmas and Halloween parties were something that all the kids in Newark looked forward to. Growing up without anything, he always tried to give back to the kids who were living his struggle. When the streetlights came on, kids knew that Dora better not catch them outside.

If your lights were about to go out, you had no food in your fridge, or you couldn't pay a bill, Dora's secretary was the person people called on, because there wasn't nothing he wouldn't do for anybody.

He was taking care of his community, but the judicial system deemed him a monster who moved with caution. He was suspected of killing and carrying hits out on dozens, but it couldn't be proven. Not even his niggaz knew just how many bodies he had under his belt—but it was a lot.

Dora rolled over in his king-sized bed, exhausted from a long night at the club. Not making it home till 6 a.m., he felt like he had just closed his eyes. Looking at the digital clock, reading 9:49 a.m., he knew it was time to get up and start his long day. Every day was long for Dora, but Fridays were always longer because most times he didn't make it home until Saturday afternoon.

Damn, I don't want to get out of bed, Dora thought, knowing that he had to. Shit fell to pieces when Dora tried to take a day off.

Getting up and throwing on his red Ralph Lauren terry cloth robe and matching slippers, Dora headed toward the shower. Standing in the shower, he enjoyed what was going to be his only quiet moment of the day.

Dora's life consisted of very little down time, but he didn't mind because it benefitted the people around him.

He thought about the blue-eyed beauty he'd met in Boston. *Damn, why she ain't answering a nigga's calls*? he kept wondering as he lathered his muscled, ink-covered body with Dove soap.

Before leaving the house, Dora stopped and looked in his full-length mirror at the front door. Looking in the mirror, he was pleased at what he saw, though he wasn't hung up on his looks as others were. Dora's only interest was being crisp from head to toe, and he never left the house any other way, not even to go to the mailbox or to the store for a carton of milk. Seeing his crisp black and red Prada sneakers, black cargo shorts, and red Lacoste shirt, he was ready to hit the streets.

Hopping in his red Porsche truck with bulletproof tinted windows, Dora headed over the bridge to Newark. Living where he conducted business wasn't an option. When Dora made it home, he rested his head in New York on the fortieth floor in a duplex condo that overlooked the Hudson River. Dora loved Jersey, so he chose to live where he could see his real home at all times.

Hopping on the New Jersey Turnpike, Dora popped on the CD player. Listening to Lil Wayne's "Mrs. Officer," his thoughts were interrupted by his cell phone.

"Yo, what's good?" he answered.

"What good, nigga," his right-hand man Bryce asked.

"I'm just stepping out the house. I'm on my way to the hood. I got mad shit to do before I head to the club tonight."

"Well, I'm down South Jersey getting this week's profits," Bryce informed. "I called to see how shit went in Boston. Ever since I got off the plane from the Dominican Republic this morning, I been trying to call you. My phone hasn't stopped ringing, though."

"Shit went love, my nigga. We getting the ice cream sundae with a cherry on top," he said, which meant that the deal was sealed with only half to be invested upfront.

"The basketball team did their thing and came in second in the tournament." Dora sponsored a traveling summer basketball league that he tried to see anytime they were close to home. "Them niggaz in Boston be balling though. Mission Hill took the title. Our boys did their one, two though. I met this bad ass broad," Dora said, and his whole face lit up.

"That's what's up, my nigga," Dora's best friend said, hearing his smile through the phone. Laughing, Bryce said, "Sounds like she got your ass wide open."

"Nah, not yet. But she got potential."

"Get the fuck outta here, son. I'm not believing my ears right now. Damn, did you hit it, 'cause you sound like she got some whipper snapper to have you talking like this," laughed Bryce.

"Nigggga, don't I wish. She wasn't even tryna come up off the digits. I had to call in a favor. The craziest part is she's my probation officer."

"What did you just say?" Bryce questioned, as if he heard his nigga wrong.

Dora cracked up laughing. "Yo, I met shorty, she didn't swing the number. Just so happens I caught a bullshit DUI case and she works at the courthouse. I slid the lawyer an extra two grand to get me her as a P.O. I thought I was doing something but she flipped like we weren't at the club talking the night before," laughed Dora. "She gotta man who better watch out, because I'm in the wings, waiting for him to slip."

"Nigga, when you ever had to wait for someone to slip, you usually take what you want."

"I know, right," laughed Dora. "I'm trying to play nice with shorty though."

Bryce cut Dora off. "Matter of fact, nigga, speaking of taking things, I heard some funny shit. Nigga, word is that you took over the hoe houses too," laughed Bryce. "When the fuck did you do that shit? I was in the barbershop and overheard some niggaz talking about it this morning."

"Oh, a few days ago," Dora answered nonchalantly. "They were getting good dough, so we needed in. I went to each house and told them I'll be back at the end of the week for my half and if they didn't have my shit there would be no hoe houses, simple as that." Bryce's body was paralyzed with laughter to the point where he was choking. "What the fuck is so funny?"

"Nigga, you got your hands in everything."

"Fucking real, if me and mine ain't eating then ain't no one fucking eating."

"I hear that, my nigga. I just didn't know about adding hoe houses to our list of businesses," Bryce said, still laughing. "I was in the barbershop listening to niggaz talk about how you went house to house and the bitch ass niggaz running them bowed down. I was in the fucking chair in stitches, like only my nigga."

"Word is born, son. I told niggaz my nigga is shot the fuck out but only he could do that. But yo, do what you do my nigga and I'll meet you at the club at four," Bryce said.

"That's what it do. I'm about to head to Jersey City and then to Newark. Buddah should be in Patterson. Kollar Dollar is meeting me in Jersey City, so we'll meet at the club at 4:00 p.m.," said Dora.

When the infamous fire-engine red Porsche with dark tents and specialized plates rode through any hood in Jersey, people knew who it was. Dora was always in a hood being the hood Santa, checking something or someone or collecting, so his car was known. Hopping out on 11th Street, Dora got out, not locking his doors or putting the windows up in his truck, and knocked on the brown, well-maintained, single-family home.

"Hey, Dora." An old lady, old enough to be his grandmother, greeted him.

"Hi, Miss Perlene," Dora greeted her with groceries in his hand and stepped into the house.

"Thank you, baby. I was wondering what time you were going to get around here. I was going to run out to get my hair and nails done but decided to wait for you."

"Thanks, Ms. Perlene. I was trying to get a little rest. So I slept in."

"Was it a good week around here?" Dora questioned.

"Good enough. The police was up and down, but they didn't stop shit. They just like to pretend like they doing some shit." That was just how Dora liked it.

Unlike most hustlers, niggaz who were down with the Murder Mafia paid taxes to hustle. Instead of paying taxes to Uncle Sam, they paid taxes to Dora and the Murder Mafia family. It was a $200 a day tax to hustle, and it was to be paid weekly or biweekly, whichever they signed up for. No one was getting small time change, so $200 a day was like a normal person buying a $20 bag of weed. Everyone gave their contribution to the hood nana in the hood they hustled in or closest to. There was even a detailed, tracked report of who did and didn't pay by Talia, Dora's secretary. When you evaded your taxes, you got shut down not only from hustling on the block, but from being able to even score a package, so niggaz usually paid their taxes.

Dora had long surpassed dealing drugs, although he was the one who made it possible for his niggaz to sell the best of the best coke and crack in Jersey. In return, they gladly paid homage with their taxes and everyone was happy.

"I got your money in the back, be right back," Ms. Perlene said as her big frame went heading down her long hallway. Returning with three huge envelopes, she gave Dora a total of $70,000.

Newark was a drug goldmine, and Dora was getting paid without hand-to-hand selling anything. He got paid from his wholesale distributions to his immediate squad and those paying the taxes.

Handing Ms. Perlene her $2,000 weekly cut, Dora headed toward three other hoods in Newark to collect from the other hood grannies.

The police never expected grandmothers and great-grandmothers to be holding, so it worked in his favor. They loved him and he loved them more than they knew. He kept them paid enough to pay their bills, have food in the fridge, play the lottery, and keep a roof over their heads, and in return they housed all his drugs when the guys needed to re-up and collected his tax payments. Leaving the Tremont

Street projects, Dora decided to stop by his barbershop before heading to the club.

Pulling up on Avon Ave, Dora tried to call Tavares for the third time in the last two hours. He reached her voicemail. He had called and called, sent flowers, called and called, and still she wasn't answering. Dora parked his truck and went into his barbershop, King Cuts, and hollered at his mans and them. Dora had taken a lot of his soldiers and put them in legal positions when they were ready to make the move. The only rule was you had to be fully ready to get out of the game. He didn't allow illegal shit in his legal establishments. Just off of Dora's name, the clientele was crazy and the barbers were getting money like they were still hustling, so they were good. *Damn, it's 1:30 and it's this crazy*, Dora thought, looking around his barbershop. All the chairs were full with at least twenty people sitting around waiting to be serviced. Everyone was watching one of the ten flat screen TVs, the kids were in their own world playing the video games on three out of the ten TVs and snacking on the free goodies.

"Hey, Dora, can I holler at you?" a short, brown-skinned hoodrat with a lisp asked no sooner than he walked in the barbershop.

"What's up?" he asked the girl he knew from grade school. "Timmy, you sit right here, Mommy will be right back." Giving the kid $50, Dora headed toward the back of the barbershop toward his office.

Teeka was an around the way chick who'd been trying to holler at Dora for years, but he wasn't beat, not in the least.

"Yo, what's good, Teeka?"

"I just wanted to holler at you and ask you when you gonna stop playing games. I been at you for years and you been giving me the run around for years."

"Is that right?" Dora chuckled.

"Yeah, I need a nigga like you in my life."

"Teeka, it ain't nothing personal, Ma, but no thanks. I'm a nigga keeping it real, and you just ain't my swag or my flow. So, no can do."

Teeka was crushed.

"Damn, Dora, it's like that?" Teeka said, upset at his honesty. "You got that though," Teeka said, walking away to keep what little of her pride that she still had.

Handling his business and kicking the shit with his mans and dem, Dora was on his way to handle more business.

By the time Dora had collected his profits and made it to get up with his niggaz, he was mad Tavares still hadn't called him back.

Walking into Kings, Inc., the club that he and Bryce owned, he walked to the bar and grabbed a drink without saying anything to anyone.

"Damn, hello to you too," Buddah said, sitting at the bar.

"I had a long day, nigga. And the shit ain't even really started yet. A nigga ain't gonna make it home till tomorrow and I'm fucking tired. I swear I need a vacation," Dora said, throwing back his double shot of Patrón.

"Well take a vacation, my nigga. You know we got you," Buddah said.

"I wish I could, but right now ain't a good time. I got too much on my plate."

"Well nigga, we ain't gonna let shit fall to pieces. You can take a break and your empire will still be here when you get back. Ain't that what you pay us for?" asked Buddah, confused.

"I know, right?" Dora asked, forgetting that as hard as he worked, he paid people to work in all the jobs that he filled. *I really need a break*, Dora thought, wanting to take him up on his offer.

"Well, let's get down to business," Dora said, pointing his finger, motioning everyone to get up from the bar. Bam Bam, Oh So, Buddah, Pure, Bryce, Dominic, Kollar Dollar, KJ, Maniac, and Hawk all followed Dora upstairs to the soundproof VIP room called King's Playpen. Everyone grabbed a seat on one of the various leather sectional couches or king-sized chairs.

"Any new business?" Bryce asked his fellow brothers.

"Yeah," said Buddah. "Word is there're some niggaz from New York over here, talking real greasy. Running their mouths and shit, talking about they're over here getting money and ain't no one going to stop them."

Dora's whole demeanor changed. First he chuckled, then he paused. Everyone in the room knew what that chuckle meant.

"I love niggaz who disrespect what we stand for. It's nothing to make an example out of someone. Let them niggaz get some money and then send their asses home in a body bag." Disrespect was the one thing that Dora didn't tolerate from anyone. "Be sure to send the money to their families so that they can be buried or have a memorial or something."

"How you want it done? Buddah style—chopped to pieces, or Bryce style—somewhere found full of holes?" asked Buddah.

"Doesn't make me a difference, flip a coin for all I give a fuck. Next order of business," Dora said, not even blinking twice.

"Bryce, what's up with the kids' trip to Great Adventures?" Dora asked.

"Well, I got the shit all set up. Well, wifey has it all set. Shit's a go for August, right before school starts. We have kids from Newark, Patterson, Camden, Trenton, and Jersey City going. There will be a pickup point with three buses for every town. All the pimped out buses have DVD players, video games, and will be stocked with junk food and shit. Kids under twelve have to be accompanied so the family knows that they're on volunteer status for the day. So we got more than enough chaperones. And the kids will all be given $50 apiece to spend in the park. I've also worked it out so that all the kids spend $20 to eat and the park will just bill us. So that's what it do, my nigga," Bryce said, having his shit together.

"I'm glad to hear that's a go," Dora said, cracking a smile. He truly had a soft spot for the kids.

"Just a heads up, this shit is running us about three hundred grand."

"It's no big deal. Each of our companies will donate the money and then we'll write it off on the taxes," Dora said. "All the kids been asking if it's going to go down, so just make it happen. Spread the word like wildfire and let the parents know that the kids have to be signed up by next week, because I need a head count so I know whether or not to get more buses."

"Dominic, how much did we collect this week?" Bryce asked.

"Without what Dora collected, we got nine hundred thousand."

"Well, I got a little over four hundred grand, so we hit our million dollar mark," Dora said, seeming a million miles away. "Bryce, do me a favor, you take that shit and put it away," Dora said rubbing his forehead. "We'll get up later."

"What's up, my nigga, you feeling alright?" asked Oh So. "You don't seem like yourself."

"I'm good. A nigga just need a vacation, that's all."

"Nigga, don't talk about it, be about it," replied Oh So.

"Yeah, yeah, yeah," Dora said. "Oh shit, before I forget: Bam Bam, I need you to go down on Chadwick Street with me, your block of course, so we can holler at them little niggaz who ain't been going to school. They just been congregating in front of Ms. Wilson's house like I play that shit. We'll do it before the weekend is out," Dora said.

"No doubt, son. I be telling them niggaz to go to school," Bam Bam said, trying to smooth it out.

"Bam Bam, that's your sector, so if you're telling them and they ain't going, that's a whole another problem my nigga. It's not too often or for too long that the kids are on my block during school hours, so that shit will be taken care of by Sunday."

"Well, now that we got that shit out the way, can one of you niggaz put some haze in the air?" Buddah asked.

"Old ass going to have a heart attack," KJ joked as he pulled out a pack of backwoods and started to roll the whole pack up.

KJ was cute and knew it, so he was always running his mouth and talking shit. Buddah was the oldest at thirty, but looked like he wasn't a day over twenty-one, with his reserved schoolboy looks and waist-long dreadlocks.

"I need you niggaz here on time tonight," Bryce said in between his blizz to the face.

"Ain't we always here on time?" Buddah asked.

"Hell fucking no! Why the fuck you think I just said that shit?"

"Well, I'm going to be here a little late," Dora said. "I gotta run back to New York. I didn't grab my clothes."

"Nigga, you better hit the mall," Bam Bam said, knowing that Dora wasn't coming back if he went home to New York.

"Better yet, Imma call my little bitch Jade and have her shoot to the mall and grab me something."

"Now you're talking," Dominic said as he passed the blunt to Maniac. Dora left his niggaz blowing it down while he went to call Jade.

Relaxing in his tall, plush red leather chair, he picked up his office phone and called Jade, one of his most steady bitches at the moment.

"Hello, sexy," Jade answered.

"What's up, lady?"

"Ain't shit, I'm at Garden State Mall getting something to wear for tonight. What's going on with you?"

"I'm at the club getting ready for tonight. I caught your ass right on time though, I know that."

"Why you say that?" Jade asked curiously.

"I need you pick me up something to wear tonight and you're already out shopping."

"Oh yeah, you def caught me at the right time then. I got you," she responded eagerly.

Jade liked when Dora asked her to do stuff. It made her feel like she was his bitch, even though she knew she wasn't his only one.

"Anything in particular that you want?"

"Well, you know it's Friday, so it's grown and sexy night, no jeans or sneakers. Don't forget an undershirt, socks, and boxers too."

"I got you, baby. I will hit you when I get back to Newark. And please don't forget to put me on the VIP list because that line be around the damn corner and you know I will not be happy if I'm standing in it."

"I got you," Dora said, making a mental note to put Jade and her girls on the VIP list.

~ CHAPTER 6 ~

Do it blindly and play it by ear.

Dora went back in the VIP room where he had left his niggaz smoking.

"Alright my niggaz, it was a good week, now it's time for me to go up to Montclair to see my moms."

"Tell Ms. D we said what's up."

"Sure will," Dora said, giving his niggaz dap.

"Nigga, don't get lost," Bryce said, giving his best friend dap.

Just as Dora got in his truck, his cell phone started ringing. _It never, stops does it?_ Dora thought, picking up the unfamiliar number.

"Hello, may I please speak with Abdora?" a very sweet and sassy voice on the other end of the phone asked.

"Speaking, who is this?"

"Your probation officer," Tavares said, politely sarcastic.

Happy, but mad it took her so long to call him back, Dora had to give her the blues.

"Well, about damn time you called me back," Dora said, not out of disrespect, but pure frustration of wanting to talk to her. Only it came across like he was checking her.

"Excuse me?" Tavares said, taken aback, thinking this nigga done bumped his head.

"You heard me," Dora said, having to smile at the tone she tried to check him in. "I been waiting on you to call me back all week. I usually get call backs within minutes, and I'm not being cocky. I'm keeping it real with you. So know that you're pushing it with this week bullshit," he said, pushing the envelope now.

"Listen, I think that you have me confused or twisted with someone else. You have to, because your mouth is totally out of control and I am so not her. So we're going to hang up and try this again," and the line went dead.

In total shock, Dora cracked up, laughing. *Damn, Ma got balls*, he thought to himself as the phone rang.

"Hello," Dora sang.

Not liking him one bit, Tavares snapped. "Now that we've gotten that out the way, let me explain something to you one time and one time only. I don't know WHO you thought you was talking to before, but don't you ever talk to me like that again. I get back to my clients within three days' time."

"I'm not your client," Abdora interjected.

"You are my client. Didn't you read the papers that you signed in my office?" Tavares asked sarcastically.

"You have a real smart mouth, word you do," Dora said, chuckling, liking it on the low.

Tavares almost forgot why she had called till she looked around the room at all her floral decorations that had been delivered every day for the last week.

"I'm breaking my job protocol, but I just wanted to say thank you for the flowers. They're beautiful, even though they're taking over my office," joked Tavares.

"They're beautiful, huh?" Dora questioned. "And they're taking over your office? That's nice, but too bad I didn't send them," Dora said, dead serious.

Confused, Tavares paused because she had just known he sent them. *Who else could have sent them?* Tavares asked herself. Sounding disappointed, Tavares replied, "Oh, my bad. They're all signed from 'your secret admirer,' so I thought it was you."

"I don't know why you thought that," Abdora said. "It ain't no secret that I admire you," he said, playfully sarcastic.

"Excuse me," Tavares snapped.

"Yeah, it ain't no secret 'cause I told you right to your face," Dora said, shutting her down nicely.

"You know what, I made a mistake even calling, so you have a—" and Dora cut her off.

"No, sir, I sent them," he said and burst into laughter. "I'm glad you like them."

"You know what...?" Tavares said, and caught herself from almost going in on him. Tavares was blushing even though she was a little steamy.

"So tell me, Miss Apple, when am I going to see you? Why don't you and some of your friends come to Jersey tonight and stay till Sunday. I got you, I'll pay for everything, all yawl have to do is get here."

Tavares was tempted for a free weekend getaway but knew better.

"I want to get to know you better," Dora said, sounding so genuine.

"Well, considering that you're on probation with me till the end of the summer and I have a boyfriend, I'm not sure just how much you think you can get to know me," Tavares said flirtatiously.

"So you're going to make me settle for our office visits? You should just come down this weekend. All you would be doing is going out of town for the weekend with your girls, so what's the big deal?"

"I'm not fooling with you," Tavares laughed at how innocent he tried to make it sound. "You're my client, that's it. But thank you again for the flowers."

"I can respect it," Dora said, not feeling being shot down.

"I have to get back to work, have a nice day," Tavares said before hanging up.

Only one more hour, Tavares thought, looking at the clock that read 4:30 p.m. She wished she could go to Jersey just to get away for the weekend, but she didn't want to add fuel to the fire.

Hearing her cell phone vibrate, Tavares reached under her desk and grabbed her blue denim Dior purse and retrieved her pink Blackberry. Seeing the message indicator, she opened her text messages and couldn't help but smile her pearly white teeth from ear to ear. She read…"I just wanted to say thank you for putting a smile on my face for the day with your call."

This dude is too much, Tavares thought. She stopped mid-thought and said, "Wait, how the fuck did he get my cell phone number?" It was the same number that had been blowing her up for the last week. Her work phone rang and diverted her attention for the moment.

"Good afternoon, P.O. Del Gada speaking."

"What's up, boo?" Randee said, happy like she had just hit the lottery.

"Damn, you sound overly happy," Tavares said.

"Shut up and let me conference call Mona-Lisa in."

On hold, listening to the boring elevator music, Tavares thought, *I can't believe he has my cell phone number.*

The elevator music silenced and Randee asked, "Tavares, are you there?"

"Yeah, I'm here. What's up, Mona-Lisa?"

"I'm sitting at my desk shopping online talking to yawl."

"Let me find out, you get paid to go to work and talk to us and shop," Tavares joked.

"Something like that," Mona said in her small, squeaky voice. "I do my job and the lawyers love me, so what can I tell you."

Mona-Lisa was an administrative assistant for two high-priced divorce attorneys who loved her to pieces and highly overpaid her.

"As long as their stuff gets done we're cool and the gang."

"Listen here bitches, I have to get back to work before one of my patients dies," Randee interrupted. "I just called to see what was good for this weekend so I can let Garvey know if the kids are spending the weekend with him or not."

"Yo, it must be nicccce," Mona stressed. "I can't get my bum ass baby's father's fat ass to take the kids on a bad day and here your baby's father babysits any time that you say so. He be like 'Okay Randee, no problem,'" mimicked Mona-Lisa.

"Shut the fuck up," Randee laughed. "We just got an understanding, that's all. So fall back and get off me."

"Yawl know that I'm with whatever," Tavares said, "but I wish we could go away."

"Let's go to the city for the 4th," Mona-Lisa said. "I wanna pick some stuff up for the twins so we can shop by the day and then we go uptown to Harlem and tear up the club up at night."

A bell went off in Tavares's head. She wasn't fucking with Dora for the sake of her relationship and job. But if they were in the same place at the same time, that was outta her control.

"Oh, I'm so wit it," Tavares said no sooner than the bell went off.

"Damn…you said that fast as hell," Mona-Lisa said, reading her girl's mind. "Don't think you're slick, I got your card, hooker. I spoke to Jazz earlier," Mona-Lisa said, shutting Tavares down. "She told me that the fly guy from Jersey has been showering you with flowers all week."

"Here you go! You're all on me and you don't even know what you're talking about," Tavares said, trying to hide the fact that she was busted.

"Tavares, you book the rooms, and Mona-Lisa you rent the car, and I'm going to call Jazz and Leslie to get all the money we owe yawl," Randee informed.

"Where do yawl want to stay?" Tavares inquired.

"It doesn't matter to me," Mona-Lisa said.

"Times Square," Randee volunteered. "Alright ladies, it sounds like a plan has formed to me," Randee said. "We can bounce first thing in the morning on Saturday, so, Mona, reserve the car for that Friday till Tuesday."

"Will do," Mona-Lisa said.

"Ditto," said Tavares.

Hanging up, the ladies all went back to work, anticipating the weekend getaway.

Dora pulled up to his mother's grey house that was decorated with multi-colored rose bushes in the front and realized he always felt at peace when he came to the suburbs to kick it with his mother.

Going through what he did never made him love his mother no less. She was his best friend. She was the one person he confided in about everything: legal, illegal, bitches, business, problems, or advice, she was his number one girl. His mother was always around, regardless of her habit, and in his eyes she made him the man he was, even if he did become a man at ten. When she got clean, all it did was strengthen their bond.

Walking through the bright red door, Dora screamed, "Ma!"

Startled, Dhara came out the kitchen, yelling back. "What the hell are you screaming for? You almost scared the fucking shit out of me. Don't be trying to give me no God damn heart attack, you big head bastard."

Dora just laughed, because that was his girl. She was where he got it from. Dhara was from the old school.

A diva in her day who had it past going on. She was five-foot-nine with long, toned legs. A medium build with a bodacious butt and no gut. Her slanted eyes and Indian-colored skin made her look exotic, and was still beautiful through the storm.

Her looks were one thing, but her attitude was another. She was hood to her heart and would knock you the fuck out if you fucked with her. Going on forty-three, she would still tell you off and fuck you up and keep it moving like nothing ever happened, which was why Dora called her his female alter ego.

Following his mother into her chef-sized kitchen, Dora took a seat at her rectangular kitchen table that sat twelve.

"I was just in here cooking because your brother is going to bring the boys over later."

"That's what I'm talking about. Let me get a plate right now, before them greedy little bastards come over."

"Nigga, you're a greedy bastard, don't be talking about my grandsons like that."

"Yeah, yeah, yeah. Mummy, what did you cook?"

"Don't get slapped," Dhara checked her son. "I made barbecue chicken, fried fish, macaroni and cheese, collard greens, yellow rice, and biscuits."

"Damn, Mummy," Dora said, looking at his mother like she had lost her mind. "It's Friday, not Sunday."

"I don't cook based on no damn day of the week. I cook what the fuck I wanna eat. Don't come in here starting no shit," Dora's mother snapped at him.

"Relax, Killa Granny, ain't no one fucking with you and your Sunday dinner on a Friday," Dora said, cracking up laughing.

Making her son a plate, Dhara sat at the table and proceeded to grab her sugar jar. Coming out with a pack of cigarillo rollies and a fifty-bag of weed, she started to break her weed up like it was nothing.

"I know that's not where you keep your stash," Dora said, with his big green eyes staring at his mother in amazement.

"Shit, why ain't it," Dhara stared right back at him. "I keep my shit wherever I'm at. I was in the kitchen so my weed was in the kitchen. Never know when I need to twist something up."

Shaking his head, Dora said to his mother, "Ma, you's crazy. Hurry up and twist up though, 'cause I'm going to be ready to smoke when I finish eating." Dora went to scarfing down his mother's extra tasty cooking.

Dora and his mother sat at her table and blew it down like they were old homies.

"Ma, shit is crazy in the hood."

"Shit been crazy down there in the bricks and throughout Jersey and you've handled it this long," Dhara said as she heard the stress in her son's voice. "You're one man with a lot of people on your back. You have people who look up to you, depend on you, who need you and honestly wouldn't know whether they were coming or going without you and your direction, so I know that shit is stressful. Remain solid and be true to who you have been all this time and you'll be fine. God gave you a gift, blessed you with the quality of being a leader, and as long as you stay true and grounded, God will have your back. And plus I raised you, so I know you'll be fine," Dhara said, taking the blunt out her son's hands.

"Ma, I don't know. Every day it's something. Sometimes I just wish I could walk away. But I can't, too many people need me."

"Baby Boy, you need you first and foremost."

"I know, mummy. I swear I just need to take a vacation to get my mind right."

"Well, Boo, do what you need to do. But you know I always got your back. I'm your true ride or die," Dhara said as she inhaled the smoke from her blunt, but she wasn't joking in the least. Dhara and her son were like best friends. There wasn't nothing that her son couldn't talk to her about or come to her for help with.

"On a lighter note, Ma, I met this bad broad when I was in Boston." Dora's face was glowing.

"Oh, shoot," Dhara said, interested to hear about the young woman who had her son smiling from cheek to cheek. "Let me find out, she gave you a piece and got your ass open because you're smiling hard as hell."

"Ma, not even. She's beautiful though and she ain't no hood chick. She's just a good girl who survived through these streets. She's in school, taking up criminal justice, works at the courthouse, and ain't one of these gold digging bitches with a shovel on her back. She's actually my probation officer." Dora laughed.

"Probation officer? How the hell are you trying to push up on the probation officer? I know you don't think you're that good."

"Ma, please! I am that good. But I actually met her before she was my probation officer. I only copped to probation just so that I could get at her! It's gonna take some work though, because she's playing hard to get 'bout her job, but Imma wear her down. You know your son. I usually get what I want," Abdora said with a sneaky look on his face.

"You just got it all worked out, huh?" Dhara asked sarcastically.

"Ma, just know if baby girl slips up and gives me an in, it's a wrap, game over. I'm playing for keeps."

"Son, I ain't mad at you. If you can work magic and get her to come up off some airtime, then more power to you."

"I ain't even got her yet and she got me open. Imma gangster, I don't be on no lovey dovey shit with these nothing ass broads. Ma, all I do is fuck these chicks and deal with them lightly. Then I do it moving."

"And that's a problem," Dhara cut him off. "I'm not saying don't live your life, but sometimes you gotta know when the right one comes along so that you can stop all that wild shit. So if you think she's the one, get her and do her right. I'm about sick and tired of meeting bitches periodically, then they're gone a few months later. Get your shit together," Dhara said, trying to school her son.

Dora's mother couldn't help but keep it real. She had seen too much in her life to bullshit. Dhara's phone interrupted the conversation.

"Grab that," Dhara told her oh-so-fine son.

"Hello?"

"Hi, may I please speak with Dhara?"

"Ma, it's for you. I don't know why you didn't just answer your own phone in the first place." Taking the headset, Dhara talked to one of the girls she sponsored for a few minutes, gave the young girl some encouraging words, and finished up her conversation with her son.

Dora kicked it with his mother, left her some money, and headed back to his hectic life.

Arriving on 11th Street, Dora met Jade, took his bags, peeled $1,000 from his money clip, tapped her cheek with a kiss, and said he would see her at the club.

Driving to Bryce's house, Dora was lost in the zone, thinking about Tavares. *Why am I feeling a chick that I don't even know? And she gunned me down*, he laughed, being even more intrigued at how open she had him. He just didn't understand how or why, though. Beating his brain till he gave up, Dora said fuck it, for once in his life he was going to do something blindly and play it by ear. His number two rule: never walk into a situation not knowing the consequences of the outcome.

Pulling up to Bryce's ranch-style house, Dora got out of his truck, grabbed all his bags, and got his mind focused on the long night ahead of him. Entering Bryce's house with his spare key, Dora headed downstairs, where he knew Bryce was falling back in his theater. Bryce had a built-in movie theater in his house where he loved to watch movies and blow it down. Entering the nice-sized room, Dora's best friend passed him the blunt. Taking a seat in the movie theater style chair, Dora reclined and blew the sour deez down. After watching Donnie Brasco, the fellas shot the shit. Dora's phone stopped their debate about who was finer, Stacy Dash or Nia Long.

"Hello," Dora answered his phone all hostile.

"Hey, Dora, this is Ms. Claudia. How you doing?"

"I'm good, Miss Claudia. How are you?"

"I'm good. I just wanted to call and let you know that Callie ain't been home in a few days. I've seen the kids coming and going but no Callie. I know that you're the only family those girls got, so I just wanted to call and give you a heads up that no one was watching over them."

"Thanks, Miss Claudia, I'll take care of it." *I can't stand that stinking ass bitch*, Dora thought as he picked up his phone to make a call. Dora called one of his homies that was on that side of town.

"What's good, Dora?" Vato asked.

"I need you to swing by 1445 S. Orange Ave and drop something off for me."

"No problem my nigga, what you need?"

"Third floor, drop off three hundred dollars. Tell them I said to get some food and call me if they need anything. Let them know I'll be by there tomorrow."

"Will do, my nigga." They hung up and Dora went back to defending Stacy Dash as the baddest black broad to ever be on TV.

~ CHAPTER 7 ~

Rules ARE meant to be broken.

It was Friday again already. By the time Tavares got home from work, she was exhausted. Approaching the back porch of her brownstone, she could hear Dame and all his friends. _I swear these dudes think this is the party house._

Walking up the back stairs that led into the kitchen, Tavares could hear "Hard Knock Life" blasting from the TV room that was off the kitchen. Hearing multiple voices singing like they were Jay-Z's back up singers, Tavares couldn't help but laugh. "Hey, Apple," "What's up, Apple?" "Hi, Baby," everyone said when they heard the door shut. Tavares kicked off her black Jimmy Choo pumps and walked into the doorway of the TV room.

Tavares loved to tease Dame's friends, who never seemed to want to go home. Tavares was the coolest of their girlfriends. Never was she bitching, complaining about hanging out or riding Dame with bullshit. Tavares was always chillin,' cooking, cleaning, and shopping, as far as they ever saw. The TV room was even their designated area. They had a 7seventy-two-inch flat screen TV, two large, oversized sectionals, surround sound, a pool table, and video games to keep them occupied.

"Don't yawl have homes and girlfriends who want yawl in them? I swear I might as well be running a shelter as much as I see all of yawl."

They all laughed because they knew Tavares loved to give them a hard time, but she never put them out. Sitting on the swirling stool at the kitchen island, she began to rub her feet.

Tavares went up to the third floor, grabbed her slippers, and came back downstairs. Damien came in the kitchen and asked, "What's for dinner? We're hungry."

"Hello to you too. No 'hi, how are you, how was your day?'"

"Sorry, baby. I was just starving, that's all."

Tavares snapped, "I do have a job and am good for something besides cooking for you and the greedors."

"Damn, my bad baby. I'm just trying to eat something before we head out."

"Alright, Dame, I'll drop some wing dings and French fries in the deep fryer. But hold tight because I need to do something on the computer first."

"Cool," Dame responded, and put a kiss on Tavares lips.

Walking in the opposite direction, Tavares walked through the living room and into the computer room. Tavares sat down and printed the hotel confirmations out. The phone rang.

"Hello," she answered.

"What's up, Boo-Face?"

"Shit, just got home from work."

"Well, what's all that noise I hear?"

"I got a house full of niggaz. I'm about to make something quick for them eat, so they can get the hell out."

"Them niggaz act like you're the community girlfriend or something," chuckled Leslie.

"Bitch, who are you telling? I told them, I might as well be running a shelter. What are you doing, though?" Tavares asked, heading back into the kitchen to cook.

"Nothing, braiding Tay's hair, it's so damn long that I can't do nothing else with it."

"Are you ready to go?" Tavares asked as she grabbed her seasonings.

Sprinkling black pepper, Lawry's seasoning salt, and Sazón on the chicken, Tavares got ready for the bullshit to come out her friend's mouth.

"Yeah," Leslie said with a strong confidence.

"Riiiiight," Tavares said, to say "yeah right." "We're out at 7:00 a.m., so you and your slow ass better be ready."

"I will be," Leslie said, knowing that being on time was the last thing that she would be. Being slow was a part of their common nature. Sucking her teeth, Leslie said, "Don't start, heffa. You're just as slow as me. I'm just a little worse than you."

"Hold on," Leslie said, clicking over to answer her other line.

"Hello."

"What's up, Leslie," asked Jazz.

"Nothing, just braiding Tay's hair and talking to Apple."

"Tell her I said what's up. Ask her can we go to Jersey instead of NY," Jazz laughed. "No sir, I just called to see if we were going out."

"We got an early morning ahead of us, so ain't no way in hell my slow ass is going anywhere. Plus ain't no one called and said nothing. I would assume we're falling back, since we're going to party for the weekend," Leslie informed her girl.

"That's what's up," Jazz said. "Imma go holler at my friend."
"Your friend who?" Leslie asked, being nosy.

"There you go," Jazz laughed. "Come on, you know they don't call us the secret squirrel club for nothing. We're the best at being inconspicuous," Jazz reminded her girl.

"Oh shit, bitch, I got Apple on the other line. I'm just a running my damn mouth, let me hit your ass back."

"Aight."

"Hello," Leslie said.

"Damn, hoe, was that—God? I hope so the way you just left me on hold."

"Nah, that was Jazz. She wanted to know if we're going out. I told her nah, since we're leaving so early in the morning. She's about to go secret squirrel."

"With who?" Tavares asked, exhibiting her nosy trait that she and her friends shared all too well.

"Shit if I know, she wouldn't tell me. Apple, let me finish Tay's hair and I'll call you back after I drop her off."

"Cool," Apple said, hanging up and going to work to feed eight grown ass men.

By the time Tavares had finished dinner, she was ready to take a shower and do nothing but relax. Contemplating whether or not to text Dora, Tavares decided to play the text game. Making her way to the third floor, Tavares crawled in her king-sized platform bed and texted Dora, "My girls and I will be in the City this weekend if you care to bump into me on accident...lol!" *Ding Ding*, her phone chimed within seconds. Reading "where so I can be the best accident you ever had?" Tavares burst into laughter. *This dude is crazy*, she thought as she texted him back. "Staying in time square call you tomm." She gave him no time to respond.

Just as Tavares powered her phone off, she heard Dame's size-twelve feet coming up the stairs. *Perfect timing*, she thought.

"Hey, sweet thing," he said, coming in and plopping on the bed.

"I'm tired," Tavares whined.

"Well, take your ass to bed. Me and Winky are about to make a few moves."

"What's new?" Tavares asked sarcastically. "All you two do is eat and rip and run. I don't even know how yawl function. Lord knows that yawl run from sun up to sun down."

"Don't start because you ain't complaining when you're paying the mortgage and got your hand out."

"Whatever," Tavares said, getting up off the bed and sliding out of her tan pencil skirt, wide camel-colored belt and black button up blouse.

"Speaking of which, I need some money to go to New York this weekend."

"Who's going to New York?"

"Me and the girls. Mona-Lisa wants to go shopping and I do too, so we made it a weekend trip."

"I told you, you talk shit about me getting money but you sure ain't got no problem spending it when the occasion arises. Yawl just hopping up and hitting the city on a humma. Let me find out yawl got some niggas out there."

"Well, then let you find out," Tavares said, throwing it right back at him. Feeding into Dame's shit talking, she gave it to him as good as he dished it out.

"Me and my friends like to get up and go, and you know that. Yeah, we're going away on a humma, but shit, New York is convenient. How much planning does it take to go to the city, really? What's the problem again? You and your boys go out of town, so why can't me and mine?"

"I didn't say yawl couldn't, but you just came out the cut with it."

"It's close and Monday's the holiday," Tavares defended, knowing she had won.

"That's what's up baby, I got you. Niggaz are gone and Winky is cleaning up. I'll be back later," Damien said, kissing Tavares as he grabbed one of her fully erect nipples.

"I bet you will," Tavares said.

Tavares slipped on some Capri sweatpants, a wife beater, and her slippers that had huge ducks bouncing off the top. A Valentine's Day gift from Dame, Tavares rocked them hard in the house. Tavares grabbed her cell phone. Making her way downstairs, she took a seat at the kitchen island and powered her phone on.

Her message indicator popped up and when Tavares opened it she read, "Can I keep you for the night?" Tavares laughed, texting him back, "no, you can't. We're breaking ENOUGH rules." Tavares wiped the counters down and mopped the floors. She finished cleaning the kitchen before responding to Dora's text, "Rules are meant to be broken." Cleaning the house from top to bottom and texting Dora stole the evening.

It was 12:00 a.m. before Tavares knew it. Showering and getting in the bed, Tavares flipped the sixty-four-inch flat screen TV on. Tavares picked up her phone and called Dame. Listening to the phone ring and ring, she got irritated that it took him so long to answer.

"What's up, sweet thing?"

"Sounds like you're up to no good. What took you so long to answer?"

Sucking his teeth, Dame said, "Here you go starting shit. Don't fucking start. What are you doing?"

"Nothing. Just got in bed. I'm about to watch a movie," Tavares stated, really not liking him right now. "I was calling to see what time you were coming home, so we could lay up before I go away for the weekend."

"Baby, it's Friday night and the first of the month, you already know that it will be real late when I come in."

Tavares couldn't help but suck her teeth. "I swear, one day you're going to wish that you took the time to take care of me."

"I do take care of you, and if I laid in the house with you, there would be no taking care of you. Don't you need spending money for New York? Please let's not act like I can give you a few punk hundred dollars and you're good to go."

Tavares knew he was right, but she was right too. *I'm glad he knows though*, Tavares thought to herself. *I can only buy a pair of shoes with a few hundred dollars.*

"Well, if I'm asleep when you come in, just wake me up."

"You got it, baby. I'm pulling up to holler at my peoples but I'll make sure I wake you up."

Pulling up to the brick apartment building sitting on the corner of Blue Hill Ave and Mattapan Street, Dame beeped the horn of his black

Benz. Walking out of the building, he couldn't help but smile at his chocolate bunny.

"What's up, little mama?" he said, passing her three ounces of coke to throw in her pocketbook.

"Nothing, Daddy."

"I see you're looking real good for a nigga."

"Always, that's what a woman's supposed to do for her man." Dame couldn't help getting lost in the sauce with the hoodrats. They went to way far extremes to get his attention and to try and fuck with him.

"How many people do we have to go see?" questioned the hood chick.

"It's busy, so pass it to me when I tell you to." Cruising the town with a hoodrat, Dame made play after play to hood niggaz needing their supply of crack and blew it down with his favorite hoodrat of them all.

She was his favorite because she took it how he gave it, got up with him at his convenience, and had the best head game since super head.

"Let's take a break, I want to suck your dick," she whined.

"And that's why when I fucks wit you, I fuckssss wit you," he said, tilting his head to the side laughing and pointing his finger at her.

Hitting Mclellan Street off Blue Hill Ave to get his pleasurable blow job, he pulled over and reclined the seat all the way back. Dropping his red monkey jeans, his multi-purpose hoodrat took all of him into her mouth and continued to swallow him deep. After twenty minutes, he was convulsing and putting his babies down her throat.

"Damn, that was good, daddy." *I would never kiss this bitch,* Dame thought, sliding his jeans back up.

"I'm hungry," complained the thick-lipped, smooth-toned, chocolate girl.

"What do you want to eat?"

"Can we go somewhere and sit down?" she damn near begged.

"Come on, Ma, you already know that ain't happening. One, I got a wife at home, and two, I don't got time for that shit. I have to get this money."

"Well, I'll settle for Flames in Grove Hall."

Flames had the best West Indian cuisine in Boston. *This bitch really think that I would take her somewhere to sit down and eat, she's starting to get it fucked up,* Dame thought, staring at her. Four hours later and $30,000 dollars richer, he was dropping his hoodrat off and heading home to his real girl.

As soon as Dame came up the stairs into the kitchen, he knew why he loved his girl. Smelling the freshness of the house, Dame knew that Tavares had spent the evening cleaning before she went away in the morning. He loved that she did her own thing but also was a good woman who took care of house and home. Walking upstairs to the third floor, Dame slipped off his clothes, dropped $5,000 on Tavares's night stand, and decided to take a quick shower to wash his guilt off before sliding in bed.

At 7:00 in the morning, Tavares was rolling out of bed, wondering why no one had called her. Looking at her cell phone, there were no missed calls. Dame was snoring like a baby, so she slipped out of bed quietly. Tavares headed downstairs to the second floor bathroom to shower and get dressed. Turning the shower on in the brown and orange colored bathroom, Tavares was getting ready to step in the shower when her phone stopped her. She reached for her blaring cell phone.

"Damn, what fucking happened with your extra on-time ass?"

Mona sounded like she was about to have a nervous breakdown.

"Yo," she exclaimed, "shit is real crazy right now. We're going nowhere fast."

"What the fuck is wrong, and why ain't we going nowhere?"

"Randee is in jail!"

"What the fuck do you mean Randee is in jail?"

"The nutty bitch called me an hour ago. I went to the station to get her, but the bondsman said he wasn't coming out."

"Oh, hell no," Tavares said. "What did the crazy bitch do?" she asked, knowing that it could have been anything when you were messing with Randee.

"Randee got real crazy. You know she ain't wrapped too tight," laughed Mona. "This fool went over to Garvey's and acted real crazy about some chick who called her phone talking shit over him. Chick didn't wanna meet Randee after she talked all that shit, so Randee called him. He acted like it was no big deal and to just let it go, so that shit pissed her off more. She went to Garvey's, busted his windows out his car, flattened his tires, and threw Drano all over it, so the paint is gone. When he came and saw his shit, they got to arguing. The nosy ass old white man from next door decides that he's going to come outside and tell super crazy to take her stupid, nigga bitch ass in the house with her ghetto drama."

"WHAT?!" Tavares exclaimed, knowing that was where the story went wrong. Everything else was typical Randee.

"You know she whipped crazy on that man faster than a tornado. She spit on him faster then the speed of lightening and beat him down. He called the police. End of story. Only this nut would get arrested the morning we're leaving," Mona-Lisa said, mad as hell.

"That's Randee for you, but we're good," Tavares said, thinking it coulda been worse.

"I'm jumping in the shower and going to call in a favor to my homeboy whose father is a bondsman. I'll be ready in forty minutes. What station is she at?"

"B-3," responded Mona-Lisa.

"I'll meet you there in an hour." Tavares got dressed, left Dame a note thanking him for the money, and headed toward B-3 Station on Blue Hill Ave in Mattapan.

Two hours later, the jailbreak went down, everyone had their luggage in the truck, and they were on the Mass Pike headed to the city.

"Randee, why did you think it was okay to spit on the man?" Jazz asked in between rolling up a blunt.

"She's looney," Tavares said, like she was stating the obvious.

"No, boo, I'm not crazy. That motherfucker calling me a nigga bitch had to be crazy. He had the right one, forget the wrong one. He didn't even know about feeling the spit of a nigga bitch. A nigga bitch?" Randee asked, still appalled.

"What, it didn't even cross your mind about whether or not to spit on him? That shit just went flying, all over his face. That is so disgusting," Mona-Lisa said, crunching up her face. The ladies laughed, blew it down, listened to music, and were in New York in two and a half hours.

Pulling up to the valet parking in front of the Times Square Hilton, they entered the hotel's modern décor and retrieved the keys.

"Why do you have your own room?" asked Leslie as Tavares handed them their keys and still had an extra one in her hand.

"Come on, boo! Get off me! I need some space," chuckled Tavares.

"Sure you do," hissed Mona-Lisa, already knowing the deal.

"Well, let's drop our stuff off in our rooms and meet in the lobby," suggested Leslie. Leslie didn't get away too often and was ready to get the weekend popping. Everyone made their way to their rooms. Randee and Mona shared a room, and Leslie and Jazz roomed together. Making their way back downstairs within ten minutes, they headed out, ready to shop.

Dora and Bam Bam cruised down Avon Avenue in the heart of Newark.

"Tonight's going to be crazy," Dora said, "We're going to the City to get up with my Bean Town Baby and her girls. She's in NY for the weekend, so that's the flow for the night," Dora said, all smiles.

"Let me find out, she got a stomp down gangsta getting all mushy and shit. You been gangsta since the womb, let me find out my nigga!"

"I'm feeling Ma. I'd drop all these bitches on my team for her."

"Damnnnnn...it's like that?" questioned Bam Bam, really shocked to hear the words coming out of his man's mouth.

All the chicks went crazy over Abdora. His selections were major, so Bam Bam couldn't believe his ears. "Yo! You mean that shit, my nigga?"

"Yeah, she got it, my nigga. She got everything a nigga need, and she don't even know it. From that first time I saw her in Boston, I knew I had to have her ass. She got ass and class," Dora laughed. "A nigga had to catch a case to holler at her, so yawl better know she's the one."

Bam Bam was cracking up that he took probation for something he didn't do, just to get at her. Taking probation for a chick was crazy in his book, but more power to his man. Dora wasn't a desperate dude, so to be going so hard, baby girl had to be big business. Every bitch wanted him and threw themselves at him daily, so if he was chasing, it was no doubt she was serious. But probation was just a high price to pay for Bam Bam.

Pulling up on Bam Bam's block, he and Dora hopped out of the cherry red Porsche truck.

"What's good, Dora?" the little niggaz asked, excited to see their idol.

"What's good?" Dora asked, ever so cool. "How about yawl tell me? Because the waves I'm catching on my phone lines ain't too hot about yawl. You little dudes wanna be stupid ass niggaz who go nowhere in life? You have to, because you clueless ass little niggaz ain't been going to school, huh?"

The truancy suspects dropped their heads while Abdora went in on them.

"But yawl think yawl gonna come out here and get a few dollars? Nigga you can't fucking do nothing with a few fucking dollars if you're a fucking dummy. Any idiot can stand on a corner and sell drugs, but your purpose is pointless if you can't take the money, plant a seed, and make it grow into something that takes you off the fucking corner."

~ 130 ~

Dora didn't say anything for a moment, and the little dudes went to pleading their stories and cases all at once.

"Let me tell you something before you think to even open your stupid mouths and say shit. Everyone in my camp, in my organization and around me and my niggaz, goes to school and has finished school. I got niggaz with degrees around me, doing big things, 'cause that's where school took them. But if school ain't for you, then do the minimum and fucking finish high school. I don't do kids hanging on the block all day. I ain't into breeding dummies. The game is always gonna be the game, but your brain is a terrible thing to waste. So if you niggaz wanna sit out here, HERE, and get fucking money, take your little fucking asses to school," Dora said, real edgy and icy.

"You get money out here after school hours only. Because if you don't, you won't be getting a motherfucking dollar at all," Dora said calmly but loud and clear.

The youngins knew that the king had spoken and they would be off the block and back in school because they weren't trying to feel the wrath of Abdora. They'd seen what the wrath had brought to other dudes who hadn't listened in some way, shape, or form.

~ CHAPTER 8 ~

Sometimes you just gotta let loose and live life.

After shopping the afternoon away on Madison and Park Avenue, the ladies went and had dinner in Times Square at Carmines. The ladies arrived at the hotel and decided on some naps to sleep off their nigga-itis from eating lasagna, chicken cutlet, angel hair pasta with freshly made Italian meatballs, and cannolis family-style.

Tavares wasn't really tired. She decided she would try on her clothes to see what she would be rocking for the evening, keeping in mind that she was out of town and had to stunt. Tavares's thoughts were interrupted when her cell phone rang and it read "My Dude."

"Hey, boo," Tavares answered.

"What's up, baby? Just checking to see what's up with you."

"I'm in the hotel, about to take a nap before we go out. Where are you?"

"I'm in the hood, just bullshitting around. Niggaz are chillin,' doing a whole bunch of nothing and I always need to be doing something because I'm that dude."

"You're fucking retarded, that's what you are. Where did I ever find you?" Tavares said through eyes teary from laughing because he was past dead serious. He was in his own world when he said that one.

"You didn't find me, I found you. I saved you. I was your hood knight in shining armor."

"Oh, you got jokes, huh? That was cute. Yeah, you saved me but you ain't let me go since. You've been something like a stalker," laughed Tavares.

"Girl, please, you wish a fine ass nigga like me was stalking you." Together they just laughed because they were both stuck up, with good reason.

"Where are you going tonight?" Tavares asked while looking in the mirror, admiring her new outfit.

"Niggaz might go to the casino."

"I think you should go," Tavares said, encouraging him.

"Why is that, because you're out of town?" Damien said, puzzled, because usually Tavares hated when he went to the casino.

"Nope, so can you win me some shoe money," joked Apple.

"Apple, please! I found a receipt from Bally's in my car for eight hundred dollars, so you don't need any shoe money. It was dated last week, if my memory serves me correctly," Damien said, sucking his teeth.

"Here you go, Mr. Investigate the Receipts," Tavares said, hating when he talked shit about her shoe habit.

"It's my car. I can check what I want. And since it ain't your car, you should take all your shit, including trash, when you get out," Damien set her straight.

"Okay, fine! You found it, whatever," Tavares screamed. "This is a new week. That was last week so don't bring up old shit. You want to be on some bullshit, keep your punk ass casino winnings, yo," Tavares said, mad as hell at herself for leaving that receipt in Damien's car.

"What the fuck ever, Apple! You got life fucked up with your spoiled ass! You just blow dough on shoes and bags and shit like we got a money tree. Damn, we got money, but if you buy every fucking Chanel, Dior, Louie, and Prada bag and shoe, we ain't gonna have no money! I love your spoiled ass, but goddamn," Damien laughed. He loved his boo, who thought it was okay to spend at least $30,000 a month at the mall.

"I love you too, boo," Tavares said, sounding sad to make him feel guilty.

"Have fun, baby. Call me tonight when you get in," said Dame.

"Will do baby, I love you," and the phone hung up.

Tavares showered and was watching TV. Before she knew it, she dozed off. Waking up from her nap, Tavares could hear her message indicator going off on her phone. Picking up, she could see she had three missed text messages. The first text was from Mona-Lisa and said "meet in my room at 11:00." The second was from Dora and it said, "what hotel are you at?" The third message was from Dora. "Ur location, Ma, will be in NY @ 11. Be ready." Looking at the clock that read 10:35, Tavares knew she had to get moving real fast.

Working well under pressure, Tavares was ready in thirty minutes flat. By the time she was done, she looked like she was straight out of *Cosmopolitan* magazine. Rushing down the hall toward Mona-Lisa and Randee's room, Tavares tapped on the door, knowing she was late. Tavares greeted her crew, "Hey, Boo-Faces." That was their personal nickname for each other. And if everyone was together, you never knew who the other was calling, but it was alright because everyone would respond.

"You're so slow but you know I wasn't the once cussing you out," said Randee when she opened the door. "Boo, I'm used to it, these bitches are the ones who act like they don't know."

"Shit," interrupted Mona, "Leslie and Tavares are slower than fucking molasses on a good day."

"I'm working on it though," said Leslie, with her small frame sprawled across Mona's bed, looking at *Law and Order* on the flat screen TV. Jazz had finished rolling two blunts and looked up.

"Apple, you look cute," Jazz said, referring to her grey Rocka Republic skinny jeans, blue Gucci stiletto heels, and a corset with a blazer over it. "The blue eye makeup is killing them. It brightens your eyes."

"Thanks," she said, and took a seat on the bed.

"Listen up, bitches," Tavares said, a little hesitant. Everyone turned to her. "We're going to go to hang with a dude that Jazz and I met from Jersey. They're going to meet us at Madison Square Garden to go to New Jersey."

Jazz's eyes lit up. "That's my bitch! I want to go to Jersey to see if it's popping out there. I am so with it," said Jazz.

"How the fuck did that happen?" laughed Mona-Lisa. "I thought from the sounds of the conversations we had the last few weeks, you wasn't messing with him."

"I ain't messing with him," Tavares said, with her eyes almost popping outta her head, letting her friend know she had it all twisted. "I called and thanked him for the flowers and he invited us to Jersey for a weekend on him, but I said no. Then when we decided to come out here, I figured hey, since we in a group setting it's okay to see him. Plus he's going to treat us all, so why not?"

"Shit, had you said he was paying from the beginning, this conversation wouldn't even be going on," Mona-Lisa said.

Within thirty minutes, the ladies were headed toward Madison Square Garden.

Tavares's phone rang as they were in motion.

"Tavares, where are yawl," asked Dora with impatience in his voice.

"We're on our way. Sorry we're late, we got lost," Tavares said, lying because she didn't want him mad at her.

"Well, you need to come on, the concert is going to start."

"Alright. But I thought we were going to New Jersey."

"I never said that, sweetheart. I said to meet me at Madison Square Garden."

"Alright, we're two minutes away."

Hanging up, Tavares informed her friends that their sponsor had secured tickets to the 4th of July rock out concert at the garden. "Then we're going to club VIP."

"Yo, Tavares, how the fuck did that nigga get tickets to the rock out concert? That shit been sold out for months," Leslie said, shocked.

"Bitch, please don't get me to lying," Tavares said, shrugging her shoulders. The ladies arrived in the nick of time. Jay-Z, Lil Wayne, Young Jeezy, Monica, Keyshia Cole, and Rihanna were about to Rock The Mic.

Dora was outside when Tavares and her girls approached. Handing them five tickets, he waved and said, "I'll catch you ladies after the show," and made his way to his skybox seats.

"Damn, this shit is packed," Randee said, walking down the stairs toward their front row seats.

Dora and his friends were in their skybox watching the show, getting tore down. This shit was nothing to him. He went to most concerts that passed through the city or Jersey. He gave Tavares and her friends the tickets that he was going to use, and just partied with his mans and them in the skybox.

"Thank God for NJ," praised Mona-Lisa, "because this is unbelievable."

This is what's up, Tavares thought looking around the crowd, trying to spot Dora, but she didn't see him anywhere in sight. The girls listened to the best of the best in the industry do their thing and couldn't have been more pleased. The adrenaline rush was crazy. It was pure amazement to look around and see Madison Square Garden packed to capacity and everyone on their feet singing along to every song being sung or rapped. Damn near losing their voices from singing along, the girls was amped and ready to party. Exiting Madison Square Garden, Tavares called Dora.

"Hey what's up, where are you?" asked Tavares.

"I'm getting in my car. We'll meet you around the corner in front of Penn Station. I'm in a red Porsche."

Once in the rental, Tavares and her girls made it around the corner and pulled up behind Dora.

"Tavares, is that his truck?" Randee questioned.

"Yeah, I guess."

"It's nice," Leslie said.

"That shit ain't nice, that shit in rear," Randee informed them. "How many fucking niggaz you know running around the hood in a Porsche? Bitch, that nigga got some long ass dollars. Do you know what the shit will do on the highway?" Randee loved fast cars and thought she was a NASCAR driver. She always thought someone was trying to test her, so she always ended up somewhere racing. "He needs to let me push that," Randee said, shaking her head.

Blowing it down and discussing the concert, the ladies followed Dora.

"Keyshia Cole is the shit," raved Tavares, ready to get at anyone who disagreed. Of course no one did, because Keyshia was the hottest thing rocking. Keyshia had brought Tavares to tears singing, "You've Changed," "Sent From Heaven," "Just Like You," and "Love." Keyshia Cole was the face of every hood chick's pain, especially Tavares's. Tavares had spent many nights crying to Keyshia Cole when she and Dame fought, had it out, or he didn't come home. She would cry and Keyshia Cole would pull her through the pain and hurt. "I fucks with Keyshia hard body. I love that bitch like a play play cousin!" Everyone fell out laughing because Tavares was for real. Keyshia Cole was the first CD that Tavares had ever purchased in the store and not from the bootleg man. Tavares wasn't into music, only what they played on the radio. But Keyshia got Tavares's money at Best Buy with no problem.

"I love Keyshia too," Mona-Lisa said. "She makes you feel like she's singing about your story and pain. It's like she was really there when the shit was going down and then went and wrote the song for you."

"Ahh, you sentimental ass hoes," screamed Randee, who was just always tough. "I love some Keyshia when I'm at home and alone, but Lil Wayne and Jay-Z rocked that shit."

"Jigga my nigga can't be topped," Jazz cosigned.

"If you think about it, everyone was the shit," Leslie said, deadening the debate.

Talking about the concert all the way to the after party, the ladies pulled up behind Dora in valet parking. They were ready to drop down and get their eagle on. It wasn't too often they partied till the wee hours of the morning, but when they did, they did it for real. Dora paid the valet $200 for each car and made his way toward the door.

"Damn," Dora said, admiring Tavares's sexy outfit. Tavares and her crew had stopped short of the door to fix their makeup, so Dora took advantage of the moment and viewed all Tavares's sexy bumps and curves.

"How about one of you niggaz push up one of her girls, that way I'll for sure get her back out here. I'll pay for it and all," said Dora.

"I got you my nigga," Dora's brother said.

As the ladies approached, Dora's brother Middeon went in hard body. "Hey, ladies, I hope yawl enjoyed the show," said the mocha-brown man with a sexy pretty boy hood swagger and monotone voice. They couldn't help but laugh at how coolly he'd said it. Everything about him screamed too cool for his own self.

"Yeah, it was off the hook. That shit was hot. Enjoy myself is an understatement," the ladies responded.

Middeon approached Mona-Lisa and playfully pulled her hair that was to the middle of her back, "You're cute, where's your man?"

"Probably with your girl and get your hands out my hair."

"Damn, you're feisty, I like it."

Mona laughed and said, "Nah, I don't have a man. I have a set of a twins and a bum ass baby father. Nothing more, nothing less."

Everyone fell back and conversed like they went way back before entering the club—everyone except Tavares. She stepped away to call Damien. With no answer, she left a message. "Baby, I'm trying to call you but you aren't answering, so I assume you're in the casino WINNING." Hanging up, Tavares made her way inside.

Club V.I.P. was packed to capacity. Making their way through the crowd, they stopped and all took pictures on the huge adult-size swings that draped from the ceilings.

Dora escorted them upstairs to their private room. Their private party room had exotic circle chairs, sectional couches, and glass cabinets with their ordered choice of liquors for the evening. There was a personal bar stocked with appetizers, ice, and glasses.

"This is crazy," Leslie said as she took a seat next to Randee.

"This is what I'm fucking talking about," Randee said, knowing that they were about to have a good time in their club inside the club.

"Who wants a shot?" Dora asked. Everyone surrounded the bar while Dora popped three bottles of Don P and poured eleven shot glasses with Patrón. Tavares, Dora, and all their friends started taking shots, getting the party started.

Meanwhile, Damien was in the casino hotel with his little freak bitch looking at wifey come across his caller id. He would tell Tavares he was on the tables when she called. *Tavares is going to kill me if she ever catches me*, he thought as he looked down at his exotic black and Chinese side bitch sucking his dick like she was bobbing for apples.

"Damn…" he said as his head fell back and his eyes rolled around his head. Thus far he hadn't got caught because Tavares was a homebody except for when her and her girls were out of town. She had been through enough with Damien that she learned that when she stayed away, she didn't have to fight, stab, or end up in jail with him and his drama. Tavares played her role and it was at home. In return, he kept his dirt from circulating.

Two hours later, after rolling in the sheets like two dogs in heat, Damien left his freak in bed and headed to the shower. Coming out fully dressed, he looked at the naked fixture and said, "There's some money on the dresser for you to gamble. I'm going back downstairs."

Hopping on the elevator, he looked in the mirror and felt guilty. He always did after cheating, because he had no reason to be cheating on Apple. Apple was truly what every nigga needed in their life. She was beautiful, intelligent with book and street smarts, took care of her man, was a go-getter, and a pure freak in the sheets. Dame just didn't know how to reject all the other pussy that was thrown at him.

Spotting his mans and them, Damien gave them dap and caught up on who was up and who was down.

"Damn Winky, you down $5,000 and still trying to come back, you better go take the broad upstairs and blow her back out."

"Nigga, Winky ain't never down," he said in his usual cocky tone. "And don't worry about me tapping her, just be glad I can't tap Tavares," Winky joked.

They all laughed, but little did they know he wasn't joking. Winky was Damien's best friend, so he would never cross Damien, but he was secretly crushing on Tavares. He hated that Damien cheated on her with no-good bum bitches. But that was his man, so he just rolled with it.

"I'm up and need three more thousand to take home to my baby," Damien said, taking a seat at the blackjack table.

Tavares and her girls partied the morning away with Dora and his friends. They drank, blew down some chocolate tie, laughed, joked, and danced till the early morning. Exiting the club, they waited at valet parking for their cars. Middeon approached Mona-Lisa and playfully pulled her hair.

"You seem to like my hair. You been touching it all night."

"It's real, so what's the problem?"

"These is tracks, stop tripping."

"Girl, please. They don't even sell hair this pretty from no horse," he said in his sultry low, cool tone. Everyone fell out laughing. Tavares stood to the side trying to sober up because she was on a mean wave at the moment.

"Tav, we gonna all go get breakfast, is that cool?" asked Mona.

"Yeah, I'm hungry anyways," Tavares said, catching Dora's eyes on her. He was staring past Jazz at her. Hopping in their respective cars, they all traveled to the Village to a soul food restaurant that was open all night.

Arriving at the Pink Tea Cup, "Table for eleven," said the biggest of all the men. At six-foot-seven, with three hundred pounds of solid muscle, Bryce looked like he should have been a linebacker for a professional football team. The hostess said ten minutes, and they shot the shit till their table was ready.

An hour later, the ladies were having a good ass time with these niggaz they had just met but felt like they knew for forever, laughing, joking, and clowning.

"Damn, you got a lot of food on that plate, what you eating for three?" Pure said to Randee.

"I know you ain't talking, as big as that head and stomach are, you look like you are three people." Everyone cried in laughter. After eating steak, crab cakes, scrambled eggs, waffles, bacon, pancakes, grits, bagels, English muffins, sausage, home fries, and orange and cranberry juice, everyone was stuffed.

"Check, please?" asked Leslie, who was getting ready to pass out from nigga-itis.

"Damn, you paying or something?" Bam Bam asked like he'd missed the memo.

"Nah, but you are, smart ass," Leslie replied, and started laughing so hard that she had to grab her chest.

"So tell me when yawl going to come to Jersey?" asked Middeon with his low, sexy voice, handsome face, and pretty braids that touched his mid-back.

"It's Tavares's birthday in a few months, so maybe we could come see what's up in the Brickz," Jazz said, eyeing the prize.

"When's your birthday, Tavares?" asked Dora.

"October 1."

"Get the fuck out of here, lil mama? That's my birthday too." Dora almost died inside at the mere coincidence.

"Shut the hell up, it is not." Tavares was blushing from ear to ear, thinking how crazy that was.

"Well, good, now we really need to come see what's popping out in Jersey," Jazz said, not letting up on Dora.

"We are New Jersey," said Dora so nonchalantly that the seriousness of the statement was clear.

Tavares wasn't trying to get close to Dora. Her attraction was too strong, and seeing as though she had never cheated, she knew she had to stay clear of him. She knew she couldn't play herself with trying to deal with Dora. So she was going to play it cool.

"Excuse me for a moment," she said, excusing herself for a cigarette.

"Where you going, shorty wop?" asked Dora instantly.

"Where my feet are about to take me," Tavares said, and turned around and went about her business.

Walking away, all his mans could see why she was his type. She had a strong presence, fly as hell, and wasn't bowing down to their man, like most women did. She was a lot like him and they could see why he wanted her for a counterpart. Dora was on her and they could see it. Exiting the diner, the ladies and new their new friends were exchanging jokes and laughs. Saying their good mornings, the ladies headed toward their rental car.

"So did you enjoy yourself?" Dora asked Tavares as she stood under the streetlamp, looking bashful.

"Yeah, I did. I had a ball, to be honest. Thanks, because you treated not just me, but all my friends."

"No thanks needed, babegirl. The pleasure was all mine. Tomorrow yawl gonna come out to Jersey to a cookout at my grandmother's house," Dora stated. Tavares wasn't sure if he had just asked or told her. "My grandmother does the damn thing in the kitchen. There will be more than enough food."

"Sounds like a plan," Tavares said, knowing that her girls wouldn't mind some free and tasty cookout food. "I'll see you later today," Tavares said, and headed toward the car to meet her friends.

"Damn, I want to smoke," said Jazz.

"You always want to smoke," said Randee. "What else is new?"

"Shut up bitch, you do too."

"I know, but you're always the one to suggest it."

"Yawl are stupid," Leslie said as she crawled in the back seat.

By the time the ladies got to the hotel and twisted up, it was 7:30 a.m. All lying across each other on Tavares's king-sized bed, blowing it down, they cooed over their fantastic night. Tavares mentioned Dora inviting them to Jersey to a cookout at his grandmother's.

"Let me find out you got the hots for homeboy," Randee half-joked.

"Not even," Tavares said nonchalantly. "He's cool, but I got that other dude, you know the one I live wit and call my boyfriend," Tavares said, jokingly sarcastic.

Jazz's phone interrupted them.

"Jump off, jump off, who got a booty call, on the straight early morning," Mona-Lisa said, looking at her girl real suspect.

Jazz looked at the phone and hit ignore. "Shut the fuck up, bitch. Even if I wanted to go jump off, we're a long ways from home," Jazz said, exhaling the smoke.

Tavares looked at her phone and couldn't believe that Damien hadn't called back.

~ CHAPTER 9 ~

If you knew better, you would do better.

Damien was at the Casino hot on the blackjack table on the early early a.m. He was up $6,000. He had hit all night.

"I only got two more G's to go, niggaz," he said. "My baby's going to be mad at me for not calling her, so I got to bring her five grand, which means I need two more."

Rollo looked at his right hand man and said, "Damien, get the fuck up, you're killing us tonight with your hot ass." Some of them were up, but not like Damien.

"Damn, Dame," Squizzy said. "Get the fuck up and let someone else break the bank."

"You niggaz is stupid? DO I kick niggaz off when they hot? Hell no, so you niggaz can kick rocks and keep losing."

The dealer on the blackjack switched because Damien was killing the casino. That was his fourth dealer, so he was calling it quits.

"Alright, you niggaz win, I'm betting five grand and win, lose, or draw, I'm walking away."

"Word," his mans said, and the one outsider, a Chinese man, nodded his head. Damien watched the dealer lay a ten down and knew that if it wasn't a high card, he was screwed, because the dealer had an eight. When Damien's second card was an ace, he burst into laughter how lucky he had just made out. His mans and them shook their heads in disbelief.

"What the fuck, nigga?" Winky yelled. "You fucking come down here with some hot pussy and get lucky. This is some fucking bullshit," he said, only holding fifteen.

Damien tripled his money with blackjack. Getting off the table like he said he would, he fell back and watched his mans win, before he went and cashed in on his $30,000. He started with $1,000, so he was more than happy with his night's profit of $29,000. Tavares could have $10,000 because he felt really fucked up tonight. He fucked bitches, but he never tricked on them like he did tonight and that had him feeling some kind of way.

Heading upstairs for round two, he pushed his guilt to the side and his wifey out his mind for one last go round. Walking in the room, Damien pulled his clothes off and climbed in the bed next to Jazlene, who was sleep. Feeling him slide in the bed next to her, she instantly woke up and went to work. Jazlene thought fucking Damien real good would make him leave his girl. She sucked his dick for forty-five minutes before climbing on top of his long dick and riding him under the bright morning sunshine. After they both exploded, Jazlene rolled off of him ready to snuggle up.

By the time Tavares and her girls woke up, all lying on one another, it was 1:00 p.m.

"Alright," Mona-Lisa said, twisting the last of the three morning blunts. "It's 1:30. Let's meet in the lobby at 2:45. That's enough time for everyone to go to their rooms and get ready."

"Tavares and Leslie, even yawl should be able to be ready," Mona-Lisa said sarcastically.

"Shut up," Tavares said, eating a banana. "I'm not as slow as you try to make me out to be."

"Apple, only in your world ain't you slow, Boo."

"Yo," said Randee. "When you're just as slow as Leslie, you know you're slow."

"Shut up, I'm not slow," Leslie defended herself. "I'm time management challenged." They all fell out laughing.

"Well, like I said, she's time management retarded too then, if she's slow as you," Randee said matter of factly. Smoking and reminiscing about their night, the ladies headed to their rooms to get ready for their day.

Exiting the hotel at 3:00, the ladies were ready to start their afternoon. Going to get their hair, nails, and toes done for a total of thirty dollars, it was times like this you had to love New York. Ten-dollar wash and sets, and manicures and pedicures for twenty dollars made beauty day just all too cheap. Tavares got directions from Dora and they headed toward Newark to get their grub on.

Mona-Lisa's phone interrupted their conversation. "Hello?" she said hesitantly, looking at the unrecognizable number.

"Yo, what's good Mona-Lisa? I just swung through your spot and laid on the bell. Your car's there so where are you and where are my kids?" Mona-Lisa laughed.

"Walter, who the fuck are you talking to? You be killing me how you just call up out the cut and shit. Your kids ain't heard from you in months, now you talking about you was just ringing my bell, oh please. Your kids are away for the weekend. I'll be sure to have them call their daddy dearest back when they get home."

"Yo! Mona-Lisa, I don't got time to play with you. I want to see my kids today, so if you know like I know, you'll just tell me where they are and I'll go get them, since you're somewhere tramping through the streets."

Mona-Lisa looked at the phone and looked at her girls, then she looked back at the phone and said to her girls, "Yeah, this nigga has definitely got to be smoking. Are you serious? Walter, whatever you're smoking, I would advise you to stop because that shit has got you losing your motherfucking mind. My kids aren't sitting around just waiting for you to play sometime daddy. So when they get home and I get home from tramping around the streets, as you say, I'll have them call you," and she hung up.

"Walter sadly got me twisted. Gonna tell me he wanna see his kids and can go pick them up since I'm tramping around in the streets."

"Yeah?" asked Randee, like she knew for sure Mona-Lisa's baby's father had lost his mind.

"That nigga has got to be smoking," cosigned Tavares. "Niggaz kill me how they want to come around and play daddy when it's convenient for them," Tavares said, shaking her head. Mona-Lisa was pissed off that her baby's father had just tried to ruin her good day.

"Don't even let that nigga get you mad," said Leslie. "We just had a good night, morning, and in a few minutes we'll be in Jersey hanging out and getting it in."

Dora and Middeon were headed to their grandmother's house for their Sunday ritual. No matter what they did, they made it to their grandmother's for dinner, unless they weren't in town. The 4th just meant bigger and better for their grandmother, who loved to get a party popping.

Mid sat in the passenger seat and said, "Ole girl Mona-Lisa is cool. I need a headstrong broad like her in my life."

"You sure the fuck do, because all you do is find stupid bitches to put your dick in their mouths, who ain't got no conversation for you."

"Nigga, it ain't my fault that hoes like to slob my knob. Shit, you think I don't want one who can have a conversation and not just suck dick like a pro?"

"Mid, please," Dora said, knowing his brother. "You ain't trying to settle down."

"Yes the fuck I am!"

"I gots to see it to believe," said Dora.

Arriving at their grandmother's house, they could see they were the last to arrive. Getting out of Dora's Porsche, they saw their mother, aunts, uncles, cousins, friends, and family scattered everywhere. Saying their hellos, they made their way into the house and could smell their grandmother's cooking a mile away.

"Me-Ma," Dora yelled.

"I'm in here, baby boy," said Dora's grandmother.

Dora's grandmother was the head of their family. She was a lady who had been in the streets in her days and wasn't nothing to fuck with at fifty-nine. Only sixteen years apart from her daughter, they resembled sisters rather than mother and daughter. She still rocked high heels, a dooby-wrap, and wore the flyest name brands. She was at the gym four times a week and even had her a little PYT that kept her glowing from the great sex. Draped in jewels, she was glistening in diamond studs, a necklace with a diamond pendant, and diamond rings on all her fingers, not to mention the six bracelets on her arms. Me-Ma was too fly to be a nana.

"There go my favorite boys, you know it ain't a party without yawl," said Me-Ma, giving each of her grandsons a hug and a big kiss. Me-Ma had taken care of the boys when their mother was off and getting high. Me-Ma was their rock and the best grandmother you could ask for. She talked and kicked it with her grandsons about any and everything under the sun. There wasn't nothing that her grandsons didn't hesitate to talk to her about. Women and money were their favorites, though, because Me-Ma had a lot to say on both.

"What's up, fellas? Yawl ain't been to see me in a few weeks."

"Me-Ma, we ain't been in town or you know we woulda, so stop tripping." Taking a seat at the kitchen table that was covered with multiple desserts, Dora and Mid kicked it with their grandmother and waited for their friends to arrive.

Tavares and her friends arrived at Dora's grandmother's house and couldn't believe the amount of cars that were parked outside and around this lady's house, which was in a cul-de-sac.

Tavares called Dora. "Hey, I think we're in the right place."

"Why do you think that?" Dora shot back. "Why ain't you sure?"

"Don't get smart with me, boy. Didn't you say we were coming to your grandmother's house? This is too crunk to be your grandmother's house."

"Girl, stay right there. You're in the right spot. I'm coming," he said and the phone went dead.

"He's coming," Tavares informed her crew.

Looking around at what might as well have been a block party, the ladies waited for Dora.

"This is way too poppin' to be nana's house," Mona-Lisa said, looking at all the cars.

"Hey, ladies," Dora approached, looking good.

Damn...he looks good every time I encounter him, Tavares thought. In a red polo wife beater, some tan shorts, and some red and tan beef and broc Timbs, he was sexy. The detailed tattoos that sleeved his shoulders, arms and neck, were just so thugaliscious on him underneath the strong sunshine. *He is so fine*, Tavares thought, and knew her girls were thinking the same.

The ladies tried to not stare at the ice that was definitely blinding them. Dora dropped $20,000 on his bracelet and $50,000 on his platinum chain that had an iced-out D on it, and $30,000 on his ring. His ice was meant to blind people, so he was glad it was doing its job.

"Come on, yawl, there's mad food out back, drinks, cards, gambling, gossiping or whatever you want," joked Dora.

Following Dora, the ladies entered the crunkest family cookout they'd ever been to. There were three moonwalks for children of all ages and a below-ground swimming pool with about fifty people lounging in it. Rented water slides. About thirty picnic tables occupied by guests. There were eight food tables with entirely too many choices and selections.

"This is crazy," Randee said in total disbelief at the mounds of people crowding the overly massive backyard.

The ladies and the guys shot the shit and cracked jokes, enjoying the warming festivities around them.

"I'm hungry," Jazz said, admiring all the food across the huge backyard.

"Yeah, we definitely need to be making that happen," Leslie said, snapping her fingers and pointing to the food, to motion *let's go.*

The ladies made plates and sat down at one of the empty picnic tables.

"Yo, this shit is bomb," Leslie said, pointing to the potato salad on her plate. "His grandmother definitely made this. It just got nana written all over it," Leslie said, licking her fork slowly, savoring the taste.

"I ain't bit into shit that wasn't good," Jazz said, eating some chicken ziti and broccoli. "His grandmother put her foot in this shit," Jazz said, wanting to suck her fingers.

Dora came over and said, "Excuse me ladies, do yawl mind if I steal Tavares for a minute?"

Tavares was tearing a piece of BBQ chicken up and really didn't want to move, but she didn't object. Getting up from the table, Tavares followed Dora into the house.

"Where the hell are you taking me?" Tavares said, poking him in his long, firm, toned back as she walked behind him.

"Damn, you act like you can't talk to me one-on-one," Dora said, stopping in the mudroom of his grandmother's house.

"I never said that."

"Well you sure ain't tried to get me alone, Ms. Lady."

"Whatever, Mr. Santacosa. I told you, I'm not messing with you. We can be cool though, since you're so hella handsome. You're quite a character, if I may say so," Tavares informed him as she tried to hold back her light chuckle. "But I can't fool with you. It seems like our friends are hitting it off, so we'll see each other in passing, maybe."

"You got a lot of shit with you, Apple. But I got more with me. So we'll see who wins in the end."

"Is that a threat?" laughed Tavares.

"Nah, Ma, threats are idle words, so I don't make threats. I don't say things that I can't make good on."

Tavares looked at him and loved the swagger that parted his sexy full lips with each word.

Dora grabbed Tavares's hand and led her into the kitchen where his grandmother and mother were talking.

"Here go my two favorite ladies."

"Hey, baby boy," Dora's mother said. "I was just talking about you."

"Good things of course, because you know how sweet, great, and loving your son is. Ma, I think Miss Boston needs you to tell her to stop giving your favorite son a hard time and be nice to me."

"Mrs. Santacosa, I'm not giving your son a hard time. He's giving me a hard time."

"I believe it, baby. He's good at that and good for that," Dhara said, shrugging her shoulders, letting it be known that she was just keeping real.

"Ma," Dora said, looking at her sideways. "How are you going to take her side?"

"Hey, I'm just keeping it real."

"I know yawl better leave my grandson alone," Me-Ma said, pointing a wooden spoon at her daughter and grandson's friend. "My grandson is the best nigga in the world, and if you don't know, his Me-Ma just told you so. So get it right and get it tight about my baby." Tavares laughed while Dhara looked at her mother like she was crazy.

"Ma, that's why that big baldhead nigga got it twisted now. Listen to your grandmother if you want to, but you know I'll break you down." Tavares laughed at them, because they were too cute in their relationship. She kicked it with Dora's mother and grandmother for a little bit before returning to join her friends.

Dora's mother and grandmother instantly fell in love with Tavares and her bubbly, happy, outgoing personality. They could see that she was a good girl with her head on straight. She didn't have that aura about her as if she was in it for the fame game or a few dollars. In their eyes, she was a potential keeper from their first encounter, but even more so because Abdora saw something in her that just made him light up when he talked about her.

Dora brought very few women home. The few he did bring home didn't make him sparkle the way Tavares did. Nor did any of them seem to have their own dreams and ambitions other than trying to get Dora to be theirs. He was a very powerful man in the streets and women were trying to grab him every day, so they wanted him with someone who was truly about him and not just the benefits that came along with him. Dhara liked anyone who kept it real and was down to earth. She just wanted someone to make her son fall in love and let him experience the beauty of love, because she knew that it was a beautiful thing. When Dora loved, he loved hard, so Dhara wanted him to get the same love reciprocated.

Tavares returned to the backyard to find that her girls were in no way worried about where she had disappeared to. The ladies were engaged in two card games. Leslie and Randee were playing spades against Pure and Buddah. At the table next to them was Mona-Lisa and Jazz kicking Bryce and Maniac's asses in whist.

"Damn, you niggaz ain't looking too happy," Dora teased his boys.

"Man, they whooping our asses and taking our damn money," complained Maniac.

Tavares just laughed because her and her girls were beasts when it came to cards. Not many chicks could play like they did, so it was funny when they sat down and played with men, because they never expected the blindsided ass-whooping.

They spent the evening laughing, joking, eating, playing cards, drinking, and just having a downright good time. Before everyone knew it, it was 2:00 a.m. and the party was still going. It seemed like no one was tired and the yard seemed to be even more full than it was earlier when the ladies arrived. It wasn't until 4:00 a.m. that the ladies stated their thank yous and said their goodbyes.

After a fun-filled weekend, Tavares and her friends hit 95 North at noontime and headed home to the Bean. Blowing it down, they tried to figure out what the hell Tavares was going to do about Dora. Tavares looked at her friends with pleading eyes that read, *don't I wish*, as she inhaled the sour deez blunt.

"I can't fuck with him, yawl," Tavares said, shaking her head. "So stop trying to even tempt me. Dame's a handful enough so there ain't no room to be creeping on the side."

Leslie turned around and looked at her home girl like she had lost her mind.

Mona-Lisa said, "Girl is you crazy or just plain foolish? Please let me know," in a serious tone. "Tavares, when the fuck have we ever passed up a good thing, and that nigga right there is a good thing for sure."

"Yeah, so get your mind right," Leslie said, taking the blunt and turning back around. Jazz was feeling some kind of way that she was at him and got nowhere, so she just kept quiet on the matter.

"Yeah, Tavares, if you let that slip through the cracks you need to be slapped," Randee added to the conversation.

"I hear yawl, but hmmm, I don't know. I never been one to take on more than I can handle." Tavares was feeling them, but knew better than to play with fire, no matter what her girls were suggesting. Abdora was definitely fire and she wasn't trying to get burned for playing with him. The conversation of Damien and Abdora took up a lot of time, because before the ladies knew it they were outta Connecticut on the Mass Pike entering Massachusetts. Tavares heard her girls loud and clear, but she wasn't too sure this was one time that she would be taking their advice.

Tavares entered her large home that felt empty when she was the only one in it. Going to the TV room, Tavares saw that Damien and his friends hadn't been tearing her house up, as she had assumed they would have. There wasn't a DVD or a video game out of place. All the colored suede pillows were nicely on the sectional couch, with no plates or cups in sight. Tavares was impressed for once. She took a seat on the couch to relax and smoke a blunt to the head.

What the hell am I getting myself into? Tavares thought as she split the cigarillo down the middle and emptied the guts into the special blunt trashcan. *This isn't a movie or a book*, Tavares thought, *if I fuck around and get caught slippin', it'll be my ass for real.* Tavares rolled her blunt, sparked it, and inhaled deeply as she listened to India Arie drain the room through the surround sound stereo. The more Tavares inhaled, the more she knew the answers. If she just didn't fuck with Dora she was good, no problems; life goes on. If she did get tempted to see him again, outside of work, then she would be the only one to blame for whatever happened.

Damien came in the house and saw the bags in the doorway and knew Tavares was somewhere in the house. Hearing the music, he followed the sound and found his shorty totally passed out. She was in some small cotton hugging shorts and a tank top, with her hair everywhere, on the couch with neo soul playing. Slapping Tavares's huge, round tight ass, she jumped up like a bolt of lightning.

"What the fuck, Dame?" Tavares said, with her cheeks rosy red.

"Get your fucking ass up. You always wanna come in here and smoke and take your ass to sleep. Who fucking wastes a high like that? Plus, I ain't seen you, so get the fuck up and twist another blunt so we can kick it."

Tavares just looked at Damien with a look that let him know he had her totally fucked up.

"Damien, I ain't twisting shit up. I was high and sleeping peacefully, and you came in here fucking with that, so you roll," Tavares said, grabbing the remote to put on a movie, not even giving him a second look.

"What we eating?" Damien asked as he gave the backwood its last lick.

"Damien, do me a favor, please? Leave me the fuck alone. You woke me up and right now all I want to do is smoke and go back to sleep. How about you work dinner out? Go get plates from Ma's house or get Dining In. They deliver from any upscale and medium-scale restaurant you want."

"Well, call them and order Legals," Damien said, handing her the blunt and pulling $200 out of his pocket. "Get me double-stuffed twin lobsters and a side of clam chowder with extra crackers." Tavares just busted out laughing.

"Why are you giving me the money, Damien? Like Yo! Who was I fucking talking to when I just said work dinner out? Did you not fucking hear me or did it go in one ear and out the other?"

Sucking his teeth, Damien took the money back and dialed the Dining-In number that he actually had stored in his phone.

"Don't smoke the blunt till I come back," Tavares said. "Wait, what do you want to eat? Get me a seafood casserole and a clam chowder with extra crackers."

Needing to take a shower because she woke up crabby, Tavares stopped in the kitchen, grabbed her phone out of her Louis Vuitton bag and climbed two flights of stairs to the third floor. Entering the bathroom, Tavares looked at her phone that had been on silent and noticed she had a message. Opening the message, Tavares knew she was either in for a smile or a good laugh. Reading, "Miss Lady, u home safe? Hit me when and if you can. I dig u got a man, so just let me be your friend?" Tavares wasn't messing with Dora, but somehow texting him back showed something different. "Not calling u. home safe though. Thanks for everything." Getting in the shower, Tavares washed and washed till she felt like she couldn't wash anymore. Tavares realized that she couldn't wash the confusion away about whether or not to pretend she wasn't feeling him and let him kick rocks or follow the attraction and settle for being his friend.

Dame was the one that ladies thought that they wanted every night with his light chocolate skin, handsome face, and long dick. But

Dora was the one that every woman needed in her life every night and every day. He was the best example of, "if you knew better, you would do better."

Dame was fucked up at times, but Tavares figured, what nigga wasn't in real life, so she dealt with the bullshit. She figured no nigga was perfect, so you picked and chose your battles. Damien had a lot that came with him, but he had a good heart, didn't beat or abuse her, and was a good provider. His only downfalls were his whores and street ways.

After showering for thirty minutes, Tavares stepped out the shower feeling fresh, clean, and replenished. She dried off, lotioned down, put her deodorant on, and slipped into her pink and purple tee-shirt nightgown from Victoria's Secret. Slipping on her matching terry cloth slippers, Tavares grabbed her phone and saw that she had another text. Opening it, it read, "Apple, you didn't answer the question of are you going to let me be your friend? If you want me to fall back, I will. I'm not that dude." Apple sucked her teeth because now she really had the ball in her court and she didn't know what to do with it. "Don't get feisty with me, I'm sleeping on it. Good night," Tavares texted back, putting a smiley face on the end. Powering her phone off, she went downstairs to kick it with her boyfriend, who she had enough problems with.

Tavares and Damien spent the whole night in the house together, to her surprise. They feasted on lobsters, seafood casserole, clam chowder, chocolate cake, and blew blunt after blunt while they snuggled up and watched movies. This was the old them, not the new them—which had Tavares even more confused.

Damien had rolled four blunts and didn't feel like rolling. "Yo babe, you gotta twist up."

Tavares looked down at the lime green weed and said, "I'm not rolling, Damien. So let's make a deal. If you roll for the rest of the night and not complain, I'll rub your fucking back until you cry."

Damien knew her skills. That was more than a deal, so he hopped on it. "Okay. But when it's time for my backrub, I want no static."

"You got it," Tavares said, slipping *Love Jones* in the DVD Player.

"What better else to watch," Tavares said as she looked out the huge room's bay window to the right and saw the rain falling. *Love Jones* and shots of Patrón was the evening aphrodisiacs that caused them to make sex linger from the first to the third floor, where the royal rumble went down between the silk sheets of their king-sized bed. Damien got his back rub twice over and got put to sleep like a baby after Tavares gave him the business.

~ CHAPTER 10 ~

You can't teach an old dog new tricks.

Waking up, Tavares got ready for a long day. It was back to work, school, and hustling. Tavares was only on her way to work and she was tired already. By the time she got to work and saw the long line of people waiting for the courthouse to open, she knew what kind of day it was going to be and prepared herself mentally. By noon, Tavares was popping two aspirins. In four hours she had processed over two hundred intakes, met with twelve trifling ass clients, and was just ready for the day to be over. Tavares could hear her phone chiming in her Chanel bag in her desk. Digging for it, she saw the message indicator and actually cracked a smile. Reading: "hey beautiful, I hope you're having a good day. If not smile for me and have a better day till I see you tomm for my office visit since you won't let me be your friend." She couldn't help but smile, because he was right on time and didn't even know it.

Tavares made it through work and school and was definitely tired. Having to go see two of her fiends, she was ready to go home and climb in the bed. Sitting at the red light on Washington Street and Blue Hill Ave, Tavares thought her eyes were buggin.' But she was definitely seeing correctly.

Damien was across the light going up Blue Hill Ave stuck at the other red light. Only he wasn't alone, he was with a bitch who seemed to be smiling real big. Tavares didn't trip. She went on about her business and would deal with his trifling ass when he got home.

All Tavares could think was you couldn't teach an old dog new tricks. No matter how good she thought things were going between her and Damien, somehow, some way he seemed to show her that he couldn't do right. *Damien got me twisted*, Tavares thought as she pulled up on Devon Street.

Damien got home, thinking that he would find a plate in the microwave and Tavares in the bed knocked out or watching TV. Only to his surprise, he found the complete opposite and he wasn't happy about the no food thing. Tavares always cooked, so he was mad there was nothing to eat. Hearing the clicking of the computer, Damien made his way through the kitchen to find out why he was starving and there was nothing cooked.

Tavares was in the computer room looking up airline tickets.

"Where you going and why there ain't no food?"

"That bitch that you was on Blue Hill Ave with shoulda motherfucking fed your ass. 'Cause yawl was looking real chummy chum chum. And when you start worrying about home, you can ask me questions about where I'm going." Tavares turned back around to the flat screen monitor, letting it be known she was done with the conversation.

"Don't fucking turn your back on me when I'm fucking talking to you," Damien said, instantly getting hot as fire. "Don't get disrespectful, Tav, for real."

Sucking her teeth, Tavares kept on about her business.

"Tavares, you didn't see me with no bitch," Damien said, dead ass serious, truly sticking to his story.

If Tavares had a hint of doubt, he would have convinced her she was losing her mind and didn't see him, but she knew exactly what she saw.

Damien wasn't giving up. "I didn't fucking have a bitch in my car, so cut the shit."

"Oh, okay, you didn't have no bitch in your car, it must have been Puff the motherfucking dragon that I saw you with."

Damien needed an Oscar as hard as he was going with his lie. Tavares was trying not to let him get the best of her, but the more he lied, the more he was asking for it. Tavares hopped up out of the tall leather chair and looked up at Damien.

"Yo! You know what, Damien? Do us both a fucking favor and just stop before you fucking dig yourself a hole that you can't get the fuck out of. Don't bury yourself alive. Because I know what the fuck I saw with my own two eyes."

Tavares was rolling her eyes, snapping her neck, and pointing her finger right in his face, ready to give it to Damien, who was a good foot bigger than her. "So save that Sideshow Bob shit that you're trying to put on right now. I ain't about to be talking about I seen some shit that I ain't seen. Ain't no one fucking call me. I sawwww you with my own two fucking eyes that work perfectly fine. I was really ready to go to toe to toe with you, but for what? This bullshit is for the fucking birds, and I ain't got time for it," Tavares said, slightly shrugging her small shoulders.

"What the fuck ever, I ain't got time for this bullshit," Damien said, storming to the kitchen, knowing that Tavares had seen him because he had actually seen her first. He got caught at the light on Blue Hill Ave first. Looking to the left, he saw Tavares coming down Washington Street. He knew it was her from her specialty license plate that read "Apple." Her light was red like his, so he knew she was going to get stopped at the corner of Washington and Blue Hill Ave. He just prayed that she was on her bluetooth, running her mouth and paying no attention to the other cars.

Damien cursed himself for being on the main streets with another bitch in his car, especially when it wasn't even late at night, during empty street hours. Dame knew he was in the doghouse and would be there for a hot minute. *Fuck*, Dame said to himself, so mad at himself for being so reckless.

Dame knew he might as well get comfortable in the doghouse, because it was where he would be for at least the next month, easy. Especially because, as bad as she wanted to scream and go off, she didn't, so he knew she was going to go extra hard with the silent treatment. Tavares went hard or went home with the doghouse treatment.

Dame hated when Tavares was mad, because she would block him out of her whole existence without a problem in the world. Tavares lived around him, like he was another house fixture or something. Sleeping on his pillow-top mattress was an out. Showering in his stand up marble shower wasn't happening, and neither was lounging in his round Jacuzzi-style tub. He was downstairs in a spare bedroom, in a regular bathroom. Cooking wasn't his thing for nothing in the world, and he hated takeout on a regular basis, so he would be starving at home. Tavares always found joy in eating something good and leaving evidence of all that he missed out on. She would leave the scent lingering, with no leftovers. Only dishes in the sink and him looking mad and hungry. Nine times out of ten, he went to his mother's, but he hated that he couldn't eat at home.

The most extreme thing Tavares had done to Dame while in the doghouse was have a friend at the bank completely delete his bank account. Taking all the money out of his account, Tavares put it into five various kinds of accounts that he didn't know anything about, although they were legitimately in his name. Her friend had even been able to cross over the transaction histories from the one account to the five accounts.

Dame was tight when he went to get a large amount of money, and his account was nonexistent. By the time this had happened, he and Tavares made up, so he just went straight flip mode on the bank about his money that had disappeared into thin air.

For a week Tavares kept quiet. She even let the bank go forth with an investigation and watched Damien stress over where his $500,000 was. The bank tried to convince him that he had $500,000, but that he had his accounts confused. His total amount in investments was $500,000 and he had divided his assets into CD, money market, and dividend accounts, not one account. He wasn't buying it or the bullshit they were kicking. He knew he had one account, not five damn accounts.

When Tavares came clean, he was madder than mad, but what could he do, report her for bank fraud? So she won once again.

On top of being evil, there could be no sex, no conversation, no nothing, and it drove Damien mad when she got that cold. Sometimes he wondered if doing the shit he did was worth the repercussions he caught at home. Never did Tavares let him get away with his bullshit or let him think he was getting off the hook in the least. Tavares knew leaving wasn't in the plans, but letting him slide with the bullshit wasn't either. She stayed and put up with his bullshit, but when it was time to give hell, she was even better at that.

Damien had her twisted and she didn't know why he thought he didn't. Every time Tavares went to try to forgive him, she couldn't help but think, *Hell No! He had the nerve to be riding with that bitch in his car like he ain't got a girl at home.* The silent treatment continued for another two weeks. She fixed him. She didn't talk to him, feed him, fuck him, suck him, or wash his clothes. Instead, she went to work, school, and partied, and put getting money last on her things to do. Damien was heated. He was going out his mind. Tavares was cool as a fan as she kept busy through text messaging. He felt Tavares was getting out of control and had proved her point after going hard for a month. Dame was good and tired of being Mr. Invisible. He was getting in her good graces before she headed back to school.

Damien got out the bed, wishing that he was upstairs in his bed that felt soft as cotton. The bed he had slept in was good, but nothing like his $3,000 California King mattress he should have been laying on. "I'm tired of this shit," Damien said, knowing that he was about to drop some heavy cash. Dame took a quick shower, threw on his True Religion jeans, brown tee, wheat Timbs, and called Rollo to come get him. Rollo and Dame were shopping all day to find the perfect gift. Damien had shopped long and hard, and dropped every dollar that he knew he was going to have to in order to get out the doghouse.

Arriving home, Damien couldn't believe that he had even got corny and put a fucking bow on it. "This shit is fucking crazy," Damien said out loud as he went in the house. Dame busted in the TV room like a bat straight out of hell. Tavares looked at him as she laid on the couch on the phone, kicking it with her girls on the four-way. Tavares paid him no attention, like he wasn't even there.

"Okay, bitch, you fucking win. I fucked up. I'm fucking sorry. I was wrong, out of pocket and the whole nine. Here," Damien said, tossing some keys at Apple, who caught them right on time.

"Uhhh huh," she said, really not even mad any more, but just dragging it out for the sake of him deserving it for going on with the lie.

"Hold on, yawl. Damn right, Imma bitch, and the only reason I ain't going to call your mama a bitch is because I love her like my own. What are these?"

"Go outside and find out." Before Damien had it clean out of his mouth, Tavares was rushing past him, down the stairs to the back of her brownstone.

"Hellll to the yeah, bitches!" she yelled.

"What, what he get us? Tell us!" her girls were yelling.

"This nigga got me a 2010 cherry red Acura Truck. Oh my god, and the shit is laid out with satellite radio, a twelve-disc CD changer, heated seats, TVs, and everything. It's fucking cute to death, yawl. Okay, it's Saturday, get the fuck up, we are so in the streets," Apple said.

Tavares and Damien made music notes with their private parts, as always from the first floor to the third floor. After screwing their brains out with makeup sex, they laid in the puddles they created underneath them. They were too weak to move.

After napping and waking up sticky and gooey, Tavares made her way to the shower to wash her body and hair that also felt like it was a bit sticky. Damien changed the sheets and laid out his clothes for the night. He was ready to go out, ball with niggaz, and celebrate his girl finally being off the bullshit. When Tavares had him in the doghouse, it fucked up everything he had going on, whether it was business or pleasure.

After showering, their bodies hadn't had enough. Damien came out of the bathroom in a towel while Tavares was on the bed naked, lathering her body with Victoria's Secret vanilla lotion.

"See, here you go," Damien said.

"Here I go what? I'm not bothering you. I'm simply putting on lotion. You just wanna be nasty, so you wanna flip it on me."

"Sure do," Dame said, walking toward his bed, dropping his towel and diving on top of Tavares.

"Get outta here!" Tavares screamed and laughed at the same time as she tried to wiggle from underneath him. "No, Dame, I just got out the shower and we just changed the sheets, hell no!"

Damien slipped two fingers between her legs that she hadn't bothered guarding, and it was on from there. Before Tavares knew it, she and Damien were back at square one. Sticky, gooey, laying on soaking wet sheets.

"This is fucking ridiculous!" Tavares screamed as she snatched the sheets off her bed, that could truly be rung out, after how bad she had orgasmed all over them.

"Don't be mad at me that you cum like a never-ending water fall."

"Shut the fuck up," Tavares said, throwing the wet sheets at him.

"I got enough of your pussy on me, get them sheets out of here," Damien said, jumping out of the way. Together they cleaned up, showered, dressed, and got ready to hit the streets. They had sexed all day and needed to rebuild their energy for after the club when they came home.

It was the same shit, different day for Tavares all summer. She was hustling at night, going to school in the evening, and working at the courthouse during the day. Dora was making his mark by trying to wear her down, but she hadn't caved. His smile melted her heart. Fine wasn't even up for debate. His words were smooth as they rolled off his tongue in his East Coast accent. His body was so sexy that it made Tavares have naughty thoughts of him throwing her over her desk and giving her the business. It was way too overwhelming.

What started out as an ice cream on his first visit turned into edible arrangements showing up, and next it was lunch being delivered every day. Her favorite was a steak and cheese sub from Ugis. What was so crazy was that Ugis was directly across the street from the courthouse and Tavares knew for sure that they didn't deliver. It was always a place that she loved—he did his homework. Olive Garden, Fridays, Legal Seafood, Margianno's, or something tasty to hit the spot.

Tavares was finishing her lunch when Mr. Santacosa decided that he wanted to come strolling in fifteen minutes early for his visit. Mad as hell that she had to throw her seafood casserole away from Legal, she tossed it in the trash and headed out front to escort Dora back. Before Tavares could say, "please excuse the smell," his smart ass beat her to the punch. Playfully raising his eyebrows and curving his semi-thick, juicy lips up, Dora said, "It smells fishy in here."

"Oh yeah, well you gotta holla at the person who gets my lunch. Or did you forget that you feel the need to deliver me food every damn day?"

"Well, I have to remember to not have seafood delivered on days that I have to come, that after-smell ain't too pretty."

Dora took a seat and slouched slightly in the cushioned chair and put his toothpick back in his mouth. Dora kept a toothpick in his mouth. It was his official trademark because it was rare he didn't have one in his mouth. Providing his proof of residency and employment to his probation officer, he utilized the time to kick it with the chick that he played text tag with after work hours and on the in-between time with her boyfriend.

"I can't believe that you can't come to Six Flags with me and all the neighborhood kids next week. You won't come see me for a weekend and now you won't even let me treat you to Six Flags with busloads of children? Damn, what a nigga gotta do to get some airplay?"

"If I didn't have to do all the ripping, running and coordinating, and attending of my boyfriend's mother's birthday party, I would so be there with yawl," Tavares said, meaning it. "Me and my friends would be there. We love amusement parks, but I can't miss this party."

"You always telling me why you can't see me past visits to your office, this is some real live bullshit," Dora said, not feeling like he had made any progress in the last month.

"EVEN if I did want to holler at you I can't because of my job. Nosy people go into criminal justice. I don't need the conflict of interest because some nosy person knows I'm hollering at one of my clients."

"Whatever," Dora said, still mad that he couldn't get her to come back to Jersey since she was there for the 4th of July. All he got was office and text time.

"I think you be forgetting that I have a boyfriend. And that you and I are just cool. I know he's an asshole, but he's my asshole, so you better stop acting all crazy," Tavares said, rolling her eyes. Tavares was a tough cookie, but Dora was going to get her.

~ CHAPTER 11 ~

When you look for trouble, you find trouble.

Looking around the only half-decorated lavender and silver hall, Tavares complained, "Come on yawl, we have to hurry up. We have to get the decorations up, go to the mall, and make it back here in less than three hours. I still have to get something to wear and pick the cakes up."

"How you got the nerve to be rushing us, when this is your project?" asked Randee. "You always plan these huge extravagant parties and then we always get stuck bailing you out, so don't be rushing us and talking no shit," Randee said, climbing up on the ladder to stream silver 45s from the ceilings. "It's going to all get done, Tavares, just relax."

"I know that's right," added Mona-Lisa.

"Tavares, how about you leave us here, shoot to the mall, and by the time you snatch something to wear and get the cakes we'll have finished everything. You know we work better under pressure anyways, so just relax."

"This is what we do! We can just wear something out of our closets."

"Nah, six hands will go faster than four, so let's just get to it and then I'll just shoot to the South Shore mall," Tavares said, placing lavender tablecloths on the twenty round tables.

An hour later, the hall was beautifully decorated in lavender and silver for Damien's mother's forty-fifth birthday party. The tables were immaculate with lavender tablecloths and silver place settings, with a lavender and silver champagne glass in front of every seat. The centerpieces were silver shooting stars that doubled as candles. Silver 45s dangled from the ceilings with lavender and silver balloons floating throughout the room. *Happy 45th Birthday* streamed from door, and the girls were officially done decorating.

"Alright, who's rolling to the mall with me?" Tavares asked.

"We might as well all go, then we just all get dressed at one house and shoot to get the cakes and go to the party together," suggested Mona-Lisa.

Walking out the hall, Tavares called Damien.

"What's up, sweetness?" he answered.

"Shit, where are you?"

"I'm at the house about to get dressed in a little bit, then I'm going to get my mother. Where are you?"

"I'm about to go to the mall and I'm just going to get dressed in the hood instead of coming way down to the house. I'm going to be a little late, because I have to pick up the cakes."

"Ain't shit new. Baby, you're always late. How does the hall look?"

"It's beautiful. We did the damn thing. Everything is perfectly coordinated with the lavender and silver. I gotta hurry up though, because the party starts in two hours. The DJ was setting up as we were leaving and the picture man called me and said he was on his way."

"Alright baby, go ahead, do you need anything from the house?"

"Just some little slippers in case my feet start to hurt."

"I got you. Love you," Damien said and hung up.

By the time Tavares and her girls arrived, the party was in full swing. Damien's grandmother rushed over to Tavares and gave her a big hug and said, "Do the damn thing girl! You hooked this place up, you make sure you're the one planning my sixty-fifth birthday party next year."

"For shizzle, nana, I got you."

"That dress is bad," nana said. Tavares had on a black dress that was halter-topped and fit all the way down to her waist, where it became fringed at various lengths.

"Nana, you ain't looking too bad yourself in the that wrap dress and all that junk in the truck."

"Girl, I'm sixty-four and I still got it! I'm like fine wine, I just get better over time. Instead of dropping it like it's hot, now I just drop it like its warm."

Tavares laughed and said, "Nana, you're too much."

"Get settled and then come meet me on the dance floor," Nana Dancy said.

Tavares watched nana walking toward the dance floor, thinking she was hot shit. Nana got it in and was still that chick. She didn't look a day over fifty. She had men in their late fifties for male friends that she always refused to call boyfriends. She said she was too old for that bullshit. *I love nana*, Tavares thought as she sat the two strawberry shortcakes down on the table. Tavares made her rounds greeting her boyfriend's mother and family.

Damien was in the corner, trying to get his baby's mother to leave him alone. Tavares instantly turned mad on the inside but kept her game face on.

"Tavares, don't pay that bitch no attention," Randee said, knowing her girl all too well.

"Oh, it's nothing, Randee. She just better stay the fuck out of my way, because I'm not even in the mood for her tonight."

"You already know it is what it is," Randee said, letting her girl know she had her back.

"We didn't come here to act up, but if she starts, we'll be sure to finish it." Tavares was heated. "I'll be right back, yawl."

Tavares walked outside and was standing on the stairs when Damien's coolest aunt of them all walked up.

"Oh shoot, there goes my girl!" she yelled in her small squeaky voice. "Why ain't you in there walking it out or two-stepping?" she asked while getting her two-step on.

Tavares cracked up at the lady who was forty years old really walking it out and having it down pat.

"Nah, that's you, Aunty Danny! You got the bounce in the ounce. I'm loving that shirt, let me get it," Tavares joked, admiring her white shirt with angel-wing sleeves and funky silver designs everywhere.

"Girl, you know I'll give it to you right off my back, it ain't nothing, but you got to give me something else."

"Nah, Aunty, I was joking," Tavares laughed at the lady who loved her so much that she would give her the shirt off her back.

"Where is my fine ass nephew?"

"He's in there," Tavares said dryly.

"So then what're you doing out here?" Danny asked, schooling the young lady.

"I'm just tired from running all day, so I came out here for some air."

"Okay, well don't be too long. Let me go in here and show these old bitches how to get down," Danny said with her petite, sexy frame, not looking a day over twenty-five.

"I'm right behind you. I just need to get my mind right."

Before Tavares knew it, she had drifted off thinking about Mr. Santacosa when the door flew open. Sucking her teeth, Tavares knew it was about to be some bullshit.

"Can I talk to you?" asked Damien's tall, chocolate, round, crater-faced, long haired, jealous baby's mother all crazy.

First Tavares looked at her real stupid. Then she sucked her teeth at Damien's immature baby's mother, in a real disgusting tone, and asked, "Talk to me about what? We don't fuck with each other so what would we have to talk about?" in a real snooty tone with her nose in the air.

Tavares's face was tight as hell. Her expression read that she would be taking her shoe off and shoving it down Shaunda's throat if she even thought to come sideways. Shaunda didn't back down, she loved to keep drama brewing. Instead, she simmered her original tone down to a low boil.

"What's this I hear that you and Damien are getting married? And if it's true, you should be woman enough to tell me, since it means that you'll be my kids' step-mother." Tavares just burst into laughter. The bullshit with Shaunda was just so petty and ongoing. Shaunda definitely acted more her shoe size than her age. They had been through so much that it was just truly comical to Tavares now.

"Is that what you hear?" Tavares asked sarcastically, like she was even more shocked than Shuanda was. "Hmmm...I can't confirm or deny that for you, but either way what does it fucking matter because I'm already in your kids' lives. They stay in my house. We do our thing and have a good relationship. I have never mistreated them and won't ever, so what is this bullshit really about? Matter of fact, don't answer that, because I don't give a fuck. If and when we do decide to get married, you'll be the first one to know." Tavares just chuckled because Shaunda was a real joke.

"You ain't fucking gotta get smart," Shaunda tried to yell, but really wanting no problems. Shaunda really had a problem and just didn't know it. She loved drama more than she loved herself. She didn't know what to do with herself if she wasn't entangled in drama. Tavares just laughed at the bum broad with no class.

"Shaunda, me and you are right here, so save your bullshit drama antics for another day and another time because this ain't it." Tavares walked back in to the party, just shaking her head, mad that she even had to be bothered with that bucket head ass bitch. Shaunda was left dumbfounded. Tavares took her seat and her girls read her face.

"Yo! What the fuck did that bitch say to you, Apple, because I will smash her right here in the middle of the party," Randee said, with her face letting it be known that even though she dug Doll, she would shut her party down. Fighting ran through Randee's veins like her blood.

"Nah, it's cool, boo. That bitch wants no part of me. She's just so fucking retarded. She's so past motherfucking retarded that it gets on my nerves," said Tavares.

"What happened?" asked Mona.

"The bitch came outside, talking about what's this she hears about us getting married, that I should be woman enough to tell her since I'm going to be her kids' stepmother."

Tavares laughed again, because Shaunda didn't even get how stupid she was. "Shaunda can fuck with me tonight if she wants to," she said. She really wasn't trying to be the one to ruin what was supposed to be a very nice and special night for Doll, but if Shaunda kept pushing, it was going to happen.

Mona-Lisa's peaceful but crazy ass wasn't feeling the drama. "Yo, Tavares what's fucking with this? How about you tell Damien to deal with his own bucket head ass baby's mother? You ain't got no kids with her or no reason to even be bothered with her ass. She's his attachment."

"I know, Mona-Lisa, trust me I do. I blame Dame but the broad is just so damn retarded that I don't think she's even within help range. She be buggin' on some immature shit because she feels like if anyone should be taken care of it should be her, because she's the baby's mother."

Jazz was walking into the party, late as always. "Damn…Doll's party is crunk as a motherfucker," Jazz said, approaching her girls while dancing at the same time. "My bad I'm late, but I was getting up with my little thing thing," Jazz said, dropping it like it was hot. "I lost track of time."

"What else is new?" asked Mona-Lisa.

"Let me get a plate, eat me some food, and then I'm going to take my shoes off," Jazz said, real sweet and calm. Looking confused, everyone just stared at Jazz.

"Why are you going to take your shoes off?" questioned Randee, puzzled as hell.

"Oh, because I saw Shaunda when I walked in and she was grilling me like she had a problem. So I'm just going to take my shoes off before I bust her ass, so I don't break my heels." They cried in laughter because Jazz was dead serious and was really going to be coming out of her shoes with no problem.

"You're so fucking stupid," Mona-Lisa said, already knowing how the night was going to end if Shaunda dared get out of line before the night was out.

Shaunda felt she had a point to prove. She was the number one bitch in Damien's life because she bore his kids. She knew that Tavares and her girls were on her like a hawk, so she was going to show them who the boss bitch in Damien's life was. She was. She was the baby's mother, right? Shaunda walked up on Damien like she had an attitude or something, or even more like Damien gave a fuck.

"Excuse me, can I talk to you outside for a minute?"

Never turning around from his conversation, he sucked his teeth and said, "Nope. Your child support gets there on Fridays, so you're a day late to have any reason to be talking to me. Damn nigga, what was I saying?" Damien said to his brother, like Shaunda wasn't even there.

"Damien," Shaunda whined. "Do yawl hear something?" Damien asked his brother and homeboys. Feeling totally embarrassed, Shaunda stomped off, crushed as hell.

As she made her way through the crowd, seeing her kids talking to Tavares, that just enraged her more. That was the straw that broke the camel's back. Shaunda was tired of everyone being pro-Tavares and anti-Shaunda when she was the baby's mother. Storming over to the picture stand where they had all just taken pictures together, Shaunda was ready to act up.

She threw her hand on her hip and said, "You two get the fuck over here. Who told yawl that yawl could take a picture with her? I don't give a fuck if she's your father's girlfriend. I didn't tell yawl it was okay."

Hanging their heads, because they really liked Tavares, they walked toward their mother.

"Ma, we were just taking pictures," said DJ, Damien Junior.

"Don't talk back to me, just—"

Cutting her off, Tavares said, "Yo...Shaunda, you're a real petty bitch."

"What the fuck you call me?"

"You heard what I called you, but you got that for now, because now ain't the time or the place. Unlike you, I know that. But we'll finish this conversation in the streets."

Seconds later, Tavares heard a loud scream. Turning around, she saw the cakes go flying in the air off the table that was being pushed between her and Shaunda. Shaunda snatched a knife off the cake table and was storming toward her back with it.

Chaos broke out. Tavares's girls came running her way. Doll came running from behind Shaunda, DJ and his little sister Ashaunda went running for their father, while the crowd just watched. Damien had his mans take his kids out the back.

Tavares jumped across the table—knife or not, it was fucking on. When she got there, she was beat to the punch, literally. A left hook sent Shaunda backwards. Nana Dancy started to stomp Shaunda.

Everyone just looked while Dancy stomped and screamed, "Didn't I tell you not to start no shit? Didn't I?"

No one was surprised. Everyone who was there was family or a close friend and knew that Dancy was known for handing out harsh ass whoopings. She was nothing nice and still had it at sixty-four, and had no problem getting it popping.

"Nana, get off of her!" screamed Damien as he pulled his grandmother and her foot from Shaunda's head.

"Get her, get her!" screamed Shaunda.

"Get me? No bitch, they better get you," Dancy said, laying her hair back in place and walking back to get the guests, settled as if nothing had happened.

Getting up off the floor, Shaunda thought it was over. But Tavares swung her back to the floor. Tavares dove to the ground and commenced to giving her face a real bad beating. She grabbed her by the neck, and started banging her head on the floor. Before anyone could get Tavares's hands from around her head, she blacked out.

The crowd had security blocked because they were trying to see the circus act that was going on.

Breaking through the crowd, the hall's security team screamed, "Party over, party is over."

It was twenty minutes before everyone was actually out of the hall. It was ruined. Food and cake were everywhere. Decorations seemed to be falling. Chairs and tables were upside down. A beautiful hall not too long ago, now looked like horror.

Cleaning the hall up, Tavares and her girls exited with Damien's mother, grandmother, and aunts. Tavares and her girls contemplated their next move.

"Yo, the party is over, we can smash that bitch again for GP," Jazz said.

For sure, we're going to that punk bitch's house. That hoe tried to stab me, so she owes me another round. I don't give two fucks about what Dame's talking about, I'm smashing her face again," Tavares said, with tears streaming down her face.

"Don't NO one have time for this fucking drama. I'm totally embarrassed. Totally. How the fuck Damien got me at a family function and his baby's mother tries to stab me and I beat her half to death. I'm not no trashcan type bitch. This is some real Jerry Springer shit that is real beneath me," Tavares screamed.

"Tavares, just calm down," said Mona-Lisa as she patted Tavares's back.

"Damien isn't to blame this time," said Jazz. "That hoe just acts like she's two, so don't point the finger at him."

"Fuck Dame, he's why I even got to be bothered with that whack-minded ass hoe. Yo, this is what it is, take my truck keys, go to my house, get me some sweats, some sneakers, and a change of clothes, and then call me. By the time yawl do that, I'll have made it back to Doll's."

"Let one of us stay with you," pleaded Mona-Lisa.

"You know that hoe ain't nothing but drama. Her and her girls don't shoot the ones, they like to jump bitches," Randee reminded her girl.

"That's the last of my worries, nana Dancy and Doll got me." Tavares had to laugh at her O.G. granny posse. "So go ahead, because that hoe is going to get the ass whoopin' of her life in about an hour. She thought I gave her the business in there, she better not dare let me get my motherfucking hands on her tonight," Tavares said, ready to really kill Shaunda with her bare hands. Parting ways, the ladies headed toward Tavares's house to get her stuff to finish what Shaunda started.

Doll was with her sisters and mother waiting for Tavares. It was Dalila, Danny, and nana Dancy.

"Baby, I'm so sorry," pleaded Doll, whose real name was Devin. "I didn't know that the night was going to turn out like this. I thought her simple ass would come here and act like my grandkids' mother, not like a fucking maniac or else I would have sent her packing when she walked in the door."

"It's cool, Doll. Don't even worry about it. Shaunda's going to learn the hard way." Dalila, Damien's outspoken aunt, laughed.

"Girl, she been a stalker since she was a kid. She used to peek in my backyard looking for Dame, and I would run her scraggly ass away. So now that she got some babies with my nephew, she's his headache for life. Good luck, girl."

"Dalila, close your mouth," snapped Dancy. "You always running your mouth, why don't you shut up sometimes?"

Doll, her mother, her sisters, and Tavares left the hall and headed toward her house. As her cell phone rang, she thought to herself how this was some bullshit, that her forty-fifth birthday party was just ruined.

"Hello?"

"Yeah, Doll, you want to take sides with that bitch, I bet you won't see your grandkids no more."

"Don't no one got time for your fucking shit, Shaunda. So save it, because I will beat you down. I will fucking beat you down to the ground and you know it. Trust me, I will see my grandkids. You talk all the shit you want, bitch, but we both know that you will not be keeping my grandkids from me. You not bringing my grandbabies to see me is hurting them, not me, so grow the fuck up."

Snatching the phone, Dancy said, "Bitch, keep them kids over there with your retarded ass, all you going to do is make them retarded like your stupid ass." Dancy hung up on Shaunda, tired of her.

Tavares just laughed because she was about to ring this silly bitch's neck. By the time everyone had made it to Doll's house, Damien was there, parked out front, reclined in his car. Dancy tapped the window to wake him up.

"Come upstairs, boo." Tavares was so mad she couldn't even look at him. Upstairs, everyone shot the shit about the night, drank, blew it down, and talked about how stupid Shaunda was. Tavares kicked it for a minute. She just sat quietly as everyone around her spoke about the crazy night, because she was ready to finish it.

Seeing her girls calling her, Tavares said her goodnights.

"Just stay here tonight," pleaded Doll in her motherly, convincing voice.

"Nah, Ma, I'm going home. I'm good. I just need to take a hot shower and get my mind right. I'll see yawl tomorrow."

Closing the door, she could hear Damien say, "I'll meet you at home."

"Yeah, right," Tavares said, climbing down the stairs to her truck.

Meeting her girls on Washington Street, Tavares changed her clothes right in the middle of the street. She was ready to stomp Shaunda's face off. Pulling up on Dale Street, she rang the bell. No one answered, so she continued to lay on the bell. She could see someone peep through the blinds.

Ashaunda waved from the window. Opening the window, DJ said, "Tavares, my mom isn't here."

"So who's home with yawl?" questioned Tavares, now infuriated.

"No one."

"NO ONE!" screamed Tavares. "Put yawl stuff on and pack a bag. I'm going to take yawl to nana's."

"My mom is going to be mad," said DJ.

"Don't worry about it, DJ, she isn't going to be mad."

"Okay," DJ sadly responded and went and did as he was told.

Fifteen minutes later, Tavares and her crew were back at Doll's with the kids. Walking through the door, everyone looked puzzled to see Tavares back, especially with her friends and her step-kids. Ashaunda ran to her father and wrapped her arms around him for dear life.

"Baby girl, it's alright. It's late, you and DJ go get in nana's bed and I'll be in there in a few minutes to tuck yawl in."

"Alright," the little girl said in her sad voice, giving her father puppy dog eyes as she exited the kitchen.

"Where the hell did all of yawl come from?" asked Dancy, knowing what was good.

"Don't worry, Ms. Dancy," said Randee, "we didn't kidnap the kids, that's not our M.O. Secret Squirrel Crew loves the kids." They all laughed to cosign her truth speaking.

"That stupid heffa bag left them at the house by themselves," Mona-Lisa said in disgust, as a mother of two kids. "Who does that?" she asked sincerely.

"I swear, when I catch her it's going to be on," Tavares said, with tears starting to stream down her face.

"What the fuck do you mean she left my kids alone?" asked Damien, like he didn't really understand that his babies' mother had done something so crazy.

"What, you can't hear or something?" asked Doll. "The sick bitch left your kids alone. I'm just saying, son, if you need me to say it a sixth or seventh time, let me know."

"Ma, here you go. Save the smart shit right now."

"Did they say where she went?" questioned Dalila. Dalila was sucking it all in while she puffed on a Newport in the corner.

"Nope. I didn't even keep digging," said Tavares. "I just told them to pack a bag and I brought them here."

"Let's roll, yawl," Tavares said, ushering her friends.

"Wait," said Damien, looking stressed as hell now that his babies' mother and wifey were at war. They fought and argued before, but tonight Shaunda crossed the line with the weapon.

"Wait for what?" asked Tavares.

"Don't go home and do nothing stupid," pleaded Damien.

"No, that bitch did something stupid by deciding to grab a knife like she was gonna stab Apple," Leslie said, with her face slightly turning up and a sarcastic chuckle that said *nigga please.*

"We don't start shit," said Randee, "we just finish it."

Randee wasn't a troublemaker, she was just a bitch and didn't mind letting it come out of her.

"Tavares, don't be fooling with that nut," said Dancy. "You know she just be acting all crazy, carrying on and whatnot because she ain't got no damn sense and because you got her damn baby daddy."

The girls knew they had to listen to nana Dancy preach. If not, she would be the one going off next because she took no shit and still got it popping in a serious way. They wanted no parts of nana.

Thirty minutes later, Tavares and her girls pulled up to her house and no one was in sight.

"Come on yawl, we might as well go inside and have a drink." Walking in, the phone was ringing.

"Grab that, Mona-Lisa. I'm going to make the drinks," Tavares said, looking at the clock that read 2:30 a.m.

"Hello" was as far as Mona-Lisa got when the person on the other end started screaming, "Bitch, where the fuck are my kids?"

"First of all, I'm not your bitch, second of all, they're your fucking kids, so if you don't fucking know where they are, then that sounds like a personal problem," Mona-Lisa shot back. Recognizing that it wasn't Tavares, Shaunda cooled her tone down.

"Where is Tavares?" she asked snidely.

"Shaunda, what the fuck do you want? You tried to stab my homegirl. So really what do you want to talk about?"

"I want my fucking kids."

"We don't got your kids, bitch, so let's talk about how you got on some real bum bitch hoodrat shit tonight. You ruined your kids' grandmother's birthday party on some dumb shit. Then you try to stab Tavares, are you crazy? You gotta be, what else can explain your actions, but if you want to come over, we got an ass whooping waiting for you."

"I know that bitch took my kids, because my neighbors said they got in a red truck with a light skin bitch."

"Well," Mona-Lisa said calmly, in a sarcastic tone, "in that case your neighbor should have been watching them and not watching them be kidnapped by some mysterious light skin women in a red truck. Your kids ain't here. So good luck finding them," Mona-Lisa said, slamming the phone down.

"That bitch got me tight, but Damien got me tighter because he plays with that bitch and that's why she acts all retarded and crazy," said Tavares, coming in from the kitchen.

Jazz jumped to Damien's defense. "Tavares, that nigga takes damn good care of you. He can't help what she does."

"Yes, he can," snapped Mona-Lisa.

The phone rang again and Randee snatched it up, "What, bitch?"

"Excuse me," said Damien. "Randee, why are you answering my house phone like that?"

"Because your BITCH baby mother was calling. She's looking for her kids. You might want to call her simple ass and let her know that they're with you."

"Fuck Shaunda. I ain't been answering her calls. Let me speak to my wife."

"Hold on. Tavares, Damien wants you."

"What's up, Damien?"

"I know shit is crazy right now, but is it okay if I come home and we talk about this?"

"Do what you want," Tavares said, slamming the phone down, mad as hell about his baby mother drama. Damien came home, but none of the ladies were moved by his eyes that said *stop drinking all the Patrón on my bar and please get the fuck out*. It was only after Tavares said something that they started making their way toward the door.

Making their way home, the ladies knew that from there on out, wherever they saw Shaunda at, it was going to be drama on site.

~ CHAPTER 12 ~

God isn't too fond of the pretty, but He sure doesn't like UGLY.

Shaunda was mad as hell that Damien's stinking ass high-maintenance bitch made her look bad. First at the party and then she came and took her kids from her house. Shaunda didn't feel like anything was her fault, because Damien was her kids' father and Tavares was just the girlfriend. Taking her kids had pissed her off more than anything, though. Her nosy, in the window, ANY time she heard a car neighbor saw the red car and the light skinned girl with four friends. Who else took them, damn sure not no nighttime kid supersavers.

"I can't stand that bitch," Shaunda said, mad as hell at 5:00 in the morning.

Sitting in the empty apartment, Shaunda rolled a blunt in a backwood and called her forbidden fruit. He was just starting his day at this hour, so Shaunda knew she was in business.

"Yo," the smooth, deep voice answered. "What's up with you?" he asked as he was moving down a back alley in the theater district.

"I had a real long, fucked up night. I'm sitting here smoking a blizz and just called to see what you were up to."

"Why, you want some company?" he asked, all hard and seductively.

Shaunda only called when she wanted a mean dick down, which worked for him. Shaunda knew that it was going against the grain to be messing with him. So she only called when she really needed his magic touch. His and Damien's hoods were at war, so she had no business fucking with him. Shaunda knew that Damien would kill her if he ever knew that she was sleeping with someone that was shooting at him and niggaz from his hood.

"I gotta get a few more dollars. There's crazy money all around me. But make some breakfast and I'll slide through there in about an hour."

Shaunda killed time cleaning her house. No sooner than she went to call her creep buddy, her phone was ringing.

"Hello," Shaunda answered sweetly with her naturally flirtatious voice.

"I'm on my way. I hope my food is hot and my pussy is wet." Shuanda couldn't help but laugh at his joke.

"I'll see what I can do for you," Shaunda said, hanging up the phone.

Shaunda was in the kitchen, piling the eggs, waffles, bacon, grits, home fries, and toast on the plate when her bell rang. Buzzing the bell and opening the door, Shaunda knew that she was about to get what she was overdue for, a serious dick down. As he was coming in the door, looking like a ruggedly sexy replica of Jim Jones, Shaunda tried to feel bad but couldn't.

He was sexy like no one's business. He had long, pretty, thick silky braids. He was rocking the sexy scruffy face. His face was natural in beauty, with a pretty boy swag and a look beneath the surface that said hood nigga to the heart so please don't get it twisted. Tall, slender and bow-legged, he looked so scrumptious in his red and grey True Religion hoodie, dark denim jeans, and grey tee with matching red and grey Air Max 95s.

I love this nigga's swag, Shaunda thought, looking him up and down. He started blushing when he saw the look in Shaunda's eyes. "Stop looking at me like that and let me in the house." Shaunda stepped aside and closed the door the behind them. She led the way to kitchen, where the fresh scent of cooked food was lingering. Taking off his hoodie and washing his hands, Shaunda's friend got comfortable at the kitchen table and twisted up a blunt.

Blowing two blunts of haze, Shaunda and her forbidden fruit kicked it about the latest hood shit and how the war between his hood and her kids' father's hood needed to end, since it was old and over nothing that was truly worth so many lives.

"Man, them niggaz been on some bullshit ever since Markey got killed. Niggaz live the life and know what it is. Sometimes death is the consequence that you have to pay when you're out here in these streets."

"You know what, I won't even dispute that," Shaunda said, feeling where he was coming from. "But sometimes there needs to be a limit. For example, I can't believe your niggaz shot at Russ at the grocery store while he had his kids with him. Come on now, that's some fucking bullshit. Kids are innocent and don't deserve to lose their lives because grown men want to be stupid, shooting at each other and shit."

"Yo, Ma, what you want me to tell you. I personally don't blam at niggaz when they're with their seeds, but some niggaz do. They see it as war means war." The debating back and forth went on till the Jim Jones look alike was ready for his plate.

"Damn," he said, looking at the plate of food piled high on the plate. "I said breakfast, ma, not breakfast, lunch, and dinner."

"You need to eat with your little ass, so sit down and shut up. I'm gonna go put a load of laundry in while you do you. After that we can do each other," Shaunda said, rolling her eyes and exiting through the door that led to her basement. While Shaunda got it in with what she knew was the second best thing to Jim Jones, across town her baby father was being cussed to pieces.

"Damien, I'm fucking done with your fucking stinking bum bitch, chickenhead ass baby's mother. I be trying to respect that bitch on the strength of the kids, but you know what, she don't give a fuck about how she acts in front of the kids, so neither do I. Every time I see that bitch, I'm whooping her fucking ass. All you do is put up with her fucking bullshit. Well, you know what? You can deal with the fucking headache by your motherfucking self. I don't got time for you and that simple-minded ass bitch."

"Tavares, this is some real fucking bullshit. For real it is. Do you think I condone that stupid bitch trying to stab you with a knife? What the fuck?" Damien said, mad that Tavares was cutting into him like he gave the bitch the knife or something. "I don't condone what the fuck she tried to do. She deserves to get her ass whooped every time you see her, but come on. I got kids with her. Unfortunately she is my kids' mother, so what the fuck do you really want me to do? Just tell me. I can't go over there and beat the bitch up. How the fuck do I explain to my kids that daddy kicked mommy's ass because she can't grasp around her head that I don't want her? Get the fuck out of here, Tavares, that's some real bullshit and I'm not doing it. But I'll keep that bitch clear of you, before you fuck around and kill her."

Tavares was hot as hell. Damien was always putting up with Shaunda's stunts and antics and she was real tired of it.

"Damien, you know what? I don't want you to do a motherfucking thing." Tavares said nothing else. She got in bed and turned her back on Damien, with the sun in her face. Damien drifted off to sleep while Tavares just lay there with tears staining her pillow because she was real tired of the bullshit.

Bullshit seemed to be circulating in the air among Tavares's team. Mona-Lisa was lying in bed when her baby's father's phone went off. Not even supposed to be lying up with his stupid stinking ass, she was mad that some bitch had woken her up. Walter showed up drunk saying he wanted to work it out and be a family bullshit. Mona-Lisa wasn't listening, though. Mona-Lisa had stopped buying Walter's dream's a long time ago. If he couldn't take care of Jayla and Layla, then there was nothing he could do for her. He was drunk and she didn't want him driving, so she let him stay; the dick was just extra.

Getting up, Mona-Lisa picked up her phone and looked at the missed calls and text messages, reading, "baby where are you, why didn't you call me or come here last night." "Baby, I need the car." Mona-Lisa kindly took a seat on the bed next to her baby's father and called the number back.

"Hey, baby, where are you?" asked a voice way too bubbly for 6 a.m..

"Well, I'm not your baby, but my bum ass baby's father is laying right next to me. Would you like for me to wake him up?"

"Excuse me," the girl said. "I know he's not at your house in the car that I pay the note on. He told me he doesn't talk to you."

"Well, boo, the nigga lied, something he's good at. He's in my bed knocked out. But don't worry, he's on his way now."

Mona-Lisa picked the lamp up and crashed it over her kids' father's head. Walter jumped up, holding his head.

"What the fuck, Mona-Lisa?"

"Nigga, get your shit and get the fuck out. I didn't tell you to come here on no drunk I love you shit. And not that I bought that shit, but nigga you don't even get to rest your head in my bed as nasty and full of shit as you are. Take your phone and bring your bitch back her car," Mona-Lisa said, throwing Walter's stuff down the stairs.

"See, Mona-Lisa, this is why I don't fuck with you."

"I know, I was thinking the same exact thing," Mona-Lisa said, looking at him like he was stupid. "Get your shit on, Walter, kiss your kids goodbye, and get the fuck out my house," Mona-Lisa said, uninterested in anything he had to say.

By the time Shaunda was done with her duplicate Jim Jones, she couldn't even be mad at herself. He touched, tasted, licked, and caressed her to a pleasure that was past A+. Shaunda was totally dumbfounded by his crazy bedroom skills on top of his being drop-dead ruggedly pretty boy handsome. Her and her kids' father weren't together, so why should she feel bad? He was living his life with his girlfriend. So it shouldn't matter who she slept with. Shaunda knew that girlfriend or not, Damien would bug if he found out. As long as Damien didn't find out, she was good in the game.

Tavares was hot with Damien for the next few weeks to come, due to his lack of anger over his kids' mother trying to stab her. Tavares was in the house little as possible. When she was home, she was cold to Damien. It made him not want to be in the house with her. He tried everything, and Tavares wasn't budging. She wasn't stunting Damien.

She was doing her, texting Dora in the in-between time. She was showing Damien that she was tired, because telling him hadn't got her anywhere. Except almost stabbed in the back.

Summer had come and went. It would be time for Tavares to go back to school in a few weeks. Dora was making his office visits like clockwork, wearing Tavares down with each visit. She hadn't caved, but he was wearing her down slowly but surely. She was more and more tempted in the few weeks that she hadn't been speaking to Damien.

Seeing Dora always brought a smile to Tavares's face, but she had enough going on with the nigga that she had at home. Dora was too much of a handful to take on. He wanted all or nothing, and Tavares couldn't give him that, so it had to be nothing, nothing but friendship that is.

Dollar was in the window when Damien pulled up to her building. As she came downstairs, Damien couldn't help but wonder why she always did this when he told her not to. Getting out of the car, he headed to the second level of the condo apartment building. Dollar's small one-bedroom apartment was nice. Damien couldn't believe how lavish Dollar was living to be a straight up crackhead.

"Damn, Dollar, the new crib is fly."

"Thanks, I always had nice shit. I just lost it all fucking with that shit. But I got a come up and did the right thing with the money and got this new place."

Damien liked Dollar, because from the door she was always like, *as long as I got the dollars don't ask me no other questions.* Never did she hang around or stay the night in the crack houses. She would smoke and then say she had to go home because she had money to make the next day. That was how Damien got to calling her Dollar. Dollar didn't turn tricks to smoke. She spent what she came with, what others shared with her, and then she was gone. As Dollar started to smoke, her habit progressed. She went from coming around sometimes to get high to being an everyday smoker.

When Dollar hit rock bottom, she never lost her beauty or morals. Her habit never resulted to turning tricks to get high. Damien respected her for that. He could tell that something drove her to crack. She wasn't like the people that she hung around and got high with. He had a genuine liking for the strung-out lady.

"Alright, how much money you got, Dollar?"

"I only wanna spend $200," Dollar said, passing Damien two crisp $100 bills.

"Dollar, you know that it's Friday, I'm not coming back out here tonight. You better get what you want while I'm here."

"Naw, Damien. $200 will get me through the night." Damien gave Dollar a look that said, stop playing yourself. Damien gave Dollar her money's worth.

"So you partying alone tonight?" Damien asked, looking around the empty house.

"Yeah, ain't no one popped up and that's cool for me. Less of my shit I gotta share."

"I heard that, Dollar," Damien said, giving her dap, and headed home to his shorty before he hit the streets.

No sooner than Damien walked out the door, Dollar got to making her a new homemade pipe with a nip bottle that she had downed earlier. Dollar smoked in peace and was glad there was no one to blow her high. Before she knew it, she was down to three twenty-rocks and knew that would be gone in the next hour. Dollar knew she needed more. Knowing that Damien wasn't going to come back, she was going to have to troop it to the hood. It was Friday, why not? A little money to blow, with some in the stash, Dollar got motivated.

She got up, got dressed, and cleaned herself up to look decent in a pink and white capri sweat suit, some crisp white 54-11s, aka Rebook Classics, and thought she was too cute. Throwing her jet black hair into a ponytail, she called a cab to take her to the projects in Boston.

Dollar hopped out of the cab by the park and saw that it was still the same shit, just a different day. Niggaz were in the park gambling, playing tonk and dice. Blunts were flying all over the place. Niggaz were talking shit in between serving the fiends that were everywhere, like roaches that had taken over. Boogie was in a wheelchair but still had his swagger and gangster. He was cussing a fiend out.

"Nigga, you always come with this fucking $40 dollars for a fifty; if I was selling forties then the fucking price wouldn't be fifty fucking dollars, asshole. What you think this is?" he asked, not really even giving a fuck about the short. But he couldn't let the fiend know it didn't matter. The difference between the projects and a phone hustler was that in the projects money was always coming and flowing, so it was short. The fact was that so much of it came, that shorts really didn't affect the intake.

Dollar watched fiends counting change on corners, fiends cussing each other out on how they were going to split the crack among each other. Flunkies were on the corners, serving as middlemen so they could get the free hit they were searching for. There were clean, dirty, decent, white, black, young, and old fiends moving about the projects. It was like a zoo and the animals were the crackheads.

"I sure don't miss this shit," Dollar said, looking around the projects that she didn't frequent too often.

Tavares made some salmon, broccoli, and wild rice. After her and Dame tore it down, they had baked brownies together. Damien had been on the get right ever since the fallout with his baby's mother. He didn't take the silent treatment too swell, so he was trying to stay in her good graces. They were snuggled up in the TV room watching *August Rush* under the cool air conditioner when Damien's phone went off. Grabbing it, Tavares read, *Dollar*.

Passing the phone to him, Tavares asked, "Who is that, your Puerto Rican stripper?"

"Shut up, Dollar is a fiend."

"What's up, Dollar?"

"I need to see you."

"Oh, fucks no. I'm not driving way the fuck back out there. You should have got all that you needed when I was there. I knew you was going to call," Damien yelled.

"Calm down, Damien. I caught a cab to the projects. So can you please shut up and come see me?" Dollar said, knowing that he wouldn't gun her down.

"Meet me at Stacy's house in a half." Stacy's was a local crack house that Damien had in the projects. It was always rumping with crackheads ready to spend.

Finishing the movie and wetting up the sheets, Damien knew he was already a half hour late. Damien got up and took a shower while Tavares changed the sheets. Tavares had placed her black sheets on the bed when her phone went off.

Picking up the trap phone that was used solely to hustle off, Tavares said, "Hello."

"Hey mama, I want you to meet me down in the projects in like twenty minutes. I got $2,000. That should hold me for the weekend," the sweet, Spanish-accented lady said.

"That's what's up," Tavares said. "I'm about to jump in the shower, I'll meet you on Eustis Street."

As Damien came out of the shower, Tavares was rushing in and telling him she had to go down to the projects too, so finish making the bed and that if he was gone when she got out, she would call him later.

Damien called and said that he was on his way and would be there in forty minutes. Dollar had time to kill and definitely needed a drink. She was on her way to the store to get her a bottle of Hennessey Black, enjoying her day and evening so far. Just as she got to the bottom of Eustis Street, she saw a face that angered her every time she encountered it. *Stinking bitch*, Dollar thought as she spun the corner to go into Dearborne Liquors.

Parking her car and waiting for Tavares, the lady got out, hoping that Dollar would say something to her. Coming back around the corner, Dollar bumped right into the lady.

"What the fuck?" Dollar yelled, not even wanting to bust this bitch's ass today.

"What's up?" the lady asked politely, with a hidden snide tone.

"Listen, I don't got time for your bullshit. Shouldn't you be somewhere doing what you do best, hiding your habit from your husband?"

"Don't worry about me, my habit, or my husband," the pretty woman snarled.

"You kill me," Dollar laughed in a confident tone. "Your husband? Yeah, he's your husband, but he's everyone else's man," she laughed. "Only difference is you got a ring, but he's slinging dick and dollars all across town," Dollar taunted.

"Fuck you, bitch, you just mad you didn't get the ring."

"Is that what I am?" laughed Dollar. Dollar hated the bitch standing before her, who thought she was so much better but wasn't shit but a manipulating, jealous ass bitch. Once every blue moon they would bump heads in the same place they chased crack, and when they did it wasn't pretty. After arguing, the women came to blows.

Damien was coming down Harrison Ave and could see Dollar and his girl's fiend going at it real hard. Pulling over, Damien hopped out.

"What the fuck are you two doing?" Not even giving a fuck what they were arguing or fighting about, Damien screamed, "Yawl are making the block hot as shit. Dollar, get the fuck down the street and meet me at Stacy's house."

Dollar was mad that after all these years, her and Lilly was still fighting in the street. Dollar was mad as hell as she scurried down the street because she was still fighting over a man she hadn't seen in decades.

Damien looked at Tavares's fiend and said, "You're buggin.' Meet Tavares and get the fuck from down the bricks." Damien wasn't trying to be disrespectful, but he was serious.

Three minutes later, Tavares came to the intersection and saw Damien and his fiend on the corner, looking like shit wasn't right. Getting out, Tavares asked, "What's wrong?"

Me and this bitch just got into it," the Guatemalan and Italian lady said, with a clear hate present in her voice. Damien cut Lilly off.

"Babe, I don't know, nor do I give a fuck what it was about. I'm out of here, I gotta go holler at Dollar." Damien hopped in his car and headed to Stacy's.

"What the hell happened?" Tavares asked, touching the lady's knot on her forehead. It was clear that someone had just given her a for real beat down.

"Me and my enemy from way back just had it out."

"Mita Mami, you're too old to be out here in the streets fighting," Tavares said, disapproving. "I thought fighting was for a purpose, when someone did something to harm you or your family. Not just to be looking stupid over some bullshit. Bitches and hoodrats fight for those reasons, not ladies," Tavares said, disappointed in Lilly.

"She deserves what I gave her," Lilly said, not realizing she was the one to catch the beat down. "She's a stinking whore bitch," the lady said, with disgust in her heavy accent. "Me and my husband weren't married yet, but we had courted each other early in life. We grew up together in the North End. When I was about eighteen I heard that word on the street was that they were building to be doing big things with this chick from over here in the hood. He thought I wouldn't come to his stomping grounds, out of my comfort zone of the North End. He was supposed to be wining and dining her around town. He got her a nice laid out apartment and was acting like he didn't have a woman. I wasn't having that. So one night I had a friend of mine accompany me to the

Sky Cap on Warren Street and all hell broke loose. First me and that bitch, and then me and him. I shut it down. I was young, but where I came from it was a respect thing. I wasn't some whore and he wasn't going to treat me like one. He owed it to me to keep it real with me."

Tavares cut her off. "Lilly, you're right, he owed you. Key word being he. You had no reason to be bugging off that lady. Her loyalty was with him but his should have been with you. She didn't know you. His loyalty was to you, so you need to be mad at him and only him." Lilly stopped and thought. She knew Tavares was right.

"After that night I told him that if I ever found out about him and her, I would leave him forever and he would never see our baby boy."

"Lilly, you have kids?" Tavares asked, surprised.

"No, I was bearing his first born son at the time. I told him if I heard of him having anything, absolutely anything to do with her that I would take his son away and he would never see him again. From there he never looked her way and I never heard nothing about them again. We got married when I was seven months pregnant and had our son. Sadly he passed away of SIDs," Lilly said, her eyes dropping.

"Damn, how awful," Tavares said, but really thinking *that's fucked up but GOD don't like ugly.* "I'm sorry to hear that, Lilly."

"Yeah, I still go see his grave. My husband doesn't though. It's like he forgot him over the years. Losing my son's actually how I started smoking," Lilly said, like it was just yesterday she smoked crack for the first time. "I was broken from losing my son, and my husband was distant and not showing any emotions about our loss, so one night I smoked with a friend of mine. Been undercover smoking ever since."

"Then it's just my luck when I come down here, I bump into that no good bitch. I still hate that bitch after all these years," Lilly said. "She was the only one to give my relationship havoc."

"Lilly, let that shit go. Fuck her. Don't let that shit get you down. It ain't about nothing. You got him, he married you, so you won all the way around the board, except for the loss of your son. Lilly, I love you to death, so I gotta tell you that you using your baby like a pawn was foul as fuck, though. That was some low down trifling shit you did just to keep a man."

"I know it was, but I was desperate to keep my husband and my family. So I did what I had to do. I'm not proud of it at all, trust me, I'm not. It was the personal with her that I couldn't swallow though."

"Well, at least you know the error of your ways, so that's a good thing."

"Let me get your shit." Tavares gave Lilly a carton of cigarettes out of the car. In return, the woman gave her a hug and slipped the money in her hand.

After departing from Lilly and her drama, Tavares decided that it was too nice to be in the house. Instead, she made her way to her hole in the wall bar, Packy's, where she loved to drink. Tavares ordered her some chicken wings, sipped on some wine, and had good conversation with the chatty bartender for a few hours. Stuffed as she could be and feeling a little tipsy, Tavares made her way home to relax till Damien found his way home.

Tavares was knocked out on the couch in the TV room when she heard Damien come in the house on the phone.

"Yeah, my nito, I need to make a power move. I got this little hoodrat bitch who's willing to traffic the shit, but the problem is that she wants more than to make a few dollars, she wants to swallow a nigga's babies, and after the bullshit I been through with Tavares I can't afford no more mishaps." Tavares got up off the couch and appeared in the doorway, scaring the shit outta Damien. "Damn, baby, don't be sneaking up on me."

Tavares just looked blankly at him and said, "Don't put your dick down that bitch's throat for a few dollars, 'cause I'll find out," and she went upstairs to bed.

It was time to go back to school and bang out her senior year of college, and Tavares was ready. No more friends, Damien, hustling, or work till she graduated. Tavares had done so well with her four-year paid internship that they offered her a job full-time after she graduated.

The last Saturday of August was always the West Indian Carnival. Carnival was always bananas. Floats went from one part of the city to the other, with the crowd alongside them rocking to the tunes coming off the Caribbean floats. All the floats stopped at Franklin Park, and it was nothing but a massive, out of control block party of thousands of people. Damien and Tavares threw an after party for Carnival and Tavares's going away party. First they both went to Carnival and played the packed streets with their friends. From Warren Street and MLK Blvd all the way to Blue Hill Ave where Franklin Park was, there were people in the streets hanging, congregating in groups, dancing, selling food and drinks, and partying on a level of go hard or go home.

Finally making it to Blue Hill Ave and Columbia Road, Tavares and her girls posted up in front of Stash's Pizza Shop. They were laughing, joking, and kicking it with people they knew who passed by, enjoying the street party. Tavares looked straight ahead through the crowd, and by luck she could see Damien in some broad's face. He was laughing and smiling real hard. Tavares didn't trip, she just looked to see how far it would go. Damien must have had God on his side, because Tavares didn't have to come across the street and bust him in the head to the white meat. His body language read that he was shutting the girl down.

Picking up her cell phone, Tavares called Damien and interrupted his conversation.

Before he could get a hello out, Tavares asked, "So what's her name? You been talking to her for about three minutes, you didn't get her number yet?"

Damien just busted out laughing and walked away from the girl without saying goodbye.

"Tavares, what do I look like a fool to you? Do you really think I'm going to be somewhere hollering at some bitches when I know that you're close by? Hell fucking no," Damien laughed. "It's packed out here but I still ain't no fool. I do crazy shit, but I ain't no fool. And where the fuck is your ass that you see me? The streets are on fire all the way from Warren to way up here, so just how in the fuck did you end up anywhere in eyesight of me?" Damien asked, looking around.

"Stop looking around, you aren't going to find me," Tavares said, already moving out of his view. "And don't worry how I ended up where you are. Just know that I got my eye on you."

"Of course you do, you're part of the eye spy crew."

"Whatever," Tavares said, not even feeding into Damien. "Don't worry about us being the eye spy crew, just worry about the fact that we got all eyes on you!"

"What time are you going to head home to start the party?" Damien asked.

"I'm going home in about a half hour. It's only 7:00 and I figured the later the better, since we'll be partying all night. Plus I set up everything this morning after you bounced," Tavares informed.

"Alright, well Imma grab the ice and meet you at the crib in an hour," Damien said.

Tavares couldn't believe how a medium-sized party on her rooftop deck had turned into an all-out, packed house party by 11:00. It was all family and close friends, so it was cool, but it was people everywhere. Damien's mother, grandmother, and aunts were doing their thing in the kitchen. They were getting it in drinking Hennessey, smoking cigarettes, and gossiping at the large marble kitchen table. Doll went in her Coach pocketbook and retrieved her mixed greens.

"Doll, I know you're not about to roll that shit up."

"Why ain't I, ma?" Doll asked her mother with a tone that said *I'm grown.*

"Just because you don't smoke anymore doesn't mean that everyone else has stopped," Doll said, shaking her head and continuing to break up her weed.

"That shit don't smell right," Dancy said, curling her nose up.

"Ma, you wasn't smoking good shit like this, so unless you're smoking with us, keep your comments to yourself."

"You know what," Dancy yelled and hopped up with the heavy wood pepper shaker in her hand. "I will knock the shit out of you. Keep talking shit."

"Nana, don't hurt her," Tavares laughed, knowing that nana would crack Doll for sure. Nana was about that life. "I'll be back," Tavares said, getting up, leaving them to check on the kids.

In the TV room Damien's kids were playing video games and eating ice cream with the other children who were there, acting like they were old enough to hang. They were in their own world with all the games, candy, ice cream, and a huge TV. Before Tavares headed upstairs, she peeked in the formal dining room that was closed off from her kitchen. People had moved the centerpieces and were playing bid whist at one end of the table that seated eight, and spades at the other end.

Making it to the second floor, Tavares found three different dice games going on and didn't hesitate to speak her piece about them.

"Listen here, don't you niggaz go acting crazy and stupid over no dice game in my motherfucking house," Tavares said. Dice games always resulted in problems in the hood, and Tavares wasn't letting that bullshit get started in her house.

"Damn, Apple, don't act like that," said Breezy Baby. Breezy Baby was a loud, arrogant, flashy, always-under-the-spotlight type nigga.

"Don't 'Damn, Apple' me. I know as well as yawl do that no matter where niggaz are, as soon as yawl go playing dice the bullshit pops off. And Breezy Baby, I want you to pull those fucking sagging ass jeans up on your ass. You ain't no little ass teenage nigga, you're a grown man. No one wants to see your boxers, which I hope are clean. Then take all those damn gold chains off. You look like Jim Jones and

Kris Kross done had a car accident." Everyone burst into tears laughing, but Tavares was dead serious. He always looked way too off the video for Tavares.

"You always trying to go in on a nigga," Breezy Baby said, knowing that he was on clown time. "I can't help if I'm a star. The chains are my thing, so get off me."

Tavares just said, "Whatever, just remember what I said, no fucking bullshit over dice, because I swear to God you'll be barred for life." Tavares opened the door that lead up to her deck and went where the party was on and cracking. The music was going, people were laughing, joking, talking, dancing, smoking mad blunts, and having a ball. Tavares found her homegirls in a heavy blunt rotation and got in where she fit in.

"So Tavares, what're you going to do about homeboy?" Jazz asked, passing her girl the blunt. Jazz always asked the wrong questions at the wrong time.

"I have no fucking clue. He's cool as fuck and I'm kind of digging him, but what the fuck can I do? I got a boyfriend who I ain't gonna walk out on. We been together too long."

"Damn, you ain't gotta leave Damien, but we should definitely keep Dora," Leslie said. "He got that major benefit package thing going on," she joked. "Boo, you know we're all about the benefits," Leslie laughed, reminding her friend of their rule number one, when it came to men.

"His benefits seem like an upgrade from Dame's," added Mona-Lisa.

"So shit, keep being cool with the nigga, you might decide to go have some fun with him. Lord knows you ain't having none with Dame," Leslie said.

"Damien be on some bullshit, sometimes yawl, but I love him. Sometimes I really be wanting to leave him, but we been together so long that it would just seem crazy. He's the only nigga I ever loved—or slept with, for that matter."

"Speaking of the devil," Tavares said, looking down at her phone that started ringing. "Hello?" Tavares asked, with her eyes scanning for Damien, who was occupied smoking and talking to his friends.

"What's up, Ms. Thing? I wish I could have seen you before you went back to school, but you know how you do."

Tavares sucked her teeth and said, "Don't start. I can't just be up and bouncing and coming to see you. I told you work and my boyfriend doesn't permit it."

"Well, work is over and I don't give a fuck about your boyfriend," Dora said.

"You ain't right," Tavares said, chastising.

"I hope with you going back to school, you'll have a little more free time to speak to a nigga. Your run around game is wearing me out," Dora said, even though he was having fun chasing and flirting with her.

"We'll see," Tavares said, simply put. "I got a house full of people right now and Damien is coming my way, so let me call you back tomorrow before I head back to school."

"Later," Dora said, not liking that he was being dismissed because her boyfriend was coming. Dora knew she had a man and shit, but actually being told that she had to go because he was coming had somewhat struck a nerve.

"Dora plays no games," Tavares said out loud to no one in particular.

"Why, what happened?" questioned Randee.

"He told me that he's getting tired of chasing me and he hopes when I go back to school I'll have more time for him."

"You're killing me," Mona-Lisa said. "That nigga is fine as fine gets and he's all the way into you and you be treating him like a stepchild," Mona-Lisa said, rolling her eyes and sucking her teeth.

"I told yawl, he's cool and I dig him, but I'm not walking out on what I know for what I don't know. So like I told him, we'll see." The ladies let the conversation go abruptly because Damien was just a few feet away.

"What's up, eye spy crew?" Damien asked as he approached his girl and her friends.

"Here you go," Leslie said, playfully slapping Damien in the back of the head.

"Yawl enjoying yourselves?"

"Of course we are," Jazz said, answering for everyone.

"You threw Tavares a popping party, sending her off in style."

"Yawl know it's nothing but the best for my baby," Damien said, running his fingers through Tavares's hair. "So baby girl, you ready to bang this last year out?"

"I sure am. And I know while I'm gone the eye spy crew will have their eyes on you. Eight eyes is better than two so I know I'm good," Tavares said.

"That's my cue to roll," Damien said, handing Tavares a "7" of some granddaddy purple haze. Kissing Tavares, Damien made his way back to the other side of the deck to blow it down with his boys.

Tavares couldn't have asked for a better night. After partying till 4:00 a.m., everyone made their way home. Tavares had no energy to clean her house, which was truly crazy from all the people, food, and drinks that had passed through it during the course of the evening.

"Don't worry about that shit, Tavares, I'll call a cleaning service to come out tomorrow or Monday."

"Sounds like a plan, because I'm not up to it," Tavares said, winking at Damien.

Tavares left the kitchen, where bottles were sitting everywhere. There were empty Rémy, Hennessey Black and Privilege, Absolut, Cîroc, Corona, Heineken, and Patrón bottles in multiples in the corner on the floor. Tavares went and checked on the kids and made her way upstairs to the third floor to take a shower.

Entering his bedroom, Damien could hear the shower running and quickly shed his clothes, headed to the shower on a mission. As he was opening the tall steamed glass door, Tavares screamed.

"Oh shit, you scared the hell out of me," Tavares said, lathering her body, waiting for Dame to get in and shut the damn door. Damien and Tavares showered together, with their hands gliding over each other's bodies. They were clean and ready to finish what they had started in the shower in their king-sized bed. Damien had every intention of giving Tavares the business. He had mastered her body inside and out; he knew her body better than she did. He had taught her the art of her own body.

Tavares lay down on the bed, but before she could pull the covers back, Dame dove and attacked her like a football player. "Ahhh!" screamed Tavares as Damien grabbed her hands, held them tight, and put them over her head, being slightly aggressive. Damien sucked her melons real slow and let her scream, squirm, and melt all at the same time. Tavares's nipples were so sensitive that if he just ran his tongue across her big, thick nipples, she would instantly get wet.

Tavares's eyes were watering from not being able to control the waterfall that had her thighs soaking wet. Damien let Tavares go and slid down to make the real waterfall come. After multiple strokes of the tongue across Tavares's clit, Damien got what he was looking for. He kissed Tavares up her chest, on her chin, and stopped at her lips. Giving her a real intense dance with his tongue, he grabbed her body and flipped them both over. Tavares loved being on top, especially when she was as wet as she was.

Standing up, holding the headboard, Tavares slowly lowered her body and thick butt down on Dame's dick. Getting up and sliding down over and over, she had Damien's eyes rolling and his toes curling. Picking up the rhythm, Tavares splashed Damien in the face every time she came down on his dick. He had her cumming in overtime. Riding Damien for twenty minutes, Tavares turned around with her ass and back facing him and continued to ride him with the same intensity. Grabbing her waist, Damien assisted Tavares, who was riding the shit out of his long dick. Damien knew the exact way and place to touch, lick, and fuck Tavares so that she wet the sheets every time.

"Yuck," Tavares said, looking at all the wet puddles on the sheets as she got up to change them. Tavares loved sex, but always needing to change the sheets made sex a pain in the ass. There was no such thing as them having sex and being able to sleep on the same sheets. Damien was in the shower washing Tavares off of him, while Tavares put the bed back together.

Damien's personal cell phone started to ring. Tavares looked at the clock that read 5:37 a.m. and didn't hesitate to remove the phone. Looking at the name Jazz come across the screen, Tavares politely picked up.

"Damn, Dame, why you ain't been answering. I been blowing your phone up all night." The woman took no breaths and waited for no answers.

"I'm going to Jamaica with my girls Tuesday, and I wanna see you before I leave. And do you think you could take me to the airport too? Hello? Dame, you there?" the woman asked when she heard nothing in response.

"No, this isn't Dame. It's his girlfriend," Tavares said dryly.

"Oh, hi, Tavares," the chick said, knowing she'd fucked up the church's money but had to try and save face. "I can't wait to meet you, Damien told me so much about you."

"Is that right?" Tavares asked, letting it be known that she didn't give two flying fucks about what the hoe on the other end was talking about. "That's odd you've heard so much about me, because, bitch, he's never mentioned your existence to me. And bitch, you don't fucking know me, so stop talking to me like we go way back or something. So tell me, why is it again that you need to fucking see Dame before your trip, and why do you think you're so important that my boyfriend would be taking you to the airport?"

The young girl was quick on her feet. "I wanted to snatch some weed off of him. I just needed a ride, and since we're cool, I figured he wouldn't mind."

"Riiiight, Jazz. I guess you take me for a fool, huh?" Tavares said, cracking up laughing.

"No, not at all," the girl said, knowing that she had fucked up by calling Damien's phone so early, even though he was usually up and out the house trapping during this time.

"Bitch, you must think I'm a fool to be shooting me this bullshit." Dame's girlfriend was giving it to her and now that she'd got him in trouble, he was for sure going to give it to her. "So if I can assume correctly, you've been fucking my boyfriend and you want him to dick you down before you leave and see you off at the airport," Tavares said, knowing that she was right on the money. "Well, Damien is in the shower right now, washing me off of him. As soon as he gets out, I'll be sure to relay your message. What time does your flight leave again?" Tavares asked sarcastically.

"Noon," the girl said, so low that Tavares could barely hear her.

"Don't get quiet now," Tavares snapped. "I'll be sure to let Damien know that you need a dick down and ride before you leave for Jamaica," Tavares said, hitting end on the phone.

Tavares was mad, but she didn't even know why she wasted her time. Damien was a motherfucker and she knew it. Tavares had definitely had enough.

Coming out of the shower, Damien found Tavares sitting up in the bed with her arms folded. Damien sat on his side of the bed and dried off. He turned around and looked at Tavares, who wasn't moving.

"Damn, I know you have to be done as wet as those sheets were," Dame said, thinking she was mad because she wanted some more. Tavares wasn't cracking any smiles.

"You had a phone call while you were in the shower."

"Who was it?" Damien asked, expecting her to say a fiend, because wouldn't no one else be calling this early in the morning. As soon as Tavares answered, "Jazz," he knew the wrath was coming.

"Jazz says she needs to see you before she heads to Jamaica and she needs you to drop her off at the airport. Let me find out you done went from a drug dealer to a motherfucking cab driver. Last time I checked, if my memory serves me correctly, you don't have a hacker's license. If I'm wrong, please let me know." Damien was silent. "Okay then, motherfucker, in that case you don't have a hacker's license. I didn't think you did. I think you forget sometimes that I'm your bitch. I should be the only bitch that you're taking anywhere. That is, unless you're Jazz's fucking man too, or you're dicking her down in your in-between time. Yo, you fucking disgust me," Tavares said.

"Tavares, I'm not fucking Jazz. What the fuck, yo?" Damien said defensively. "I'm the fucking weed and coke man. Do you think I can fucking control when and at what time people desire to get high?"

"Damien please, it's fucking 5:30 a.m. in the motherfucking morning, that bitch wasn't thinking about no fucking blunt. She needed another kind of high. She should've been fucking calling another weed man if she was waiting on your fucking ass till 5:30 this fucking morning. What the fuck you take me for, a fucking idiot or something? But you know what? Keep going hard with your story about her just wanting some smoke. It's cute, so keep rocking with it," Tavares said, flaming mad.

"But tell me this: why the fuck does Jazz think you would even take the time out of your day to take her to the airport? She got niggaz she's fucking and sucking for that. If they ain't good for a ride to the airport, then she shouldn't be fucking them. So that's why she asked you, she thinks that she's worth it."

"The bitch is from around way, would you relax?" Damien said, knowing he had no out. "She buys smoke in weight off me. I have no fucking clue why she'd think I'd take her to the airport. Maybe the bum ass niggaz she fuck with ain't got no cars. How the fuck should I know?" Dame said like he was telling the truth.

"Damien, you're full of fucking shit. Save the lies for someone who doesn't fucking know better. You would think that you would know better than to be so fucking sloppy with your bullshit. But of course not. You just don't get e-fucking-nough, do you?" Tavares asked, mad as all hell.

"What the fuck, Tavares? I'm sure she told you we ain't fucking, I'm telling you that we ain't fucking."

"And what the fuck does that mean?" Tavares asked him, like he'd bumped his head. "So I'm just supposed to believe you and some tramp bitch that's calling your phone during the wee hours of the morning? Get the fuck out of here," Tavares said, getting up off the bed. Walking into the bathroom, Tavares slammed the door behind her. She got in the shower and got her mind right. She let the water trickle off her body for forty minutes, wishing she could wash the anger away. She realized that she was beyond pissed, but wrinkled from being in the water so long, Tavares stepped out the shower under the heating lamp and dried off, hoping Damien was sleep.

Exiting the bathroom, Tavares's first thought was to stab Damien as he slept like a baby. Instead, she gathered her pajamas and made her way downstairs to the spare bedroom. She didn't want to look at Damien, never mind sleep with him.

Tavares woke up and knew that she wasn't in the mood for Damien. She was still pissed. Making her way upstairs to get dressed, she was more than happy to find Damien gone. *It was always some bullshit*, Tavares thought. They would be doing good, and as always Damien would show his fucking ass. She pushed Damien out her mind for the moment and did all the last-minute cleaning and packing before the kids woke up.

Tavares was in the kitchen mopping when the kids came downstairs.

"Morning, Tav," they both said.

"Hey munchkins, take a seat at the table or the island and I'll get your breakfast. Just watch your step on the floors because I just mopped." Tavares spent time with her step kids, got them dressed, and headed to say her goodbyes. Pulling up to Shaunda's house, Tavares could see her simple ass in the window. Giving the kids hugs and kisses, they told Tavares how much they were going to miss her. As the kids turned to go in the house, Tavares gave Shaunda the middle finger while the kids couldn't see her, got in her car, and headed to Randee's house.

Making her way upstairs, she found everyone lounging in Randee's smoke room. Tavares tossed Leslie an ounce and told her to twist up. Leslie whipped out a fresh box of cigarillos that she always kept in her purse and rolled up five blunts. The ladies laid on the beanbags and futons while they smoked with the lava lamps going. Tavares told them about Damien's latest bullshit.

"That nigga got a lot of shit with him, Apple," Mona-Lisa said, feeling bad for her friend who was so pretty, sweet, and kindhearted, and took so much bullshit from her boyfriend.

"I'm sure you got enough dough saved to do you," Randee said, knowing her friend well enough to know she wasn't broke.

"I do, but let's see how it all plays out after I graduate. If shit don't change in the next nine months, then I'm good with Dame. I mean, like, really good with him. I'm going to take the L and just walk away and rebuild my life."

"Good for you," Leslie said, knowing that her friend meant it. The ladies reminisced about how fun the summer had been before saying their goodbyes to Tavares.

Damien went to Jazlene's house and tore her a new asshole. Damien gave her a verbal lashing that was so brutal that he might as well have put his hands on her the way she was crying.

"You fucking stupid, silly, marble-minded bitch. Why the fuck would you call my fucking phone that fucking time of the morning? You gotta have a fucking brain full of rocks to call and just start running your diarrhea ass mouth."

Through tears and choked up words, Jazlene kept saying, "I'm sorry. I'm so sorry, Damien."

"What the fuck you mean, sorry? Have you lost what little bit of brain you got?" he asked, really not understanding what would make her call his phone so early in the morning.

"Please, please, please, let me make it up to you," Jazlene said, dropping to her knees. Damien was mad but he wasn't turning down the blowjob that Jazlene was offering as a peace token. Getting his dick sucked, Damien busted all in her face, pulled up his jeans, and left

~ 219 ~

Jazlene on her knees with nut streaming down her face while he headed to his mother's house.

"Doll, Damien ain't never going to change," Tavares said, sitting at the table rolling up a blunt of some Canada Dry. Tavares was venting to the only mother-like figure she knew. Even though it was Damien's mother, Tavares didn't care; Doll was a mother to both of them.

"I be trying to be a woman and stand by him, but your son makes it hella hard. I just don't get him. I'm a good chick and go hard for him and he still abuses it and takes me for granted." Doll looked at the pain, stress, and hurt in Tavares's eyes.

"Tavares, let me talk to you woman to woman, and not as Damien's mother. Tavares, I know you love my son, but you got to love you and put you first and foremost. If Damien isn't doing right by you, then you do it moving. Simple as that. I love my son and don't want to see him lose you, but I love you too. I want to see you happy and getting all the love you deserve in return. I know Damien means well and loves you, he just got a crazy way of showing it. But if you feel like he ain't doing his job, then let him be by himself. It won't change shit between you and the family. You are one of us, just as well as he is. Put you first," Doll said, inhaling the good weed. "Damien doesn't know that he has a good thing. So if he has to lose it to find out, then that's on him. I want to see you happy too, so don't stay with Damien because you feel like you have to, because baby, you don't."

Damien came in the house and entered the kitchen. Finding his mother and Tavares, who had stopped their conversation short, let him know he was the topic of conversation.

"Don't stop the conversation on account of me," Damien said, snatching the blunt out his mother's hand and taking a seat across the table from Tavares.

"If we weren't done, we would have carried on," Tavares said, getting smart with him.

"Is all your shit packed, smart ass?"

"Sure is, hot dick."

"Apple, I don't got time for your fucking bullshit. If you're going to let me take you to the airport, fine, if not what the fuck ever. I told you, I'm not fucking her. So no, I'm not kissing your ass about this." Tavares laughed at how funny it was to listen to Damien go hard with his lie. He was true to it: if he didn't get caught red-handed, then it didn't happen. Tavares wasn't a fool. But it was cool. Tavares was ready to go back to school and do her own thing.

"This is what I need you two to do, shut that bullshit up in my house," Doll said, looking at both of them. "If yawl are going to be together and do this shit, then do it. If not, split the fuck up and go your own damn ways. I really don't care what yawl do, just don't be bring all that negativity up in here."

Tavares saved her cab money and rode in silence to the airport with Damien.

"So you're going to go back to school on this bullshit, huh?"

"Bullshit? I'm glad that's what you call it, when a bitch is calling you during the early a.m. like you ain't got a girl at home."

"Tavares, I keep telling you I'm not fucking that broad. I don't fuck every bitch that calls my phone."

"Damien, I can't cosign that, and that's a problem. I don't care what you say, how cool she is, or how much weight she buys, she should not be fucking calling your phone at no 5:37 in the goddamn morning. How would you feel if some nigga, who I said I was cool with, was calling me that time of the morning?"

Damien wasn't liking the sound of that and it showed all in his facial expression.

"My sentiments exactly. Damien, you got me fucked up. I'm getting sick and fucking tired of all your fucking bullshit."

Damien could hear the seriousness in her voice and knew that he had really fucked up. Arriving at the airport, Tavares and Damien exchanged goodbyes with cheap kisses. Tavares headed back to school to start her last school year, which wasn't starting out too well.

~ CHAPTER 13 ~

Can I giftwrap the globe and give you the world?

After being back in school for almost three weeks, Tavares was excited that in a week it would be her birthday and she and her girls were definitely going to be somewhere loose on the goose, off some Patrón. The girls were coming down for the weekend. They were definitely balling out for Tavares's birthday. If they didn't, it wouldn't have been right, because she was turning twenty-one.

Tavares was in her Senior Research Methods class when her professor announced that there was going to be a big storm hitting and Savannah was going to have to be evacuated. *What the fuck*, Tavares cursed to herself. Her birthday was in four days and her girls were flying down the following day to party with her and her homegirls from school. Class ended and Tavares hurried through the busy hallways of Payne Hall to her car. She called her friends as she headed home, mad as all hell. Informing them that they would have to change their plans, she was so mad that she told them she would call them when she got home. Tavares hung up with them, wracked her brain, and listened to Keyshia Cole. As Tavares drove down Skidaway Road, she contemplated what the hell she was going to do, now that she had to evacuate Savannah by tomorrow afternoon.

Tavares's phone rang and she pressed talk, knowing she needed to hear the voice on the other end. "Hello, how was your day?"

"School was school, same shit just another day. I just found out a big storm is hitting down here, so we have to evacuate."

"And your girls were coming down, right?"

"Yesssss." Tavares answered like it was the end of the world.

"Damn, so what are you going to do for the birthday?"

"Good question. I have no clue."

"Well, you know since we got the same birthday, yawl can meet me and my niggaz in Atlanta and we can party like it's 1999."

"Damn, Dora, that sounds tempting," Tavares said, actually strongly considering it. She was still mad at Damien for the stunt he pulled before she came back, so it was daring.

"Why is it tempting? Just drive your ass to the A and let me do the rest." Sighing, Tavares knew she really didn't have another choice on such short notice. Getting home, Tavares called her girls' phones one by one. Everyone was with the plans and called and changed their tickets.

Tavares called Damien. "Hey, birthday girl," he answered his phone.

"Hey, baby. I was just calling to tell you that there's a storm coming. We have to evacuate."

"Are you coming home?"

"Nah, my girls are going to meet me in Atlanta."

"Damn, why don't you just come home?" Damien asked.

"I don't want to party at home for my birthday." Tavares really, *really* didn't want to party at home and it had nothing to do with meeting Dora in Atlanta. Yeah, they had been talking every day since she returned to school, but it wasn't all about him. It was a rule, never party in the home state, so she was going to Atlanta.

"Be careful and call me in the morning before you hit the highway."

"I will. Love you."

"Love you too," he said, and they hung up.

Tavares arrived in Atlanta and called Dora as she hit Highway 78.

"Hey, birthday girl."

"Hi, birthday boy."

"Where are you, Ma?"

"I just got into Atlanta. Where are you?"

"I'm downtown on Peachtree. Come to the Ritz-Carlton. I'm in room 5012."

"Alright," Tavares said, knowing exactly where he was due to all the time she'd spent in Atlanta. Fifteen minutes later, Tavares was valet parking and making her way to Dora's room. Knocking on the door, Tavares could hear that Dora and his boys had already got their weekend started. Entering the laid out room, everyone said hello to Tavares. Tavares waved to the familiar and unfamiliar faces who were in the living room of the suite playing video games, drinking, and blowing it down.

Dora led Tavares back to the oversized bedroom. "Damn, you look good," he said, eyeing Tavares from head to toe.

"Thank you," Tavares said as she stood in front of him in a red and white Adidas track sweat suit and some matching Adidas sneakers. Taking a seat on the king-sized bed that was soft as silk, Tavares wanted to fall out.

"So are you ready to do the damn thing?" Dora questioned, walking over to the large cherry wood desk and posting up on it, with his hand cupping his chin.

"I sure am," Tavares said, thinking naughty thoughts of what she could do to him in the bed she was laying on.

"My girls should be here in about an hour."

"Well, I have a birthday planned that you'll never forget," Dora said, handing her three hotel keys and four sets of car keys.

"You got them cars too?" Tavares asked in utter shock.

"Yeah, but they gotta work out who's driving what. There's an Aston Martin, Lamborghini, Porsche, and the Ferrari. The Bentley is all us," laughed Dora. Tavares stood up with all the keys in hand and just looked up at Dora, who towered over her.

"What am I going to do with you?" Tavares asked, shaking her head, not believing how hard he was going for her birthday. Damien would never have done something nice for her and her friends.

"Hopefully you'll keep me, Ms. Tavares." Dora wanted to give this girl the world and just wished that she would wake up and see it.

"Well let me go to my room, get settled, and we'll meet in the lobby at 7:00 p.m." Tavares made her way to her room and couldn't believe it. Dora had got her a suite that had a huge, oversized living room, with a sixty-four-inch flat screen TV, a Nintendo Wii, and a stereo system with surround sound. There was a built-in bar, filled with bottles of Patrón and Don P along with Moet and Rémy, Cîroc, and Hennessey Privilege. There was a dinner table for ten and a full stainless steel kitchen. There were two identical bathrooms, one in the common area and one in her bedroom. Both had a Jacuzzi-style tub, a glass standup shower, and a separate, closed off area where the toilet was. There were full-length terry cloth robes hanging up in the closets.

Tavares was shocked to find a dozen roses on each nightstand. "He definitely knows how to get his romance on," she laughed. On the bed were three boxes. Tavares sat on the bed and was going to open the boxes, but noticed she had a balcony. "Oh my god," she gasped when she walked out on what she thought was a small balcony. It was actually a huge balcony that wrapped around her whole bedroom. There were two patio sets with umbrellas over them, an outside bar, and a pool.

Tavares was deep in thought when her phone rang. Sprinting to catch the call, Tavares made it just in time.

"Hey, chica," Tavares answered.

"Where are we coming to?" Mona-Lisa asked. "We just touched down. We have to pick up the rental car and then we're on our way."

"Well, take a cab, because Dora got yawl an Aston Martin, a Porsche, a Ferrari, and a Lamborghini."

"What?" Mona-Lisa said like she had heard Tavares wrong.

"Same thing I said, Mona. He's too much, right?"

"Girl, when that nigga does it, he does it for reallll!"

"Well, hurry up, because we're meeting him and his crazy ass friends in the lobby at 7:00. I left yawl's room keys at the front desk, so just come to my room when yawl get settled. I'm in room 5016."

Mona-Lisa hung up with Tavares and informed her girls that Dora had taken care of everything.

"Yo, that nigga did everything, yawl. We don't even need the fucking rental. All we have to do is get there. Tavares is already there."

"What do you mean, everything?" asked Jazz.

"He got us rooms at the Ritz and got us cars."

"Damn, he got more than one car?" Leslie asked.

"Yeah, he got a bunch of expensive toys to play with for the weekend. I know for sure he got a Porsche."

"I am so in the Porsche," Randee said, knowing that this weekend was about to be on and popping.

Arriving at the hotel, the ladies retrieved their room keys, dropped their bags off, and went up to Tavares's room. Everyone was in shock seeing Tavares's suite.

"Damn, Tavares, this nigga is balling out of control," Jazz said, admiring the hotel room that was bigger than most people's apartments.

"Girl, that ain't shit, let's go out on the patio."

Walking on the private balcony, Mona-Lisa screamed, "Tavares, you gots to keep this nigga. I know you got a man and all but this right here is what life is all about." Tavares shot Mona-Lisa a look that said "let's not even go there."

"What's in the boxes on the bed?" Leslie questioned.

"I have no clue. I didn't open them yet. I'll open them later."

"We had boxes in our rooms too," Jazz said. "Well, open them, and let me know what's in them."

"Let's meet in the lobby at 6:45 so we can take some pictures," Leslie said.

"Alright," everyone cosigned and made their way to their rooms to get dressed.

Jazz entered the room and went straight for the boxes on her bed. Opening the first box, Jazz was shocked.

"What is it?" yelled Leslie from the bathroom.

"It's a fancy pink invitation that reads "You are cordially invited on a shopping spree and spa day with Ms. Tavares Del Gada for her 21st birthday. A limo will arrive to pick you up Saturday at 12:00 p.m. sharp. It's a surprise so please don't tell the birthday girl." It had a spa day VIP pass for a facial, manicure, pedicure, and one-hour massage.

"Oh, shit!" Jazz yelled.

"What is it?" Leslie yelled from the bathroom, where she was preparing her shower.

"The second box has $500 in mall gift cards inside. The last box has a silver Tiffany bracelet with a friendship charm."

"Tavares got a good one this time around," Leslie said, coming out of the bathroom and opening her boxes to find the same thing. "If she don't want him, we're for sure pulling straws for him," Leslie joked.

"Shit, I seen him first," Jazz stated nonchalantly, but mad inside that she hadn't bagged him like she tried to.

The hotel phone rang and Jazz answered.

"What yawl doing?" Randee asked.

"Nothing, we just opened our boxes."

We did too. Shit, that's why I'm calling yawl. Yo, this nigga is going really hard for Apple's birthday. He's A to the okay with me," Randee joked.

"Tell me about it," Jazz said.

"Tavares is going to be so surprised tomorrow."

"Hell yeah," said Randee. "I can't believe he's funding our trip and giving us spending money," Randee said, feeling like this was a real good vacation.

"I need a nigga like him," Mona-Lisa said in the background.

"Alright, well get dressed bitches, we'll see yawl at 6:45," Jazz said, hanging up to get dressed.

Arriving in the lobby before Dora and his friends made it downstairs, the girls posed and took about fifty pictures. By the time Dora and his loudmouth crew came down, the girls were sitting on the lobby couches looking like divas.

"Damn, are these the ladies of the evening?" KJ said. Everyone exchanged hellos and made their way out to the valet parking to retrieve the striking vehicles. All the ladies hopped in the passenger side with Bryce, Hawk, KJ, and Mid getting in the driver's sides.

"Where are we going?" Tavares asked.

"You'll see when we get there. Do you have to know everything?"

"Yes, I do. But you seem to love to challenge me," Tavares said as she relaxed in the butter soft leather seat. KJ and Leslie were in the car, laughing at how cute Tavares and Dora would look together.

"Real talk, Leslie. My man's feeling your girl. I don't know what she did to him, but he got it bad."

"Shoot, Tavares got it bad too, because once upon a time, we would have never been here, no matter what. Tavares ain't into cheating. That's on everything," Leslie said, not believing how open Tavares was. "Actually they both are open," Leslie said.

"What's this?" Mona-Lisa asked Middeon as he pulled the Lambo into Benihana.

"It's a Japanese steak house. You sit around a huge rectangular table that's also a grill, and they cook your food to order right in front of your face."

"Hmmm, sounds good to me," said Mona-Lisa, down for whatever. Her go-with-the-flow attitude was part of her natural demeanor. Taking a whole table to themselves, everyone took a seat and became entertained by the chef, who did tricks and played with fire while preparing their food. After stuffing themselves with drinks, chicken, steak, and shrimp they headed toward the cars.

"Where to now?" Jazz questioned Hawk as she stretched out in the Lamborghini.

"Who knows with Dora? You just have to follow the nigga's lead."

Mona-Lisa was loving Mid. His smooth, laid-back, catering demeanor made her feel warm. But he wouldn't know it because showing too many emotions wasn't her speed. Mona-Lisa was all about her kids, and she knew that she could never half-ass with a nigga. But she thought he had potential if he got his mind right.

"You know what?" asked Dora, looking so fine driving the Bentley.

"What?" Tavares asked curiously.

"You're just like me," Dora said, like he was stating a fact. "I just watch you, ma, and you're my twin. Why else you think we were born on the same day?" Dora's phone went off.

"Hey, Talia, what's up?"

"I was just calling to see if you made it to the game yet."

"Nah, we just now left dinner and we're on the way there."

"Let me speak to Bryce."

"Is this Bryce's phone?" Dora asked his secretary like she had truly lost her mind.

"No, but ain't he right there?"

"No, he's not. My future wife is," Dora said, looking Tavares up and down. Tavares couldn't help but shake her head no.

"Oh, yeah," Talia asked sarcastically. "And who is that, this week?"

"Talia, do me a favor? Save the bullshit because you ain't never heard me tell you anyone was going to be my wife. That's hate I'm sniffing coming up off you, and it's a foul smell. So I'll hit you later."

Hanging up, Talia was about to get on her homework to figure out who this chick was that had Dora balling out of control. She had booked and purchased everything for the trip, so she knew the total tab of $200,000 was only on bookings, not to mention what he was spending out of pocket. *Hmmm... I need to do a background check*, Talia thought.

Arriving at the Atlanta Falcons and Patriots game, the large group stopped at the concession stand and bought beers. Making their way to their seats, Randee whispered, "Yo, Apple, do you realize that we're at a football game with ground seats? We could end up on TV with these seats."

"Uhh, yeah, I know. But what the fuck? We'll just say Leslie's people invited us to the game." Tavares shrugged her shoulders. *What else can I do?* Tavares thought to herself. They made their way to their seats, ten deep. Everyone got loud on the Patriots side, as they were smashing the Falcons.

The niggaz were in their glory while the ladies just laughed and chuckled at them being so uptight about the calls and plays. Before the ladies laughed themselves to death, the Patriots won.

"Damn, you'd think that yawl's asses were the ones from Boston," Randee said.

"Yawl was all into it, rooting for Boston."

"Fuck that shit," Hawk said.

"Yawl from the Bean and yawl with us, so we was holding it down. And them niggaz won."

"I'm glad because I won some money," Dora said, smiling at the quick, easy twenty grand he'd just made.

"Yawl ladies enjoy yawl selves?" Bryce asked.

"Yeah," they all said.

"Where to now?" Mona-Lisa asked.

"Well, ladies, we're going to park the cars."

"Park the cars?" Randee asked, but was really thinking, *why would we do that?*

"Yeah, Ms. Randee, park the cars," Dora joked.

"Whatever, yo," Randee said smiling, liking Dora, especially for Tavares, because you could tell he was all into her and not just for her looks.

Arriving back at the hotel, everyone was greeted by a not-so-average party bus that was waiting for them.

"Oh, my fucking God," Mona-Lisa said when she saw the party truck.

Jazz looked at Hawk and said, "Yo, but did yawl really rent a double stretch Cadillac party bus? This is *crazy*."

"When your boy said money is no issue, he really means it," Leslie said. "I can only imagine how much liquor is on there. That nigga is crazy," she said, just shaking her head as if to say, *hey, if he wants us to have a good time, then I'm all for it.*

"Trust there's about $3,000 in liquor on there," Hawk laughed.

Everyone boarded the huge party bus and it was a party from there, real bananas. There were blunts on top of blunts on top of blunts being passed in a heavy rotation. The bus was ventilated, thank God, because there were way too many blunts being smoked in the large, confined area. Ten people had no business blowing twenty blunts at a time. Every hand had a blunt, with the other hand holding the next blunt for them to smoke. Everyone was throwing back shots and sipping on Don P. Dora was trying to convince Tavares to let him take body shots off her.

"Come on, lil mama, just let me taste you."

"Ohh, no, I'm not fooling with you. But lay back and open up and I'll put the shots down your throat," Tavares tried to compromise.

"Naw, I wanna suck 'em off you."

"Ohh, you're fresh," Tavares said with lust in her eyes. She laughed and walked toward the stripper pole, where her friends were playing.

The girls were so fucked up that they were fully clothed, trying to maneuver the two stripper poles in the middle of the bus. They weren't doing a good job, though. For their effort and not being afraid to have fun, Abdora and his boys were throwing hundred dollar bills at them.

Tavares couldn't believe that she was having such a ball. They were dancing, smoking, talking shit, drinking, and getting fucked up with a driver to get them home safely. Tavares was blowing it down with her girls when Dora came up behind her and lightly brushed his dick across her ass. Tavares jumped at all the dick that had just poked her in the rear end.

"Can I steal her for the moment?" Abdora asked, handing them four blunts to add to their six-blunt rotation.

"Go ahead, fair exchange ain't no robbery," Randee said, taking the blunts.

Before they knew it, they had partied on the bus and club-hopped through the morning. It was 6:00 a.m. when they were dropped off at the hotel and stumbled upstairs to their rooms. Tavares knew that she wanted to give Abdora some, but it was out of the question, drunk or not. Tavares blew her girls kisses as they got off the elevator on the forty-seventh floor. Next was the forty-eighth floor where Abdora's boys were.

"And where's your room?" Tavares asked, realizing that it was just them. Dora just chuckled as the elevator rose to the fiftieth floor.

"I don't have a room. I was hoping I could crash with you."

"Is that what you was thinking?" Tavares asked, trying to contain her laughter. "Glad you don't get paid to think, then."

"You gonna leave me with no place to sleep?" Dora said real mellow and sexy.

"Of course I will. You knew you needed a place to stay when you booked this trip."

"Well, I gave you my room, so you really gonna leave me to sleep in the hall?"

"Of course I will," Tavares said with a straight face.

"Damn, that is fucked up."

"Not even, you tried to be slick, and now it's biting you in the ass."

Exiting the elevator on the fiftieth floor, Tavares asked real serious, "Are you joking, Dora?"

"Nope, I don't gotta room. I couldn't afford it."

"Whatever," Tavares said, bursting out laughing, knowing that he was definitely full of shit now. "Well, what do you want me to do? Give you a pillow and a blanket to lay on outside my door?"

"What the fuck I look like, a dog or some shit?" Dora said, scrunching his whole face back, like shorty had truly lost her fucking mind. Tavares burst out laughing.

"Oh, relax. I was just playing. I guess I'm stuck with you for the night," she said, looking him up and down and walking toward her suite. *Lord, please don't let me get myself into no trouble,* Tavares kept pleading in her mind.

"Hold on, let me run in my room and get some smoke and rollies," Abdora said nonchalantly.

"You fucking play too much," Tavares laughed as she stopped in her tracks and put her hand on her hip. "I thought you didn't have a room?"

"Come on, baby girl, you should have known better than that. But you already done said I can stay, so it's too late to reneg. I'll be right over," Dora said, going a few doors down to his room.

Before Tavares made it to the couch to kick off her five-inch heels, there was a light rap at the door. Letting Abdora in, Tavares made her way back to the couch. She plopped down on the couch and kicked off her purple Jimmy Choo heels and rubbed her feet.

"Let me do that for you," Abdora said, watching and taking a seat next to her. With no objections, Tavares stretched her legs across his body and let him go to work. Tavares dropped her head back and dozed off as Abdora hit every pressure point in her soft feet. Not wanting to wake her, Abdora picked up her small frame and placed it in the king-sized bed.

Tavares woke up. "Damn, it was that good that you put me to sleep." She was good and tore down. Patrón made her feel easy on the body and ready to get her back dug out doggy style. Tavares looked at Abdora wishing, but knew better. She wasn't going that far and came back to reality from her dirty thoughts.

Dora was moving the boxes at the foot of the bed when Tavares asked, "What's in those boxes?"

"Why don't you open them, crazy? Actually nah, open them in the a.m. Let's get our sleep on, because I see the Patrón is doing the same thing to you that it's doing to me."

"What?" Tavares asked like she was lost.

"That look in your eye. I'm feeling the same way. So don't deny it, please."

Tavares caught on and just laughed.

"Just don't try to take advantage of me," Dora joked.

"Don't you wish," Tavares said, laughing with her eyes closed. "I'm not moving to change my clothes," Tavares said, knowing that moving from the spot she was in was impossible.

"You ain't got to." Together they cuddled right there in their clothes and went to sleep.

Jumping up from the overly loud, ringing phone, Tavares groggily said hello in a half-awake tone. "Hi, Miss Tavares, this is your 11:00 a.m. wake-up call."

"I didn't call for a wake-up call, you have the wrong room."

"Well, it says 11:00 wake-up call and your car will be here at 12:00 p.m."

"Alright," Tavares said, slamming the phone down, knowing that this was the work of the body lying next to her.

Tavares didn't wake Dora up, she just slid out of bed and proceeded to prepare herself. Tavares loved Patrón because it was like she was never drunk hours before. She slept the alcohol off and was ready to get her day started. She quietly laid her clothes out before heading to the shower. Taking a shower and putting her make up on, Tavares was sliding into her jeans when Abdora turned over.

"Hmmm… I like that look, jeans with a bra."

"Be quiet. Where am I going?"

"I don't know. You're the one getting dressed, so you tell me."

"Dora, don't play games. I got a wake-up call and the lady said the car will be here at 12:00."

"I don't know, but hopefully the car takes you somewhere nice," Dora said, playing completely stupid.

"You play too much," Tavares said, slipping on her red bottom pumps as she buttoned her white shirt.

Tavares slipped on her butter soft, fire-engine red leather jacket, threw on her Jackie O shades and said, "Fine, play games, I'll see you later."

"Don't you want to know what's in the boxes?" Dora asked, knowing she would need them. "You got five minutes before the car comes, slow down."

Opening the boxes, Tavares found a spa day gift certificate for the works and $5,000 in mall gift cards in the first two boxes. The third box had a silver Tiffany bracelet with a friendship charm dangling from it, with a pair of silver ball earrings and a silver mesh ring.

"You and all your girls got matching bracelets," Dora said as he looked at Tavares. She was looking at the boxes in utter shock. Tavares thought time had stopped for a moment. She was blown away by his efforts.

"Yo, like what the fuck am I going to do with you?" was all that she could manage to say, still in shock. Her heart was fluttering back and forth out of gratitude. "You make it real hard for a chick to just get rid of you. You do the most thoughtful and considerate shit. It's like you thought and planned out everything to the T, to make sure I had a ball. I'm totally blown away."

"I'm glad, because I wanted your twenty-first birthday to be special beyond words." Tavares was so at a loss for words for how far he'd gone for her birthday. She hugged Abdora tight and planted a sweet, tasty kiss on him for the first time.

"Thanks, Mr. Hella Handsome."

"You're welcome, Apple."

"So, what are you going to do today?" she asked. "It's officially your birthday too."

"I'm going to go to my room and take a shower, and then, Imma go play big boy style. After I get dressed me and my niggaz are going to get some upscale massages," he laughed, knowing that the upscale part was the perk of the blowjobs that came along with the Swedish massages they'd scheduled. "From there we're going to have lunch, kick it, and then we'll get up with yawl tonight." Dora sent Tavares off on her day of shopping and beauty as he got ready to do the same thing with his niggaz, gangsta style.

After a day of sipping on mimosas, being pampered at the spa, and shopping till she dropped, Tavares thought that she had really died and gone to heaven. If she wasn't in heaven, it sure felt like it, looking at all the bags around her. Victoria's Secret, Saks, Neiman Marcus, Banana Republic, Sephora, Louis Vuitton, Tiffany's, BCBG, Chanel, Michael Kors, and Foot Locker. Her friends had even used a portion of their money to buy her gifts. Tavares's body was totally relaxed from the full body massage; all she wanted to do was go back to the hotel and lay down.

"Apple, can you please keep Dora? If not for no one else, for me, boo," asked Leslie.

"Shut up," Tavares said, knowing that Dora was spoiling her and her friends.

"Boo, we gots to make him a community boo," said Mona-Lisa. "He doesn't just treat you good, he's good to us, so we say he stays around as the community boo. He's the fucking best! Someone second the motion," Mona-Lisa said, raising her right hand.

"Seconded," Leslie said.

"I third it," Randee said, rolling her eyes.

"He's community boo," Mona-Lisa joked, but she was dead serious at the same time.

A community boo had no problem treating and being good to your friends like he was to you, because he respected your bond. Tavares didn't know how she was going to keep him around, but she knew that she wanted to.

Tavares and her friends arrived at the hotel and made their way to their rooms to try on their new clothes and prepare for only who knew what, messing with Dora. Tavares picked up the phone and called Damien. He had left three messages, so she needed to call him.

"Hey, birthday lady," he answered, happy to hear from his girl. "How was your birthday?"

"It was a memorable day," Tavares said, filling him in on her day, but failing to mention that Dora footed the bill.

"Damn, baby girl, it sounds like you had a ball."

"I did. I really had the most bombest birthday ever. Imma take a nap, then we're going out."

"When you going back to school?" Damien asked.

"The evacuation is over Monday, so Imma head back Monday night."

"Well, your birthday presents are in the mail. I'm sure you'll be pleased, because you ain't got a slouch nigga."

Only if you knew, Tavares thought, thinking nothing he was sending was going to top her weekend with Abdora.

"Well, mama, I just wanted to make sure that you were enjoying your birthday. I'll see you very soon, I'm sure of it. You can't sit your ass at school if you wanted to."

"Shut up, because you be telling me to come home most times. I be down here getting my school on and your ass be telling me to come home because your horn dog ass wants some, so kiss my ass."

Damien laughed because she was telling the truth. He fucked other bitches, but nothing was better than his in-house pussy.

Tavares hung up the phone with Damien and called Dora to see where he was and what the plans for the night were.

"'Sup, birthday lady," Dora answered with a lot of noise and music in the background.

"I was calling to see where you were, how your day was, and what time me and the girls should be ready?"

"I'm at the strip club, my day was excellent, and you and the ladies should be dressed to kill and in the lobby ready to roll at 9 sharp."

Out of all Dora had said, all Tavares could respond was, "Ain't it a little early to be throwing dollars at some pussy?" Dora just laughed.

"Babe girl, this was what my niggaz wanted to do. Should have learned by now that I don't trick no money on no pussy. We 'bout to head up outta here anyways because we gotta come back and get dressed. So I'll see you in a little bit."

Tavares hung up the phone with Dora, called the ladies, and told them to wear something nice and to meet in the lobby at 8:45 sharp. Feeling like she was running off of fumes from only four and a half hours of sleep, Tavares decided that she was gonna get a power nap in. She had two hours and was gonna take full advantage of it.

When everyone made it to the lobby, out front was a stretch hummer waiting for them. Tavares wanted to ask questions, but Abdora beat her to the punch by saying, "Don't even waste your breath. Just get in the limo." She giggled and did as she was told.

Upon entering the limo, the large group was welcomed by bottles of Don P and the freshest, loudest weed. Sipping and smoking made the time fly by as they rode to their destination. Tavares thought that with everyone in dresses and suits, they were for sure going to some kind of five-star restaurant, but to her surprise, when they exited the limo they were at an airfield.

"Dora, what's going on NOW?" Tavares asked.

"Don't worry about it. Just get onboard and see when we get there." Tavares's girls weren't asking no questions because they knew that whatever it was, it was going to be a good time. Abdora had already proven that he was all about showing them a good time.

One hour later the plane landed and they were at a dock in Miami. Tavares's girls and Dora's boys were chopping it up as they made their way to the huge fifty-foot yacht that was obviously waiting on them. Tavares just stood in shock, not moving.

"Are you coming?" Dora asked.

"Abdora, like really, where does it end with you? You just flew us from Atlanta to Miami and now we're getting on a yacht. This is all too much for me."

"Tavares, I told you I wanted to gift wrap the world and give it to you. You've given me the pleasure of gracing me with your presence for our birthdays, so I just wanted it to be extremely special, that's all." Tavares was fighting back her happy tears for the simple fact that she didn't want her eye makeup to run and make her look like a blue-eyed raccoon.

"Dora, everything with you is just so over the top and it's becoming a little overwhelming for me. I'm used to nice shit, but you give nice a whole new meaning."

"Well, good, because life is too short not to enjoy it, so let's get on this yacht and do the damn thing."

Aboard the yacht, Tavares decided to take a stroll alone to see just how outrageous Dora had got. Dora had a seafood buffet with lobsters, seafood casserole, king crab legs, fried shrimp, scallops, and clams, with corn on the cob, baked potatoes, and salad to go with it. There was a carving station with filet mignon, fried turkey, and ham, and there was a dessert station with every flavor of cake, cupcakes, and cookies to satisfy their sweet tooth. In the center of the dessert table was a huge, three-tiered red and silver birthday cake that had shoes and purses from all Tavares's favorite stores decorating the cake.

A bar was on each of the three levels. A DJ and a club were on the second level. Tavares was in shock to see her favorite DJ, DJ Roxbury. After turning blush red and screaming, Tavares asked, "How the hell did he get you here?"

"Man, listen," Roxbury said, "the nigga is digging you and went hard to get me here. I had a heavy rotation this weekend in Europe and he paid me what each job was going to pay me, plus he paid me for the night and covered all my expenses. You're my homie, so I know what it is with you and your man. But this nigga is a good catch, Apple." Apple just had to smile to let Roxbury know she heard him loud and clear. Making it to the third level, she found a casino, and Tavares was hoping she got lucky and won a few dollars.

She enjoyed her alone time taking in all the beauty that was around her. As she looked out at the water, she had a million thoughts running through her mind. *Damn, is this real? Where does it end with this man? How can I not fall for him, as sweet and romantic as he is? Could I ever really just walk away from Dame and all the history that we have? Don't I deserve to be treated like this?*

Dora had been looking for Tavares everywhere and finally found her on the top deck alone, overlooking the water.

"What's up, ma? You alright?"

"Yeah, I'm good, Dora. I was just having a little alone time to get my thoughts together from all the shock I was in."

"Baby girl, if you let me in your life for real, this is nothing. This is just the tip of the iceberg." Tavares loved his fine ass looks, but his personality was what drew her in more and more.

"Dora, Imma tell you, you drive a hard bargain and make it hard for a lady to not want you in her life. You even got my friends advocating for you. They're certifiably Team Dora!"

"I can dig it," Dora said. "They all know I'm a good catch, you're the only one who seems not to know."

"Dora, don't start," Tavares said, giving him the evil eye. "I know it, but you know I got a situation at home."

"Yeah, and it's a bad situation and I don't get why you don't want to walk away from it." Tavares wished she had an answer for him, but she didn't.

"Dora, I don't know, but I do know that I do dig you. I know my home life isn't perfect or even great for that matter, so to be honest I'm just going with the flow to see what happens."

"I can accept that for now. So let's get back to it. We can dance and gamble, and then I wanna feed you chocolate-dipped strawberries." Tavares just busted out into laughter.

"What?" Dora asked, not getting the joke.

"You're just too fine and too gangster to have such a romantic side," Tavares informed him. But she followed his lead and continued to enjoy their birthday.

By 5:00 a.m. everyone had stuffed their bellies, blew it down till they were just too high to smoke anymore, sipped on the best champagne, partied, and gambled the night away. Everyone was feeling good and aching to hit a bed. They were watching the sun rise above them as they exited the yacht and made it back to their private jet. It was 6:30 a.m. when they arrived at the hotel. Everyone was partied out and ready to do nothing but sleep the day away before they journeyed home the next day.

The last day in Atlanta, Tavares and Abdora spent solo. Abdora had informed both of their friends that they were on their own for the day, because after all he'd spent on the weekend, he'd earned some alone time with Tavares. They lay in bed for half the day, doing absolutely nothing except watching movies and relaxing. By the time they made it out the bed and got dressed, the sun had gone down.

"Abdora, I really don't want to do anything. Can't we just stay in and do nothing?"

"No way, babe girl. Get your ass up, put some clothes on, and let's rock and roll."

"I'm not a fan of being punked," Tavares joked. Dora kissed her on her forehead and made his way to his room to get dressed.

While Tavares and Dora were doing who knows what, their friends were doing them. They had went to Gladys Knight's Chicken and Waffles, enjoyed the Atlanta Aquarium, went to Buckhead and shopped, and were dressing to get ready to hit a few clubs.

Tavares was dressed and ready to roll when Abdora came back to her room. "My, my, my don't you look casual and sexy," Adbora said, referring to Tavares's tight, black jeans, sheer black top trimmed in pink, and her matching pink platform heels with a black and pink clutch.

"Thanks," Tavares responded. "But I would much rather be makeup-less, in my pajamas."

"Well, we can't always have what we want in life, now can we?" Abdora said sarcastically.

Abdora looked good in anything he put on, Tavares concluded. He was rocking a red, black, and grey plaid True Religion shirt, some black True Religion jeans, and some black ACG boots—and he looked dead right. *Damn, we look good together*, Tavares thought as she looked him up and down.

Tavares wanted to ask where they were going, but decided against wasting her breath. When the Bentley stopped, they were at

Capital Grill. "Hmmmm, good choice," Tavares said. It was three hours later and Tavares and Abdora hadn't touched their food. They had got so caught up in conversation and enjoying each other's company that they didn't eat. Two prime rib dinners and six drinks later, Abdora paid the $500 bill and was ready to party for real.

When Tavares looked out the window and saw they were at the strip club, she started to talk shit, but said *fuck it, anything goes with this dude,* to herself. Making their way in the club, it was as if Bobby and Whitney had just entered, the way they had all eyes on them.

"Damn, do we got a red dot on our foreheads?" Tavares asked.

"Nah, Ma, they just know fineness when they see it," joked Dora.

Getting a table and ordering a few bottles, they were greeted by stripper after stripper. Tavares turned them all down.

"If I'm going to buy you a lap dance, she has to be a badddd bitch," Tavares said.

"Who told you I want some bitch giving me a lap dance?"

"Well, then why the fuck are we here?" laughed Tavares.

"Maybe I wanted to buy you a lap dance," Abdora said, real seductive with his sexy lips curling up.

"Alright, let's make a deal. You buy me a dance and I'll buy you a dance."

Tavares and Abdora ended up have a ball, balling out at the strip club. Abdora never balled in strip clubs, but him and Tavares were having such a good time drinking, clowning, and throwing money at the big booty strippers that he ended up spending $5,000. By the time they left the club, they were good and drunk and ready to curl up in bed.

Tavares and Dora staggered to the car. Wasted was an understatement. Tavares leaned back with her eyes resting when all of a sudden her phone started blowing up with Damien's ring tone.

"What the fuck?" Tavares said out loud, not meaning to.

"Who's that, your mans and them?" Dora asked, catching a slight attitude.

"Yep, and I don't understand why he's calling this late. But I ain't answering."

Damien was in the telly with a jump-off when he a got a phone call from his man that was on business in Atlanta. His boy informed him that he was at Magic City and saw Tavares in VIP balling out with some nigga. He informed Damien that they was straight into each other, popping bottles and getting lap dances. Damien told his boy that he was mistaken, because Tavares was with her girls. The nigga said the DJ gave a shout out to the birthday shorty who had just threw a stack in the air, and Damien was convinced and on fire. He hung up and immediately left the bitch in his bed, got up and called Tavares.

Tavares not answering convinced him that his man was right. He couldn't believe that Tavares had lied and wasn't with her girls for the weekend, but was instead stunting off with some nigga. He knew she was awake because his man had said he just saw them leave. Damien called and called.

"Yo, this nigga is blowing me up, something has to be wrong," Tavares said to Dora, who really didn't give a fuck. He was blowed that Tavares's man was trying to rain on his parade and ruin a perfect night.

"Do what you gotta do," Dora said, playing his position.

"Hello," Tavares said with a slight attitude.

"Who the fuck you with, yo?"

"What?"

"Don't fucking act like you didn't just hear what the fuck I said. Who the FUCK are you with?"

"Damien, that's a fucking stupid question, so what the fuck are you talking about at 4:30 in the morning?"

"No, bitch, it ain't a stupid question, it's a fucking question I'm waiting for an answer to."

"Bitch?" Tavares asked, pulling the phone away from her ear and looking at it like Damien could see her twisted face. "Nigga, I got your bitch and I'm with my girls."

"Stop fucking lying, Tavares. My man just seen you at Magic City balling out with some nigga."

Tavares froze and was quick on her feet. "Okay, and what the fuck does that mean. I'm in Atlanta, and I was in a club, so what's the big fucking deal if I was kickin' it with a nigga? The girls got drunk a little too early and didn't want to go to the strip club so I went dolo. I caught a cab and kept it moving and he just dropped me off."

"So, you trying to tell me you just went to the strip club dolo."

"Nigga, you know I have no problem rolling by myself, so let's cut the fuckery right here and right now. Yeah, I met a nigga. Yeah, I was talking to the nigga and hanging with him. It was his birthday, and he was dolo too, so we was hanging, big fucking deal. Tell your rat ass boy he should of brought his bitch ass over and spoke and bought me a drink instead of being a rat bastard. I wasn't sucking the nigga, fucking the nigga, or being trashy, so what are you really calling me about?"

"You know what, Tavares? You got a lot of shit with you. Say what you want but you was with that nigga. My man said yawl was rocking hard body like yawl went way back like babies and pacifiers. He wasn't just all into you, feeling you and balling out on you after just meeting you in a club full of bad bitches. He had a club full of bitches to choose from and he just chose you, huh?"

"And why wouldn't he? Nigga, I had on clothes and was still the baddest bitch in there, so I think you need to check trap and get your mind right. Motherfucker, you're the trick dick in this relationship, so this not so bad "Bitch" is hanging up, and you have a nice fucking night," Tavares said, hitting end on the phone and powering it off.

Dora couldn't front. Tavares was nice with it. She didn't gel up or break under the pressure. Instead, she went hard in the paint and put her nigga in his place. Instead of touching the conversation at hand, he just drove in silence.

Tavares couldn't believe that she was all the way in Atlanta and someone that Damien knew had spotted her in the club with Abdora. Tavares really didn't give a fuck in her drunk state of mind, though. She rationalized it that she wasn't fucking Abdora, and Damien stuck his dick a little bit of everywhere, so he better leave her the hell alone. She knew Damien was going to be mad that she turned her phone off, but she didn't care. She would deal with him and his bullshit when she got back to school.

Arriving back at the hotel, Tavares was ready to come out of her shoes and her clothes.

"So is it your room or mine?" she asked on the elevator.

"Don't make a difference," Dora responded.

"I just want to smoke a blunt and get in the bed," Tavares said with her eyes half open.

"Well, since the smoke is in my room, we'll take the party to my room."

School was going good and Dora was keeping Tavares with a smile. They were keeping it on a friendly level, but growing closer and closer beyond their control. Damien was under the impression that Tavares was deep in the books, since she was mad at him for accusing her of cheating. She was, but she was getting deeper into Abdora with all the time she spent talking to him and texting him whenever she wasn't in class. Damien was free to play, so he wasn't objecting to Tavares being at school. Damien loved when his girl was home, but had no problem keeping busy while she was away, getting her school on.

Tavares was lying in her bed, studying, when her phone rang. Looking at the private number, Tavares debated picking it up. Letting it ring, Tavares kept reading her book. *I don't do private numbers*, Tavares thought, looking at the word *private caller* come across the caller ID for the third time. The person wasn't giving up.

"Hello," Tavares asked as nastily as she could.

"Is this Tavares?"

"You know it's fucking me, as many times as you done called and waited for me to pick the fuck up, so who the fuck is this and what the fuck do you want?"

"I was just calling to tell you that you ain't got to be talking to Damien all nasty."

"What, bitch? Did you really just fucking call me and tell me how the fuck I should be speaking to loose dick ass Damien. Bitch, you got life real fucked up. I talk to Damien any fucking way I want to."

"If you keep talking to my daddy like that, you're going to lose him."

"Bitch, let me tell you something, if you want him, have him, but I ain't going a motherfucking place till I'm good and goddamn ready." Tavares flipped her phone closed and was ready to give it to Damien.

"Hello," was as far as he got.

"Listen here, motherfucker. I don't know what bitch you was around talking to me, but you better keep your bitches in their place. One of your smut butt whores just called me talking about she don't like how I talk to her daddy. Damien," Tavares said, pausing to take a deep breath. "I don't got time for this bullshit."

"Tavares, that was a hoe bitch that I knocked. I was with that bitch when I was arguing with you last week. I had the phone on speaker. That bitch is retarded," Damien said, in disbelief that the hoe bitch called his girl.

"Damien, I don't give two fucks who the bitch is or where you found her, but you better keep your bitches and your side professions in order," Tavares said, hanging up the phone. *I'm way the fuck in school and still going through this bullshit,* Tavares thought, thinking fuck the books and pulling out her stash of weed. Drama with Damien was so tired and played that the love she had for him was fading with each passing day.

~ CHAPTER 14 ~

Love complicates everything.

It was midterms already. Tavares had been deep in the books, taking test after test, and she wanted to fly home for the weekend, so she came out of class and immediately flipped her phone on and called Damien.

"What's up, baby?" he answered.

"Ain't shit. I just got out of class. I been taking tests all week. I'm glad that I have no classes on Fridays, because the last four days have been hectic."

"Well, it'll be over in less than six months."

"I know, right," Tavares said, ready for it to be over right now. "I wanna come home for the weekend, can you get me a ticket?"

"I can get you a ticket baby, but I gotta go out of town. I'm leaving in the morning, gotta go to Miami to take care of some business."

Damien had business, alright. He was flying down to Miami for the day to see his bad, exotic Miami sensation. She was past bad and had a head game that was grade A, so he didn't mind bringing his girl home, but he was still going to Miami.

"Ahh, damn, if you aren't going to be home, I might as well wait and come next weekend."

"I don't care if you come home both weekends."

"Nah, I'll just wait until next weekend. Maybe me and Asia will get into something. Maybe we'll go to the outlets and shop."

"Alright, well I'll get you a ticket today to come home next weekend."

"That's fine," Tavares said.

"I'll text you the information once I've booked it."

"Okay, love you," Tavares said and hung up.

Tavares was in her car, bumping to her mix CD that was currently playing Keyshia Cole's "Trust." Tavares was ready to get home and peel off her clothes and relax. School wasn't hard for Tavares, but studying and doing the work had become a bore and a pain. She decided that she was just gonna go shopping over the weekend and do some school work. Damien was off and running, so why not. Tavares was just about home when her phone interrupted her thoughts.

"Hello?"

"What's up?" Dora asked harshly.

"Damn, is that hostility I hear in your voice?" Tavares asked, trying to hold back her laughter.

"Why ain't I heard from you in three days?" Dora barked.

"Do we have an agreement for me to check in every day?" Tavares said, being smart but only playing.

"Nah, but I can draw one up if that's what you need to get your mind right and call me every day."

"Hey, do what you gotta do," Tavares said, not backing down. "I been crazy busy with school, taking tests, and writing papers. You know I wait till the last minute to do everything."

"Tavares, please, it takes thirty seconds to pick up the phone."

"Ahh, who's mad?" Tavares said, taunting Dora.

"Mad, nah, ma, too gangster for that soft bullshit, but I don't appreciate not hearing from you. I think you should make it up to me."

"Ahh, now you're milking it."

"You tried to play me the last three days by not calling me. Now you need to make it up to me."

"Okay, fine, what do you want?" Tavares asked, feeding into his already thought-out trap.

"How about you meet me in New York in a few hours?" Dora said, real mysteriously.

"Oh, hell no!" Tavares yelled. That's asking a lot. How you want me to just fly to New York to see you. Alone?"

"Yeah, why not?"

"You know me, and you do not do visitation alone."

"Damn, you act like a nigga is going to hurt you if you come without your friends or some shit."

"Not even," Tavares sucked her teeth. "It's harmless when we party as a group, but we might get into too much trouble if we're together just me and you," Tavares laughed. She wasn't even trying to set herself up for failure.

Dora knew that she might say no, so he had a way to soften the deal.

"How about you bring one of your girls? I'll bring one of mans and we can just all hang out together."

"Hmmmm," Tavares said, taking a deep sigh. "I don't know."

"Come on, why not? You don't have classes on Fridays or Mondays. Stop being all scared and come see me." Tavares liked that he knew her schedule."What the fuck else are you doing? Not a goddamn thing, so cut the bullshit and come fuck with your boy for the weekend," Abdora said, real sexy and demanding. "Yawl can fly back Monday."

Tavares surprised Dora and gave him no headache. She simply said fine.

"Oh my god, did you just say fine and not give me a fight?" Abdora had to look at the phone to make sure he'd heard correctly.

"Yes, I did. Because you're right, what the hell else am I doing?"

"Your tickets will be at Delta, what's your homegirl's name?"

"Asia Caviet."

"Alright, well everything will be set. Just get to the airport when I call you back with the times."

Tavares headed back to her apartment to go pack her bags. Pulling up to her two-bedroom townhouse-style condo, she knew that she had to pack fast. Tavares screeched in the parking lot and rushed in the house.

"Other Half!" Tavares walked in screaming.

"Damn hoe, why you yelling? I'm upstairs in my room."

Racing to the top of the stairs, Tavares dashed into Asia's black and gray decorated room that had pictures everywhere of Asia living life, balling out.

"Yo, bitch, I got a dilemma. I'm going to see my homeboy in the city." Asia's eyes brightened and her pretty yellow cake-batter colored skin started to turn red.

Hopping up, Asia screamed, "Hoe, is you crazy?" in her native New Orleans accent. "You ain't never cheated on Dame, not in the three years we been in school. You're on some other shit, bitch. That nigga is fucking you up in the game. Homeboy is weakening you every time you talk to him," Asia laughed.

"I know, but we ain't fucking."

"Not yet," Asia snickered.

"Shut the fuck up and listen, bitch. It's not cheating, we're just hanging out innocently. Plus, you're going to come with me."

Asia looked blankly at Tavares. "Bitch, you wanna do some really daredevil shit, and then you want me to take the nosedive with you? Hoe, I got mad engineering homework and a test to study for Tuesday. I ain't got time to fool with you."

"You can study on the plane. We'll be back early Monday, so you'll be good."

"I don't have money to just go ball out. I paid my half of the bills for the house and all my credit cards. I got dough but not to just ball outta control. My parents aren't depositing any money into my account until Monday."

"You don't need no money."

"Yes, I do need money."

"Dora is paying for everything. And plus you if you need money I got you. I'll get it from Damien."

"What the fuck you mean that you're going to get it from Damien? That's some fucked up shit."

"Hey, ask no questions, and I'll tell you no lies. You need money, so I got you. You love to shop, so just pack your shit and let's go. He got a friend for you and everything."

"Girl, I'm not getting put on with no flunky ass friend."

"First, I thought you weren't going. Now you ain't getting stuck with no flunky ass friend. Imma need you to make your fucking mind up."

Seeing her desperation, Asia knew she was packing her bags and homework with no notice to head on a weekend adventure with her road dog. "Bitch, all I know is you owe me. Not only does your ass owe me, you owe me big."

"Thanks, Asia, I love you more than you know right now. He knows that you're coming and is getting you a room and everything, and no, it doesn't have nothing do with his friend."

"Oh, as long as flunky boy knows it ain't that type of party we're good," Asia said, walking to her closet, ready to get divalicious.

With a natural model frame, standing at five-feet-eleven, Asia was an Amazon Goddess. She had golden yellow skin, long, thick, wavy jet black hair, hazel eyes, and a sexiness that represented mixed women everywhere. Asia was Cuban, Guianese, and black and was drop-dead beautiful.

As Tavares and Asia headed to the airport, they laughed and reminisced over the last three years of school.

"Girl, shit was crazy the last three years, but we had a good time," Asia said. "I'm so going to miss you. Remember when we first got down here, we was like having a total culture shock like a motherfucker? You were from Boston and I was from New Orleans and Savannah was like a small little hick town to us."

"Asia, I didn't even believe I could make it here four years in this small ass town, but we did. This shit down here ain't nothing like up top. But I can't lie, we did have some good times. After we hooked up, we def put this school on the map," joked Tavares.

"The end was when our New York Crew came through and fucked with us like they little sisters," Asia said thinking about all the haters they accumulated because of the NYC niggaz.

"Shit ain't the same without them," Tavares said, missing her friends who had graduated a semester ago. Tavares and her girls were like the first ladies of their crew.

"All the bitches on campus were giving up pussy trying to get in with them like us and that shit didn't even work." Tavares laughed at all the hoes that got dragged through the mud trying to use their pussy to get in where they fit in.

"Tavares, the best time we had down here so far was the homecoming party, sophomore year. That's when all our peeps were here. Dame and his niggaz, your girls from home, my girls from home, niggaz from New York, the Chi town boys, every hood nigga on campus, the groupie crews, and even the lames. I really didn't think that the whole campus would come, but they did," Asia said with pride and sass.

"That shit was the party of the year," Tavares bragged. Tavares and Asia always gave parties that started out with good intentions but just got out of control with so many people showing up because of all the free liquor and food they never ran out of.

"Yo, Asia but remember when Pootie, repping the Lower East Side, was going to really stab Dre at the party that year? Like he wasn't his man and shit," Tavares laughed.

"That was exactly why we said no gambling," Asia said, remembering how their argument escalated so bad over $100 that they shut the party down.

"Asia, stop, you know niggaz don't listen to us."

"Of course not, they just rather kill each other over a punk $100," Asia said, frowning her face at her hard headed homeboys.

"Asia, you must admit, we did have some crazy times, but at the end of the day, they were all good times." Laughing, the girls pulled up to the airport, ready to park in long-term parking and head to the city and see what was to come in the city that never slept.

Approaching the counter to check their luggage and get their tickets, Tavares made a mental note to call Damien no sooner than she was done. Not really trying to answer her phone for the weekend, Tavares had to tie up some loose ends.

"Hello, Sweetness," Dame answered, hearing Tavares's ring tone of "Monica's Angel of Mine."

"Hi, baby. What are you doing?"

"Shit, out here with niggaz, blowing it down. It's still nice and shit in late October, so we're sucking up the good weather."

"Hmm…ain't that cute," Tavares sassed. "Too bad I don't know nothing about that. Savannah is nice year round," Tavares teased. "Baby, I was just calling to tell you that me and Asia're going to Jacksonville for the weekend. We're going to do a spa day, gonna do some shopping, eat good, and just relax."

"And I guess I'm funding your half of this weekend adventure?" Dame said, knowing the answer.

"Nope."

"Excuse me? Is there a bad connection or something?"

"No, smartass, there isn't. I paid for it myself."

"That's what's up. In that case, have a ball."

"Actually I figured when I told you I picked up the tab that you would give me some spending money for being a good sport and paying for it myself."

"Yo, Apple, you're nuts. You kill me how you try to word shit," Damien laughed. "You make it sound like you did something major by paying for your own damn weekend getaway. But I'll deposit a grand in your account."

"Appreciate you, Baby Cakes."

"I know you do," Dame said, giving himself way too much credit. "Well, enjoy your weekend. I'll call you Sunday."

Damn, that was a burden lifted, Tavares thought. She didn't know why she was so worried. "My boo really knows that I won't cheat," Tavares said, not knowing why she thought it would be hard to say she was going away for the weekend. She did it all the time. Only this time, she had altered her destination.

Stepping on the plane, they made their way to their first class seats for their 6 p.m. departure. In the air, Asia realized that these tickets had to be a grip as she sat in the overly large seat.

"Tavares, how much did these tickets cost him? Not only did he buy them today, they're fucking first class seats."

"I don't know," Tavares said, real nonchalant, in a way that let it be known it hadn't even crossed her mind. With Dora, money was never an issue, so she didn't worry about it. "He said our tickets would be at the airport and there would be a car there to pick us up when we touch down."

"A car? What the fuck do you mean a car? He isn't coming to get us?"

"No, he said he would meet us later at the hotel."

"Tavares, what kind of nigga sends a car for you? Any nigga I ever went to see outta town came to get me. I was there to see him, so he came to get me. Not one of his friends, but him. So he's going to have one of his niggaz just come pick up us and drop us off? Bitch, this nigga better not leave us stuck in no hotel all weekend."

"He's not like that. Just shut up, enjoy the flight, and drink the free Rémy."

Three hours later, Tavares and Asia landed at the airport. Stepping off the plane, they could feel the crisp October night air.

"Damn, it's kind of brisk out there," said Asia, who truly wasn't used to the cold. Asia lived in New Orleans her whole life and only visited warm states. Going downstairs to get their luggage, Asia and Tavares approached the luggage area of JFK airport and saw a dude holding a sign that read, *Tavares and Homegirl.* What was even odder was that he was a big, burly black dude with too much belly, rocking a blazer and blue jeans, with Timberlands.

"This cannot be possible," Asia said. "Please tell me they don't got a hood dude with a hood sign."

"Girl, yes they do," Tavares said, still in disbelief. Together they fell out laughing.

Approaching, Tavares said, "Hi, I think you're looking for me."

"Yeah, and I'm the homegirl," Asia sassed as she rolled eyes at him and his sign.

"What it do, ladies? I'm your driver. Let's grab your luggage, so we can shake and bake." The ladies just laughed and said okay. He grabbed their luggage and they made their way outside.

They were even more in shock at what he was about to transport them in. Following him to a long, black Escalade truck limousine, they looked at each other.

"Yeah, right. He is NOT driving this," Asia said.

Tavares just looked and said, "Wow, this is crazy."

As he opened the door for them, they stepped in the limousine, totally surprised. There was some fireweed that was fresh and potent, various rolling materials, waters, juices, sodas, and bottles of Moet. Tavares and Asia got comfy, rolled up, and sipped all the way to the hotel.

"This is what I'm talking about," Asia said, stretched out with her legs crossed and a wine glass in her hand, looking real Hollywood.

The limo stopped and the ladies were high and buzzed, not ready to get out. Opening the door, Tavares and Asia were welcomed to the fast-paced Times Square area of New York. The whole city was lit up. People were talking fast, moving fast, trying to squeeze through each other on the crowded sidewalks. Everything about New York always seemed full of life and fast at all times. Asia was in awe as she came to New York for the second time.

"Damn, I thought Bourbon Street got crazy, but this is insane. Look at all these damn people in one place."

"Girl, and it's like this every damn day of the year. New York is the craziest place to live in the United States. I could never fuck with New York other than to visit," Tavares said as they entered the hotel. "Damn, I know we smell like weed," Tavares said, hating to smoke and then go in public.

"Who gives a fuck?" Asia asked, not giving two fucks who knew that she had just blew two blunts of some fire ass weed. Before they moved, Tavares sprayed herself down with some Gucci Rush perfume and did the same to Asia.

Making their way to the forty-fifth floor of the Marriott Grand Marquis, Tavares and Asia went to their respective rooms. Getting dressed, Tavares called Asia.

"Yo, hooker, you ready to roll?"

"Actually, if you don't mind, you can roll dolo. My cousin who lives in Detroit just posted on her Facebook that she's here for a conference, so me and her are going to hook up. I know you ain't mad because double dating ain't never been our swagger anyways."

"Yeah, it's cool."

"I'll get up with flunky boy tomorrow."

"Sounds like a plan to me," Tavares said, not really wanting to be alone with Dora.

"Behave and don't do nothing I would do," Asia laughed before hanging up.

Forty-five minutes later, Tavares was walking downstairs, not knowing what to expect of the evening. Tavares took one last look in the long double mirrors next to the elevator. Seeing her jeans that were hugging her tight, Tavares knew she was looking past juicy thick. Her butt was ridiculous in Lucky Brand jeans. The red silk, off-the-shoulder shirt looked good as it showed off her cleavage a little bit. Her Chanel earrings and five-carat diamond ring sparkled just right. Tavares was hot to death, stepping in her red thigh-high boots. Exiting the hotel, Tavares saw the man of the hour looking way too luscious for his own good. His honey skin was perfect against his chosen color attire. Rocking a chocolate brown leather bomber jacket and chocolate suede Timberland boots so tough, the rest of his outfit was unimportant.

"Damn, little mama, that's how you doing it?" Dora said, admiring the sexy but classy getup.

"Doing what?" Tavares said, playfully nudging him.

"You gonna hop on?" he asked Tavares, who was looking at the motorcycle like he was crazy.

"I know you don't think I'm getting on the back of that bike. I love my life, and I don't know how well you operate that thing," Tavares said, rolling her eyes seductively.

"Do you think I would put you on the back of this bike if I didn't know what I was doing? Girl, don't play with me. Put that helmet on, climb on the bike, and put your big ass in the air so we can ride." Tavares was hesitant, but she did as she was told after giving him a look that let him know he won for now.

After taking a ride through the city, they parked the bike. They took a walk through Central Park, had dinner at Justin's, and walked up and down the busy streets of New York, shopping.

"Genius, when you we decided to start shopping, did you forget that we're on a motorcycle?"

"Do I look like a fucking idiot to you?" Dora said, quick on his feet. "We can either both take a cab and I'll come back for my bike, or I can take the bike and put you in a cab, smart ass."

"Whatever," Tavares said, heading in Neiman's. "I just want to get some makeup and we can be done."

"Get what ever you want, Ma. What my nigga T.I. say, 'Ma, you can have what ever you want. It ain't tricking if you got it,'" Dora sang on key and burst out laughing. "I definitely got it, but it's far from tricking because I ain't no tricking, wet dick ass nigga, ma. I like you and we're having fun, so buy the makeup counter out if you want."

"I know you got it, but I don't want you spending all this dough on me. It makes me uncomfortable that you spend so much on me."

"Man, listen, Ma. I never over overextend or overspend. Dudes be wishing they could live the life that them niggaz in the industry rap about, but I do live that life. I'm that nigga, mama. I'm not bragging by far, 'cause that ain't my style. But what I'm saying to you is that we can do whatever, however, because money ain't an object for me. I worked hard to be able to say them words, so let me worry about the spending and you worry about smiling." Tavares just looked at him with eyes that said she hated being defeated.

They made their way to the makeup department, where Dora didn't wait for Tavares, and he started picking out stuff for her. He picked out everything from brushes and toners and cleansers to multiple colored lip glosses and eye shadow. It seemed like he picked out a little of everything. He went hard with the bright pinks and blues and green eye shadow. Tavares was tickled pink watching this gangster ass nigga pick out makeup for her.

"Excuse me, miss, can you please get five of those fire engine red lipsticks, three cherry red nail polishes, and three mascaras, and then you can ring us up?"

"Yo, after this you ain't buying me nothing else. Nothing fucking else."

"Why not?" Dora asked, confused, thinking all chicks liked gifts. Dora wasn't too sure though, because he wasn't in the habit of giving them. But last time he was in the loop, it was the in thing to buy a chick you liked presents. "How the fuck you going to tell me how to spend my money and shit, like you worked for it? Shit don't work like that, Ma."

Tavares didn't care what he said, he wasn't buying her nothing else. "Who in the hell comes to MAC and gets probably like $2,500 in makeup? I ain't accepting shit else, so don't waste your money," Tavares said, walking away from the MAC Counter.

Dora paid for Tavares's $2,650 worth of MAC makeup and was blown away that she could tally her makeup that close. Dora wasn't stunting Tavares. He took his time and even stopped to snatch her some Dior Addict and J'Adore perfume before he headed out of Neiman's.

Dora headed directly across the street into the Gucci Store.

"Damn, ain't you done shopping yet?" Tavares said, thinking she never thought she would say those words. Tavares loved shopping, but her four-inch heels weren't made for shopping. She had done enough walking and shopping in her heels for the night.

"I'm done after this," Dora said. "Go look around. I want to snatch a purse for one of my shorties. I like to pick out my own presents for my shorties," he embellished, referring to her shopping for Majors.

"What the fuck?" and then Tavares stopped short and chuckled. "Is that right, Pimpin?" Tavares said, with a long gaze from head to toe. "Well, in that case let me help you out. That way, she's sure to love it." Tavares wasn't even entertaining him.

"I got it," Dora said, leaving her standing there in the middle of the store as he left to do his own thing.

Tavares was a shoe freak, so she hit their shoe department. It was nothing for her to drop $500 or more on a pair of shoes; she loved Jimmy Choo, Gucci, Christian Dior, and Prada. She never forgot where she was from, though. Tavares still loved Kenneth Cole, Charles David, Carlos Santana, Anne Klein, BCBG, and anything else that was cute and a good shoe. If she liked them, she bought them, was her motto. Tavares was feeling the bowling ball sneakers that she had in her hand, though. *Five hundred thirty-five dollars isn't too bad*, Tavares thought, staring at the sneakers. Dora broke her trance as she debated whether to buy them or not.

"Tell the lady to bring your size."

"I thought you were getting a purse for one of your chicks, what happened?"

"I am, she's ringing it up now. That's why I told you to get those, if you want them."

"Nope."

"What you mean, nope? You got them in your hand, so you must like them. Get them shits and come on. Get off that bullshit, Ma."

"Alright," Tavares said, knowing that they would have been there all day, debating back and forth, if she didn't agree. "I'll meet you at the counter," she said, waving the Asian sales lady down. "Hi, can I please have both colors in a size 6 and a 13? Here's my American Express, please ring them up at the other register in the corner before my friend sees you."

"No problem," the lady said, winking.

Dora had been at the counter for ten minutes when he went to find out what was taking Tavares so long.

"Damn, baby girl, where is she with your sneakers?"

"She didn't have my size in one color, so she had to go back and check in the other color."

"Well, she needs to hurry up."

"Excuse me, ma'am. Here are your shoes. Can you just sign the receipt, please?"

Looking at Tavares, Dora shook his head, chuckled, and said, "You ain't shit."

"Call it what you want, but hold these because they belong to you." Tavares signed the receipt and turned her attention back to Dora. "I can buy my own stuff. Shit, I was even nice enough to buy you

~ 268 ~

something, so be glad you got something in the process. You been buying us stuff all night." Tavares paused and smiled. "I told you I wasn't accepting shit else and I meant that. Now, go pay for your broad's bag and I'll meet you out front," Tavares said, heading toward the door.

Dora just shook his head, looked at the back of her head; he wanted her for keeps. She was too much, and especially too much like him.

She was meant to be his queen and he knew it. As long as he ripped and ran, no one chick had made him want to give the game up—Tavares did, though. Sucker for love ass nigga was past the last thing he was. He stayed with a chick chasing him, not the other way around. Chicks went hard to get at Dora, but he wasn't really interested in settling down with any of them. He hollered at them when he felt like it, but kept it moving most of the time. He was still sliding with Jade on the strength of pussy, but she wasn't who he was trying to wife. Tavares had him ready to give up all the freelance pussy, and he hadn't even touched hers yet. *Yeah, it's serious*, Dora thought as the door shut behind her big butt, long hair, sexy heels, and tight jeans.

Tavares hopped in a cab with their gazillion bags while Dora hopped on his bike. Tavares sat in the back of the cab surrounded by tons of shopping bags and thought about how much fun she had with Dora. She loved that they always had a ball together and that he kept her laughing when they were on the phone. Never was there any bullshit between them, and that was to be appreciated with all that she went through with Damien. Tavares was trying so hard to not fall for him, but he was making it real hard. Tavares just fell back and enjoyed the cab ride. Pulling up to the hotel, she found Dora leaned up on his big boy toy looking sexy to death.

"Damn, how did you get here so fast?" Tavares said getting out of the cab with all of the bags.

"I was bobbing and weaving through traffic. I'm on a bike, in case you forgot."

"Don't get smart, just take these bags and carry them upstairs."

"What the fuck I look like, Mr. Belvedere or something?"

Tavares laughed so hard that she cried, because that was her show when she was a kid.

"Naw, you're much cuter then Mr. Belvedere, so get to decorating your hands with these bags." Dora just cut his eyes at Tavares and picked all the bags up. Strolling through the hotel lobby with over twenty bags, they made their way to the elevator, upstairs.

Entering the suite, Dora went to the living room and dropped the bags. Taking a seat at the desk, he started twisting up a blunt.

"Okay then, who wastes no time with the drugs?"

Dora looked at her like she had lost her mind, "Drugs? I don't do drugs, Ma, I smoke and blow hella good weed. And weed ain't no motherfucking drug. It's from the earth."

"Sweetheart, say what you want, it's drugs," Tavares sang. "It's cool, though," Tavares said. "Me and my friends smoke drugs, weed that is, but we definitely call them what they are: drugs," she said sarcastically.

"Ma, you is fucking crazy, but I fucks with you, word I do."

"I can dig it, Mr. Hella Handsome. You make that happen, and I'm going to take a quick shower."

"The blunt waits on no man," Dora said, letting it be known that he was sparking it.

"Whatever," Tavares said, knowing that there was more weed, so she wasn't sweating that one blunt.

"Hurry up," Dora called behind Tavares as she headed down the hall to the bathroom.

Tavares showered while Dora blew the blunt to the face and watched TV. Getting out of the shower, Tavares dressed and was so ready to smoke and relax. Knowing there was a blunt waiting, she went into the living room ready to blow it down. Seeing no blunt in sight, Tavares started looking around like she was lost.

"Uhh, excuse me, where's the blunt?"

"I smoked it. Didn't I tell you the blunt waits for no man?"

Tavares sucked her teeth with a look that said, "you gotta be kidding me." "Okay, well since the blunt couldn't wait for me, then you need to twist up another one."

"Yeah, is that what I need to do?" Dora asked, giving a snide chuckle.

"Yeah, you do. I want to smoke, just like you smoked when I was in the shower. So yeah, I would appreciate it if you would get that cracking." Dora just laughed at her smart, sassy mouth, snatched the haze off the table and rolled another blunt.

"Your mouth's out of control, lil mama."

"Is it really?" Tavares asked, clueless.

"Yeah it is," Dora said, giving Tavares some playful attitude.

"Well, I've heard your mouth and you're the last one who should be talking."

"There's a difference," said Dora, "I get smart when I need to be, you get smart just because."

"Same, difference," Tavares said, taking the blunt out of his hand and sparking it as she sat on the couch next to him. Instead of hitting the streets, they opted for a lower key sort of scenery. They watched movies, ordered room service, smoked, talked, and laughed the night away.

Waking up to the phone ringing, Dora picked up because Tavares wasn't budging.

"Hello?" he asked, groggy but still sexy.

"Can I speak to Tavares?" the female hesitantly asked on the other end of the hotel phone.

"She's sleeping. You want me to wake her up?" Dora asked with his eyes only half-open.

"Naw, don't bother. This is Asia. Thanks for the ticket."

"You're welcome. It's nothing. I'm just glad that you could convince Tavares to come see me."

"No doubt," Asia replied. "Just tell her I went to see my cousin again. We haven't seen each other in three years and I'm sure you want the time with Apple all to yourself anyways. So I'm going to spend the day with my cousin and everyone's happy. Tell her I'll call her tonight when I get back."

"Will do, shorty," Dora said, laying the phone back on the cradle and closing his eyes, grateful for how the weekend played out. Asia had been his blessing in disguise to get Tavares to New York to see him, and he'd even got alone time with her, for once. Tavares was knocked out. Dora rolled over and curled back under her body that fit his so perfectly and drifted back off to sleep.

~ CHAPTER 15 ~

I know a GANGSTER when I see one.

Tavares and Dora both rolled over at the same time. Always playing and talking shit, Dora said, "Stop trying be like me, punk."

"Whatever," Tavares laughed. "Damn, have we been asleep all day?" she asked, still not really wanting to get up.

"Yeah. Your girl Asia called earlier," Dora said, relaying Asia's message.

"Even better," Tavares said. "Now I don't have to rush to get up to do no double date bullshit."

"How can it be double dating when you don't call what we do dating?"

"Here you go," Tavares sucked her teeth, knowing he'd caught her on that one. "Leave me the hell alone, you know what I meant, you goddamn trouble maker."

"I will leave you alone," Dora said, getting up out the bed, as bad as his body wanted to stay. "You lay up and relax for a little while. Keep my spot warm," he said as he puckered his luscious lips in the air. "I gotta go get dressed. I'll be back in two hours, so be ready," he said, slipping on his clothes and Timbs.

"Sure will," Tavares said, snuggled under the covers, not wanting to move. Dora came back out of the bathroom with a fresh mouth and a toothpick between his lips. He looked good even though he was dressed like yesterday from head to toe.

"Where are we going?" Tavares asked, shifting her body on her side.

"Does it matter?" Dora responded as he stood in the doorway, looking more scrumptious than he knew. The brown bomber jacket, tan cashmere sweater, and suede brown Timbs was doing things to Tavares. "Don't answer a question with a question," she sassed him.

"You do it all the time," Dora said, looking at her out the corner of his sexy, sleepy eyes with his lips turned up and the toothpick still in place.

"Well, I need to have an idea of what we're doing so that I know what to put on."

"We're going to paint the town. Sexy and classy is what I like. So you use that to put together an outfit." Dora pulled his toothpick out his mouth briefly to kiss Tavares on her forehead. He headed to his house to get changed and prepare for the evening.

A few hours later, Tavares and Dora entered a comedy show to see Kat Williams.

"Damn, it's packed in here," Tavares said as they walked down to the front row of the auditorium.

"I think you're working that dress a little too much," Dora said, walking behind Tavares, looking at her snug money-green form fitting wrap dress that was hugging her butt perfectly. Tall chocolate knee boots gave the dress a sexy look as she strutted.

"Thanks," Tavares said, recognizing the compliment. Taking a seat, they never stopped laughing from the time Kat came on stage. Kat Williams looked down and saw the cute couple and went to town on them.

"I know a gangster when I see one, and that toothpick in the corner of your mouth says, 'nigga, Imma gangster and what.' You probably got your gun up in the motherfucker waiting to blast a nigga and shit. Nigga, I'm trying to get paid, don't shut this shit down, you fucking hear me? You got all that ice on like you got Jacob the Jeweler on speed dial, let a nigga get a loan."

The audience and Tavares were cracking up.

"Damn, that's your girl, super gangster," he said, looking at the beautiful lady seated next to his victim.

Dora just smirked and let Kat do his thing, because he was a fan and knew it was it all in good fun. "Nah…" Dora answered him.

"Well then, nigga, you need to get your pippin' up and gangster down and get her blue-eyed ass on your team," he said as if he was schooling the brother. "Her blue-eyed ass is what we call a bottom bitch. Did you hear me, pimpin', a bottom bitch? You see she got on money green, with blue eyes and blond hair, so trust me, she's bottom bitch material. Let her play #1 on your team and your money will be busting out the seams." Everyone fell to tears, including Tavares and Dora.

After two hours, as Dora and Tavares exited the auditorium, you would have thought that Dora had just come off the stage, the way people were stopping and talking to him. Just as Tavares thought they were going to make it to the door, Dora stopped to talk again for the tenth time. Tavares rolled her eyes and stood in her four-inch boots that were killing her feet.

"I'm going to wait for you over there, Mr. Important," Tavares said, walking toward a long row of benches. Having to look like you weren't in pain and being bubbly at the same time wasn't easy. *It definitely paid to look good, even though it hurt*, Tavares thought, taking a seat.

"What's good?" Dora said, giving the Dipset Harlem looking nigga dap.

"Ain't shit, my nigga. Just kickin' it in the city for the weekend for my shorty's birthday. Speaking of shorties, yours is bad," the young dude said, spinning the conversation. "Where did you find her?" the youngen asked, looking in Tavares's direction and loving what he saw.

"Pick your mouth up, lil nigga," Dora said to his man who was all over Tavares. "She's bad, right? I'm trying to make her mine but she be playing. If she knew better she would do better," Dora laughed. "She got a man and shit who got her open and you know hating ain't in my blood. I'm trying to get her though. But right now, shit ain't looking too promising," Abdora said, keeping it real.

"Damn, now I see why Kat was on yawl. I was wondering who the super gangster and blue-eyed bottom bitch were," the dude laughed. "Shit, I would make her my bottom bitch faster than she knew," the light-skinned, scruffy-faced, cute dude said, shaking his head and rubbing his cheek at the same time. "You better get that," the youngen said before giving Dora dap.

"Nigga, you ain't gotta be no stranger when you slide to Boston either. I know you dipping and dodging and shit, but damn nigga, holler at me."

"I know, my nigga. I just be moving fast, with little time to spare. So I don't be hitting you up less need be. But I swear the next time I'm out there we gonna get up," Dora assured his homeboy. "That's my word, my nigga. But yo, Shorty's looking mad and shit, so let me go," Dora said, giving his homeboy dap.

Damien was fresh home and his phone was blowing up. Looking at the very familiar number, Damien knew he would be going back outside even though he had no desire to. He was drained from his fun in the sun rendezvous, but never did he turn down dough. Damien made his way up Warren Street, through Grove Hall, down Washington Street to Codman Square.

Handling his BI in a matter of minutes, he was about to go home when Dollar called. "What's good, Dollar?"

"I need to you to come to my house. It ain't no money here, but I got a few dollars."

"Alright, give me thirty minutes and I'll be there." Damien hung up and made his way down past Ashmont Station to head to the highway. He arrived at Dollar's and made his way upstairs, out in the brisk air. Damien gave Dollar her drugs and he looked at her all cleaned up.

"Yo, Dollar, you look good all cleaned up and shit. You shoulda made you some babies because they would be pretty as a motherfucker. I bet if you had some girls they'd be the baddest broads on the block," Dame laughed.

"Dame, in the last eleven years you've known me, have you ever heard me talk about kids or any family for that matter? I only have me," Dollar said, extending a hundred dollar bill to Damien.

"Damn, Dollar, you got real loud with a nigga. It wasn't that serious, so Imma let that shit go, but don't you ever fucking talk to me like that again," Damien said, looking Dollar straight in the eye as he snatched the money. Dollar just hung her head and eyes to the floor until Damien walked past her and out the door.

Dollar felt fucked up for going off on Damien. She was aggravated like she always got whenever anyone mentioned having kids or talked about kids. Dollar had no kids and that broke her heart every day. She had wanted so badly to be a mother and it didn't happen for her, so kids were a sore spot. Dollar's pain was deep and she did what she did best. She pulled out her homemade crack pipe, loaded it up, and smoked till she couldn't smoke anymore.

"Damn, must you stop and talk to everyone?" Tavares asked, definitely tired of working the crowd like they were the president and his wife.

"Damn, what you want me to do, just walk by people and not speak?"

"No, you just need not to know so many damn people," Tavares said, getting in the car. "At that, we ain't even in Jersey, so how do you know so many damn people?"

"I'm international, ma, I got niggaz everywhere."

"Who was that you was talking to?"

"Why, you like him or something?" Tavares sucked her teeth so loud that she didn't feel the need to even entertain the comment.

"Dora, are you for real? Please get it together. I asked because yawl were talking about me." By the confidence in her words you would have thought she was standing there and heard them. "Don't look all crazy and stuck on stupid. I'm good at reading body language and I was definitely the topic of conversation," Tavares said, winking her eye. "It's cool, though."

"Whatever, Miss Lady! You swear you be knowing shit. You were not the topic of our conversation," Dora said. "That's my man Holly Hood. He's a good little thoroughbred nigga. Pretty boy thug, getting money, stacking dough, busting them thangs, and fucking mad bitches."

"Ain't that what every nigga in the hood is doing?" Tavares asked, unimpressed. That was every hood nigga's story. And she was tired of that being all they did.

"Holly Hood ain't like other lil hood niggaz, he got a brain that's going to carry him out of that hood."

Tavares and Dora spent the weekend talking, laughing, joking, and partying hard. Tavares didn't know why it was a never-ending fun time when they were together. He made her laugh and smile and it was priceless to her. What was good about what they had was that they were friends, even though they knew deep down that the other one wanted more.

They kept it real. Tavares told him about Damien, he spoke about chicks he messed with. He gave Tavares her pocketbook and told her that he would never buy no chick shit while he was with her, but he wasn't going to front like he didn't have chicks. Tavares loved that he kept it so real that it hurt.

Tavares was glad that she brought Asia, but was even happier that she ended up getting stuck alone with Dora for most of the weekend. Asia joined them for breakfast Monday morning before their flight. Asia had to admit that Dora was past fine and definitely had to be running a swagger factory. His swagger was so mean that he had more than enough to share with niggaz who were on the waiting list trying to find some swagger.

"So Dora, what are your intentions with Tavares?"

"Oh my God, you don't have to answer that," Tavares said, staring at Asia with big, bright eyes.

~ 279 ~

"Nah, Ma, it's cool. My intentions with Tavares are to grow from friends to lovers, show her the world, give her some babies and make her mine. But all those intentions need her to be on board, so until then, my intentions are to hang out and be friends. Now, are you beautiful ladies ready to get to the airport so you can get your school on?"

After stuffing themselves with grits, salmon cakes, waffles, and eggs, the ladies were stuffed and ready for their journey back to school.

Arriving home, Tavares was exhausted. She brought her luggage upstairs and called Damien.

"What's up, Mumma?" he answered.

"Nothing, we just got back so I was calling to let you know I made it home safely." Tavares plopped on her bed, exhausted from such a good time.

"That's what's up, did yawl have fun?"

"We had a ball," Tavares said, even though they were thinking of two different yawls. "Yeah, we went shopping, ate, went to see Kat Williams, and partied hard."

"Kat Williams was in Jacksonville this weekend?" Damien asked.

"Ohh, no, not Kat Williams, the little pimp dude. She's this big, black country chick that's funny as fuck," Tavares said, kicking herself for almost giving herself away. *Fuck, fuck, fuck,* she cursed herself in her mind.

"Boo, she reminds you of a more fucked up, raunchy version of Samore and Mo'nique put together."

"That's what's up, Boo. Because I was about to say, how the fuck you see Kat Williams unless you was in NY? Niggaz was trying to go to that shit but I had to go to Miami."

"How was your business down in Miami?" Tavares asked, flipping the conversation as fast as she could. Damien had a flashback and got hard thinking about his Brazilian and black sensation that he tore down all day Saturday.

He had met his Brazilian wonder when he was on business with Holton a year back.

"It went good, baby. I sealed and closed the deal," Damien said, knowing that was exactly what he'd done.

"That was a fast trip."

"Yeah, I was in and out. No need to hang and linger around when the business is all taken care of."

"But you love Miami."

"Yeah, baby, I do, but it was business, not pleasure. So what are you about to do now?" Damien asked as he headed from one fiend's house to the next, getting money.

"I'm about to relax. I got some homework to bang out for tomorrow. Other than that I'm not doing nothing for the rest of the night."

"Alright, well get some rest and call me in the a.m.," Damien said.

Tavares hung up and called Dora, who was in Atlanta until Wednesday.

"So what are yawl going to do before yawl go home?" inquired Tavares.

"We're going to have dinner at Justin's, then we're going to hit Magic City."

"Magic City, huh? I like Magic City," Tavares said, not even knocking his choice of club. "Sounds like a plan, just don't make it rain on no buss down, bum bitches."

"First of all, Ma, you best believe I got better shit to do with my money than make it rain on any bitch, taking her clothes off or not. I get money, not throw it away. I give back to others who need it, but not by making it rain in no strip club. That was a one-time thing because I was with you. I'm going on the strength of niggaz wanting to go, but making it rain is out! I own a fucking strip club, so I can respect the hustle, but I'm not throwing my dough at some sweaty pussy bitches like every other stupid nigga in the room. Get the fuck out of here." Dora laughed at the mere thought.

Damien wasn't in the mood for his baby's mother, who had been calling him since he got back from Miami. "Why is this bitch blowing me up?" he asked, ignoring her calls.

He wasn't fucking with Shaunda. She was on some slime ball sucker shit, sliding with a nigga he had beef with. She was still denying it, but word in the street wasn't lying on her. Damien wanted Shaunda to keep lying because she wasn't getting shit out of him till she came clean.

Picking up her seventh call, he answered, "What do you fucking want, Shaunda?"

"Nigga, I been calling you for two fucking days. Why you ain't been answering? What if something was wrong with one of the kids?"

"Shaunda, there ain't shit wrong with the kids. You would have called my mother, so let's cut the bullshit. What the fuck do you want?"

"Damn, can't I just call to speak to my baby's father?"

"Hell fucking no," Damien said harshly.

"Dame, you're on some fucking bullshit." Shaunda didn't know for the life of her how word had leaked that she was creeping with one of Damien's archenemies. But it did, and Damien had been acting shitty ever since he heard it. "Damien, I need a hundred dollars."

"No."

"What do you mean, no?"

"What part didn't you get, the n or the o?"

"Your kids need new sneakers."

"How the fuck do the kids need new sneakers when I bought them each three pairs less than three weeks ago?"

"They're kids, Damien, they're rough on their shit."

"Shaunda, what the fuck do you take me for? You got the wrong nigga, so you better go on with the bullshit. I ain't got a hundred dollars for you," Damien said, hanging up on his stinking ass baby's mother.

Damien got dressed and bounced from his house, which seemed way too big and empty when Tavares was at school. Damien went to see his grandmother and mother before he got deep in the streets for the day. Seeing his two ladies always brightened his hectic days. Damien spent the day ripping and running, seeing fiend after fiend and delivering weight.

The sun had just set when Damien got down to the projects. Approaching the park, Damien found his niggaz entangled in a tonk game and drinking some Henny. Picking the bottle up, Damien poured himself a shot, took a seat, and proceeded to twist up.

Damien was good and high when he saw Dollar coming down the block. She didn't call him because of their spat, but it was nothing. It wasn't a big deal to him. It was her who got all bent out of shape.

"What's good, Dollar?"

"Shit, can I holler at you?" Damien got up and walked underneath a tree with Dollar.

"Yo, my bad about yesterday."

"It's nothing. I just don't get why you get so bent out of shape when people talk about kids, but it's your business. So what can I do for you?"

"I need a quarter."

"Damn, you spending like that?"

"Yeah, I need it."

"Well, go to Stacy's house. I'll meet you over there in fifteen minutes."

Damien wrapped up his session with his niggaz and went to meet Dollar. Damien entered Stacy's house, which always had a fresh scent of crack lingering. He wasn't surprised, seeing as it was a crack house and it was rare that people weren't smoking. Dollar kicked it with Damien for a minute about life, his girlfriend, the hood shit, and they parted ways. Dollar headed to a bedroom upstairs to smoke her crack while Damien hit the streets to party. Dollar sat in a corner by herself and loaded the nip bottle that she had converted into a pipe. Dollar took each hit, trying to run faster and faster from her past.

Dollar was born and raised in the Dominican Republic. Coming to America at ten with her mother, she quickly adapted to being the pretty girl with a thick accent in America. Developing into a beautiful, thick Dominican chick who was badder than bad, Dollar could have had her choice of any nigga she wanted. But Dollar wasn't the one to be chasing boys. She liked for them to chase her, because even though she never gave in, they entertained her. No one had been able to crack Dollar and boys had been trying since she was eleven.

Dollar was on her grind with school. She was determined to be something and take advantage of the American dream. She always liked nice stuff that her mother couldn't afford, so Dollar vowed to go to school so she could have a good career and make mad money.

Dollar was rushing to work when she bumped into the finest man that she had ever seen. "Sweep you off your feet fine" was what Dollar called him. He was tall, with broad shoulders and an athletic build. He had fair skin with a deep rich olive-color that glowed radiantly. He had strong facial features that were attractive and hard to miss. His eyes weren't grey and they weren't green—they were their own perfect combination of the two, and had a deep, dark tint to them with the bright colors mixed in. He definitely had no nigga or spic running through him; with wavy hair, you could tell he was something though, Dollar thought, looking the man up and down.

Damn, she thought, rushing down Warren Street to Dudley Station. *Damn, who the fuck is that?* thought the man. *That girl right there got more ass and hips than I've ever seen*, he thought to himself. Not to mention her thick round cheeks and long eyelashes. *Damn*, he thought, thinking about the young lady who'd just whisked by him.

Going back the very next day, he waited for Dollar to come out. Not giving in so easy, Dollar made him come back for two weeks before she would agree to go out with him. One date turned into two dates, and from there they were going out whenever Dollar wasn't in school or at work. They were hot and heavy and into each other without a doubt.

Until Lilly made her presence known. Unknown to the present day, Lilly had done something or said something, and never again did Holton take her calls or come see her. Dollar spent the evening reminiscing about her past and getting high as she tried to escape life as she once knew it.

Shit was getting crazy the more time that Tavares spent with Dora. She didn't mean to keep going to see him. But it was so much fun that it was hard to resist the invites. They were always sliding somewhere different. Tavares's favorites were the Poconos, Atlantic City, and Hilton Head Island. Tavares had too much on her plate with two men and school.

Going to Newark the last three weekends had Tavares feeling like finals came too fast. She told Damien that her work had her too busy to fly home. Ironically, work was the last thing she was doing. Studying had been the last thing on her mind when she had the option of seeing Abdora. *Damn, you better hope you pull this shit off*, Tavares thought, praying she passed the finals she hadn't picked up a book to study for. Tavares picked up the first book and got ready to cram for three different finals. Tavares studied all the way through the morning with no sleep, only books and coffee.

Tavares was ready to take her finals and then she was heading home for the next month. She had a long list of things to do. A party, Christmas, New Years Eve, her friends, and Damien. First on Tavares's list was a party that she wasn't in the mood for. Dame just said they were going to a party on Saturday. He said nothing of what kind of party it was. He just told Tavares to be on her A game. She loved when he put the pressure on, because she did her thing.

Tavares showered, drank some more coffee, packed her suitcases, and got ready to go take her finals. She threw her bags in the car and headed to school to bang out her last tests of the semester before she headed home for Christmas break. Two tests down and one to go, Tavares was confident. Strolling to her history final, Tavares prayed to God she had all the dates down pat, because that was the key to her passing. Taking test number three, Tavares knew she was good in the game. She was confident that she had got at least Bs on all the tests she had crammed for. Tavares exited Payne Hall and headed toward the parking lot where Asia was waiting to drop her off at the airport.

Tavares's cell phone rang and she looked down and said, "See, this is why I'm in the position I'm in now. Hello?" she answered in her sweet, sassy voice.

"What's up, Beautiful?"

"Nothing, headed to the airport. I was going to call you when I got to there."

"Damn, I was hoping I could convince you to take the plane to Jersey, because I got something real pretty with your name on it." Tavares just chuckled to herself like this dude be for real, what's wrong with him.

"I can't take the plane to Jersey," Tavares said, knowing she better not, or there would be hell to pay later.

"Come on, all you have to do is get on the plane. The price doesn't matter. If you want, I'll send my jet."

Laughing, Tavares said, "You don't have a jet."

"Okay, you got me," Abdora laughed. "I don't have a jet. Although I do have a prepaid flying time on a jet, which is available anytime I need it," Abdora said pleadingly, wanting to see his breath of fresh air, who he was loving more and more the more time they spent together.

"I have to go to Boston on Friday anyways. Just say that you're flying home tomorrow. You can come here for the night and we can go to Boston together tomorrow."

"Uhh uhh," Tavares said, shaking her head from side to side like he could see her. Asia just laughed.

"Why not?" Abdora, asked mad as hell.

Tavares was the only one who gave him hell to get what he wanted, and he loved her for it everyday, just not at the present moment.

"What do you mean, why not? Because I can't. How am I just going to come to Jersey when my boyfriend thinks I'm flying in tonight? In about four hours, if you want to be exact."

Sucking his teeth, because he didn't accept no from anyone but her, Dora responded, "Call me and let me know you landed safe."

The line went dead and Tavares just started laughing. "Oh, he's mad, Asia."

"Tavares, that nigga is feeling you fucking hard body. I want to know, what are you going to do? Like really, what are you going to do? He makes the good time too easy and innocent because he doesn't bad mouth your nigga or tell you to leave him, that nigga don't even try to sleep with you. What's really going on?" laughed Asia. "He just be wanting to hang out and see you and be with you and get to know you."

"I know," Tavares sighed, feeling him way too much to have been in a relationship for six years. "He's just so sweet and rough all in one that I don't know what the hell to do with his ass or how to just stop seeing him."

"I love Dame, but I just go through so much drama with him and his baby's mother, the streets, and the bitches—and he'll keel over in agony if you dare say he's fucking them. Not to mention that I love him and his family like my own. I just can't walk away from history."

"Dame is Dame, Tav. We all know he loves you, he just be doing too much," Asia said. "With him it's either take it or leave it. You need to figure out if you want to be with a guy that you're obviously falling in love with, or the guy you have an undying loyalty to."

"I know, and I'm tired, but when you love someone, how can you just walk away? I love him, that's my dude. How can I not when he put me through school and held me down from day one? My heart won't let me walk away. I'm too loyal for that."

"Tavares, if he had your heart and was all that you needed him to be, you wouldn't be spending so much time flying high in the skies with Mr. Santacosa. But if you say you love him, then true love will prevail."

"Asia, I do love that nigga, especially the magic we make," Tavares said as she started to blush. "When he touches my body we don't make nothing less than magic," Tavares laughed. "So no, I'm not leaving him. Asia, listen, okay? I like Abdora, word I do. He makes me smile, laugh, and gives me butterflies every time I hear his voice or am around him, not to mention he's the most perfect man that I've ever laid eyes on, but how can I just leave Dame? I don't think I can. So Dora's just gonna be my best kept secret."

Tavares shrugged her shoulders like she didn't see the big deal, even though she really did. She knew she was lying to herself about the fact that Dora was making her weaker and weaker each day. Never in all the years she'd been with Damien had she been tempted, and now temptation was knocking hard.

"Like I said," Asia repeated, "just don't fall in love. Love complicates things."

"Whatever," Tavares said, rolling her eyes, because she wasn't falling in love—so she thought. Tavares took what Asia said to heart more than she knew, gave her a hug, and headed home to Boston. Exiting the car, Tavares was more than ready to get on the plane and get her mind right.

As Tavares got on the plane and got comfortable in her seat, she was glad she was going to Boston, because her heart was telling her to go to Jersey. Four hours later, Tavares stepped off the plane and was back in the freezing cold, dressed in blue jeans, a cream cashmere hooded sweater, a brown leather blazer, and chocolate knee boots. Savannah was sixty-five degrees when she left, but she was prepared for the brisk Boston weather.

"It's fucking cold," Tavares thought as she trucked through the exit with her luggage. "Damn, where is he?" Tavares said, turning around and not seeing Damien. Just as she was about to get mad, she saw him parked behind the orange and red checkered colored taxis.

Damien gave Tavares a big, juicy kiss on her MAC lip-gloss-covered lips. Damien threw her luggage in the car while she got warm on the luxury of a heated seat. They headed out of Logan International Airport toward Back Bay.

"We got mad shit to do in the next week," Damien said. "We have to go Lilly's birthday party."

"Lilly, as in my Lilly?" Tavares asked, confused that she knew nothing of a party.

"Yeah, her husband is my mans and them. He's giving her a surprise birthday party. He invited us and knows nothing of you knowing her."

"Well, how come I'm just hearing that you know Lilly's husband?" Tavares asked, confused.

"Baby, I had no clue all these years that Lilly was his wife until he invited us and I saw her face on the invitation. I've known her husband since I came up. He was always in the streets and when he saw a nigga getting money he fucked with me. So you can have my credit card to get her a gift and something to wear. We also need to get the Christmas tree up and bang out the Christmas shopping for my family."

"What do you want for Christmas?" he asked Tavares as they exited the Ted Williams Tunnel onto 93 South.

Dame could see the sadness in Tavares's face. Holidays always made her depressed because she didn't have a family to call her own. Tavares really didn't know what she wanted for Christmas.

"I don't know, surprise me. I ordered mad stuff, though. You didn't open my boxes, right?" Damien sucked his teeth.

"Why would I fuck with your boxes, do I look like a big ass kid?"

"Yeah, you do," Tavares said, politely smoking him. He laughed because he knew Tavares knew he'd fucked with the boxes. Arriving home, Damien carried the bags in the house while Tavares went in the kitchen and went through the bills.

Tavares threw the bills back in the bill box and got ready to do what she do and get it in for the next month. Ever since she'd been in school, she still hustled when she was home on breaks. She had her four or five loyal customers who loved her and always copped off her when she was in town. Summer break and Christmas break were when she went hard. Tavares grabbed the water and the baking soda and went to get some coke out of the stash.

When she was done cooking the coke and waiting for it to harden into crack, Damien walked in and was like, "Damn, you don't waste no time, huh? So are you going to go back to the courthouse or are you just going to hustle over Christmas break?"

"I don't know yet," Tavares said, shaking the glass with crack forming at the bottom of it. Not looking up, she said, "and don't disappear either. I need you to pull my car out and warm it up."

As Tavares let the crack dry, she picked up her phone and called her favorite fiends. Saving her best for last, she dialed Lilly.

"Hola, Mama," Lilly answered, loving to hear from Tavares.

"Hi Lil, I just called to tell you I'm home and I'm on and popping. The cakes are baking as we speak."

"Glad to hear that," Lilly responded.

Lilly only bought crack from two people to conceal her habit from her husband. Tavares was one of them. Tavares loved Lilly because outside of being a fiend, she was the sweetest and prettiest lady you ever wanted to meet. Lilly was only a fiend because she smoked crack any chance she got, not because she looked like it in any way. Lilly had to be in her early forties, but definitely passed for early thirties. She was always immaculately dressed, with her long, beautiful silky hair in one braid because it was too long to do anything else with it. She had big, bright brown eyes and a smile that would melt anyone's heart. You would only know she was a fiend if you caught her with the pipe in her hand.

Lilly always spent big money. Tavares had met Lilly the summer of her junior year of high school. Tavares was parked on a side street waiting for Damien. Unknown to Tavares, Lilly was searching for her other connect and found Tavares instead. She pulled up looking like death and started talking to Tavares.

"Hi, I spent all my money getting high, but I promise if you give me some gas money, I'll pay you back. I have money but it's at home. I come to Boston to get high and I spent all that I had on me. Please help me out."

Tavares could look at the lady and see that she came from money. She was pushing an Escalade, with at least ten carats on her hand. Her clothes were expensive. Reaching in her back pocket, Tavares gave the lady $20 and said, "I hope you make it home with this money and don't use it in one of these crack houses." Lilly took Tavares's telephone number, promising that she would be calling with her $20.

"I promise, I'll bring you the money back. I just need to get home before my husband finds out I wasn't in the Bahamas, but in Boston getting high for the last week."

How ironic, Tavares thought, she passed on a sunny vacation on the beach for some crack. Tavares was in disbelief that a woman with so much money and so much beauty was wasting her life getting high. Tavares gave Lilly her number and, true to her word, Lilly called two days later.

After repaying Tavares with a crisp $100 bill, she said, "Alright, well now I need to go cop me some shit before I go home," dressed in her expensive sundress and Dolce and Gabbana shades. Tavares told her that she was on, and from that day Lilly had been spending thousands with

Tavares. Lilly's spending alone was the main reason Tavares had her own pretty little nest egg.

"Lilly, I'm here till Jan seventh, so just call me," Tavares said, knowing she would see her before that at her surprise birthday party.

"I sure will, mi bonita mija."

Tavares hung up and went to unpack. Damien carried Tavares's luggage up three flights of stairs and wasn't happy about it. She unpacked while Damien warmed the car up, parked it, and was back in the streets, ripping and running. Tavares was tired by the time she unpacked. Showering and hitting the bed, she tossed and turned and finally closed her eyes.

Damien went and collected a few dollars before going to scoop his right hand man, Winky. They blew it down and went to hook up with some groupie bitches for a few drinks. By the time 3:00 a.m. rolled around, when they dropped the broads off, they were bent.

"Yo, nigga, I can't fucking believe that my baby's mother is fucking that bitch ass nigga from Walnut. I caught that little bitch ass nigga coming out her crib on the late night. I didn't have my girlfriend on me or I would've laid that nigga out, right there on the sidewalk. Shaunda's a trifling, stinking whore bitch. She's just lucky she's the mother of my kids," Damien said, really wishing he could shoot her too.

"Let's go through Grove Hall and see if that bitch ass nigga is in front of 7/11. He be out there on the late night getting money. That's his spot because he got a bitch he fucks with hard who lives on Cheney," Winky said, getting his boy amped up. "He be thinking he's hot shit, like he can't get touched," said Winky in his burly laugh.

"I'm going to touch that nigga, alright," laughed Dame. Coming up Stanwood Street to the corner of Warren, Dame stopped, spotting their victim of the morning. Winky fell out laughing.

"There go that bitch ass nigga right there with his back turned," Winky said, slapping Damien's shoulder. "Yo Dame, he's sleeping, we can get that nigga." They threw on their all black champion hoodies and skully hats and loaded their .45 and Beretta.

"We're just going to roll up on the block and pop that nigga," Winky said, falling out in laughter with no remorse. They slowly approached the corner where their target was standing. A fiend started to yell, but it was too late. Turning around to see what the hell the fiend was yelling about, he felt it first. Trying to whip out, he couldn't. He was already on the ground. He just laid there in pain with bullets in his back and legs.

The phone ringing woke Tavares up. Groggy, Tavares answered. "Hello?"

"Yo, Baby, wake up. I got a code red and need you to get up right now." The words "code red" woke Tavares up in seconds. She sat straight up in the bed that was too big for just her and wiped her tired eyes.

"What's wrong?" Trouble was in Dame's voice.

"Throw something on quick and hurry. I'll be at the house in five minutes. Come downstairs and bring your car keys."

Rolling out of bed, Tavares threw on some of her Victoria's Secret sweatpants, a tank top and a hoodie, some Timberlands, and her puffy coat.

She hurried down two flights of stairs. Opening the front door, she heard Dame pull up. Coming down the outer stairs, she saw Damien and Winky. They were sitting in the red rental car that Winky had picked Dame up in. They both got out of the car and met Tavares at the bottom of the stairs.

"Listen, baby, I need you to take this car and drive it to Adams Street."

"For what?" Tavares asked, as she looked at Winky with the evil eye. "Why can't one of yawl drive it?"

With stress lines in his forehead, Dame said, "Not now. I have no time for questions. Just park it on any side street. I'm going to drop Winky off in your car and then I'll pick you up."

"What the fuck is going on?" asked Tavares, knowing something was up. At times this ride or die bitch thing was just a real force to whoever had created the term.

"Just do it and I'll explain later." Asking no more questions, Tavares hopped in the rental, took a left at the end of her street, and took off down Columbus Ave. As Tavares got to the end of Columbus Ave where Ruggles Station was located, she saw two Northeastern University campus police pull out behind her. Not panicking, Tavares decided to take an alternate route to be sure they were following her.

Instead of going her original route, Tavares took a major detour down Melena Cass Blvd. Looking out the rearview mirror, she saw that there were two more campus police cars behind the two cars already following her. Tavares didn't know what was going on, but started to worry that it was something that was about to have her in two silver bracelets. Turning right on Shawmut Ave, going through Dudley, Tavares headed up Warren Street.

"Why the fuck did I pass the police?" Tavares cursed herself as she passed the Roxbury police station that was dead smack in the middle of Dudley on Warren Street. Dudley was an area where there were major businesses. Barber shops, multiple eateries such as Chinese, Jamaican, sub shops, and soul food. Dudley had everything—sneaker stores, clothing stores, hair supply stores, beauty salons, a fire station, a bus station, a police station, a courthouse, and a library. Tavares kept driving, trying not to be afraid because it was only campus police behind her. She slowed down at the red light, at one of the busiest intersections in Boston, where Warren Street ended and turned into Blue Hill Ave.

Out of nowhere, a mass of Boston Police came from every direction and surrounded Tavares. There were five blue and white Boston Police cars, two unmarked cars, and a patty wagon. They had Grove Hall on lock as the sun was trying to rise. Everyone got out with guns drawn. Two white police officers in an unmarked car screamed, "Get out with your hands in the air."

Pulling over, Tavares looked around and asked herself, *what the fuck?* A black officer who'd been in the other unmarked car approached Tavares and told her to put her hands behind her head until a female officer came to search her. Tavares showed no fear or panic in her face. She was far from scared. But deep down she was past mad because she knew she was about to go to jail.

A female officer approached the scene, patted Tavares down, and informed the other police officers that she was clean.

"Madam, you can sit in the car. We need to ask you some questions," the black detective with bad breath informed her. "What's your name?"

"Tavares Del Gada."

"Do you know that this car was used in a shooting tonight?"

"Is that so?" Tavares asked, portraying clueless but believing them.

"Someone was shot tonight, and this car fits the description of the vehicle that the shots were fired from. The casings were found right there at the store to the right of us. Do you have any idea who could have fired those shots?" asked the bad-breath cop. Quick on her feet and street smart, Tavares got on her A game.

"Officer, I have no clue what the hell you're talking about. I didn't shoot anyone. This is my rental car that was rented in my mother's name. Your officers just searched the car. Yawl patted me down in the middle of Grove Hall and found no gun. I don't play with guns. Guns are dangerous," Tavares said, sarcastically serious. "All I can tell you is that I just got out of bed and was home all night, so this is not the car that you're looking for."

"So where are you headed this time of morning?"

"I'm on my way to my mother's house to bring her the car. She rented it while my car was in the shop. My car will be ready today, and since I have to be to work at seven in the morning, I'm returning the car now."

Tavares was hoping this car was rented in the older woman's name that Winky had been dealing with. Knowing him, it was. Mad that she was quick on her feet, the black police officer started boiling inside. He snapped at Tavares.

"Miss, we know that shots were fired out of this car, so you might as well help yourself out. All we have to do is test your fingers and the car for gunpowder residue."

No fool, because she was a criminal justice major, Tavares knew that they couldn't test it right there on the spot, with no proof or anything to go on except a description.

"Well, go ahead, because my fingers are clean and so is the car. I just have one question," Tavares said, slightly chuckling to herself. "Before you test me for gunpowder residue, what makes you think I had the ability to shoot someone out of a car?" she asked sarcastically. They were looking for two black males, and she didn't fit that description, so she was good and knew it.

"Wait here," the black detective said, with more attitude than necessary. "We'll be right back."

Walking away to talk to three uniformed cops, the detectives were getting mad that they couldn't break Tavares.

"She's a smart one," the older white detective said to his co-workers. "You'd think the little bitch was one of us."

"Well, pull her card and tell her she's going to be arrested and brought to the hospital to be identified, and if the victim says it's her, she's going to jail for attempted murder," the black cop said. "I bet the black bitch will break then."

Meanwhile, Tavares was cursing Dame for setting her up and not giving her a heads up. *I'm going to kick this motherfucker's ass*, Tavares thought, as she heard feet approach.

Approaching the car, the white detective said, "Ms. Del Gada, we're going to have to take you with us."

"What for?" Tavares asked, as if he'd lost his cotton-picking mind.

"We're going to take you to Mass General Hospital and if the victim identifies you, you'll be placed under arrest for attempted murder."

"Oh hell fucking no!" Tavares screamed, because they were on some real bullshit.

"Yes, that's right. If the victim says it wasn't you, then you're free to go and can pick your car up."

"Yawl are on some bullshit, but I won't mind a laugh for the morning, because yawl got the wrong car and the wrong person."

~ CHAPTER 16 ~

When do you realize enough is just enough?

Tavares was handcuffed and placed in the unmarked car with the black detective and his fat Puerto Rican partner. The police tried to make conversation and ask questions in a roundabout way.

"Ms. Del Gada, so you were home all night and no one had access to this car?"

"Isn't that what I said the first time?"

"Well, why would someone give a partial of your license plate number?"

"Maybe someone wants to see me go to jail. I can't speak for why people do what they do, but obviously you believe them, so what does it matter what I say or think? Real talk, you just need something to do, so entertain yourself for the moment."

"We think you're protecting someone," the Puerto Rican officer said. "Now's the time to come clean if you are."

Tavares laughed so hard that they knew every tear coming down her eyes was real.

"Officer, no disrespect, but like I told you, I have no idea what you're talking about and even if I did, I'm not a snitch bitch."

They rode in silence the rest of the way. Arriving downtown at Mass General Hospital, Tavares was uncuffed and escorted into the emergency room with a police officer on each side of her. Walking through the sanitized-smelling emergency room, Tavares saw multiple police officers outside of one room and knew that was where she was being escorted to. Tavares was left outside in the hallway with the officers on police detail while the detectives went in and had a few words with the victim. Too stupid to close the door, Tavares listened to their every word.

"Hi, Mr. Danby," the black cop said, "We want to know if you would mind identifying a potential suspect."

As their victim looked at them, he had to really remember that he was talking to the police.

"Yo look here, I told you I don't know who shot me. So, how about you and your suspect do it moving? I don't know who yawl thought I was, but I'm not that nigga. I'm no rat. So even if you brought a nigga in here, don't even waste your time thinking I would point at the nigga and say, 'yeah, he shot me.' That's some bitch shit and I'm not no bitch ass nigga, so how about you close my door on the way out?" the victim said in his low, raspy voice. He lay in bed and closed his eyes because he was full of anger. It was war with the niggaz who shot him, but he didn't need or want no type of help from the police.

The police exited the room and the black police officer grabbed Tavares tightly by the arm and shoved her into the room.

"Open your fucking eyes," the Puerto Rican cop shouted. "I don't give two fucks about your 'I'm too fucking gangster to snitch shit.'" Opening his eyes, ready for war, the victim got the shock of his life. Staring at the thick, sexy, blue-eyed shorty, he was fucked up in the game. They locked eyes. *Oh shit, it's the beautiful, ocean blue-eyed beauty that was with Dora.* They were on the same page because Tavares's first thought was, *That's Dora's boy. Damien shot him, so what's really good?* she asked herself. *Is this dude from Boston?* Tavares wondered, because she for sure didn't know him.

"Do you know this lady?" snapped the ugly, crater-faced Puerto Rican cop.

"Nah, I ain't never seen her," Holly Hood said, wondering as to how she even came to be a suspect. Tavares stood in shock, but didn't let her eyes give it away.

"So this lady didn't shoot you this morning?" said the Spanish officer.

"Didn't I just tell you I never seen her, so how could she have shot me? To get paid all the money you do, you sure ain't got no common sense," laughed Holly Hood.

"Now, am I fucking free to go?" Tavares said, ready to flip out on the police.

Staring at the nigga in the bed, she was really fucked up in the game. *He was talking to Dora at the comedy show*, was all Tavares kept thinking in her mind. Tavares wouldn't forget his face, he looked like he was Jim Jones's twin.

As Tavares rolled her eyes at the police, she turned and said, "I'm sorry you got shot. Thank you for letting these assholes know that I had nothing to do with it." Tavares looked at his face, trying to figure out why her boyfriend shot him. Something was funny money.

"No problem, shorty, please close the door behind you." Holly Hood was racking his brain, trying to figure out how shorty was connected to him getting shot. Past Dora, he had never seen her. But he knew for sure that Dora didn't do this shit. *Who the fuck is she and who else is she fucking with that did this?* Holly Hood wondered. He didn't know, but he was going to find out for sure.

Mad that Tavares was free to go, the police led her out to the lobby. She exited Mass General Hospital and walked toward Government

Center, steaming mad. Tavares thought she could feel heat coming off her body as she wiped the tears that were rolling down her face. Angry and hurt, Tavares couldn't believe that Damien had set her up blindly, knowing he'd just did some grimy shit and threw her right in the middle of it. Now, even worse, the guy was a friend of Dora's. Tavares was steaming inside.

Approaching Park Street station, Tavares walked down the stairs of the Red Line station and cut through the tunnel to the Orange Line. Tavares waited on the bench for the train and thought of all the ways she was going to cuss Damien out when she got home. Taking the Orange Line train to Back Bay station, Tavares was ready to go home and set it off. She exited the station, crossed the street, walked past Copley Mall, and power walked down the path that led to her house.

Approaching her big, beautiful house that was far from a home, Tavares could feel her blood boiling more and more. Walking up the steep stairs, Tavares knew it was on from the moment she crossed the threshold. As Tavares entered her house, she could hear Damien in the computer room, on the phone. Standing in the middle of the kitchen, she listened.

"Look here, bitch, let me tell you something and tell you one time only. You ain't gonna say shit. Let my bitch hear any—" and Tavares dropped her keys.

You stupid bitch, Tavares cursed herself as she bent down and picked them up. Damien came out of the computer room, through the living room, and saw his girl with a look that said it all as she stood in the middle of the huge kitchen.

"Umm, if you're done talking to your bitch in my house, I need a few words with you," Tavares cut into Dame.

"First off, let me tell you something, don't be fucking talking to your stinking half of a dollar ass bitches in my motherfucking house. Because you and that fucking phone will get kicked the fuck out. But right now I'm more upset that I almost went to fucking jail fucking with you."

"Jail?" Dame said, shocked.

"Jail, motherfucker, what are you deaf or stupid? Who the fuck is that nigga, and why the fuck did you shoot him?"

"What the fuck do you mean, why did I shoot him?" Dame said, totally thrown by the line of questioning. "Obviously he needed to be shot, if I shot him." Damien wasn't trying to tell his girl he shot the dude, not only because he was the enemy, but also because he was fucking his baby's mother.

"I shot the nigga 'cause our hoods got beef, why else?"

"Damien, you know what? That's some fucking bullshit and you know it. It's not like you fucking bumped into the nigga and shot him on some hood shit. He was shot out of a fucking car. That means you were lurking and went looking for him. I know you. This was personal. Maybe you schooled me a little too fucking well," Tavares said, getting mad because something wasn't right and she knew it.

"Either you fucking tell me why the fuck you shot that nigga, or I'll go back to the motherfucking hospital and ask him why you shot him," Tavares said, not meaning it but definitely sounding like she did.

"The hospital? You and that nigga were face to face?" Damien asked, surprised that the police went so hard. "Apple, I shot the nigga because our hoods got drama. They killed my man, Rondell, RIP my nigga. So I bust at any of them niggas when I see them, no ifs, ands, or buts about it." Tavares just laughed and shook her head. She knew Damien too well and he just didn't know when to tell the truth.

"Damien, it's cool. You ain't gotta fucking tell me. I'm definitely going to get to the bottom of it, though. It was none of my business, but you made it my business when you gave me the fucking car," Tavares said, with fire in her eyes. She had to laugh to keep from crying.

"This morning was some fucking bullshit and it makes me say to you, where's the limit? The bitches, your baby's mother drama, you in the streets, late nights, the drugs, just all of it is too much. And ALL I do is just fucking deal with it. So my question to you is: where's your limit? Just tell me why you would do something so reckless as to shoot someone out of a car and then give me the car? You think that low of me?"

Damien knew he'd made a bad call, but in the heat of the moment called the one person who always had his back. He never thought Tavares would get pulled over in the car. With guilty eyes, he hung his head and didn't answer.

"It's cool, though," Tavares said, with her eyes starting to tear up. "I don't understand you, but I'm not going to try anymore. All I know is I'm close to my breaking point with you. Fuck it, though, it is what it is. Right now, I'm going upstairs to go to bed, and when I wake up I'm going to do all that I need to for Lilly's surprise party tomorrow. After this party and Christmas, me and you are going to have it out, to see where we're going. I want to believe that you love me, but your actions speak louder than your words. I'm just so blown by you."

Tavares looked at Damien with such disgust in her eyes that he couldn't help but feel like shit.

"Tavares, please don't look at me like that, because I know I'm not perfect but damn, am I really so fucked up to you, for you to look at me with malice in your eyes? No, so don't look at a nigga like that."

"Whatever," Tavares said, turning around, and walked out of the kitchen and up the stairs two flights to her bedroom to get her sleep on.

As Tavares pulled her clothes off and crawled in bed, she was wishing that she'd gone to Jersey. Never did she cry or hurt when she was there or with Abdora. He only liked to make her smile and make her cheeks rosy red with laughter, not anger. Damien came upstairs and saw Tavares tucked under the down comforter, as beautiful as she wanted to be. Bright yellow face, thick hair all over the place, looking innocent. Damien felt bad and was going to make it up to Tavares. He hated fucking up because he knew he had a good bitch.

Tavares was a bad bitch look-wise and had the truest go-getter nature, which made her an even badder bitch. She was always being a good girlfriend and taking care of the home. Not to mention that she went through it with Dame and still hadn't left him. She caught him cheating, went through it with his jealous baby's mother, put up with him being in the streets, and no matter what, never left him. Looking at her, Damien knew he had to get his shit together as far as putting home first. Time was ticking for him, and he saw it in Tavares's face. Damien didn't want to lose his girl, so he promised himself he was going to get it together.

Holly Hood lay in bed, beating his brain trying to connect the dots as to how the pretty young lady that was with Abdora at the comedy show was connected to his shooting. Holly Hood had got hit up pretty bad and was going to have to do physical therapy, but he was blessed that he was going to walk again. Outside of being alive, that was all that mattered to him. After waiting hours and hours for the police to dismiss themselves from his door, Hollis Danby wasted no time calling Dora.

"What's good, son?" Dora answered.

"Yo, my nito, I don't know if you heard, but I got shot up early this morning. I took three bullets to the back and two to each leg."

"Get the fuck outta here, son, fucks no I didn't know you got shot. I would have hit your jack to check on you. So what's the drop, do you know who caught you slipping so they can be put in the room next to you?"

"That's why I'm calling you," Holly Hood said hesitantly.

Dora could hear the hesitation and said, "Nigga, if you know who the fuck shot you, what's the problem, spit that shit out."

"Dora, I don't know who shot me but I need to know what's up with shorty that you were at the comedy show with."

"Why the fuck you asking about her?" Dora snapped, totally confused how Tavares had become a part of the conversation.

"Yo, my nigg, I been sitting here busting the seams in my brain trying to figure out how shorty is tied into this shit, but she is."

"My nigga, you gots to be more specific than that shit. What the fuck would make you say that?" Dora asked, getting a little ticked off.

Hollis explained what transpired in his hospital room hours earlier, leaving Dora speechless.

"Yo, I don't know what the fuck is going on, but Tavares ain't that kinda chick. She's into getting paper, going to school, and staying fly. She would be completely out of her element setting a nigga up or having anything to do with a nigga getting shot. Especially considering that you're my nigga."

"Well, what the fuck is shorty doing in Boston, ain't she from out there?"

Nah, my dude. She's from out there."

"Say, word," Hollis said, not believing he'd never bumped into a bad bitch like her prior to seeing her with Dora.

"Yo, you said that shorty had a man, who the fuck is her man?" asked Holly Hood, trying to find anyone who was connected to her that he knew.

"Some clown ass nigga getting money named Damien."

"Get the fuck out of here," Holly Hood said in total disbelief.

"From the sound of how you said that, I take it you know the bum ass nigga," Dora said.

"Dora, Imma kill that nigga," Holly Hood said with vengeance in his voice. "Me and that nigga got beef. Rather, our hoods got beef, we ain't got too much personal, but that bitch ass nigga must of got at me because I be banging his freak ass baby's mother."

Dora laughed. "Yeah, vato, that would make sense," he said, still chuckling.

"Oh, don't worry, that shit ain't about nothing. Because give me a few weeks and that nigga is going to feel it," said Holly Hood. "He's either going to be pumped full of holes or laying in a casket."

Waking up, Tavares saw the clock said 3:37 p.m. "Damn, did I really sleep all day?" Tavares said, knowing that it was morning when she went to sleep. "Damn, how the fuck did I do that?" Tavares asked herself, hopping up.

Tavares had to make it to the mall, so she hurried up and showered, threw on a pink Victoria's Secret sweatsuit with her brown

Uggs, and pulled her hair up into a ponytail. Calling her crew, they all decided to roll to the mall at 6:00 p.m. in one car.

Spending the evening treating herself because she was mad at Damien helped ease Tavares's anger. By 9:00, the ladies were headed to the car to put the bags in the truck.

"Yo, we got mad bags," said Mona-Lisa. "Ain't no way in hell we should have shopped that much." Mona-Lisa's phone rang as she hopped in the driver's seat.

"Hello?" she said hesitantly, looking at the unrecognizable number.

"Yo, where are my kids?" Mona-Lisa laughed.

"Walter, I love it. You just call tryna regulate and that ain't how it works."

"Mona-Lisa, I don't got time to play with you. Where are my kids?"

Mona-Lisa looked at the phone and then looked at her girls. "Yeah, this nigga has definitely got to be smoking crack or sniffing dope. Walter, I could go in on you, but I ain't. Imma let you talk your shit. The kids are gone for the weekend. So when they get home, which will be Monday, I'll have them call you," and then she hung up. "Walter sadly got me twisted. Niggaz kill me how they be fathers at their convenience."

Having a baby with Damien had not been in their plans, especially not with all the drama she went through with Shaunda.

"Let's grab some food before we go home," said Mona-Lisa, pissed off that her baby's father had just tried to ruin her good day.

"Don't even let that nigga get you mad," said Leslie.

"He's just so fucking stupid that I can't help but get mad. I need to go out, on that note," Mona-Lisa said. "So everyone's going home to get dressed and meet at my house by 11:30 p.m." said Mona-Lisa.

Tavares got home, dropped her bags off, and could see that Damien had been home. Tavares took a nap and woke up at 10:50. Rushing, she went in her high-heel shoe-themed bathroom. Glass red stiletto statutes were lined along the high window sills. They were really candles that Tavares loved and lit whenever she took a shower at night, instead of using lights. Lighting the candles, Tavares thought, *I want some new shoes*, and stepped in to the shower.

Tavares showered. Stepping out of the marble standup shower, she grabbed her pink terry cloth robe.

"Who the hell is calling me?" she screamed out loud when she ran for her phone.

"Helloooo," she sang, seeing Mona on the caller ID.

"What the hell are you doing?" sassed Mona. Mona naturally had a sly, sassy, smart voice. Everything she said sounded smart, whether she was trying to be or not. She couldn't help it if her life depended on it.

"Just getting out of the shower about to throw something on and head to the hood."

"Apple, we ain't fucking with you. We're already dressed and at my house. You're slower then a hundred-year-old woman. So, we'll meet you there."

"Yawl bitches ain't shit," retorted Tavares, trying to hurry up and dry off. "I swear, give me a half and I'll be at your door."

"Yeah right, get real. Who do you think you're talking to?" Mona smoked Tavares real fast.

"Oh, shut the hell up, a half and I'm there."

Sucking her teeth, Mona-Lisa said, "Thirty minutes and we're leaving you like a bad habit," and she slammed down the phone.

Tavares quickly ran into her walk-in closet and snatched a brown V-neck cashmere sweater and some indigo blue jeans. She rushed downstairs to the room that housed all her boots and grabbed some chocolate ankle boots. Getting groomed and dressed in record time, she brushed her thick, wet, curly hair into a ponytail and was ready to go in twenty minutes flat.

Hopping in Apple, Tavares listened to Keyshia Cole sing "You've Changed." Tavares didn't want to, but she decided to call Damien and tell him she was going out. Dialing the number, she still wanted to slap the shit out of him.

"Hello," Damien answered, shocked that Tavares was calling.

"What's up?" Tavares asked dryly.

"What you mean what's up, what the fuck is up with you?"

"Save the bullshit," Tavares cut him short. "I'm just calling to tell you that I'm going out. Me and the girls are about to go the hood spot."

"You love that hole in the wall, yawl think it's the fucking black Cheers or something. It's the fat girls' club. All the fat girls go there looking for men."

"Shut the hell up, me and my girls ain't fat and we sure as hell ain't looking for no niggaz," Tavares spat.

"Well shit, yawl sure ain't too far from fat either," Damien busted out laughing, knowing he was making Tavares mad as hell.

"To hell with you, I'm thick and you just want me to think I'm fat because you're a hater. I got a mean shape and you know it, so let's say hi hater! I might stay at your mother's since you're going to be out late getting money."

"Now you staying at my mother's cause I called you fat. Get it together. Don't get mad, baby, because you're on your way to being a fat girl."

"I'm not mad, not a fucking fat girl, and damn sure ain't thinking about you, so how about you leave me the fuck alone?" Tavares said, getting out of the car, headed toward Mona-Lisa's two-family Victorian style house.

"I'm that chick and if you don't know, then you done slipped and bumped your big ass head." Damien couldn't front, Tavares was bad with her wide hips and ass, washboard belly, and beautiful eyes and face. Rapping on the heavy door, Tavares laughed.

"So what are you going to do tonight?" Tavares asked, not even caring.

"I'm shooting the shit, out here getting this money. Later I might go to the after hour and gamble a little. It'll be late when I come home, so if you go to my mother's just shoot me a text."

"If I make it there."

"Pardon me?" Damien snapped.

"I might party all night, who knows," Tavares said nonchalantly.

"Don't play with me," Damien said, getting mad.

Tavares knew she'd hit his buttons, just like he did hers. It was what they did. Laughing, she walked through the immaculately cream and brown decorated living room that had a cream sectional with brown and cream pillows, brown and cream curtains, and portraits on the wall, up the stairs toward the second level.

"I'll call you when I leave the hood spot."

"Yeah, you do that, 'cause you know you think you're grown and are trying to get beside yourself."

"I'm way past cute and even more importantly, grown."

Hanging up, Tavares walked in Mona-Lisa's oversized purple and teal colored bedroom where her crew was.

"Why are you so dressed up? We're only going to the hood spot," asked Jazz.

Looking herself up and down, Tavares defended, "I'm not. I only have on jeans, a sweater, and boots."

"You're mad overdressed for the hood spot, though," Jazz said with a look of non approval on her face. "But that sweater's cute to death," she complimented, referring to her coffee-brown colored sweater with gold sparkles.

"Whatever," Tavares said. She snatched the blunt and took a seat on the king-sized canopy bed that had teal chiffon draping from the ceiling all around it.

The hood spot was their favorite bar. At sixteen they came up on Registry-obtained Massachusetts IDs that said they were twenty-one. They'd been sliding in Packy's and other local clubs since. Only they never needed their IDs when they went to Packy's. They were true regulars. Packy's was in the center of Roxbury on Blue Hill Ave and had the cheapest drinks in town. Once upon a time it was an old-school crowd, but the twenties crowd was hip now, and it was the major hotspot.

Smoking the blunts, talking shit, and catching up on the day's gossip, they chilled for about thirty minutes and headed down the stairs and out the door. They hopped in Mona's X-5 and Tavares's Acura truck and headed toward Packy's. Pulling up, the ladies spotted a line in the dead ass middle of winter and thought they had to be buggin'.

"Who the fuck stands in a line to come to the hood spot?" asked Mona.

"When did it get this serious?" added Leslie.

Meanwhile, in Tavares's car, Randee pulled out her cell phone and called Packy Jr., the owner's son.

"Yo! This is crazy," said Tavares, in real shock. "I can remember when no one under thirty even came here, now they got it on lock."

"What's up, Randee?" Packy yelled in his normal happy, bubbly voice.

"Packy, we're all outside about to park and there's a line."

"Oh, come on now, you know yawl don't have to stand in that line. Just come around back. Light Skin is at the door."

Randee called Mona and told them to meet them at the back door.

Strutting down the block to the back of the perfectly rectangular-shaped bar, the girls looked in amazement at the people shivering in the cold, waiting to get inside the bar, and thought it was the most ridiculous sight ever. After Randee rapped three times, the door swung open, and Light Skin, the long haired, sexy, Dominican head bouncer greeted them.

"Hello, ladies."

Each hugged Light Skin and waved to the kitchen staff as they stood at the back of the bar and looked at the massive amount of people inside.

"Hey, ladies," Jr. said, coming out of his office and giving them each a kiss.

Packy Jr. was a jolly, happy white boy who'd grown up in the hood. His family owned the bar that had hood ties since the '30s. He was the coolest white boy in the hood. All he cared about was the Boston Celtics, beer, and pussy, and he was happy.

At the front of the bar were the two entrances. Between the entrances were booths and card tables where the card players got in playing spades, whist, and dominoes. The gambling was illegal, so people acted like they were playing for fun. The whole left side was the thirty-foot bar that ran from the entrance all the way to the back. With the kitchen at the back, the right side held the bathrooms and booths made to fit four people. Tables of various sizes and booths filled the interior of the bar. Flat screens and sports teams' memorabilia and photos decorated the walls. There were autographed pictures from the Boston Celtics, the Bruins, and various players on the walls. There were also posters of sports legends and icons, along with thousands of pictures of customers over the years. Although none of it could be seen with the hundreds of people everywhere.

"Go DJ" was booming over the jukebox and people were shoulder-to-shoulder drinking, mixing, and mingling.

"We so need a table," Mona-Lisa said, aggravated at all the people crammed into the bar.

"How about yawl go get a table and me and Apple will go get two rounds of drinks?" Jazz said, walking to the bar.

The ladies followed Randee, who would surely debo a table. Randee was the bully of the crew. Squeezing their way in at the bar, they waited about ten minutes to be served.

"Can I help you?" the tall, frail bartender asked.

"Ten shots of Patrón and five waters on the side, please," Jazz asked.

The bartender served the large order up nicely and said $80. Paying the bill and leaving a $20 tip, the ladies each carried a tray as if they were waitresses.

Seeing that their girls had secured a table in the corner of the bar, Jazz made her way to the table and sat the drinks down, with all eyes on them.

"Only yawl go to the bar and come back with ten shots," said Mona-Lisa.

"I see where this night is going," added Leslie.

"I'm not fucking with you two lushes," said Randee. "You know what's funny, Apple? You supervise alcoholics by day and drink with them by night, what kind of shit is that?"

"Oh, shut the hell up, Randee. I drink socially and I'm not on probation, so I can drink whenever and however." They all burst into laughter.

The ladies sat around and cracked jokes about the various hot messes coming and going through the bar.

"That bitch is for real," Randee said, shaking her head.

"She really has on eight shades of pink and thinks she's doing the damn thing. I want to know who told her all those pinks matched," Mona-Lisa, said sucking her teeth. "She looks real crazy, but please don't try to tell her that," she said sarcastically.

"I'll be back," Jazz said. "I'm going to get another round."

"Bring me some chips."

"Bring me a bag, too."

"And me too," Randee and Leslie yelled as Jazz disappeared in the crowd.

Arriving at the bar, Jazz had to do a double-take. *Damn, that nigga is way too fine*, Jazz thought as she approached him.

"What's good, my guy?" Jazz said, tapping the fine ass nigga in a black and red plaid shirt, black jeans, black suede Timberlands, and a red mink coat.

"What's up, Jazz?" he asked, slightly glad he bumped into her because he knew Tavares wasn't too far away.

"Ain't shit, the girls are up front. I came to snatch another around. Tavares know you in here?" Jazz asked, curious.

"Nah. Me and my niggaz came in here on a hummer. We got in town about a half hour ago and stopped here to get some of them famous wings I always hear about. This shit is crazy," Abdora said, looking around at all the niggaz who were trying to look gangster.

Other niggaz were whispering sweet nothings in broads' ears. Chicks who thought they looked a million bucks really looked like dressed-up chickenheads.

"Tell your girls I said what's up." Jazz knew better. He really meant "tell Tavares I'm here.? *Damn*, Jazz thought as she watched the fine silhouette maneuver through the crowd.

Jazz came back to the table and dispersed the drinks.

"Yawl will never guess who's in here," Jazz said.

Tavares didn't care, so she threw her shot back and tried to call Dame. He didn't answer and Tavares hung up when she heard Jazz say, "Abdora."

"What?" Tavares, said flipping her phone closed, not believing Jazz. Her eyes damn near popped out of her head as she sat forward and started looking around. "Where?" Tavares asked, trying to spot him through the crowd.

"No bullshit, he was at the bar."

"Damn, Apple, you got it bad," Mona-Lisa said. "That nigga got you falling in love."

"Shut up, no he doesn't," Tavares defended herself. "He said he don't fuck with the clubs when he's here, so I can't see him and his friends being in here."

"Well, they are," Jazz said.

~ CHAPTER 17 ~

Gotta love karma... What goes around comes around.

Tavares excused herself from the table and went on a mission. *Packy's is way too crowded to be a bar. This is not a club*, Tavares kept thinking as she squeezed and weaved her way through the crowd. "Pardon me" and "excuse me" got real old, real fast. Tavares couldn't believe that after the bad morning she had, the one person she needed to see was where she was.

Tavares couldn't help but shake her head when she found Abdora, Bryce, Hawk, and Dominic at a round table for eight in front of the kitchen. The food they had on the table was ridiculous. They had Packy's famous fried wings, chicken tenders, fried fish, collard greens, mac and cheese, steak tips, cheeseburgers, and French fries. They looked like they were catering a small party. Locking eyes with Abdora, Tavares said, "Hello, gentlemen." Everyone waved, not being able to speak from the food in their mouths.

"Do you mind if I take a seat?"

"Nope, not at all," Abdora said casually.

"Hi, Mr. Santacosa. May I ask you what you're doing in here?" Tavares blushed.

"Well, I told you I had to come to Boston, but what I have to do isn't till tomorrow night. We just stopped in here to get some food and have a few drinks 'cause we just got off the highway. We didn't know it got crazy in here like this." Bryce's big football frame was smashing some chicken wings. Dominic was devouring a cheeseburger wrap and French fries. Hawk was throwing back his shot of Hennessey Privilege and checking out all the big booty broads that kept strolling by, trying to get their attention.

They stood out like a white man in the middle of a housing project. Everything about Abdora and his crew screamed out-of-towners. "I had to come to your spot since I couldn't get you to come to Jersey," Abdora winked his sexy, slanted eye.

"Sorry I didn't hit you, I fell asleep last night, almost went to jail this morning, then I went shopping."

"Back up," Dora said, putting his hand up, motioning for Tavares to stop talking. "Back up to the part about you almost went to jail this morning."

"Yeah, that's a long story. It's actually why I was so mad that I didn't want to call you today. I didn't want to take my anger out on you. I had to shop it off. But we'll talk about it."

"Did you just say you shopped off your anger?"

"Yeah, what's wrong with that?"

Abdora just laughed and said, "Nothing at all, baby girl. I leave you alone for a few hours and you almost go to jail, huh? Do you see what happens when I leave you alone?" Abdora said, pinching her nose.

"Whatever," Tavares blushed.

Abdora was just chilling in his element like he owned it. He thought he was at home and in charge wherever he was, Tavares thought. He had six shots in front of him and a plate full of a little bit of everything on the table, looking like he owned the place. Abdora had a natural aura about him that said Boss, and it was hard to miss.

"Well, I'm not going to sit here for too long because the sharks are lurking, and I feel like if I stay too long I'm bound to get bit," Tavares said.

"What?" Abdora asked, looking at Tavares like she was losing her mind.

"I'm not thinking about them bum bitches," Abdora said, serious as hell. "As a matter of fact, you better not move. I'll be right back, gotta take a leak." Getting up, Abdora went in the bathroom took a leak, washed his hands, and when he came out he looked straight ahead of him to see Tavares wasn't there.

That girl is so hardheaded, he thought as he walked toward his table.

"Yo, Bryce, what happened to shorty? I was gone all of two minutes."

"She told us we were the men of the hour and she would holler at us." Abdora laughed, knowing Tavares left because of all the bitches lurking and she was trying to be under, not on, the radar.

Tavares walked in on a heated discussion between Leslie and Mona-Lisa. Mona-Lisa hated that Leslie defended her piece of shit baby's father, so it always became an escalated conversation. "That nigga ain't shit, Leslie," Mona-Lisa said, not understanding why her friend didn't get it. "All he does is lie, cheat, and be a deadbeat ass baby father. The nigga swear he be somewhere working on a career, but are you kidding me? He only be working on a career of slinging dick and being a gigolo. He just wants to come through on his time. Oh god, who does that?" asked Mona in a disgusted tone.

"Are you for real?" Leslie said, turning red. "I'm very for real," Mona said, with a look that said *don't I fucking look for real?*

"How do you figure he don't want to come by and see the kid, but he wants to come through and scrape it? Bitch, how else would I figure it from what the fuck you tell us?"

"You stay on the bullshit, Mona. Always talking what you don't know. I never said he don't come by and see the kid. And what makes you think he be scraping anything when he *does* come through? I so don't fuck that nigga, so you might want to correct that," Leslie snapped her fingers, obviously heated.

Leslie and her baby's father had a very crazy relationship, but it worked for her, so they let her be. Leslie was just trying to hold her family together, even if it meant putting up with the bullshit.

"How about this," interrupted Randee, "both you bitches shut the fuck up. Niggaz didn't come out for this bullshit. Damn, Tavares just got home, can we just fucking hang without biting each others' heads off?"

They both shut up, because it was pointless—the conversation was always the same and never went anywhere anyway.

"Alright, well now that we got that out the way, Leslie, what the hell do you want to do for your birthday?" Randee asked.

"It works out so well that your birthday is New Year's because we get to get it in and go hard and have an excuse for it," Tavares added.

"I really want to go to Atlanta," said Leslie. "I want to go down south and walk it out."

"Damn, Atlanta a week after Christmas? You hoes are buggin,'" Mona-Lisa said.

"Come on, you're just talking shit cause you're mad," Jazz said.

"Don't act like that, bitch. We're going to the A for her birthday so shut the fuck up and get with it."

The ladies were interrupted by a tall, thick-accented Spanish waitress. "Hola, mamitas. Some really, *really* big ballers at the back table sent yawl two drinks a piece and left an open tab for yawl."

"Damn, that's what's up!" said Mona-Lisa, loving the generosity.

"That's what I say too, mama," the waitress said, talking all fast as she passed them each two double shots of Patrón.

"Do me a favor," Tavares said to the waitress. "Give them each a drink on me. I don't know what they're drinking, but when you finish just come back and I'll take care of you."

The Spanish waitress knew that running between the two tables she was going to cake it for the evening, she and was already happy for the $100 tip the back table had served her for the drinks she'd just dropped off.

By the time the ladies looked up, the clock that was always set fifteen minutes fast read 1:40. "Damn, Packy's is about to close in fifteen minutes," whined Leslie. "I'm feeling good," she said, bopping to the music blaring from the jukebox. "I don't want to go home."

"Oh, yes you do," said Jazz. "You know you want your baby daddy to come through and tap that ass, while you all drunk feeling the Patrón. You know Jamie Foxx's shit said just blame it on the Patrón and you for sure done had about eight shots," laughed Jazz.

"Yeah, I do want him to come through, bitch, but he's not. Mona-Lisa's ole shit-talking ass got me going home to cuddle with the pillow," Leslie said, feeling some kind of way.

"Hmmph, better you than me, bitch," Mona-Lisa said, curling her lips up in the air. "I might not be going home to my baby's father, but it sure as hell won't be to no pillow either," Mona-Lisa reassured.

After two hours and eight shots, the ladies were good and drunk and enjoying the music when the lights came on. Over the loud speaker Packy Jr. said, "Goodnight everyone, get home safely and be respectful of our neighbors." What a joke. Everyone congregated outside like it wasn't two in the morning. Shooting the shit about all the hot messes staggering out, trying to pick someone up, the ladies spotted Abdora coming toward them.

"Can I borrow her for a moment?" Abdora said.

"No problem," Randee said, "but what you got for us?" she joked.

"Matter of fact," Dora said, "I do got something for yawl. My car is on this side street right here on Edgewood. Go in my armrest and there's another compartment in it that opens. Inside there is some fire ass weed. It's gonna slap you in the face when you unlock the compartment."

"Oh, that's what's up," said Leslie. "Boo-Face, you get your talk on with Abdora and we gonna go work this weed situation out," Leslie said with a smirk.

"Be back," Mona-Lisa said, and off they went to cop the smoke.

Walking away with Abdora, Tavares knew her time was limited because the hood was small and word traveled too fast. The last thing she needed in her life was Damien talking about she was all in a nigga's face outside the Hood Spot.

Walking toward her car, Tavares asked, "So, what's up, Mr. Man?"

"You're coming wit me is what's up."

"Oh no, we can't be doing that," Tavares said, like Abdora was losing his mind.

"I need to talk to you about something important. So you're coming with me."

Tavares sucked her teeth because she wanted to so badly. But she knew that there was no way in hell that was happening. "I want to, but you know I can't."

"Yes, you can. I'm not saying that you have to stay the night. Just come check me so we can chop it up for a sec. Because tomorrow night I have something to do, then I'm out Sunday."

Tavares's face was turning red from the cold air slapping it and her heart was beating fast as she tried to decide whether to follow her heart or her mind. "Yo, your eyes are icy blue and your nose and cheeks are rosy red, but it's kinda cute."

"Whatever," Tavares laughed.

"So what you gonna do, babe girl? You coming to fuck wit your boy or not?"

"Uhhh, I don't know," Tavares said, real soft and innocently. "How about you let me drop my girls off and I'll call you? Where are you staying?"

"Copley Marriott."

"Even better," Tavares said. "You're two minutes from my house."

"Alright, Imma wait for you to hit me," Dora said as he saw Tavares's girls spin around the corner to rescue her.

"Okay, ladies, this is the plan," Tavares said before anyone could say anything to her. "I'm dropping Leslie and Jazz off. The story is we all went to Mona's-Lisa's to smoke and fucked around and fell asleep. I was debating at first, but fuck Damien. I almost went to jail fucking with him so, uhhh, yeah, I'm going to stay the night with Dora.

Damien can believe where I stayed or not. I don't give a fuck at the current moment. Of course I'm not fucking Dora, but I'm def going to stay the night," Tavares said with a tone that let it be known her mind was made up.

"You know you're playing with fire, right?" asked Randee, but not trying to give her girl a hard time.

"Shut up, bitch," Tavares said as she snapped her finger at Randee real quick. "I got this. Just 'cause I don't be juggling on the regular don't mean that I can't do it."

Jazz asked Tavares, "You sure you wanna stay the night with that nigga? Boo, don't make Dame go upside that head."

"Oh, yeah," Tavares asked nonchalantly. "I heard that, but umm, yeah, like I said I'm about to go stay the night with Dora, so now that we got that out the way, I'm ready." Tavares was chastised for not going home to Dame, but she didn't care. She dropped her friends off and headed to see Abdora.

Having to go right past her house to get to Dora's hotel, Tavares saw that Dame's car wasn't there. She decided to go in the house for a moment.

Tavares got in the house and felt some kind of way that she was going to bounce and go see the next the nigga, so instead she called Dame to see where he was and when he was coming home. Tavares would deal with Abdora tomorrow about her not coming. Calling Damien, she got no answer. In between undressing and preparing to take a shower, she called him another three times. She was a little steamy by now, and past flaming when she called the fifth time and got no answer again.

Taking a shower, Tavares lathered her body and cussed Damien at the same time. After bathing and cussing her boyfriend out for twenty minutes, Tavares got out of the shower and decided that it was cool. She wasn't mad. He'd given her the cue to do her and keep it moving to go see Abdora.

Tavares dried off and called Damien a few more times. She was just going to use all the times she called him against him if he tried to talk shit about her falling asleep at her girl's house. After Tavares was done dressing, she called Abdora, who seemed to have been keeping busy alright without her.

"Damn, where are you, it's loud as shit," Tavares said, trying to hear herself over the loud background that was draining Abdora out. Dora went into a bathroom for a little more noise control. "I'm in my man's suite. He's having a small party. I didn't think you was gonna call, but if you coming through I'll bounce now."

"Hmmm, so you thought I wasn't going to call, huh? That's what's up," Tavares said with a mild case of sarcasm. "I came home to take a shower and change after I dropped my girls off. So time got a little stretched out, but I'll meet you at your hotel in twenty minutes," Tavares said, giving Abdora no time to respond as she hung up.

As she stepped on the glass elevator and rode to the twentieth floor, Tavares was content. *Fuck Dame*, she thought as she stepped off the elevator. *I called him mad times, so fuck his hoe ass*, Tavares thought as she made her way down the hall. Rapping on 2016, Tavares waited for Abdora to answer the door.

"Damn, you look good'n'sexy in that outfit. All tight and luscious," Abdora greeted Tavares.

"Move out of my way," Tavares said, squeezing past Abdora. "And I only have on a sweatsuit, so stop it," Tavares said in response to Dora complimenting her Patriots Victoria's Secret sweatsuit.

Tavares entered the room and was shocked. Every hotel room he stayed in was always more exotic or beautiful than the last. "So many rooms," Tavares said, passing a kitchen, two bedrooms, a dining room, and then coming to an end at the large living room with a big fire place. Abdora was so close to Tavares's face that he might as well have kissed her.

"Well, let's go sit in the living room by the fireplace so you can massage my back," he said real seductively.

"I'm doing no such thing," Tavares said as she backed up and led Abdora down the three short stairs into the cozy living room. "I swear, you're the only, and I do mean the only, person who tells me no."

"Other people fear saying no to me."

Tavares smirked. "Is that so? I don't know why that is. You ain't tough or ill," she joked. "I better let them know it's all an act and you're sweet as pie and wouldn't hurt a fly," laughed Tavares.

"Yeah, 'aight," Dora said, not even joking or laughing.

Looking at Abdora in his gray polo sweatpants and crispy white wife beater, she liked what she saw. Looking at his thick, bulging, tattooed muscles, Tavares couldn't help but admire his physical attributes. "Last time I checked, telling people "no" was free will and a choice. So now that we established that, what we gonna do?" asked Tavares.

"Since you wanna be a sucka and not give me a back rub, we're gonna sit by the fire and make s'mores and drink hot chocolate," Abdora said getting up.

"Are you for real?" Tavares asked in shock.

Abdora headed up the stairs toward the kitchen. "Very serious!" he yelled, without looking back. Taking off her hoodie and Air Max 95s, Tavares got comfy by the warm fire. Abdora returned with a tray that had graham crackers, chocolates, marshmallows, and two cups of hot chocolate loaded with more marshmallows. Tavares's heart stopped because no matter how hood he was, he was sweet and romantic with her and she loved it.

"We need to talk," Dora said with a real serious tone as he sat on the floor to prepare the s'mores for the fire.

"I already know what you're gonna say."

"What am I gonna say?" asked Dora sarcastically.

"I know that your boy called you and told you I was at the hospital with the police."

"Yeah, I guess you do know," Dora said, slightly laughing at her directness. "So yeah, how did you end up at the hospital in the company of the police as a suspect in his shooting? I had to explain to him that you ain't that type of chick. That you didn't have shit to do with him getting shot and no matter if you know who it is, you still had nothing to do with it."

"I really didn't," Tavares said, looking Dora straight in the eye. "I ain't that type of person and had I known anything about what went down, I wouldn't have been where, that led me to be brought to the hospital. From the moment he and I laid eyes on each other, I was like, *what the fuck is really going on?*"

"It's cool, Ma, you're good cause I said so. My niggaz know my word is bond. But your peoples, Ma, and I do mean *your peoples*, they got a problem on their hands."

"Oh yeah," Tavares said, tryna piece the puzzle together. "You do dirt, you get dirt. Of course I don't wanna see nothing happen to him, but what can I say? I just wanna know how the fuck does your boy know my peoples? What is so serious that their beef done came to your boy laying in that hospital bed?"

Abdora really wasn't into throwing people under the bus, so he couldn't tell Tavares the information he obtained from his man. He wished he could say, "my man's banging his baby's mother," but that would just add fuel to the fire. "I'm not sure, Tavares, but I do know that it has to do with some street shit."

"That much I know," Tavares said sarcastically. "But I also know matter of factly that there's more to it, so *spill it*," Tavares said.

"Ma, there ain't nothing to spill."

"Dora, come on, this is me and you. I don't care what it is, just tell me. I just wanna know for my own satisfaction after all the bullshit I went through. I deserve to know what really got me almost thrown in jail and I can tell you're holding back on me."

"I am not," Dora said with a straight face through his lying teeth.

"You bright-eyed, baldhead, lying, two-dollar motherfucker," Tavares spat, making Dora's eyes pop out of his head.

He wasn't used to anyone speaking to him like that, except his mother. Looking at Tavares, he was definitely in shock. But he wasn't tryna tell her what she wanted to know.

After the eleven-minute verbal lashing, Dora felt fucked up, especially because she knew he was lying. Dora was hesitant, but he gave in and told Tavares. "Yo, ma, my man is banging his BM, so even though their hoods got beef your man got a personal with him for fucking his

BM." Tavares's eyes popped out of her head and she looked at Dora like he had six heads. She knew it had to be something, but she wasn't expecting what Dora had just hit her with.

The look on Tavares's face had him feeling like a bitch ass nigga, but he wasn't going to lie to her to cover up her no-good nigga's bullshit. Tavares was heated. But she would deal with Damien when she got home. There was no way she was going to let him damper her morning with Dora.

Dora was feeding Tavares s'mores, trying to show off his romantic side. Tavares found it quite cute and let him know it. "You're so sweet. What am I going to do with you?" Tavares said, playfully patronizing Dora.

"You ain't going to do nothing with me. It's what am I going to do with your ass?" Dora said, feeling some kind of way that this girl had him slightly open. Eating s'mores and drinking hot chocolate, Abdora and Tavares kicked it about everything from politics, sports, life, and love, to religion, dreams, and favorite movies.

"Come on, Tavares. Come upstairs and lay down with me."

"I can't. I so have to go home. It's 5:00 already."

"Alright, well come tuck me in."

"No! You're fresh," Tavares said, blushing.

"You like it because you're fresh too. You just be hiding it from me."

"Whatever," Tavares said, getting up off the floor. "I'll tuck you in, but I'm not getting in."

"Deal," Dora said, excited. Tavares followed Abdora upstairs to his bedroom, which was shamefully beautiful.

On one side of the room there was a chocolate brown leather sectional couch with huge tan cushions, with a matching round chair and ottoman. There was a seventy-two-inch flat screen TV with surround sound that could be seen from either side of the room. Across the room was a huge king-sized bed with pillows everywhere. There was colorful, eye-catching modern artwork all over the walls. The rich colors and pictures on the wall gave it a warm feeling.

Abdora started to peel off his shirt and sweatpants and Tavares instantly wished she could cuddle up for the next few hours. *It makes no sense to have a body so fucking gorgeous*, Tavares thought as she watched Dora undress. His tattooed calves, back, chest, and arm muscles were so toned that it made your heart flutter to look at him. "So you tucking me in or are you getting in?" Dora asked seductively. He could see in Tavares's eyes that she didn't want to leave.

"Hmm," Tavares said, debating but truly wanting to stay. Something told her to stay.

"Just for a little while," Tavares said, feeling defeated. "I don't care how long you stay. I just want you to come lay next to me. A nigga just be needing to hold you. I tell you all the time, it's not about pussy." Tavares couldn't lie to herself, she loved for him to just hold her. It made her feel like they were bigger than the moment. As Tavares stripped down to her red lace boy shorts and matching bra, she almost made Abdora quiver.

Tavares was right in every way. Her flat stomach, small waist, baby-bearing hips, and voluptuous backside made a nigga wanna do things to her. Her full, round breasts looked like they were perfect for sucking as they sat high and perky in her bra. Crawling into the bed, Tavares curled up under Abdora. Neither of them said anything. Instead

Abdora turned on the classic movie *I'm Gonna Get You Sucker*, and together they laughed.

Tavares was waiting for Dora to try and get some, but he didn't. Little did he know that if he tried, it would have been his lucky night, but he didn't push his luck. He just held Tavares's warm, almost naked body close. Dora wasn't pressed for pussy. He had enough of it thrown at him on a daily basis. He knew that once he gave Tavares the daddy long stroke, it was going to be over, so he was being patient and waiting for her. He was hoping his time would come before she left that morning.

Dora realized he loved everything about this girl. Her smell, her touch, her hair, her body, her personality, and he hadn't even had sex with her. *How the fuck?* Abdora asked himself. As Abdora watched Tavares, who had fallen asleep peacefully in his arms, he just shook his head. *Damn, I'm feeling this chick*, he thought. Never had he been hard body for a chick, but this chick had him for sure.

What am I going to do with you, Tavares Del Gada?

Later that morning Damien pulled up and saw that Tavares's parking spot was empty. *Where the hell is Tavares?* Dame asked himself. *She's on some bullshit*, he thought, figuring she was at his mother's because she was still mad about almost going to jail.

Walking in the house, Damien went upstairs and saw that the perfectly made red and gold bedding set with throw pillows everywhere hadn't been slept in. *It's 8:00 a.m., where the fuck is my girl at?* Damien kicked off his Timberlands and grabbed the red cordless phone off his night stand.

"Hey, boo," Dame's mother answered.

"What up, Doll-baby?" Doll-baby was his nickname for his mother because she had the face of a pretty black Barbie doll and she kept her hair, makeup, and nails done. Doll looked fly at all times. She was thicker than thick but sexy for an older lady.

"Ain't shit, Boo. I'm sitting here at the kitchen table, about to eat some breakfast. You and Tavares coming over?"

"*What*, Tavares ain't there," Damien said, getting mad. "I thought she was there!"

"Unn uhh, she called me last night before she was going out. She said she was going to come over after the club, but she didn't come." "Well, her fucking ass ain't make it here either. You better talk to your daughter because she got me fucked up."

"Boy, calm down. You're always thinking some crazy shit. Stop all that damn yelling. Call her cell phone and see where she is. And where are you coming from that you don't know your girlfriend wasn't home last night?" Doll asked, knowing her son.

"Me and my niggaz went out, and I passed out at Winky's and Zeena's."

Knowing how close his mother and Tavares were, he never told her of his cheating, though she was no fool. "Is that right?" Doll asked, with a tone that let him know she saw right through his lie. Doll stayed neutral and minded her business. "If I were you, I'd start making it home so you can sleep in your own bed with your girlfriend. You got some dough? Your mother needs some pampering money. Can you help a sister out?"

"Yeah, I got you, Ma. I'll be through there later so you can go get your hair and nails done."

"Appreciate it, Boo."

"No doubt, Ma."

Damien hung up with his mother and dialed Tavares, only to get her proper perky voice, saying. "Hi, I'm sorry I missed your call, please leave me a message and I'll get back to you. Thank you and have a blessed day," *beep.*

"Apple, I don't know where the fuck you are, but it's 8:20 and you ain't home. Your phone's going to voice mail, my mother hasn't seen you, and I want to know where the fuck you are, so call me A fucking SAP."

Hanging up, Dame called Tavares a few more times, leaving a message each time. Too mad to sleep, he went and got dressed. Fully dressed in crisp wheat Timberlands, dark indigo carpenter jeans, and a brown Lacoste sweater, he grabbed his brown mink coat and headed down the stairs. Walking out the door, he saw the clock on the wall said 9:50 a.m. and he was fuming mad.

When Tavares got home at 10:15 a.m., she couldn't believe that Damien still wasn't home. "This nigga is tripping," Tavares said, plugging her dead phone up on the charger, while at the same time spotting evidence that Damien had actually been home. Tavares had to hurry up and make it to the hair salon because it got crazy on Saturday afternoons.

Getting in the shower and getting dressed swiftly, Tavares left the house to meet Mona-Lisa. She had on an orange sweater with a brown shirt, some dark blue True Religion jeans, and her tall chocolate brown Uggs. Dressed for the occasion, Tavares headed on her way.

Hopping in her car, she put in Lil Wayne and turned her phone on. The message indicator popped up. Listening to her messages, Tavares heard Damien yelling message after message and his mother warning that he was going to be calling to yell. *This nigga got a lot of nerve*, Tavares thought. *He didn't fucking call or come home, and he's trippin.' I got this in the bag*, Tavares thought as she made her way to the hair salon and nail salon, not even breaking a sweat about her boyfriend being mad. She was feeling too good from her morning adventure with Abdora and Damien wasn't stealing her joy

By the time Mona-Lisa and Tavares arrived to their lively, orange-decorated Cape Verdian hair salon, it was packed.

"Hi, Miss Luiza," they each said to their hairdresser, who was so sweet and genuinely nice. Miss Luiza had eight kids, but she had the body of a twenty-year-old and the face of a twenty-five-year-old, though she was actually forty.

"Hi, ladies, nice to see you." Taking a seat, they looked at each other and already knew.

"This is about to be an all-day event," Tavares complained.

"Who are you telling?" Mona-Lisa said, already prepared. "We needed to be here at 7:00, when Miss Luiza opened. But Tavares, just think about it, three hours is a long time, but Saturdays are the only day that we're in here so long. Three hours is a good day in a black hair salon, so you can't even complain."

The Cape Verdian hair salon didn't take appointments—strictly walk-ins—and operated very differently than black hair salons. With three wash girls who did all the perming, coloring, washing, and setting, the only thing Ms. Luisa did was cut and style. Their prices were cheaper than the black salons, so they had not only the Cape Verdian clientele but also a lot of black women clients.

Waiting in the reception area, Tavares and Mona-Lisa gossiped about the night's events. "Boo-Face, I can't believe you stayed the night with Dora."

"Boo, me neither. And I don't have one regret."

"That's what's up, boo. Damien deserved to come home and you not be there."

"I almost felt bad." Mona-Lisa just rolled her eyes. "Bitch, you'd be a fool to feel bad, when your two-timing ass boyfriend stays out whenever he wants."

Tavares didn't even get mad at Mona-Lisa because she always told it like it was.

Touching her wavy roots, Tavares said, "I need a touch up, but I don't have the time. I'm just going to get Miss Luiza to blow me out after my set and I'll be so silky I can hold out for Christmas."

"I can't believe your ass really perms your hair because it's curly and thick. Who does that? That's white people shit."

"Whatever, hooker," Tavares said, running her fingers through her thick hair that got wavy and curly rather than nappy.

After thirty minutes, the girls were ushered to the washbowl by their normal wash girls. Three and a half hours and two wash & sets later, they were on their way to get their nails and eyebrows done.

Tavares dropped Mona-Lisa off and went to see Doll. Going to Doll's was always funny, especially when it came to getting money. Walking up the stairs, Tavares could hear loud voices before she approached the door. Knocking, Tavares heard Marie say, "Oh yeah, there she go." Entering, Tavares found Doll baking a cake with her two clients at the table.

"Hey ladies, what's good? We want a double up." Doll snapped around, "Marie, I know you ain't got no motherfucking money to be doubling up. You owe me motherfucking $680 on the third and I wants mine."

Doll was nothing nice. She'd gone from smoking crack back in the day to hustling her old crack partners out of their checks every month for the last fifteen years. They borrowed money from her throughout the month to support their habit and had to pay it back on a double-up. Seeing her beat one ass, they never thought to play with her money. Doll didn't play when it came to collecting her money. Her theory was if she didn't get it, the crack man was getting it, so why not?

"Doll, you know I'm going to pay you," Marie said, all fucked up with her words slipping all over the place.

"Tavares, that bitch got $220 left, so don't give her nothing more," Doll said, never skipping a beat with her baking.

"Doll, you know why I like you," LaLa said, drunk as hell, "because you real. You say it like it is."

"You gots to go, LaLa, I ain't got no time for this bullshit. I'm too old."

"Well, Tavares, can I please get mine?" LaLa asked calmly. "I got a man ready and waiting on me. He got some more liquor for me to drink. So I gots to get back to my house."

"You're crazy," Tavares said, handing her what she came for.

"No, Tavares, I ain't crazy. I like to fuck and I like to drink and he got both, so girl, I'm rolling with him. I ain't trying to be his woman. I just want him to wax all this butt back here," LaLa said confidently, rubbing her flat ass.

Liquor and drugs had torn her down to being halfway decent, but she'd been bad once upon a time. "Lolly, why you looking around all fucking stupid and shit?" Doll asked the fiend who was sitting quietly looking around.

"I'm okay," Lolly said.

"Well, just stop looking so god damn dumb." Giving the ladies their drugs for double the money on the third, they all headed out ready to do what they did best, get high on crack. It was funny to Tavares to see them get high because she dealt and kicked it with them in the sober aspect. Tavares had eaten some of the best food out of LaLa's house, and Marie wasn't nothing nice with her bake game. *Crack was a mother*, was all that Tavares could think when she'd seen them gone and on the move, chasing their high. Tavares and Doll were smoking a blunt when the phone rang.

"Get that, Tavares," Doll said, heading to the oven to get her cake out.

"Hello?"

"Tavares, this is Marie. Girl, where's Doll? I need to talk to her right now," Marie slurred. Shaking her head, Tavares chuckled and passed the phone to Doll. "It's Marie's crazy ass."

"What?!" Doll yelled in the phone. Doll listened for a moment and then said, "WHAT," in a high-pitched tone. "Shut the fuck up, Marie! He's there now, huh? Meet me over there right motherfucking now," she said like a straight gangster. Getting up, Doll threw on her sweatsuit and Nike Air Max sneakers and grabbed her coat. She wasn't even listening to Tavares.

"Where are we going, Doll?" Tavares screamed to get her attention. "Tavares, do you know that motherfucking Dalton has been going right here out my fucking back door to the bitch behind me's house getting high? I'm about to beat that nigga down," Doll said, madder than a motherfucker. "So he thinks he's just going to be going over there, getting high with that fat bitch and her mini-me boyfriend, huh? Hmmp, well if I ain't about to go over there and whoop on some ass my name ain't Doll Stasher."

Walking out the back door to the apartment building next door, Tavares and Doll met Marie in the hallway. Doll had anger in her eyes as she spoke. "Marie, you take this jum and go upstairs and knock on the door. I'll take it from there."

Everyone followed upstairs. Falling right into the trap, Rita opened the door, and when she did, Doll pushed Marie to the side and slapped the shit out of her. "Oh, so you got my man over here getting high with you and George? Bitch, how the fuck you gonna borrow money from me and then have my man in your house getting high with you? Who the fuck do you take me for?" Doll asked, showing that she felt real disrespected as her left hand backhanded the obese, twenty-nine year old crackhead.

"But you hold that thought." Walking past George, who was on the air mattress quivering with fear, Doll stopped and turned around. "And your little pussy bitch ass is allowing her to bring him in here with you and your woman. What type of man are you?"

"Well, Doll, it's her house. You know she don't listen to me. I told her you was going to be mad."

"Shut the fuck up before I slap the shit out of your bitch ass too," Doll screamed, ready to beat the whole house down.

Tavares was just watching and laughing. Doll was a beast and had no problem letting it come out of her. Walking down the small hall to the one bedroom in the apartment, Doll found her now ex-boyfriend. "Oh, so your little faggot ass want to be over here smoking crack and shit, huh? Motherfucker, you have lost your fucking mind, backyard creeping in the neighborhood crack houses. And here I thought these last few months that you was acting different, and here you are fucking smoking crack. Who the fuck waits till they're a grown man to motherfucking try crack? You stupid, wimpy, weak motherfucker. What type of shit are you on? How are you going to move in with me, live in my house for seven years, and then decide you want to be creeping out my back door and getting high where I live? Are you fucking stupid, dumb, or retarded?" Doll screamed at her man, who was scared and quivering.

"You must not know about me," Doll said as she slapped the shit out of him. She slapped him so hard he fell out of his position on the bed with his legs and arms folded. Doll never stopped two-piecing him after that. She had him curled up in a ball on the bed, screaming like a female dog.

Doll stopped punching him and screamed, "Get your shit and let's go, right motherfucking now."

"I know you ain't letting me back in, and I don't got nowhere to go."

"Goddamn right I ain't, but guess what, you ain't living or getting high here, so get your shit and let's fucking go."

"I can't," he pleaded.

Doll slapped his ass so good he bounced right up and got to grabbing his stuff.

Tavares laughed all the way back to Doll's house as she yelled and cursed her boyfriend, who she'd just beaten the shit out of. "Ma, you're crazy," Tavares said, stopping at her car. "I can't wait to tell your son this. He's going to be mad that he missed it," Tavares said, grabbing her chest from laughing so hard.

"That nigga got life fucked up," Doll said, giving Tavares a hug and heading upstairs to beat her boyfriend up some more.

~ CHAPTER 18 ~

One man's trash is another man's treasure.

Pulling up in her parking spot, Tavares spotted Dame's car. *Here we go*, she thought as she hurried in the house, out of the cold. Coming up the stairs into the kitchen, Dame greeted her.

"It's 5 p.m. Where the fuck you been all day?" Damien asked, steaming mad. Tavares couldn't help but wear her thoughts on her face.

"Don't give me that fucking 'am I serious' face, because yeah I am fucking serious, Apple!"

"Excuse me," Tavares said, real snidely. "Oh you can't be talking to me and if you are, you sure as hell can't be serious, at least not with all that base in your voice. Dame, I almost went to jail fucking with you yesterday. Then you go out, you don't answer any of my calls after 2 a.m., and then when you do come home you wanna leave me crazy messages, because I'm not here? No, you can't be serious," Apple said, standing her ground.

"What the fuck ever, Apple, where the fuck was you last night? You said you was going to my mother's and you didn't, so where the fuck was you? Your fucking ass didn't bring your trick ass home."

"Trick? Oh, there's only one trick in this house and it sure ain't me," Tavares laughed. "I can't believe you're serious right now," Tavares said, looking quite confused. "You have got to fucking be kidding me. How can you not be?" Tavares couldn't help but laugh.

"You didn't bring your ass home and you want to talk shit about where the fuck I was. Oh, no, no, no. Considering that I blew you up and blew you up to tell you where I was and you *never* answered, you're in straight violation right now."

Tavares couldn't help but laugh even harder. "So where I was doesn't matter because you didn't answer or call back when I called to tell you where I was," she hissed as she walked right past him, up the stairs. *This nigga don't even know, I did come home,* she thought to herself, getting mad that he was trying to get over on her. Tavares paused halfway up the stairs.

"Oh, and by the way, the nigga that you shot because he was fucking your baby's mother said hello."

Damien didn't even play himself and open that can of worms. Tavares was waiting for him to reply, but he knew better. "Apple, don't fucking start no bullshit, for real."

"What the fuck ever, Dame. I'm not in the mood for this. I had a good day and I want to keep it that way."

"Well, where the fuck was you last night, since you couldn't make it home?" Dame asked, not trying to let it go. "My bitch don't sleep around."

"I know, only you do, right?" Tavares asked sarcastically.

"I'm going to ask you one more time, where the fuck was you last night, before there's a fucking problem, yo."

"Didn't I just tell you it doesn't matter," she said, giving major attitude. "What, you can't hear?" Tavares asked.

"Apple, don't fucking play with me. I'll slap the shit out of you."

"Dame, please! You talk a good one, but slapping me is the last thing you'll do," Tavares said, snapping her neck back to gesture him losing his mind.

"But if it's this serious, I was at Mona-Lisa's. We all stayed the night, got up, and had a beauty day as you can see from my hair, eyebrows, and nails."

"Word, you was at Mona-Lisa's house?"

"Ain't that what the fuck I just said?"

"Well, why the fuck was your phone off this morning?"

"Did your slow bus-riding ass ever stop to think that maybe it died?" At least that was the truth.

"Tavares, something sounds fishy, but if that's where you say you was, then that's where you was." Dame just walked out of the front door, because Tavares had him heated. He wanted to believe she was lying, but he knew Tavares wasn't out doing what he'd been doing, and he felt fucked up for using his guilt to go off on her.

By the time Tavares made it to her room, she heard his Benz speeding off. "What the fuck ever," she said, walking past and throwing her bags on her long black and white chaise. Kicking her Ugg boots off and walking toward her king-sized bed, she saw a dozen purple roses and 5 Gs on her nightstand. "To the best wifey, enjoy," the card read.

"Bastard!" Tavares screamed. And he was a guilty bastard because the card and money proved it. But Tavares would take it as repayment on what she spent getting ready for the party.

Tavares picked up the phone and told her girl Mona-Lisa what had just happened. "That nigga has me sadly twisted. I don't know who he thought I was, but you can't not fucking come home and then wanna bust my fucking chops about where I was."

"That nigga is crazy, Tav, but he loves you."

"Yeah, but he better trip off someone else with his shit-talking ass. Sometimes, I think Dame thinks I'm a bitch he found on the side of the road."

"He did," Mona-Lisa couldn't resist and burst out laughing.

"Fuck you, bitch, I was in the park, don't play with me. He got me real twisted, though. I came home, called him and called him and he didn't answer his phone. He want to play games, so I'm just showing him that I can play them better. What's killing me is that his ass didn't come home, didn't call me back or *nothing* but he wants to go off on me? Please tell me how that works and where they do that at? I must have the game twisted or something. What the fuck," Tavares cursed.

"Cause he's Damien and you know how he is," Mona-Lisa said, trying to soothe her friend. "That's just the bottom line. You know Dame thinks it's his world and we're all just in it. You been with Dame long enough to know he just gotta do him and talk shit to feel better. He don't mean that shit, Tav. But I know he probably lost it when he came home and you weren't there. The nut ain't wrapped to tight," laughed Mona-Lisa.

"Who are you telling?" Tavares said, knowing she'd crossed the line of playing with fire. "Thank God I was blowing the nigga up before hand and he wasn't answering. He had no leg to stand on. If that nigga had actually slept in the bed alone, though, he would have went straight ballistic, word he would have," Tavares chuckled. "I wish I would've saved the out of control messages. He went all the way in on me. He got issues, word he does."

"Bitch, just be glad his ass didn't come home, because we would be picking you up off the ground right now."

"I'm not even trying to imagine it. He beat me home so I know he was trippin' this morning, looking at our bed not slept in. When I got home I saw his clothes were left around to show me he was there. I got home at 10:15 and he was in and out."

"I bet that nigga didn't even so much as breathe a word about not coming home though, huh?"

"Hell, no, you know he wasn't even trying to go there."

"What'd you say to him?"

"I didn't say shit. For what? He knows he's full of shit, just like I know he is. Damien be thinking he's slick but what he don't know is that he taught me this game a little too well. I took what he taught me and applied it, so now I done surpassed him knowing a lot more than he gives me credit for. I got him very shortly, though."

"Let me find out you're about to get crazy on Dame," Mona-Lisa laughed, because she was all for it.

"Bitch, please, you know I'm not with the crazy flip mode shit that you be on. You get real crazy with it with no problem," Tavares said to her girl, having to laugh at how crazy her girl got.

"I knew I meant to ask you something last night but it slipped my mind with Mr. Man being in the building. What's good with your girl going to where her baby's father lays his head and spray painting *Quincy is a hoe bitch* on the chick's car?" Tavares laughed so hard she had tears coming down her face.

"What?" asked Mona-Lisa. "You know Leslie don't play no games! And I can't stand that punk motherfucker, so yep, I was her co-d. She def did hit the spot to let them know she wasn't a bitch to be fucked with, when it comes to her kid. I guess she called that nigga talking about your daughter needs some new sneakers. He gonna say he ain't got it and hung up on her," she chuckled, letting it be known that was where he played himself, "next thing I know she was like, 'let's go.' He didn't know nothing about your girl. We went right over there and she knocked on the door of the bitch he stays with. They didn't answer and she called him everything in the book but a child of God. I know Quincy's girl was embarrassed with her white neighbors, but Leslie don't give a fuck. Then she went downstairs and stated her opinion of Quincy on the door of ole girl's car."

"I don't even know why he thought she wasn't going to come over there like it was some sort of joke or game or something. She's crazy," Tavares said, in tears from laughing so hard.

"No, he's crazy for playing with that crazy heffa. Actually, let me take that back. He ain't too crazy because he sure got them sneakers and some outfits to match," laughed Mona-Lisa.

"Well girly, let me get dressed for this party. I'll call you tomorrow."

Tavares transformed and she couldn't believe that Damien still wasn't home getting dressed. "Oh, he's playing," Tavares thought as she looked at the clock that read 7:40; the party started at 8:00 p.m. Just as she picked up the phone to call Dame, she heard footsteps coming up the stairs. The bedroom door swung open and Dame was looking something real sexy. Tavares looked at him in his black three-piece suit on his huge six-foot-two, solid 230-pound frame, and her heart melted.

Damn, why do we go through the bullshit? Tavares thought as she looked at him looking like a million dollars. *He's so getting the business tonight*, she was thinking as she looked him up and down. The vest underneath his jacket gave him a real, 'I'm stepping out to get my grown man on' look. He kept it hood but classy in his Bally's bowling ball sneakers. The red handkerchief was the hottest though, because it was fire engine red and went perfect against the all-black suit and black and red sneakers. Not to mention it matched Tavares's dress.

As Damien looked Tavares up and down, all he could think was *I'm beating that pussy up later, mad or not.* As he looked at her from head to toe, he was proud, because he knew he had a bitch, but he'd been taking her for granted.

"What the fuck are you looking at?" Tavares snapped to break the ice.

"Stop looking at me all stupid."

"I'm looking at you and all that my money paid for."

"Oh no, boo cakes, you only reimbursed me today because ummm, I didn't take your credit card like you told me. I spent out the pocket and you just paid me back. Do you like my shoes? Aren't they sexy?" Tavares said, modeling her fire engine red leather Christian Louboutin platform pumps.

"Yeah, but that dress is sick with it. That dress was the best thing you decided on." It looked like a fitted corset from top to bottom. Every curve of her thick frame was on display. "Don't get me wrong, baby, you did your thing as a whole tonight, but that dress is going to be the talk of the night."

"Thanks, because I searched long and hard for it and I do mean long and hard. It cost me $2,000 at Karen Millen. But it was worth every penny."

"You mean it cost me $2,000. Let's not get it fucked up, miss thing, because you got your five G's off the dresser," Damien winked. "But ummm, I see you been in here making a mess with your makeup," Dame said, eyeing all the makeup on the vanity. It was his way of indirectly complementing it. Being sweet wasn't for him. It killed him. He had to do it in his own way.

"I made a mess, but it looks good on me. Admit it, because I have," laughed Tavares.

"Baby, I don't know if I'm feeling that red lipstick. It says 'come fuck my lips' and I want to, but everyone else shouldn't have those thoughts."

"What?" Tavares snapped her neck. "Fuck you! My lipstick is the sexiest thing on me. And it so doesn't say 'come fuck my lips,' you asshole. Not too many women can pull red lipstick off and I'm rocking it," Tavares said, kissing her lips proud.

"I know, and that's the problem," Damien said, looking at his beautiful girlfriend sideways. "That hot red lipstick against those sexy lips, pearly white teeth, and sky blue eyes is going to have me ready to kill a nigga."

"Don't kill no one, because looking at me is addictive like a drug. Get mad at my bum ass parents. I can't lie, whoever my donor is, he has to be somewhat cute because him and my mother created a masterpiece," Tavares said, tooting her own horn. "What you see is what you get, so grab my mink and I'm ready."

Damien knew that Tavares was looking past sexy in her red attire and she was going to be turning heads. He was glad she was his at the present moment.

Arriving at Lantana's reception hall, Tavares and Damien made their way to their table. 'Happy Birthday' was draped everywhere in the large, formal dining hall. The drapery from the ceiling held dozens of black and red balloons. The black and red decorations were beautiful against the modern room's décor.

Tavares and Damien took seats and watched a massive amount of people pour into the hall. The large room was filled with generations of men who were in the game. They were of all races: black, white, Spanish, Asian, Greek, Italian, and then some. They were accompanied by their wives, girlfriends, wifeys, and a few had even brought their bottom bitches, their best prostitutes. Everyone in the room got money in some way, shape, or form. Money could be smelled a mile away.

Damien took Tavares to meet his connect and friend Holton Montiago. Holton and Damien exchanged dap before Damien said, "Holton, this is my girlfriend, Tavares."

Holton was instantly drawn into Tavares's eyes. They were strong, bright, and icy blue. It was hard not to be drawn into them when they were so hypnotizing.

"Tavares, it's a pleasure to meet you, sweetheart."

"Nice to meet you too," Tavares said, extending her hand to Holton.

"You have the most beautiful eyes," Holton said, not knowing many women of color with blue eyes.

"Thank you," Tavares said.

"Damien, you better be good to this beautiful lady. If he isn't, give me a call, and I'll get him."

"I sure will, Holton," Tavares said, winking at Dame. Holton made a mental note to ask Damien where he met Tavares later, because she was uniquely beautiful.

"It was nice to meet you, Tavares. I hope you enjoy the party. My wife is slow and will be here any moment, so eat, drink, party, and have a good time, and let me know if yawl need anything."

Tavares and Damien took advantage of the open bar that was about to end and retrieved some scallops wrapped in bacon for appetizers. They were at the table talking when Tavares thought she was about to have a heart attack. Her eyes wanted to pop out her head and her heart was beating a mile a minute. But Tavares was unable to show any emotion. If she did, Damien would look at her like she was crazy. A lot was running through her head, though. Tavares kept laughing and talking to Dame. All the while she was looking over his shoulder at the couple chitchatting with Lilly.

Tavares waited until the couple walked away and said, "Babe, how about you go get us some drinks? I'm going to speak to the birthday lady."

Going their separate ways, Tavares didn't know whether she was coming or going. She went and tapped Lilly on the back. Turning around, Lilly said, "Hola, mamacita," with a smile plastered across her beautiful face. Giving Tavares a hug, Lilly said, "You knew about this party and didn't even tell me?"

"Actually, I didn't, Lill. Damien told me when I got home. I'm just glad we get to enjoy the night with you."

Tavares didn't beat around the bush. "Lilly, I need to ask you something."

"Anything, you know that," Lilly said in her thick accent.

"That guy that you were just talking to, was that his girlfriend?" Lilly gave Tavares a confused look as to why she was asking, when she and Damien had been together forever.

"As far as I know, that's his friend," Lilly answered with a questioning look on her face. "Why, you like him or something?"

"No, not at all, just inquiring. He's handsome, that's all."

"Uhhh huh," Lilly said, not fully convinced.

"We'll talk later, Lilly," Tavares said, winking.

"Yes, we will, Missy," Lilly said, giving Tavares a hug.

Damien was at the bar, checking out Holton talking to a dude in a black pinstripe suit with a red brim hat and red gators with a bad ass broad on his side.

"Yo, his bitch is right," Rollo said to his brother.

"Yeah, she can definitely get it," Dame said. "If that nigga let that up in the littlest way, I'm at that."

Rollo just shook his head at his big brother. "Is there a bad broad you don't try and pop? You got your girl here. Don't be an all-out slimeball."

"I'm far from a slimeball, bro, I just do what I do, when I can do it," Dame said with a slick grin.

"Nigga, there are lines that shouldn't be crossed, and trying to holler at the next bitch with your girl around is a no-no!"

"I know, my nigga, you're right, there's a time and a place for everything, and this ain't the time or the place to be trying to holler at the next chick. Imma fall back," Damien said. "I wonder who that nigga is, though," he said to Rollo out of curiosity, and he had the intent of finding out. The guy had a crowd around him and was kickin' it with the biggest of the biggest in the game. He looked to be Dame's age, so Damien was wondering how he had so many O.G.'s in his presence. Damien watched for a while before deciding that he was going to find out whose bitch he had just passed on.

Kicking it at the bar with his brother for a hot minute, Damien approached Holton, the nigga he was in question about, and a good amount of O.G.s in the game. Damien greeted the familiar faces and offered them a drink. Flagging the bartender down, she took the hefty order, but when she got to the man Damien was in question about, he looked Damien in the face and said, "Naw, I'm good, son." He said it with more than a little bit of an attitude and a tinge of a screw face.

The vibe changed once his cold words hit the air, because everyone could feel them. Holton could feel the odd tension in the air and tried to clear it. "Damien, I don't think that you and Dora know each other. Damien, Abdora; Abdora, Damien."

Neither spoke, they just stared each other down and gave a polite head nod to say what's up outta respect for Holton. Holton didn't know what the personal was all about, but it was clear Dame wasn't feeling Dora, and Dora wasn't feeling him. After paying for the $155 round of drinks, Damien made his exit.

Tavares and Damien partied the night away, dancing and drinking. They were getting along, laughing, joking, and acting as if they weren't hating each other just hours ago. They were truly having a good time. Tavares had to keep her focus on Damien because she was stealing glimpses of Dora and his date and not really feeling what she was seeing. "Baby, it's your turn to go to the bar," Damien said, giving Tavares a $50 bill. Tavares didn't even put up a fight. She was feeling alright from the Patrón, so she headed to the bar without any resistance.

Standing at the bar, bopping to the beat of Beyoncé in her own groove, Tavares's phone rang at the same time the bartender approached. Placing the order and flipping the phone open, she answered without looking at the caller ID. "Hello?" she said.

"You look stunning in that dress." Tavares sucked her teeth, because even though she appreciated the compliment, she was feeling some kinda way with Abdora.

~ 355 ~

Tavares went to hang the phone up and Abdora slightly yelled, "Wait! Don't hang up and don't turn around. I'm right behind you and you looking absolutely tasty in that dress. You know that dress is hugging those hips and that apple bottom just proper, right?"

"Is that so?" Tavares asked, real feisty as she blushed on the other end of the phone. Thank goodness he couldn't see her blush-red face right now. She was mad at him for being with his chick in her face and didn't care if she was there with her man. Tavares knew she was being selfish, but she didn't care.

"Yes, it's so, and I think I should be the one taking you out of it tonight." Dora would have left Jade in her hotel room without a problem. She would have been mad, but she wasn't his girl so she would have got over it as far as he was concerned. He was trying to see Tavares. If she was with it, Jade was going to be sleeping alone. Tavares tried to hold it, but she couldn't hold back the laughter as she picked up her drinks.

"I'm not sure that's an option, homey. Plus you have your little hot wannabe Vivica Fox to keep you busy for the night. If I was you, I would keep my focus on her. But thanks for the compliment and you have a good night," Tavares said with a slight attitude before hanging up. Abdora had to laugh because this chick reminded him too much of himself. You didn't get to piss him off and then get in his good graces easily, so he had to laugh. She didn't say so, but she was a little stung seeing him with his date and that was good, Dora thought, as he watched Tavares sashay back to her man.

Abdora passed the night with Bryce and their dates, but he was thinking about Tavares the whole evening. He kept stealing glances of Tavares on the dance floor looking like a bronze-colored Jessica Rabbit in the body-hugging red dress that she was rocking the hell out of. Her heels gave her tiny ass some height, and she was the flyest woman in the room by a landslide.

Bryce and Abdora left their dates at the table, sipping on cocktails, and went outside to kick it. "My nigga," Bryce said, half joking, half serious, "I need you to get your focus off your little cherry drop in that red dress and remember that you got a bad bitch at the table. You ain't even stunting her ass," laughed Bryce. "You been giving her half the conversation you was before shorty came up in here with her man."

"I know, my nigga, but seeing her while I'm with the next chick got me feeling fucked up. Bryce, I swear I didn't know she was going to be here. Word, I didn't. If I'd known, I wouldn't even have flown Jade out here to be my date. Me and shorty was rocking hard last night and woke up together this morning, so being here with Jade is a little smack in the face, even though she got a man. Difference is I know and accept she got a man. I know she's tight with a nigga but it ain't my fault. Neither of us mentioned that we were going to a surprise birthday party or I would have put two and two together, early. I never imagined that her nigga was getting enough dollars to be fucking with Holton Montiago. This shit was a fucked up coincidence."

"I can dig it, my nigga, you're feeling her and she got your ass open, but you're here with Jade and she's here with her man, so it is what it is, my nigga."

"I know, but do you see her ass and baby-bearing hips in that dress?" Abdora tried to reason with him. "Jade is looking good, but not that good. Tavares found the perfect dress, not just a dress."

"Nigga, I see it, her man sees it, and so does every other nigga in the room, but that shit don't change nothing. You and her are in two different worlds tonight. So let's just enjoy ourselves and you at least try to concentrate on Jade."

"Nigga, I'm gonna try since Imma be laying with her ass tonight, but she's definitely the runner-up of the evening," Dora joked.

Holton watched Tavares exit the bathroom and go back toward the ballroom. *She has a real natural beauty about herself*, Holton thought. He watched her and it wasn't her make up, her hair, her eyes, or anything else other than the natural beauty she possessed and the way she carried herself like a diva that made her beautiful. Holton couldn't help but to drift back over twenty years and think about the beautiful woman who stole his heart before he married Lilly. He loved her more than she or anyone else really knew. He wasn't supposed to fall for her, never mind be in love with her, so their relationship ended terribly. Tavares had a natural, flawless beauty and the more he watched her the more his heart skipped a beat thinking about the lady from his past, even though he hadn't seen her in over two decades.

Damien and his girlfriend partied with lust for their after-plans. Damien was ready to give it to Tavares in every inch and way possible once he got her out of her dress. Tavares got to chit-chat with Lilly and obtained a little info on Abdora. She learned that Abdora was a millionaire, even though no one really knew it. Abdora had hustled hard and invested heavy in legit businesses, and he owned massive property that made him rich. His drug money was long money, but he really just kept his street organization afloat with it. Lilly informed her that her husband considered him one of the wisest and most loyal young men in the game.

Abdora was ready for the night to be over because he wasn't feeling that he wasn't going to be the one sliding Tavares out of her red fitted Jessica Rabbit dress. Dora looked at her and couldn't help but feel like he needed her, and he was tired of not having her. Something was going to have to give, and soon.

Tavares and Damien headed home, both intoxicated and ready to get it in. Arriving home, they wasted no time coming out of their clothes and going at each other. They started at the door and there was a trail all the way up the stairs to their bedroom. Once they arrived in their room, it was like a baseball game that went nine innings. Damien was hitting home runs every time, making Tavares cum all over the place. By the time Damien was ready to nut, Tavares was good and pleased with the work he'd put in. Damien picked up his pace and started to moan loudly as he released into Tavares. For the first time, they were too lazy to move off the wet sheets and fell asleep in the puddles underneath them.

After a great night and hours of sex, Damien thought he'd gotten off the hook with the whole ordeal of giving Tavares the car that he shot homeboy from. Tavares didn't think so, though. Getting out of the bed, Tavares washed Damien off of her and got dressed. Making her way downstairs to cook breakfast, she waited for Damien to join her.

When he made his way downstairs, with a smile from ear to ear, Tavares set into him. "I hate to burst your fucking bubble and shit, but let's get down to the nitty gritty of why you shot that nigga."

"Damn, good morning to you too."

"Good morning, now back to what I was talking about. Was it because yawl hoods got drama or because he's banging your $2 hoe ass babymama? Because if you ask me, it's the latter of the fucking two." Damien sucked his teeth because he wasn't trying to get into this, fresh out of bed. Especially after the wonderful night they had.

"Tavares, I told you I shot that nigga 'cause we got beef. I don't know nothing about that nigga banging my trick ass baby's mother. Who she sucks and fucks is her business and ain't no reason for me to get salty."

"Damien, you're a fucking liar. Word, you are. How about we go to LA, Liar's Anonymous, and you just say, 'Hi, my name is Damien and I'm a FUCKING liar!'"

"Fuck you, Tavares."

"Whatever, don't be mad at me because you are a L I A R." Tavares laughed because he was busted.

"So, you gonna tell me yawl's hoods have beef and you didn't know nothing about him banging that gum-guzzling ass Shaunda? Okay, I'm glad you think I got boo-boo the fool written across my forehead. But it's cool because I can assure you, you're wearing me thin and I'm about to be all fucking set with you. You put me in a fucked-up situation because your pride was bruised that your enemy is fucking your whack ass baby's mother, but know that's the last time you'll ever play with me or my life. You got a good thing and you don't even fucking appreciate it. But know that one man's trash is another man's treasure."

"What the fuck you trying to say?" Damien asked, getting madder by the moment.

"It's not what I'm *trying* to say, it's what I just said. So don't read between the lines, read what I just put on the line!"

"Tavares, what the fuck do you want me to say?" Tavares chuckled out of sheer anger.

"The truth would be nice. I mean, it's not like I didn't just pull your card, so all you have to do is be a man and admit it."

"Oh, now I'm not a fucking man because I won't be a puppet and say what you want me to say?"

"Damien, are you a fucking idiot or just plain retarded? HOW the fuck is saying the truth being a puppet? You ain't saying what I want you to say, you're saying the truth! But I see you aren't too good at telling the truth, so fuck it, don't even worry about it."

"Fine, Tavares, I shot that nigga because he was banging Shaunda, but it ain't like that. I don't give a fuck about her, it's the fact that the nigga is from a rival hood and got the balls to be fucking my BM!"

Tavares didn't know whether to laugh or cry. "Damien, you're just sad. Sad and outside of that I have no idea what else to say to you. Your baby's mother is a trollop, a tramp, a smut, and a dog-ass mess, and you really feel some type of way that a nigga put his dick in her? WHO gives a fuck if yawl got beef, you don't fuck her or fuck with her so what the fuck does it matter?"

"Tavares, you don't get it. It's just a code of the streets."

"Damien, fuck you, fuck your street codes, and just leave me the fuck alone." Tavares threw on her Timberlands and her pink North Face Snorkel Jacket and left Damien in the kitchen looking as stupid as he was. Tavares hopped in her truck and figured she would go do some Christmas shopping.

~ CHAPTER 19 ~

Two can play that game, but I play to win.

Tavares figured she was on a roll, so she might as well call Abdora and give his ass the business too. Dialing his number, she patiently waited for him to answer.

"Hello there, sweetheart," Dora answered.

"Oh, I'm sweetheart now," Tavares said dryly. "What happened to your little wannabe Vivica Fox? I figured you fucked her brains out last night, so you'd be calling her sweetheart today. Are you done parading her around town?"

Dora looked at the phone to make sure he was hearing right. Never did Tavares talk to him all crazy and never did she comment on who he might have been fucking, so he knew for sure that she felt some type of way.

"Hello, are you there?" Tavares snapped. "I can't hear you."

"Damn babe, what's going on? Why you coming at me all harsh and fucked up?"

"Dora, like for real, really I feel some type of way about you laying up with me and then showing up to a party I'm at with the next bitch on your arm smiling like you and her got something real hot and heavy."

"Ma, slow down and pump your brakes. Since you wanna get funky and shit, Imma let you in on a secret: you was there with your motherfucking man! And furthermore, if I had known that you were going to be there. I wouldn't have brought her. Tavares, me and you both do our own thing and then meet up in the middle, so yeah, I did bring a date. but that shit don't change nothing between us. It don't alter how I feel about you or that I want to be with you. and you got a bum ass nigga that you aren't willing to leave. So until you're willing to lose your baggage, I think you're outta pocket trying to check me over the next bitch."

"Oh yeah, is that what you think? Okay, well since I'm so far outta pocket, I can stay there and you don't have to worry about me, what I think, or how I feel, motherfucker," and she hung up.

Dora tried to call her back numerous times, but she wouldn't answer. He'd hurt her feelings just like Dame did, so now they were both in the doghouse.

Before Tavares knew it, five days had passed and she hadn't talked to Abdora. It didn't bother her that she wasn't talking to Dame, but she did miss Abdora. She wasn't taking his texts or phone calls. Tavares felt some type about Abdora and his date even though she knew she was outta pocket for it. So a break was definitely in order.

She had no problem blocking a person out. She only read and deleted Dora's shit-talking text messages. She was sitting on the couch, watching a Lifetime movie, when her phone started going off. Sucking her teeth, she wondered who the fuck was trying to ruin her movie. The number was real funny, not like a number she'd seen before. It definitely wasn't someone calling from a business this late, and it wasn't a house number for sure, so who the fuck was this funny ass number, Tavares thought, and didn't pick it up. Three minutes into the movie, the same number popped up, only the last digit was different. "Who in the hell is this?" Tavares said out loud, getting agitated.

"Hello," was as far as she got before the, "You have a collect call from Damien Stasher," came on. Accepting the phone call, Tavares simply asked, "Where are you and how much is your bail?" She wasn't beat for his story.

"Don't say it like that," Damien said, not feeling her cold shoulder.

"Say it like what? Like this is some fucking bullshit? Oh, because it is, so if that's what I sound like then, hey, what can I say?"

"Whatever, yo! You gotta call the bail bondsman."

"Damien, I swear to GOD this shit is so fucking old and tired that I should just fucking leave you there. I got better shit to do then come bail you outta fucking jail."

"Yo! Tav, this ain't the time to play right now. Save your fucking shit-talking till I get outta here. Right now I need to get the fuck out of here."

"What type of money do I need to get up? Please don't say nothing outrageous because you better hope that we got at least ten thousand in the crib."

"Tavares, what the fuck did you do with the rest of the money?" "I been hitting all the house money to do Christmas shopping, duh! Where did you think I was getting it from, if I wasn't asking you for it? Sure as hell not from my personal account!"

"You be on some real bullshit, Apple. I know what was in the spot, so how the fuck did you go through that fucking much money Christmas shopping? You know what, Apple? I ain't even going here with you right now. Just call the fucking bondsman and when you find out what my bail is, call niggaz and tell them to give up whatever you need till the morning," and the line went dead.

Oh no, this nigga didn't, Tavares thought, looking at the phone. *Oh, he gotta a lotta fucking nerve*, she thought, taking her time to call the bondsman. Forty-five minutes later, Apple was aggravated and mad that she even picked up her phone. Loving Damien was just too much at times. With $30,000 bail for having a gun and $15,000 in the house, Tavares got to hustling and bustling to do what she had to do in order to meet the bail bondsman in three hours to get him out. Tavares tried to call Damien's brother Rollo and his best friend Winky, but neither one of them had their phones on. She headed to the projects for niggaz to come up with $15,000 for their nigga.

When Tavares got down to the bricks, she couldn't believe that even dead smack in the middle of winter did these niggaz hug the block. Seasons changed, but never did the weather run them off. They were keeping warm in their North Face coats, skully hats, and Timberland boots. Tavares hopped out and saw a few of her boyfriend's friends, but not the ones that he rocked with hard body. Tavares didn't care one bit. She was asking them for what she needed since they were the first ones she saw.

"What's up, yawl?" Tavares said, pulling her cute brown knit hat down over her ears. "Dame got knocked. I need $15,000 till the morning."

"Say, what?" Beefy asked like she was trippin' if she thought she was getting that kind of money from him. He was Damien's man, but he didn't fuck with him on a day-to-day basis like some niggaz.

"What, you didn't hear or comprehend or something?" Tavares asked, letting them know she was past not in the mood.

"Damn, why that nigga ain't hit our phone?" Squizzy asked, not sure if he was buying her request.

"Do I fucking look like I know? I sure wish he would have, though. Because then I wouldn't be out here in the motherfucking cold having to deal with yawl. Lord knows I got better shit to do than deal with you gutter butt ass niggas." Tavares didn't care what came out of her mouth, if it was on her mind she let it come out. "All I know is the nigga said to call yawl, but I don't have your numbers so I came down here. He said for yawl to give up what I didn't have till the morning. I'm not about to sit here and keep explaining myself. So if niggaz is on the funny shit, just let me know because I can definitely do it moving."

"Damn, why you always gotta a have a fucked up ass mouth, Shizzy?" Flores asked.

"For real," seconded Squizzy. "Because who has time for the motions? I sure don't. I told yawl what it is and yawl are looking at me all stupid and shit, so what the fuck? I gotta meet the bondsman in two and a half hours, so either yawl got it or yawl don't."

"Damien needs to tame your mouth," Beefy said, snarling at Tavares.

"Whatever, yo," Tavares rolled her eyes, not giving a flying fuck about their thoughts.

"Listen with your feisty ass. Imma go get five and these niggaz can work the rest out," Beefy said, giving his niggaz dap and walking away. After all the bullshit Tavares felt like she'd just gone through, niggaz left and went to get their portions so they could get Dame out of jail. One hour later, Tavares was straight and on her way to go get Doll.

Tavares was sitting at Nashua Street Jail with Doll as the half-bald, old, white bondsman took forever and a day to count $30,000 in twenties, fifties, and hundreds. Tavares was ready to scream, "Hurry the fuck up already," when he messed up again and started over from the beginning.

"Sir, I don't mean to be rude, but those are hundreds, fifties, and twenties, so it's not that hard to count them."

"Miss, can you please just relax, I need to make sure every dollar is here."

Tavares looked from the man to the money, then from the money to the man, and just shook her head at how slow he was. "Okay, I lost my place so now I gotta start over," the man said.

"Ma, I'm going outside before I blow a gasket," Tavares said, turning around fuming mad.

Tavares wished at times like this that she smoked cigarettes for real and not just when she was drinking, because she needed a stress reliever for real. Tavares was calming down when her cell phone rang. Looking at the number, Tavares smiled, but wasn't messing with him. He was on punishment for being at the party with the next bitch and then tryna tell her she was outta pocket for feeling some kind of way. He did brighten her face though, that much she could admit, looking at the number.

Tavares didn't know what Abdora was doing to her. She tried to figure out what she had going on in her platonic affair, but she was clueless. To be honest, Tavares didn't get any of it. She just knew that she liked him, liked him from the bottom of her heart. She thought he would stop at the phone call, but of course not. She just smiled because even though she was going hard with ignoring him, he wasn't letting up. She liked that, go hard or go home for what you want.

Looking at the message indicator, she opened the message. "So you just gonna keep ignoring a nigga, huh? I've apologized a million times. Call me when u get off dat B.S. I'm not calling no more." Tavares smiled because she knew for sure that he was mad now.

Abdora was sitting in his house, leaning back on his bed, real tight that Apple was just watching him call and text. Just like she'd been doing for over a week now. He knew her well enough to know that she never made moves without her phone, so if her phone was ringing, she was watching him call and reading his text messages. He hated that she had the ability to get to him in a way that he let no other man or woman do. Soft wasn't in his nature. But Tavares made him feel soft as pie when it came to her fine little sexy ass. She didn't even know what she did to him. He just liked everything about her, nothing more and nothing less. She was fun, funny, pretty, sexy, smart, down to earth, and made him feel so good inside.

Abdora dug that she liked him for him, not because of all the money he had or the name he had in the streets. Tavares was killing him with this nigga of hers, though, who definitely didn't know what to do with a good woman. He was trying to do big things with Tavares. She just had to get rid of her loser ass nigga and let the sky be the limit. She was loyal though, and that he respected.

Unfortunately, Tavares didn't know how not to reward disloyalty with loyalty. She didn't get the kind of nigga she was letting pass her by. Dora wasn't proclaiming to be the best nigga, but he knew for sure he was a high-ranking member of the good nigga club. Dora stewed in his thoughts and anger for about an hour before getting up to get dressed and make power moves.

Damien was sitting in the cell, mad as hell that no one had come to get him. You couldn't be bailed after 10:00 p.m. and it was nearing that. He was fuming mad as he was about to be processed to stay that night at Nashua Street Jail. He was in the cell, looking out the window that over looked the busy highway, getting madder by the second. Damien could feel fire off his body when they called Stasher.

He rose from the hard wooden bench and got ready to hit the units when the guard said, "Wrong way, you're being bailed."

Damien let out a loud sigh of relief because he didn't want to stay in jail even if it was just for the night. His girl hadn't let him down. Then again, when did she ever? He knew she was going to be cussing him out all the way home, though. He didn't give a fuck, he was just glad he wasn't going to have to stay in Nash for the night, till the banks opened in the morning. Coming downstairs with a cheesy grin, his property and shoe strings, Damien saw his mother and girlfriend when the double glass sliding doors opened.

Doll wasted no time going in on him. "I don't know what the fuck you're smiling for, 'cause ain't shit funny," Doll scolded. "Got us running around for some damn $30,000 because your dumb fucking ass wants to be picking up cases. Ain't no one got time for this fucking shit, right before Christmas," Doll said, not letting him get a word in. She spun around in her peacoat, fitted jeans, and stiletto, pointy-toed boots and headed to the car. Tavares just looked at Damien and tried to hold her words, but she couldn't resist.

"I just want to know who fucking waits till they're grown to be picking up cases. I just don't get waiting till after twenty-one to start getting arrested," Tavares said, disgusted with him for the moment. Damien got in his CL500 that Tavares was pushing and started with his mother first.

"Ma, why the fuck are you mad? It ain't like you gave up your damn money. All that dough is money I gotta give back in the morning, so cut the shit," Damien said, not feeling them.

"I don't give a fuck if I didn't give up fifty fucking cents, you still ain't had no business catching no case."

"Yawl are fucking acting like a nigga meant to get bagged up and shit. The nigga had no reason whatsoever to search the car, so the shit is beatable. Yawl really think I'm feeling fucking paying a lawyer or having $30,000 tied up in mother fucking bail?"

"Damien, you had no fucking business with a gun in your car," his mother made clear.

He started to explain that it wasn't his gun, that his man left it when he went back to the halfway house and was on his way to drop it off, but decided not to. Damien wasn't saying nothing else to his mother, because she was being an asshole at the moment. Damien and Tavares dropped Doll off at home and kept it moving to their house.

"So you're just gonna ride in silence and not say shit?" Damien asked as Tavares was quiet and looking out the window.

Not turning around, she asked, "What would you like me to say?"

"Say something," Damien slightly pleaded. Tavares turned her whole body around and faced Damien.

"I just don't think you get enough. First the hot shit you pulled with me almost going to jail, and now you end up in jail. What the fuck is going to be next? Do you know what the word 'enough' means?" questioned Tavares. "Now, you're going to be running back and forth downtown? This is definitely going to be in Superior Court if you get indicted."

"I ain't getting indicted, so you ain't gotta worry about that."

"Oh, trust and believe I'm not worried about it, but you should be because you ain't a mind reader and don't know the future."

"Tavares, you ain't gotta get all fucking nasty and shit. Hopefully my lawyer will get it thrown out from the gate. But if not, it is what it is. Let's just get through the fucking holidays. Christmas is next week, so I'm going to lay low and move in silence until then."

Before Tavares and Damien arrived home, they stopped at the gas station to get some cigarillos. Damien got out the car and waited in the long line. Tavares was waiting for Dame to come back when his phone started blowing up. His text message indicator went off. Tavares grabbed the phone. Not because she cared who it was or what it said, but because if you didn't clear the message, Dame had it set to where it would keep chiming. Tavares was checking the message just as the door swung open.

"Damn, now you going through my phone and shit?"

"Nigga please, I was clearing the message because it kept going off. Don't no one give two fucks or a lollypop about who you got calling your hoe ass."

"You better watch your fucking mouth," Damien said, without looking at his girlfriend. Tavares just wanted to get home so that she could take a shower, twist up her weed, and relax. Damien had got on enough of her nerves for the day.

Tavares's phone went off and she wasn't in the mood, but she checked to see who it was anyways. Smiling real fast without even knowing, Damien caught her and said, "Who's that? Your fucking boyfriend?"

Tavares sucked her teeth and said, "No, because your stupid fucking ass is sitting right here next to me."

"So why you ain't answering your phone, then?"

"What?" Tavares asked like he was stupid.

"You heard me, so let's not play stupid."

"Last time I checked, this is my phone, and I don't fucking want to talk so I didn't answer. So if that ain't good enough for you, I really don't know what else to tell you."

"Tavares, I just got done sitting in a fucking cell for the last four hours, I ain't got time to be arguing with you."

"So don't," Tavares said, giving him just as much attitude as he deserved.

"Oh, I'm not," Dame said, "We're going to agree not to say shit to each other for the rest of the night."

Tavares was just fine with that. Damien turned on the radio to cut through the tension that was filling his car.

Arriving home, Tavares didn't say two words to Damien. Instead, she made her way to the third floor to take a shower. While in the shower, Tavares was thinking and thinking. She couldn't help but ask herself if this was really what her life was supposed to be. Was she supposed to be with a no-good, cheating ass drug dealer who seemed to get stupider the older he got?

There was a hard knock at the door that startled Tavares. "What?" Tavares yelled, mad that Damien was interrupting her peace of mind.

"You want me to order you something to eat? I'm about to order New York Pizza."

"No," Tavares said with attitude that was evident over the running water and the locked door between them.

"Bitch," Damien mumbled to himself and made his way back downstairs. Tavares was the ultimate bitch when she wanted to be, and Damien wasn't in the mood. Damien ordered his food and went to the TV room to roll a fat blunt of some sour.

Holton was in New York, finishing up some business before he headed to meet Dora for dinner and drinks. By the time Holton arrived at Carmine's, he found Dora at the bar, chillaxing like he was in deep thought. "What's up, Dora, you alright?" Holton asked his young protégé, who hadn't even seen him approach.

"Yeah, I'm cool, Holton, was just thinking, that's all. Our table is ready, I was just waiting for you."

After a fine, authentic Italian dinner and conversing about business, the two gentlemen, who were more like father and son than business partners, shot the shit on a personal level. "Holton, I need to ask you a question."

"Anything, youngen, shoot."

"What's up with that nigga Damien Stasher?"

"I should be asking you that because I could feel the tension when he offered you a drink."

"I didn't want that nigga buying me shit," Dora said with a bad taste in his mouth.

"You got a problem with him that I should know about?"

"I only know son indirectly, but he ain't my type of nigga. He's a slimeball as far as I'm concerned."

"So why you asking about him?" Holton said, trying to figure out Abdora's angle.

Dora knew he could trust Holton, so he told him the deal. "I'm feeling his girl but she loves the no-good nigga so much that she ain't trying to give me the time of day, at least not for real." Holton's eyes widened, catching Dora's drift.

"Damien is a good nigga. I watched him grow up. He don't play in the game how you play, but he does his one, two. He worked for me and then stacked enough to fuck with me, so I fuck with him. I do know that he's a playboy type a nigga, but he does love his girl."

"Holton, Tavares is a good girl, and I do mean a good girl. I just wish she knew better so she would do better."

"Youngen, you gotta let her wake up and smell the coffee on her own."

"No doubt, because I ain't never been a hater type of nigga. I just can't grasp why she stays. He did some slimeball shit to my mans behind his baby's mother and tossed his girl in the middle, almost got her thrown in jail right before your party. I wanted to lay that nigga to rest but didn't on the strength of babygirl."

"That ain't stand up nigga shit," Holton said, not liking the words coming out of Abdora's mouth. "When you're in this game you never ever put the lady you love in harm's way. Are you and her serious?"

"A little bit, but not serious as in intimate because she's so loyal that she isn't willing to explore anything other than friendship."

"Well, you gotta respect the loyalty because a lot of these young girls wouldn't know loyalty if it slapped them in the face. My advice to you is do whatever you been doing, and in the end things will play out as fate will have it. You're a good man, Abdora, and Tavares seems like a really nice girl, with her head on straight, so eventually she'll wake up.

~ 374 ~

Trust me, all women get tired, so she will too. Just make sure if you get her you do right by her."

"Holton, come on, you already know I ain't that type of nigga."

"I know," laughed Holton, because he did know that about Abdora; he watched him grow from a roofless young gang banger to a streetwise businessman. "I still had to tell you anyways." Holton had a genuine love for Abdora and wanted the day to come that he did find someone to share his happiness.

Christmas was there before Tavares knew it. It was Christmas Eve and Tavares spent the day last-minute shopping well into the evening. Tavares and Doll went to the South Shore Mall, ripping and running in every store and were glad to be exiting the madness.

They were cracking on Doll's gay homegirl and her African girlfriend. "Doll, I want your homegirl to not be feeling an African chick with a shifty weave and a horrible dress game," Tavares said, choking on her lemonade. "Ma, her clothes be like three sizes too big and she just be looking real crazy."

"Shit, you ain't gotta tell me, I be looking at the raggedy ass bitch just like you do. Anna is the one who's blind and don't see how raggedy the fake bougie African bitch is. Girl, please, I had to fucking ask Anna if that's her woman then why the fuck was she letting her walk around looking all fucked up."

Doll had once, on the low, told the African, lesbian lady who was also married that if she was bragging about her daughter doing her hair, then she needed to send her back to hair school to get her skills up, because her hair did not look good. Doll didn't know how to not keep it real. Doll and Tavares were in the car on the way home when they spoke Anna up.

"What's up, Anna?" Doll answered.

"I'm at home stressing out. Uma is getting on my nerves. She keep talking about she's coming here to fight me because I don't want to be with her."

Doll snapped. "Anna, don't no one got time for her raggedy ass and bullshit threats. She just don't want you to leave her because of how much you do for her. That bitch just wants your money and for you to suck her pussy dry before she goes home to her husband. How many times I gots to tell you that? That bitch only sees dollar signs. Every time she comes around talking she needs this and she wants that and her husband don't do this and don't do that. Don't be no damn fool. That's why the fuck the voodoo princess wants to keep you close. She wanna control you and your estate. She don't give two fucks or a lollypop about you being with her. I keep telling you, she's a real life witch. Fruit cake bitch got toenails so damn long that she cuts her socks open and can't wear shoes with no backs. That's a creepy bitch, Anna, and you know it."

"Doll, get off my bitch, because you ain't giving up no draws," joked Anna.

"Motherfucking right I ain't. I ain't with that gay shit. I gets dicked down whenever I want," Doll laughed at her friend, who she always knew had a crush on her, but settled for them being really good friends.

"Doll, I wanted to thank you for picking up those Christmas presents for me too."

"Not a problem, just have my cash on sight, like you do Uma's," Doll joked. Tavares laughed at Doll and dropped her off before she headed home.

Arriving home, Tavares wrapped her presents in pink and silver polka dot wrapping paper to match her all-white twelve-foot tree that had only pink and silver decorations. By the time Tavares finally finished wrapping presents and cleaning the house, she was exhausted. Taking a shower, Tavares was headed to bed when her phone chimed. Opening the message indicator, Tavares read, "I just wanted to be the first to say Merry Christmas. Stay mad, but I better see you REAL soon, like today soon." Tavares laughed, then texted back, "Merry Christmas to you too. glad you think so but there's nothing that could get me there on xmas day! You are officially crazy. Merry xmas & good night." That was the first text Dora had gotten in two weeks, so he was smiling from ear to ear.

Damien wasn't home, but Tavares didn't even care. Her house was clean, dinner was in the oven, and the tree was beautiful, so she was complete for the night, with or without Dame. Tavares crawled in bed and was out before she knew it.

Damien had been in the streets all day. He planned on doing nothing but being with his family and girl on Christmas, so he was trying to get all the money he could before he took a major loss the following day. Damien was getting money till the wee hours of Christmas morning. Damien and his man Winky rode around hollering at their sidepieces, dropping their presents off in between getting money. Intoxicated from the gallon of Hennessey Privilege they'd downed, they never noticed the two cars that had been following them for the last ten minutes.

Going down Columbia Road toward Dudley Street, Damien and Winky stopped at the red light at the intersection of Quincy Street. Not paying attention to their surroundings on the empty streets, they were kicking it about Christmas.

"Nigga, what you get Tav for Christmas?"

"Some red bottoms, a Louie bag, a Gucci bag, and ten bottles of perfume."

"Damn, my nito, you went all the way in, huh?"

Drunk, high, and not on point, they never saw the two cars pulling up on each side of them. Before they realized it, shots were flying from both sides. Winky was bleeding everywhere. His body was pumped with holes. Damien lay bleeding from his neck, his legs, and his arm, fading slowly from consciousness.

"Winky, say something," Damien said as he was spitting up blood. There was no response. They both lay there on Columbia Road, Winky dead and Damien unconscious.

By the time everyone got the phone call and rushed to the hospital, it was early morning. Everyone in Dame's family was there, along with his boys and Tavares's friends. It was 5:30 a.m. and people were everywhere in the waiting room.

The police were trying to inquire and ask questions, but were being cussed by nanny Dancy to the point where they didn't even want any problems. "You know what, ma'am? Maybe you're right. Maybe we should do this a little later when things have calmed down."

"Yeah, I think you should," Dancy said, rolling her eyes. "Because these people here, these people are mourning and aren't the ones who shot my grandson or killed his best friend. Won't you go do your goddamn job and leave us the hell alone?" nanny Dancy snapped.

"If you don't, we'll slap harassment charges on you faster than you can spin your rookie heads."

The police decided to give it a rest because Dancy wasn't having it, and they wanted no problems with her because she was well connected with the City Council, the Mayor, and the Governor. Dancy was known in the hood for not liking police. She thought they were low down, crooked, and dirty, and had no problem letting them know so. Never could they knock on her door when stuff went down in her hood. She despised the police and the rats who kept them informed. That's why she kept her grandsons up on who were the old lady snitches in her hood.

Dancy was from the old school, Panther days, and got it in. She was into politics, knew many politicians, and was on every board in the community. She was all about her people and not the people against them, the Boston Police, who she thought were racist pigs. She stayed doing something to help people better themselves. When they tried to have all-white construction sites, she wasn't having it, she called and informed them she knew the law and had black men recruited. She got children summer jobs, and kept various programs going to keep them out of the streets. She organized trips for teens and seniors. Housing was something she was always connected with; when people were homeless, they somehow found their way to her door before even thinking to hit a shelter. Her aura was that of a magnet because she was so real, down to earth, and loving that you couldn't help but love her. But when you tried to fuck with one of hers she would go hard in the paint and give you her wrath, so the police exited as fast as they entered the hospital.

Damien was in a private room and everyone made their way upstairs. Doll was having anxiety attacks as she paced the floor, listening to the doctors. Her kids were her world, so she was bugging out.

Tavares's eyes were bloodshot red as she stood in the hospital on Christmas morning, looking at Damien hooked up to monitors and machines. "I need some coffee, anyone want anything from Dunkin Donuts?" she asked.

Tavares took a walk to fulfill the small order and clear her mind. *This is just too much*, she thought. "Winky's dead," she said to herself, still trying to grasp it. *Damien is laid up in a hospital bed and could have been dead too. What's really going on?* she asked herself. Tavares was thinking Damien couldn't have been anything but blessed that he was going to live and be alright after taking eight bullets. Not one bullet had permanently injured any major artery, vessel, or organ, unlike every bullet had done to Winky. Twelve shots ripped him apart.

Tavares was feeling so lost in the madness. By the time she returned, there seemed to be even more people occupying the waiting room and hallways. It seemed like the word spread like wildfire and everyone came running. Tavares noticed two sets of groups who were posted up with waterfalls falling from one chick in each group. Tavares asked Dame's cousin Hershey, in a real sarcastic tone, "Uhh, are those some cousins of yawl's that I don't know or something?" Hershey looked at Tavares as if to say, *girl, please.* "I don't know who them chickens are," she responded with her pretty face, petite frame, and pretty, vibrant, smooth chocolate skin.

"They came up minutes apart, after you left. They sat with their respective groups and ain't said nothing. Just been consoling each chick in their crew who's putting on the waterworks show."

"So this is how Damien is doing it?" Tavares asked with her blue eyes feeling like they'd just welled up with fire and turned red.

"Well, Hershey, he has to be fucking them because what other reason would they be acting all dramatic over another bitch's man?"

"Girl, I don't know. But if they are, they're straight outta pocket."

Tavares went into Dame's room. Looking at his mother, grandmother, and brother, Tavares knew that she couldn't wild out on the chicks in the hallway. It wasn't the time or the place. She was a lady first. So Tavares decided to sting them another way. She kept it lady like and walked outside to the hallway full of fans and groupies. With her eyes scanning all the hoodrat chicks spilling over in the waiting room, Tavares said, "Excuse me, everyone. Damien's still not up and even when he wakes he will not be taking any visits from fans, jump-offs, or groupies, so you can hug the hallway, but it'll be a waste of time 'cause you won't be getting in to see him."

Instead of starting anything though, they just hurled dirty looks and kept it moving. Dame's mans and them came over and hugged Tavares and told her to call them if there were any changes or if there was anything she needed. They had to go plot and get revenge for Winky's death. Everyone was gone but family. Tavares and Doll were comfortable in the two recliners in front of Dame's bed. Nana was in the chair by the window and everyone was silently thinking their own thoughts about Damien being in the hospital bed. Doll just looked at her son and kept thanking God over and over that her son had survived, unlike his best friend. Nanny was thinking the same thing, but couldn't help but look at her grandson and hope that this would be his wake up call.

Tavares was looking at Dame and couldn't help thinking, *I'm just tired of your trifling ass.*

After two hours, nanny asked to be dropped off and Tavares obliged because she needed some air. Tavares arrived back at the hospital, valet-parked her car, and made her way upstairs. When she got off the elevator she found Doll in the hallway talking to a female who was pleading to get in and see Dame. She had seen this chick before, she just didn't know where. *Damn, who the hell is that bitch?* Tavares kept asking herself as she was taking long steps down the hall toward where they were talking. It hit Tavares. She recognized the chick from the night Dame was at the light. Tavares got so mad she felt like hot lava was welling up inside of her.

Tavares interrupted the conversation. "Just who the fuck are you and how the fuck can I help you?" Doll just walked away, because she felt the chick was out of pocket for being there after she had just explained she knew Damien had a girlfriend who he lived with, but loved her son.

Caught off guard by Damien's girlfriend, Malia said, "I wanna see Dame." She was timid with her words. "I just want to see him for a minute, please," she said, practically begging.

"You have fucking bumped your head and lost your fucking mind. I don't know who you are or which night Dame creeps with you, but babygirl, you got life totally fucked up. You're a fucking sideline hoe, a bootycall, and a stunt, so there ain't no fucking way in hell that you'll be seeing Dame on my time." Tavares was so overly nasty and curt that you would've thought the groupie would have given up.

"Please, I need to see him. I love him and he loves me."

Tavares almost cocked her hand back to slap the shit out of the chick, but caught herself. Tavares laughed and said, "Bitch, what part of 'you ain't fucking seeing Damien' don't you get or comprehend?"

"Please, I love Dame and Dame loves me," she kept sobbing.

"Sweetheart, Damien fucks you during the in between time, don't confuse swallowing a nigga's babies with love. Damien might fuck you but he doesn't love you, hun," Tavares said, schooling the naïve chick.

Tavares was steaming, but the chick would have never known as she walked away and left her there sobbing. Giving up, the girl turned around and headed back down the hall, crying and balling with tears everywhere.

Early in the evening, Damien woke up and Tavares didn't care, shot up or not, she was about to give his hoe ass the business. Damien was looking groggy but he was alive and alert. After his mother coddled over him for a while, she left Damien and Tavares alone.

Tavares wasted no time going in on Damien. "Dame, this can't be my life. I'm tired and just over it. Some people can't see when enough is enough, but I can and I can't do this."

"You can't do what?" Damien said in a muffled voice. "I'm the fucking one in the hospital bed all shot up, not you, so what the fuck can't you DO," Damien said, trying to raise his voice as loud as he could.

Damien wasn't in the mood for Apple's bullshit. "I can't do almost going to jail fucking with you because you're mad about a nigga dicking your baby's mother down. I can't do your trifling ass not coming home from time to time and always tryna tell me some dumb shit that we both know is dumb shit. I can't do being here on Christmas day because you were damn near killed for who knows what. I can't do being loyal to you when all you do is fuck bitch after bitch and tell lie after lie. I'm tired of fighting and cussing and cussing and fighting. You're never going to change and I'm tired of being tired. I can't do being your wife, standing by you doing right, when your bad outweighs your good. Imma bad bitch in all departments, so I don't deserve the bullshit that you put me through. All the cheating you be doing is just trick dicking!"

"Trick dicking," Damien questioned, like that was all he heard out of everything Tavares had just said. "Tavares, you got me fucked up if you think I be out here tricking with bitches. I be out making moves, getting dough, fucking with my niggaz and doing what I gotta do for me, you, and us, so you can talk that shit elsewhere."

Tavares looked at Dame and loved his Oscar-winning performance. Damien was good, Tavares had to admit it, but he wasn't good enough. She knew him too well, but if she didn't, she would've bought it. Tavares had to pull his card before she reached out and touched him in a not so nice way. "That same bitch I saw you at the light with came up here begging to see you. Said yawl love each other. So if you ain't trick dicking, motherfucker, why the fuck does she think yawl love each other? I don't fucking hear you," Tavares said in response to Damien's silence.

He knew that Malia had done exactly what Tavares said because she was past open, young, and believed anything he said. Damien tried to think quick on his feet. When he couldn't, silence came.

"The bullshit is old now, Damien. I'm over it and just fucking tired. Like you be doing too much. You're out here living wild and rampant like you ain't got a girl. Nigga, and how long we been together? So since that's how you're out here living, why don't you just not have a girl and then you can sling your dick as freely as you want to? You had a lobby full of chicks out there crying and looking crazy. I didn't know not one of them, so that told me what that was all about. Then they had the nerve to be looking at me like I was crazy. Are you for real?" Tavares asked. "I'm fed up with you, your bitches, the streets, and most of all you taking me for granted."

"Apple, this is some bullshit. I'm lying in a hospital bed, fucked up, and you really want to rip a nigga about some bitches. Apple, look at me. Are you fucking kidding me? You're trippin' right now. Word, you are. Do you think I give a fuck about them bitches? Who the fuck do I come home to? When I get money, I bring it home to you. Who the fuck do I take care of? Whose spoiled ass gets what ever they want? So save the bullshit."

Apple just chuckled. "And because you do all that, it gives you equal playing field to fuck with other bitches and stick your dick in them when you feel like it? WOW. Okay, I get it now. Well, in that case, Damien, then you don't need me. If I can't be everything, then I don't want to be anything. I thought you loved me," Tavares said, looking at Damien with hurt welled up in her eyes.

"You know I love you, so why are we even doing this long ass soap opera hospital scene?"

"Soap opera hospital scene, is that what you call what the fuck I'm saying to you? You're a real piece of work, Damien Stasher. I don't hardly call it that. I call it me calling you on your bullshit and letting you know that I'm fucking tired of all this shit and that I'm done."

"I don't doubt that you love me, but the shit you do in the meantime and in between time is like how do you do it, if you love me? I need to get my mind right. So Imma take some me time and do me. You got your brother, mom, and grandmother here to look over you and take care of you. Not to mention the nurses, doctors, and even your entourage of bitches, so you'll be okay."

Damien was drugged up and coming down from pain medication, so he thought he heard Apple wrong. "What did you just say?" he asked through squinting eyes. "What does that mean?"

"This is what it means. I'm going away for Leslie's birthday in a week. From now until then I'm going to dig deep, do some soul-searching, and figure out what's right for me, because I'm not too sure if you or this relationship is right for me anymore. I go back to school in three weeks and I definitely need to be together to make it across that stage in May. It means that as you lay here and get better, I want you to work out what it is that you really want. And I'm going to do the same. I'll be back after the 2nd."

"So you're just going to bounce on me while I'm lying here, fucked up in the game."

"I'm not leaving you, because you have more than enough people here to care for you. You showed me that today. So you can take it how you want. I'm always here when you need me, but right now I need me, so I'm going to work it out and do what I need to for me. If you can't understand it now, you will eventually."

Tavares's heart hurt. Leaving Damien lying there felt like payback that he deserved, but doing it hurt Tavares more than she could stand.

Damien was so mad that if he could have gotten up out the bed and choked Tavares, it would have been done. "Tavares, get your fucking mind right. I hold the house down, take care of you, feed you, fuck you, and love you, so miss me with that bullshit that you're kicking. Okay, so I might fuck a whore bitch here and there, but it's a wrap; I hear you loud and clear. I'm done with that shit. So now can you cut the shit and please take a seat and get comfortable?"

Tavares had to look at Damien like he'd lost his mind. "Damien, I just told you what it was. You need to do some soul-searching because I've heard that you aren't going to cheat a hundred times too many. So I love you, and I'll see you when I get back." Tavares said nothing else. She exited the room without even looking back.

Tavares headed home and packed. Waiting for the cab, she changed her voicemail to say, "Merry Christmas, I'm on vacation until after the New Year, so leave a message and I'll talk to you in 2010."

ACID CONNECTIONS PART 2

~ CHAPTER 1 ~

Payback is a BITCH

Three hours later Tavares was pulling up to Abdora's mother's house to see no parking. There were cars in the long driveway, on the sidewalk, in front of the house, and all the way down the block on both sides. Dhara's house was packed. Tavares walked in and felt like she was experiencing déjà vu. It felt like what Doll's house would have been like on Christmas. It was just a different house and different people. This is real crazy, Tavares thought to herself. Weed smoke was lingering in the air. Kids were running happily back and forth. Food could be smelled in the air from the various plates people had. Tavares felt right at home.

Tavares said hello to the familiar and unfamiliar faces as Dora was trying to lead her to the kitchen. "Boy is you crazy or stupid if you think I'm going to roll up in your mother's house and not go speak to her," she said.

"She don't like you anyways," joked Dora.

"Whatever, nigga," Tavares said and spun around, going the opposite way of the kitchen to say hi to Miss Dhara. Dhara's eyes lit up as she hopped up off her chair. Tavares had been to Miss Dhara's house every time that she had come to visit Dora. They were cool in the game with each other. Tavares loved Miss Dhara because she was so pretty, smart, and hood all in one. It was hard to believe that she had come from being a homeless crackhead to a successful businesswoman. Tavares loved that Dora's mother was so real. Everything about her was real and she gave it to you straight-laced with no chaser. She was always spitting knowledge on life, men, the game, the streets, GOD, struggles of addiction, history, and anything else that you could think of. She was a wise woman without a doubt. That was why you had to love her. Dhara had slung dope, ran hoes, numbers, and anything else that got dough in her day. In her prime she dated only drug cartels, no low-level drug dealers for her. Dhara had shot, stabbed, and beat both men and women senseless in her wild days. Now she was a Christian woman who had been clean for 14 years, with the exception of weed. Dora definitely got his gangster from his mother, no matter how saved she was now.

"Miss Thing, what are you doing here? My son didn't tell me that you were coming. He actually told me you wasn't speaking to him. I got a present for you under the tree, so I'm glad that you made it."

"I got a present for you too. I'll have your son put it upstairs in your room. It's a very private gift," Tavares laughed, thinking about the vibrator that she had got Miss Dhara. Dhara was a born freak and still was in her older age. She was reserved but not hidden about it. One of the weekends Tavares had visited, she and Abdora attended a toy party at her house. It was a party for real. People were everywhere drinking, eating, and watching the toys being presented like they were 18 again. The lady hired to do the party was fun and raunchy with it, so the older ladies were on the edge of their seats. The men were just sitting around, waiting to catch one of them slipping. Tavares was in pure laughter watching the old-ass freaks. The funny thing was that everyone at the party with the exception of Dora, Tavares, and Dora's friends was over 40. Dhara was off the chain.

"Oh shoot, my fault," she said to her company. "Everyone, this is Tavares. Hopefully my soon-to-be daughter-in-law," Dhara announced to everyone in her dining room.

"Yeah, she got my nephew running around all lovesick and shit," joked Dora's Aunt Red.

"Miss Red, I keep telling you that's not the case, so you better stop saying that," Tavares said, blushing.

"Girl please, my baby sister don't tell no lies," Dhara said, sticking up for her sister. Tavares was okay in Miss Dhara's book. Tavares brought a smile and a look to her son's face that she had never seen before. "Miss D, I can't believe you be doing it way big like this."

"Like what?"

"You got all these people over here, like it's a huge party for real."

"Yeah girl, I gots to. I have to enjoy this big ole house. But you go enjoy yourself. Go in there and get you some food. I'll see you before you go."

"Wait, where is the original fly granny herself?" Tavares asked, realizing that Abdora's grandmother wasn't present.

"Oh, mommy and her little man thang are in the Dominican Republic," said Aunty Red.

"Oh shit... I know that's right, nana," laughed Tavares. Saying her goodbyes to the dining room full of ladies, Tavares found her way to the kitchen, where Abdora and his friends definitely had it on smash.

Tavares walked in and said hello and it was all eyes on her. Everyone greeted her with what's up's and merry Christmas. The fellas' girlfriends were sizing her up at the same time they were giving their half hellos. Tavares could feel them on her indirectly, but she didn't care. She was used to all eyes on her.

Back in Boston Damien was lying in his hospital bed asking himself several questions. Did my girl really walk out and leave me? Who shot me? Will I live next time? Is Tavares coming back? Damien asked himself these questions after calling Tavares twenty times and getting her voicemail. He loved Tavares, he really did, he just never expected for his dog ways to catch up to him enough for her to get fed up and walk out the door. This can't be life, Damien thought as he hung up from trying for the twenty-first time.

Damien decided to call his mother. "What yawl want?" Doll answered, knowing that either Damien or Tavares wanted to know if she was bringing food back to the hospital. "Ma, Tavares bounced on me. Left me here, lying here fucked up. She said that she had to do her, figure out what was best for her because I didn't appreciate her." Doll could hear the hurt in her son's voice but she had witnessed the hurt one too many times and Tavares didn't deserve it, so she had no sympathy for her son. Tavares loved her son, unconditionally, rode with him through all this bullshit, and if she got fed up and left Doll didn't know that she blamed Tavares.

"Baby boy, Tavares has been everything that you could ask for in a woman. Everything. She has loved you, respected you, rode with you, fed you, kept your house clean, laundry clean, all while going to school and working and all you have done is take her love and kindness for granted. Today when I witnessed all the women at the hospital I knew shit was going to hit the fan. Then the icing on the cake was the bitch in the hallway saying you love her. That was just crazy, son. I was surprised Tavares didn't cole cock whoop her ass because she disrespected her. But you disrespected her more because these women who you been fucking wasn't in their lane. They had NO business at that hospital crying and carrying on like they were you main lady. So I'm sorry, very sorry that you are hurt, but I can't feel bad for you. I am a woman before I am anything else and how you did that girl she deserved to walk out on you. Everyone gets tired, remember that. I have to finish making the plates and then I'm coming back up there." Damien wanted to be mad, wanted to yell so the fuck what he was wrong, but he had to eat it like man. He made his bed so now he was lying in it.

"Come with me," Dora said, grabbing Tavares by the waist.

"Where we going?"

"I told you, you ask too many questions. Sometimes you should just do as you're told," Dora said, screwing his face up at the only person who ever put up a question with him.

"Damn, I can't ask where we're going? Fine, lead the way, with your bully ass," Tavares said, rolling her eyes. Everyone watched Dora and Tavares make their exit, without saying anything. Following Dora up the tall spiral staircase, down a long carpeted hallway into a bedroom, he closed the door behind Tavares. "So what's up, punk?" Tavares asked with her hands on her waist and her head slightly tilted in a seductive manner.

"Nah, don't try to play nice wit a nigga now. You didn't even want to come wit me. I just wanted to give your punk ass your Christmas gifts." Going in the top drawer of the tall black and cream marble dresser he came out with two small boxes wrapped in pretty, shiny cherry red wrapping paper.

"Ooooh, they're little, you know what means," joked Tavares as she jingled the boxes and her bright blue eyes bulged out of her face. Taking the wrapping paper off both boxes, Tavares opened the bigger of the jewelry boxes and found a thick, heavy diamond-encrusted gold chain that had a long diamond-encrusted key on it. In the second box was a beautiful charm bracelet that had diamonds all the way around it and on the links of the charms. Huge charms were swinging. There was a heart, a shoe, a T, a purse, a sun, a moon, a scroll, a diamond ring, and an eternity symbol. Each charm was made of nothing but diamonds, making the bracelet sparkle a little too much. Tavares looked from the jewelry to Dora, from Dora to the jewelry. After doing that three times, Tavares came back to reality.

"Yo, I can NOT accept these. Don't get it fucked up, I want to. Really I want to, but I can't. You had to jack a small fortune on them and I just can't do it."

"Yo Tav, I told you it ain't tricking if you got it. Plus, I had that bracelet and chain made especially for you. They wasn't picked up out no bootleg jewelry exchange type store. My jeweler custom made them. I don't like you rocking that ring, but I knew you wasn't going to part with it, so umma let you do you for now. Just know when I come, I'm coming correct, so you can keep that one for now."

"Dora, I can't walk around with this jewelry on. Someone will take my god damn neck off for that chain and key and my wrist off for this iced-out bracelet."

"I wish a nigga might fucking wish to," Dora said, dismissing her foolish thoughts.

"Alright, I guess this is a battle that I just won't win. So thank you very much, and fyi you are right, I'm not parting with my ring. So glad you didn't waste your money," Tavares rolled her eyes.

"Dora, I didn't spend $30,000 like I'm willing to bet you did, but I did get you presents," Tavares said, feeling bad. Had Dora went to the store he might have spent that, but his jeweler was good to him as always. He had only spent twenty-one thousand on both pieces.

"Ma, I don't care what you got me. I'd been happy had you given me some socks, it's the thought that counts." Tavares laughed because if he meant that shit, that was some real sweet shit because ain't no way she would have been happy with no fucking socks.

"Damn, I didn't do you that cold."

"Well what did you get me?"

"Dang, I ain't going to tell you. That takes the fun out of it."

"Fun out of what?"

"Christmas, motherfucker, duhhh."

"I ain't no fucking kid. Christmas is for the kids and for all the greedy money-hungry whores thinking a nigga owe them something."

"Damn, that's how you feel about Christmas, you god damn scrooge."

"Yeah, because we never had shit for Christmas growing up. It was only once I started making Christmas happen, that it became a tradition. So when you're the one doing all the spending you ain't too pressed about Christmas. So now, what did you get me?"

"Nope, not telling you, you big ass scrooge. If you want to know, go downstairs to your truck and get the larger of the two suit cases."

"Damn, you got a suit case full of shit," Dora said, surprised.

"Yeah, I wasn't supposed to, but the more that I was shopping, I just kept picking shit up. So you go get the suit case and imma make my way to the kitchen and get a shot."

Ten minutes later Tavares returned with a double shot of chilled Patron Silver and Dora had made his way upstairs with the large LV suitcase. "What the fuck you got in here, a fucking body? If so, that ain't no Christmas present," laughed Abdora.

"No, smart-ass, open it and find out."

"Well, the wrapping paper is sure pretty," Dora joked, referring to the silver paper with pink polka dots.

"I love pink and my tree at home was pink and white, so shut up." Tavares got comfortable and took a seat on the bed as she watched Abdora open present after present and not even realizing that he was smiling like a big ass kid. By the time Abdora unwrapped 30 pairs of new socks, tees, and boxers, all of which were Polo, he was like damn. He moved on and found two pairs each of wheat and black timberlands, Dolce & Gabbana shades, a red plush robe that had "The King" monogrammed on the back with matching slippers, a pea coat, some Lacoste and True Religion sweaters, and some nice True Religion jeans. Smelling the Happy For Men, IssyMiake, Burberry Touch, and Versace Dreamer, he was definitely about to make her a keeper. Not because of what she bought, but because of the thought she put into each gift. Dora was totally happy and didn't even know how to express it. "Yo, you bought me shit like a woman who knows how to shop for her man. Let me find out," Dora laughed lightly, impressed at how well the gifts suited him. "You knew what to buy, like you know me and shit," laughed Abdora. "I would have truly went in the store and picked out the same shit for myself. How did you do that shit, without asking my sizes?"

"Ahhh, get off me, I got my ways," laughed Tavares, who had got all the sizes from his clothes when she had visited him. Shopping for him wasn't hard and Tavares didn't even consider that she had actually grown to know him and his style so well. After exchanging thank yous, kisses, and conversation for another half-hour Tavares said, "We been gone long enough, let's get back. I don't want people thinking I'm up here taking advantage of you," she said, poking Dora in the chest.

"Girl please, they ain't worried about us. You know you wanna take advantage of a nigga. It's okay because if I was you, I would want me to take advantage of me too," Dora said, laughing before he could even get the last word fully out. Making their way back downstairs to mingle, Tavares was happy that she had actually gotten on the plane and did what her heart was telling her, because her mind was saying to stay with Dame's trifling ass in Boston.

Damien was lying in bed hooked up to several machines, looking frustrated, angry, and hurt. He was looking at the TV when his hospital room door swung open. He really didn't want to be bothered, but his mother was the one person who he needed right now. Doll hadn't even laid the bags down yet when Damien said, "Ma I feel some kind of way."

"Of course you do. Your woman walked out on you, but guess what? You have no one to blame but you. I always told myself I wouldn't be the mother who sugarcoats when it comes to women, because you're my son. Right is right and wrong is wrong. You have done her wrong and you pushed her to leave. I'm actually glad that she had the courage to love herself more."

Damien looked at his mother with a blank stare as if she had lost her mind. "Okay, I see we're far from on the same page. Wrong or not, you're supposed to be on my side. Granted I cheated, but I WAS good to her," Damien stated with major attitude.

"I know you don't have a motherfucking attitude with me. You did this. You had the woman who everyone wants and she wanted only you, so if you're mad, you little black bastard, be mad at yourself. Your father was the same man you are and I vowed I would raise you differently, but clearly DNA makes a person. So you know what? I'm going to leave this food and give you some space to get your motherfucking mind right." Doll snatched her bag and slammed the door on her way out.

By the time Tavares and Dora returned to the kitchen they had all eyes on them. "God damn is everyone gonna keep looking at them all crazy and what not?" Bella asked with her outspoken self. Bella was Maniac's girlfriend. Tavares didn't know Bella, but was digging her style and her outspokenness.

"Shut up," Maniac said. Bella just sucked her teeth because she didn't understand why everyone was making such a big deal about Abdora and his lady friend. The fellas were in awe that he was feeling her so hard and the other girlfriends were slightly hating on her, in Bella's opinion. Tavares could feel all the other girlfriends looking at her like they had no intention of letting her into their inner circle, but what they didn't know was that Tavares didn't give a fuck. Bella had removed herself from the other ladies and was talking to Tavares to make her more comfortable.

Bella was 5'9 and all legs. She had a nice thickness to her height but was nowhere near fat. She had smooth, vanilla-colored skin and bright, bold make up on. She had a funky sense of style and a short haircut that was shaved short on one side and long on the other to let you know that she marched to her own beat, and Tavares could dig that.

Abdora was gambling and saw that all the chicks were smoking but not swinging his shorty a blunt. He didn't get mad or say nothing, he simply said, "babe girl," and when Tavares turned around he threw he a seven of some blueberry haze and some cigarillos. Tavares winked her eye because she caught the cold shoulder the other chicks were giving her and now they could kick rocks. After rolling four blunts, Tavares smoked two with Bella and excused herself outside for some fresh air. Bella said, "You mind if I join you?"

"Not at all," Tavares said and together they made their way outside to the back porch.

Tavares lit the third blunt and was enjoying the fresh air and the quiet after the long day she had. "So tell me what's up with you and Dora?" asked Bella. Tavares laughed because she loved the boldness and the no beating around the bush.

"Dora and I are friends even though it seems like a whole lot more."

"Hmmm, is that right?" Bella asked, only half buying it.

"Yeah, that's right, Miss. Bella. Maybe in the near future we'll be more, but as of the moment we're just friends. Dora's my dude though, that I can't deny. I got a soft spot for him."

"You and every other woman, so you better pay attention and act like you know. Why you think all them other huzzies are in there hating on you?" laughed Bella. "Them or one of their girls were digging him and he wasn't beat so they got stuck with one of his boys. Dora's a hot and rare commodity so I don't suggest you let him pass you by."

"I hear you, Bella, but it's a lot more complicated than that. So you weren't a Dora fan?" questioned Tavares.

"Nope, never! Dora and I have been tight since elementary school. A little nappy-headed porch monkey boy used to tease me and one day Abdora stuck up for me and been my homie every since. He introduced me to Maniac when we was fifteen. That's the love of my life, the king of my castle and the only man for me! We just got engaged," Bella said, proudly extending her ring to show off her flawless five-carat canary yellow diamond.

"Oh my gosh that is beautiful, congratulations," Tavares said. They chatted for another half-hour before Dora appeared looking for them.

"Bella Mafioso," as Dora had nicknamed Bella, "you better not be out here telling my shorty no bullshit about me."

~ 404 ~

"Oh, nigga please. I ain't telling her nothing that she don't already know," laughed Bella. "I told her how much of a dog and womanizer you are. I told her you are cheap and to run for the hills."

"Bull motherfucking shit, you know god damn well I ain't none of the that."

"I know," laughed Bella.

"Actually Bella was telling me how much of a great catch you are, so you better thank her for putting in a good word for you."

"Baby girl, I ain't gotta thank Bella because her long-legged ass is the sister I never wanted, so she just did what she was supposed to."

"Actually, negro, I did it because I figured if I can get you a NICE lady all the money hungry tricks would fall back and stop chasing you." The trio kicked the shit and blew the last blunt before returning to the kitchen,

Eating, gambling, talking, and partying the night away Tavares lifted her Christmas spirits. Before everyone knew it, it was 2:00 a.m. by the time they started to clean up and head out. Tavares and Dora were the last to leave at 2:45 a.m. Tavares and Dora were kicking it as they cruised the highway, but Tavares had a question that had been in the back of her mind since early that morning.

"Dora, I need to ask you a question," Tavares said with a serious but hesitant tone.

"Anything, what's up babe girl?" Tavares didn't want to beat around the bush. "I know what transpired with Damien and your boy and then he got shot today. Did you have anything to do with Damien getting shot?"

Abdora knew this question would eventually be coming after he okayed the hit. Dora looked Tavares straight in the eye and said, "I sure didn't. I told you I wasn't going to touch son or get at him." He knew who had popped Damien and it was his orchestrating, but he wasn't going to tell Tavares that. Tavares was a hustler, not a gangster. So although she was playing in the streets getting money, she didn't get the codes or ethics of the streets. If she did she would have known the answer to her own question. Damien got what was owed to him. Furthermore Dora couldn't have cared less if Damien lived or died. Rather than express his true feelings, he just said, "Ma, you do dirt, you get dirt," nonchalantly. What he really wanted to tell her was that Damien was a no good, grimy bitch-ass nigga who deserved what he got and just too bad he lived. Tavares didn't know if she believed Dora. She wanted to and he was real convincing, not blinking twice, but after Damien had shot his friend, she couldn't think of who else would have shot him.

Damien had enemies but it was way too coincidental to think that he had gotten shot right after Dora's boy did. Tavares couldn't prove it, but she thought that Dora knew more than he was letting on. "Abdora, so you are going to sit here and look me in the face and tell me that you honestly had nothing to do with Damien getting shot?"

"That's *exactly* what I'm going to tell you. Right now you're angry and looking for someone to blame, but mumma I'm not the person." Dora felt bad lying for the first time to Tavares, but some things he just couldn't tell her and this was one of those things. Of course she didn't blame him and knew that he was right; when you did dirt, you got dirt, but it didn't feel right if she was fucking with the nigga who shot or had Damien shot. Damien was a bitch-ass nigga and if Dora wasn't sure about nothing else, he was sure about that, and he had no regrets about the hot ones Damien caught. Mostly for the grimy shit he did shooting his man over his baby's mother, but also for all the times he had hurt Tavares. Payback was a bitch and Abdora was smiling inside…..

About the Author

Deanne is 32, born and raised in Boston and a graduate of Savannah State University. She is a SPECIAL daughter, a DEDICATED mother, a LOVING sister, and a LOYAL friend who loves to live, laugh, and love. She grew up loving the streets that she writes about and has a deep passion for the sweet love that a pen and paper make together. This is her freshman novel, but definitely not her last.